ALSO BY JENNIFER HRITZ

The Crossing

I, Too, Have Suffered in the Garden

Smoke and Glass

A Novel

Jennifer Hritz

ISBN 978-0-578-73887-1
e-book ISBN 978-0-578-73888-8

First Edition

Cover art: Stephanie Estrin
Cover design: Susan Michalski
Author photo: Dan Greenfield

For Jennifer Bloom,
who laughed and told me to write

AUTHOR'S NOTE

The first part of *Smoke and Glass* is not a linear narrative. Instead, the story moves back and forth between the perspectives of two different characters over many years. I encourage readers to place themselves in both time and locale.

I found the first piece of glass the day my father was diagnosed with prostate cancer, less than an hour after my stepmother called me with the news. I don't think he wanted me to know; if he could have gotten away with never telling me at all, I'm sure he would've kept his cancer quiet. My father has no patience for weakness, and he must be mortified by his own.

I'd been here for almost two months at that point, but I hadn't started painting. Maybe I was still getting used to the city, or maybe I was getting used to being without James. I missed him more than I wanted to admit and hated him, too, though in the months since we'd parted, I'd been trying to focus on what worked about our time together in Greece instead of that last, terrible night.

I don't think I realized how much I needed *easy* until we got to Crete. Those stories I'd told James when I was still living in Austin and he called to ask if I could help with his son were intended to assuage his guilt about taking me from my work. I'd been painting circles for months, but I didn't feel finished when I left Texas. I could use the break, I said to James, and I suppose there was some truth in that statement. Brice and I had just split up for good, and I needed distance from him and from Austin itself. Weeks turned into months; Chicago turned into Crete. I hadn't gone that long without a paintbrush in my hand in years. I knew I was cultivating something anyway, something I couldn't yet see. *Verdant.* That was the word that woke me in the morning, and I'd open my eyes and look at Henry, who was just a few months past his first birthday and slept with his arms thrown wide. In the bed opposite mine, James took shape. We might as well have been in college, when his proximity felt like a privilege.

James left for his site six days a week and didn't return for hours. After digging all day, he'd need a shower, and I'd hang with Henry while James left dirt and grit at the bottom of the tub. Then he'd take over while I went for a run, inhaling the heady scent of chestnuts along with something fruity I couldn't define. By the time I got back, we'd all be starving, and we'd walk a mile in the twilight to our favorite café, where we'd sit outside and ask for *dakos* and *raki*. I didn't drink as much as James; I rarely did. There just wasn't much I needed to escape.

I felt good in Greece, better than I'd felt in a long time and certainly better than I'd felt since I left Adam. Even though I wasn't painting, my hand was never still. I was always sketching, even with Henry sprawled out beside me on a blanket under the trees. He slept holding his stuffed bug, sunlight slanting through the leaves, and I'd sit back for a minute and take a deep breath, in full recognition of the opportunity I'd been given. I knew better than to take our time together lightly.

Once in a while, we'd leave Henry with one of James's students. James might have said he was too busy, too tired, too uncomfortable leaving Henry with a sitter in a foreign country, but instead, he was the first to make suggestions: dinner, a cab ride to a spot overlooking the sea, a walk through the cemetery a quarter mile from our accommodations. He'd describe whatever he and his students had found that day, and I'd tell him about the frog Henry saw and the books we read. There was a familiarity in those moments that I never expected, a sense of coming home. I would have never imagined the feeling so intense or sweet.

We had eight weeks in Greece before James kicked us in the balls.

So I contacted Brice, who connected me with the wife of the senator he wanted me to meet at his Christmas party the December before last. I called her from the airport before we even left Greece, and within three days, she'd offered me a place to stay in Buenos Aires and a reasonable stipend. I have no more than 750 square feet to call my own, but it's all the space I need.

My plan was to paint. My plan has always been to paint, but then Catherine called with my father's diagnosis, and I went for a run. At first, I couldn't stop thinking about my father or what he'd have to face in the coming months: surgery, chemo, the loss of his hair. I'd been through the same ordeal with Adam's father, but what I felt for George Atwater in 2005 was nothing like the emotion I was trying to pound out on the streets of Buenos Aires. I finally stumbled to a stop so far from my studio that most of my return trip I knew I'd be making in the dark. The sun slid toward the horizon as I caught my breath, and the last of the light gave me the glass.

I couldn't discern the color and still can't. That first piece has a lambent glow of its own, which makes the glass seem opaque, even though it's not, not quite. I feel like I've found the heart of something, and if I didn't know better, I'd swear it's warm to the touch. I hold the glass in the palm of my hand at night, rub it between my fingers like it's some kind of talisman. I want to unearth its secrets.

A week after I found the first piece, I started scavenging for more. I go to the beach in the mornings when it's still cool, keep my eyes on the ground while I'm running. At my studio, I wash the glass in the sink, then drain it in a colander and pick out whatever won't work. I need a substrate strong enough to support the weight of what I'm envisioning, and I find a sheet of metal at one of the warehouses near the docks. The guy at the back door watches as I circle the sheet, testing it for weakness with the flat of my hand.

At my studio, I shut the door behind him and fasten the metal to the wall, using iron brackets about two feet from the floor. I'll have to climb a ladder to reach the top, but that's fine. The height will give me perspective.

I back up, examining the angle of the afternoon sun, which lasers across the metal with a hot, white light. I feel the same tense, excited anticipation as when I face a fresh canvas.

The pieces I've chosen for the mosaic I dry under a light so bright I can only use it for short periods of time. But the light allows me to see the intricacies of each piece, and I want to know the glass intimately before I adhere it to the metal. I'm working with a fast-drying epoxy, difficult to use and a bitch to remove, so I want to be sure ahead of time that I have exactly the right piece in exactly the right place.

I make the grout myself, one part cement to three parts sand. I mix it together in a small metal pail, wearing rubber gloves because it's so caustic. The mixture's thick and creamy, hard to apply without slathering the glass, and I keep a damp cloth on my shoulder so I can wipe as I go. Some of the gaps between the glass are so tight I can't use the spreader at all, and I end up buying a box of toothpicks and sliding the thin, wooden sticks in between shards so sharp I'm still getting scratched. The process takes days, weeks, because the pieces I've chosen are so tiny, so perfect they make me want to cry.

Most artists wouldn't work so haphazardly. Most artists would have a sketch beside them, if not a diagram on the metal itself. The thought makes me claustrophobic. Isn't it enough that I have the metal in front of me, glass as brilliant as jewels?

Jennifer Hritz

Part One

Mosaic

James / Austin / February 1996

I've been staring at Joel for an hour as he scribbles across one sheet of paper after another, turning the pages in that sketchpad like he can't get whatever's in his head out quick enough. Maybe he can't. But the way he has one hand gripping that beer of his, the way he's making his way through that twelve-pack like he's checking each bottle off some kind of master list… I know what's bugging him and there's jack shit I can do about it.

Outside the trees groan with the wind and cold seeps around the window frames. I could use a cigarette but I already gave that a try when I lowered myself to the swing on our front porch after I got home from campus and found him sitting there with a pack of Marlboros and what was even then probably one beer too many. Freezin' out here, I mumbled after a few minutes and he didn't bother to respond. I stuck it out, sucking my way through one of his cigarettes until he stood up so fast the chains on the swing rattled. I followed him into the room at the back of the house where he paints. Something on your mind, James? he asked like he was challenging me and I shook my head. He picked up a pad of paper like he was thinking about drawing some but back in the kitchen he cracked open another beer and had himself a long belligerent swallow. Are you joining me in a drink or what? he asked, sitting down at the bar.

Man, I couldn't refuse him, not after the way we fought over Christmas when I gave him shit for taking money from his dad. We'd barely spoken for three weeks and each day had me digging my heels in deeper. If his dad hadn't blown into town to tell him he's getting married again I might still be holding a grudge. Joel's barely over *that* hangover and now another night's coming on thick and dark and he's buried in his sketchpad. I should be prepping for the class I've got to teach tomorrow but instead I'm in the kitchen pretending like I need to eat when really I just want to look over his shoulder so I can see what I'm dealing with here.

Aw *crap*. That's his mom.

If you want to see what I'm drawing, he says without looking up, Ask. Lemme see, I say and he shoves the pad in my direction.

She's all over the page and when I start flipping back I find her on the others too. She isn't smiling in any of them except for one where she's sitting on a tombstone. Kinda morbid, don't ya think? I ask and he scowls, yanking the pad from my hands. Why don't you just tell me what I should draw, James, he says. That's not what I meant, I mutter but he's already working away on a fresh sheet of paper. I usually like to watch him but I've got an uneasy feeling as a tree appears under his fingers. He pauses to pull on his cigarette then gives me a wink. Guess who's in the tree, he says. A fuckin' bird, Joel, I answer, How am I supposed to know? You're in the tree, he tells me, Looking down at everything. Fuck you, I mumble but he laughs, drawing me into the picture. He catches me looking nineteen instead of twenty-four and I stare with something like fascination at the way he can throw this together from memory without even taking the time to look up at me. Am I smokin'? I ask, seeing something between my fingers. You're always smoking, he murmurs.

I steal one of his cigarettes as I take in his sketch. Where're *you*? I finally ask, exhaling a big old cloud of smoke and he smirks. Now you're complicating the picture, he says but he's drawing again, a bulls-eye portrait of himself under the tree. Why aren't you up there with me? I ask. Because I'm circling, James, he says, I'm forever fucking circling.

I don't love that tone of his but at least he's not sketching his mom sitting in a cemetery. Do you want to know where she's hiding? he asks like he knows what I'm thinking. He sounds so sly he gives me the creeps and I almost shake my head. With the tip of his pencil he shades a heart in the center of his chest then holds up his hand like he doesn't want me to comment just yet. As I watch he sketches an itty-bitty shadow so faint I might've missed the pencil lines if I hadn't seen him make them myself.

You should've left me out of it, he finally says, reaching for his cigarette. I don't mind a little complication, I tell him and he locks his eyes on mine.

Joel / Austin / October 2006

I've been going through some of my work from the past year, including the first few portraits of Adam that got me into that DC gallery. Those I can't look at for long. I'm grateful for the exposure they've given me, but I'd be prepared to dump every show if it meant I could rewind time. For a few years, happiness came as easily as my own breath. Now I have to coax myself out of bed in the morning. I have to rely on a rigorous running regimen and a daily meditation practice just to stay sane. If I couldn't paint, I don't know what I'd do.

Lately, though, I've been impatient. My work these days feels stale, and looking at what I've done makes me want to empty my living room of furniture and spread canvas over the old pecan floors. Throw paint like a little kid.

I take a beer from my refrigerator. I'm indulging; I don't drink much anymore, and I can't afford the six-pack. And really, what are my options? I live alone. I don't date. James—arguably my best friend, despite what happened the last time I saw him—lives in Chicago with his wife and son. I can show up for dinner at Kyle and Scott's only so many times a week before I feel like a freeloader. If I went to a bar, one beer would cost me almost as much as the six I picked up at the grocery store this afternoon.

So I'm looking at my entertainment for the evening: a bottle of Dos

Equis and a mild frustration with my work. I'm bored with my lover, and I laugh a little, loudly enough that if my neighbor heard me through the open window, he'd assume I wasn't alone. I sit down at the kitchen table I bought last year on Craigslist for $25. My beer, when I set it beside me, leaves a ring on the faded pine. Thicker on the right, blurred around the edges. I run an absent-minded finger along one side, then cock my head. Something resonates, and I stare at the table until the outer edges fade. Then I wipe the rest of the ring away with the palm of my hand. Begin again.

I play for over an hour, pressing one cold beer, then another onto the table. I let the condensate collect on the side of the bottle and slake it off, scattering drops of water. With the tip of my finger, I pull each circle apart, then patch it back together. After a while, I try to get that first circle as perfect as possible, for the sheer pleasure of renegotiating its space. I like where I end up more than I like the beginning.

The evening started out warm, but the temperature falls with the sun, and when I open that third beer, the bottle stays cold and clean. Taking a final swig, I pour the contents in the sink; I don't need to get drunk. In my studio—the bigger of the two bedrooms in this house, though tiny compared with the space I had when I lived with Adam—I pull out my watercolors. Once I have the right shade, I touch the bottom of an empty bottle into the paint, then press it onto a thick sheet of paper.

Hello, lover.

James / Chicago / May 2007

I'm late leaving campus and late getting to the airport and Joel's already waiting for me when I stumble into baggage claim trying to figure out how much I'm to blame for everything that's happened and wondering if I made a mistake, calling and asking him to come. I haven't seen him for ten months, the longest we've been apart since we met at the beginning of our freshman year in college—except for that time he spent in Mexico back in '99—but he looks like he's not going to hold that against me. Relief comes quick and strong and I hang onto him like I might not let go. He squeezes back for a while then pulls away to take in my wild hair and a week's worth of beard, my coat stained from the coffee I gulped down on the way here. Dressed up for me, did you? he says and though I'm fighting to shut down the tears behind my eyes, the ones that aren't for me so much as for Henry since he's the one who's going to suffer I manage a laugh. C'mon, Joel sighs, Let's go see this kid of yours.

In my car he slides the passenger seat all the way back, stretching legs lean from years of running. His hair's longer than the last time I saw him and I watch, irritated, as it swings toward his chin. You look pretty great, I grunt. Why do I get the feeling that's not a compliment? he asks. I'm jealous, I admit, starting the engine. All you need is a couple of miles every other day, he says same as always. I've got a kid, I remind him and he says, I'm talking about ninety minutes a week, James. I cut my eyes at him. Are you really gonna give me shit about this? I ask, Right now you're gonna give me shit about this? I'll whip you into shape before it's all said and done, he says. Yeah? I grumble, How long are you stayin'? You leave for Greece next month, right? he says, So we have until then. What about your work? I ask. I told you on the phone, he says, I need a break. Bullshit, I mutter and he shrugs like he hasn't just offered me exactly what I need. You'd do it for me, he adds.

When he and Adam broke up I spent hours on the phone with him but I couldn't bring myself to leave Lizzie, not with her so newly pregnant, not when we'd already been through that god-awful miscarriage. Now I hate thinking that when he needed me I let him down.

But if he's still pissed he hides it well. Should we take a chance? he asks, holding up a CD I likely burned with songs from *Sesame Street*. I shrug and he shoves it in the CD player. "Bust a Move" bursts from the speakers. Oh my *God*, he laughs. It's not mine, I say right quick. Uh-huh, he nods. It's Lizzie's, I insist and he says, Now I *know* you're lying.

For the first time in months I start to chill. I've been going at full speed for so long I can hardly remember what it's like to feel rested. Last night Henry was up twice and I searched for his pacifier in the dark, shushing him, so weary I wanted to crawl right into his crib beside him. When I finally staggered back across the room to my own bed I couldn't fall asleep. I watched the clock instead, mulling over my options and coming up empty-handed. Now I feel like I've managed to light a match in the middle of a hurricane.

So did you tell Henry I was flying up to hang out with him? Joel asks. He's one, dude, I remind him, He doesn't even know who you are.

Joel looks at me like I've gone and stomped all over his heart.

Riiight. He was just talking. And anyway I'm the reason he doesn't know my son. I might try to blame Lizzie but I'm the one who let Joel leave last summer. I'm the one who didn't tell him to stay.

Sorry, I mumble and he shakes his head, the muscle in his jaw jumping all over the goddamn place like he's got something to say but doesn't want to take us down when we've barely left the airport. Fifteen minutes in and he's already disappointed with me. *Shit.* I hope this isn't an indication of what I can expect over the next few weeks. I really need this to work.

I take a good long breath and beside me like we're synchronized swimmers or something Joel does the same thing. Christ, he says, We're something else. Always have been, I agree and his expression might as well be an archaeological site. There's so much here I could excavate.

Joel / Austin / October 2006

I've worked right through lunch, caught up in the same circles that captivated me last week and haven't let go since. Now I'm starving, and I stare into a refrigerator that probably rolled off the factory floor a good thirty years ago. I don't have much in here: the remnants of a bunch of spinach, a quarter cup of yogurt, a few spoonfuls of peanut butter. Thirteen months ago, I had a well-stocked kitchen. These days, I buy my groceries one day at a time and check my bank balance the second I open my eyes in the morning.

I drive to Central Market. Even though I rent on the east side, I'm closer to North Lamar than when I lived out by the lake: small favors. I add greens, peppers, avocados, and plums to my basket, then make my way over to the seafood department and debate whether or not I want to shell out cash I don't really have for wild-caught salmon. I don't usually splurge, except for art supplies. Sometimes I think about the money I used to blow in a typical weekend in my twenties on cocaine. Or I think about the summer before last, when Adam and I were spiraling but I could still go to the farmer's market and not have to worry about dropping fifty dollars on tomatoes and peaches and artisan goat cheese, because instead I needed money for an overdue electric bill.

I ask for eight ounces of salmon and forego the wine I've been craving. At the checkout counter, I unload my basket and swipe my debit card. I've never been declined, but there's always a first time. The checker's quiet. At Whole Foods, they chat me up, ask about my plans for the weekend. They're not hitting on me; they're just friendly.

I'm grateful for the silence.

The guy in line behind me keeps trying to catch my eye. I avoid his gaze, staring down at the conveyor belt instead. He has one bottle of Veuve Cliquot. I remember the way that tastes. I remember buying bottles without forethought, just adding them to the cart on a quick run to the grocery store on a Tuesday morning. I remember the kind of hangovers I've had with champagne, as if the bubbles had made their way to my head and lodged there. I remember kissing Adam on my thirtieth birthday in between mouthfuls, in a bed newly mine.

You live on the east side, the guy in line behind me says. Startled, I look up. I've seen you running, he adds, I have a friend who lives on Chicon. Oh, I say, Yeah, I run Chicon sometimes. I've seen you more than once, he informs me. Must be a good friend, I mumble as the checker tells me my total. Punching through to the end of the sale, I hold my breath.

Approved. Hallelujah.

Shouldering the cloth sacks I've brought from home—one for the produce, one for the fish—I glance back at the guy in line behind me. Maybe I'll see you running, he says. Yeah, I agree, Maybe.

The sun hides behind the clouds like a demure lover as I head to my truck. *That shitty pickup*, Adam used to say, but it never gives me any trouble. Still, I remember what it's like behind the wheel of something better, an engine open all the way, and as if the universe has a sense of humor, I find an Aston Martin parked next to my Toyota. A DB9, the body so sleek and black even an overcast afternoon can't dim its light.

The passenger door of my truck creaks when I haul it open. I lower my bags onto the seat and ease the door shut, frowning at the front tire, which looks a little low. I should probably get that checked, and as I round the back of my truck, hoping I won't have to pay for a new tire anytime soon, the taillights of the DB9 flash. The guy who was standing in line behind me smiles. Well, of course the car belongs to him. Aston Martin probably uses him for their print ads. Tall, heavily lidded eyes, and dressed for a night out in Barcelona instead of the music capital of the world. Cliquot give you a cut? I mumble, and he lets out a surprised laugh.

Okay, that was snide. But he just holds up the bottle of champagne and leans against his car like he's posing for a layout. I'll give you a percentage, he offers, If you share a glass. I look down at what I'm wearing. Threadbare jeans, gray tee shirt, sandals two summers old. If Cliquot found out, I say, They'd never re-sign your contract. I'll land on my feet, he tells me, pairing his shrug with a smile as if he'd been born and bred on flirtation. I place his accent: prep school, with winters in Aspen. This guy has a friend who lives on Chicon?

He's watching me take him in. No fidgeting, no shifting his weight from one expensive loafer to the other. No risking the moment with the wrong question. He just lets me take him in, and for a second, I feel freer than I've felt in a year, except maybe for those few drug-induced hours last summer. He catches my expression and takes a step closer, satisfaction as familiar to him as the platinum American Express I'd bet my rent he has in his wallet. But the ache in my heart where I still carry Adam holds me back.

I open the door of my truck to the slightest lift of his eyebrows. Thanks for the invitation, I say, guilt precluding me from blowing him off entirely. He's been nice, after all, and it's not his fault I'm hurting. Anytime, he answers, with the kind of sincerity that invites me to change my mind. I give him a wave and go home.

James / Chicago / June 2002

We're living in a one-room loft downtown and it's taking both our salaries to keep us here. Lizzie likes the convenience but I hate living in one room, hate the stainless steel appliances and granite countertops that leach all the color from our furniture. I want a place for my books and I want to start a family and I can't see trying to raise a kid in a building where I'll have to take an elevator just to get outside.

So I start hunting around a little.

Please tell me you're kidding, Lizzie says when I show her the dilapidated brownstone I've found. C'mon, I protest, This has potential. Who's going to do the work? she asks. Don't you think it'd be fun to do together? I say. We don't know anything about renovating a house, James, she reminds me, And what would we do with this much space anyway? Well, once we've got kids…, I say.

We've been trying for almost a year and I finally suggested a couple weeks ago that we talk to her doctor to see if there's a problem. Sometimes it takes a while, James, Lizzie sighed but I know my wife and she's been putting me off pretty much since the day we got married. For just a second I wonder if she's taking the Pill on the sly.

She's still staring at the house, shaking her head like she can't imagine what's gotten into me and I tell her, scrambling for a pen so I can jot down the number on the sign that maybe we should look inside. She doesn't answer and before she can throw my idea away for good I put the car in drive.

The next afternoon while she's at work and I should be holding office hours I meet with the realtor I've just hired. Definitely a fixer-upper, she cautions, unlocking the front door but I made up my mind standing on the steps. When she moves aside to let me pass I feel the kind of sure I felt when I asked Lizzie to marry me. From the chandelier in the dining room to the built-in bookshelves lining the walls of the office to the nursery on the top floor with its peaked roof and window seat: this house has been waiting for us.

But Lizzie, hearing me gush that night about the art deco flooring in the front room and the corner fireplace talks about tiny kitchens and ancient windows guaranteed to leak cold winter air. Why would you want to move anyway? she asks, waving her chopsticks at what surrounds us. We're eating sushi a block from our loft in West Loop and I guess she's right about how trendy we look. Whatever, I don't even *like* sushi. We won't be that far away, I tell her. Too far to walk here, she says. Lizzie— I start but she shakes her head. I don't want to deal with a commute, James, she says, And if we have a baby...

If we have a baby? What's this *if* shit? I stab a piece of *unagi* and she reaches for my hand. It's not that I don't want to try, she says.

We're not talking about the house anymore and I listen dumbfounded as my wife admits that she's just not as sure as I am, that sometimes she wonders what our lives might be like if she doesn't get pregnant ever. Sometimes…, she says and I yank my hand from hers.

Joel / Austin / June 2002

Adam's been out of town, but he's coming back tonight, and I drift off on top of our duvet, waiting for him. I wake after midnight to his tongue circling my navel. You smell like airplane, I murmur. He laughs, coming up to kiss me. You smell like turpentine, he says. We should shower, I tell him, and his answer gets lost somewhere in my neck.

We shower in the morning, bring our breakfast to the pool. I rub sunscreen on his shoulders, down his spine. You're missing spots, he complains. You think you can do a better job? I ask. I think *you* can do a better job, he tells me, and I pull him back against my own sun-screened skin. How's that? I say in his ear, and he closes his eyes.

We swim; we sleep. I think about what I want to paint in the studio we finished renovating this past spring, mix colors in my mind. From the raft in the pool, Adam talks to his parents, then passes the phone over to me so I can say hello. I wander into the kitchen, come back with chips and salsa. Did you have to buy the spiciest kind? he asks around a mouthful.

Late in the afternoon, he makes a pitcher of margaritas. My buzz feels nice and mild, and a few laps in cool water cut right through it. I come up for air, prop myself on the lip of the pool, run my hand through my hair. I had it cut short almost three years ago, and I haven't let it grow long since.

The sun shifts, shadows lingering long on our deck. I reach for my shirt, the yellow one with the V-neck, the one Adam says makes me look like I'm still in college. You don't know what I looked like in college, I remind him, and he says, I do when you wear that shirt. He pulls himself from the pool, splits the last of the margaritas between our glasses. You want to go out tonight? he asks, and I stretch my arms above my head, looking over the lake. If we stay home, we can watch the sun set on the water. We can shower again in our own time. We'll have the perfect excuse to go out for brunch in the morning because we're out of groceries, and if we stay in tonight, we'll never run to the store. Not really, I say, stepping closer, and he invites me into a kiss. You taste like summer, he tells me. You taste like lime, I say.

It's an ordinary day, but I'm happy.

I'm happier than I've ever been.

James / Chicago / February 2006

Once Lizzie makes it through her second trimester and we can safely say she'll carry Henry to term I start working on his room. For the past three and a half years we've used the nursery at the top of our brownstone as a catch-all and the first thing I've got to do is clear some space. Lizzie can't really help but I wouldn't mind her company. She spends most of her time in bed when she's not at the office and I guess I can hardly blame her for wanting to take it easy while she can. So all by myself I strip the old wallpaper and put a fresh coat of paint on the wainscoting and the eight-inch baseboards. I read up on crown molding and install that too. After I order the furniture—a pretty white-slatted crib and a matching changing table, things I hoped Lizzie would help me find but end up shopping for on my own—I paint the walls a nice easy shade of blue.

As Lizzie's due date gets closer I register for the usual: crib sheets and bumper pads, a breast pump and bottles. The routine is that I drive out to Babies 'R Us to get a clear idea of our options—there are a helluva lot of car seats on the market—then come home hoping to talk them over. Pale and wan, Lizzie tells me to make the decisions myself. When presents arrive I open them then invite her upstairs to see what I've done. She stands in the doorway like she's afraid to come in and I go to her and pull her in my arms and tell her everything will be fine. Soon as Henry's here she'll see for herself. Everything will be just fine.

In the meantime I add what I can. A wipe warmer a colleague recommends, a piggy bank, an old rocking chair I find at an estate sale and refinish myself. The room's done way ahead of schedule and I sit on the window seat in the light from the stained glass. I can picture my son here and most of the time I'm able to hang on to that image and not give in to what has become an increasingly rational concern given the trouble we had conceiving, not to mention that second trimester miscarriage, that I'm being punished. My fear feels utter and debilitating and nothing I can confide in my wife, who despite her swollen belly looks like a shell of her former self.

Joel / Austin / October 2006

I've been opening my laptop and slamming it shut for the past week. I could call, but I need to slow time, to stretch it thin enough so there's space between the message and what I'm sure will be an instant response. I'll be lucky if Adam doesn't return my email by dialing my cell. He wants me back that badly.

I can feel his desperation almost two thousand miles away.

There's power in that realization, and panic. Seven years of therapy and a flicker of faith in some sort of inherent self-worth made me leave Adam when I found out about his affair, and despite the current of pain that runs through my every waking moment, for the most part, I've been grateful I didn't stay. My boundaries suck. If I needed proof, all I'd have to do is look at my relationship with James. I let those boundaries bleed all over the place, and just when I think we've cauterized every last vein, we start seeping.

Adam was supposed to be different. And when he wasn't, I had to make a choice. I deserve better. At the very least, I deserved for him not to sleep with one of his colleagues, someone I'd warned Adam about from the beginning. If he'd slept with anybody else, I might have stayed. But the thought that he was cheating on me with that player from his office while I was offering up my support as his father lay dying… I couldn't forgive him. Whatever excuses I wanted to make for him—and I know he had more working against him than I ever suspected—I deserved better.

I still miss him. Even a year later, I miss him, and talking to that guy with the Aston Martin at Central Market has just made Adam's absence more acute.

I could find out about him, without direct contact. I'm sure Scott talks to him, and it's likely that Scott passes those conversations on to Kyle. They've just been judicious about sharing, probably because they know there's only so much that I can handle. The last year has been too emotional, too fraught with the potential for regression. I'm discussed when I'm out of earshot, included in outings that without my presence would clearly lean toward the romantic. And since I lost my shit in their living room after I got back from Chicago in July, I haven't made it through a week without hearing from at least one of them. They might be hesitant to divulge what they know if they think it's going to set me back, but if I insist on details, they'll tell me.

I'm not sure I want details. I'm not sure I want to know what Adam's doing in Seattle, if he's rebuilding his career, if he's seeing anyone.

He's not seeing anyone. There's no way he's seeing anyone.

I'm pacing. I'm actually pacing, in front of a fireplace meant for a gas heater from the forties. The bottoms of my bare feet will be filthy; I can't afford a maid service any more than I can buy a bottle of Veuve Cliquot, and though I'm more vigilant about cleaning than I ever was when I lived on Pearl Street back in college, these floors haven't been refinished since the day they were laid. I'm grateful for this house and grateful for the grant that's paying part of my rent. But sometimes I'm so pissed I'm living here.

Maybe I'll call James.

Immediately, I reject the thought. Even if I could reach him—and between Henry and his schedule at the university, that's debatable—he'll never be able to give me advice about Adam. There's no love lost between them, and though I'm gratified by James's loyalty, I also know he's not capable of objectivity. If I tell him I'm thinking of reaching out, he'll lose his mind. *Adam doesn't deserve a second chance*, I can hear him saying, completely overlooking that a second chance is exactly what I've given James. And a third and a fourth.

God, I want a cigarette. Or a drink.

Instead, I sit down on the floor in front of the windows and close my eyes, legs crossed, palms up. One long, deep breath to center, then another. I let my attention wander until it settles on something innocuous: the hum of that old refrigerator. I have no attachment to the refrigerator. Breath in, breath out.

Twenty minutes in, I feel the answer.

James / Chicago / July 2006

I can't believe you're even making the *suggestion*, Lizzie says, folding her arms across her chest, I can't believe you'd even *ask* this of me.

She's still dressed for the office in a short black skirt and jacket, her curls pinned back in some complicated arrangement and I want nothing more in this moment than to take down her hair. Maybe then she'd relax. Maybe then I could lead her to our bed and we could make love in a way we haven't for so long, so long I can hardly remember what it's like. Instead she stands in front of me, grinding her heel into the hardwoods in a way that makes me wince. You can take some time for yourself, I say, Get a pedicure. A *pedicure*? she repeats, all tight and coiled and unforgiving, and I remind her that she said she needed one, that she wants space from Henry on the weekend. I don't point out that she has space all the damn week long. A pedicure takes an *hour*, James, she says, What am I supposed to do the rest of the time? Go for a walk? I suggest, Take one of your kickbox classes? I've lost *all* of that pregnancy weight! she cries. Lizzie, I groan, That's not what I meant.

But she's already sobbing and when I try to put my arms around her she pushes me away, her frame thin and muscular from years of exercise. She *has* lost all her pregnancy weight. There wasn't much to lose. He's my best friend, Lizzie, I say, I want him to meet my son. You say that like Henry's *yours*, she wails, Like he has nothing to do with *me*. Lizzie, I sigh and she turns on me. Don't call me that! she hisses, You make me feel like a child!

Somewhere under the weight of the past few years the memory of the way we used to be lays buried. I don't know if I've got the will to unearth it.

Elizabeth, I say, He's *comin'*.

Joel / Chicago / July 2006

God, it's good to see you, James says, throwing his arms around me, and I murmur something similar, hyper-aware that Elizabeth's hovering behind him. He must be tired; he's usually careful about touching me in front of his wife. You stop sleeping or what? I ask, taking in the pockets of fatigue under his eyes. Pretty much, he admits, but he's grinning, and he gestures me inside.

Elizabeth looks perfectly put together, like every other time I've seen her. Whatever weight she gained during her pregnancy has disappeared, and she's dressed as fashionably as ever in an ensemble that would make Kyle sit up and take notice: a dress with tiny straps, a necklace I know for a fact James gave her last Christmas, partly because he described it on the phone to me a few days before the holiday and partly because it's just like Elizabeth to wear it today. She might as well be holding a sign that says, *He's mine, cocksucker.*

But even I can see that under her pink sundress, something's off. I'm no energy reader, and I can't see auras the way my shaman back in Austin can, but this woman needs to have her chakras balanced. I actually feel bad for her. Hi, Elizabeth, I say, and she tries a smile, which trembles. I want to tell her I'm not a threat, not even single—not even after what happened last Christmas—and she probably has other issues she should address before she puts any energy into worrying about me. But there's no point, just like there's no point in pretending our relationship warrants an embrace.

I glance at James to see what he's noticing. Years ago, when he was engaged and first married, he seemed caught in a perpetual middle, wanting to behave around me like nothing had ever happened between us and at the same time acutely aware of what his wife must be thinking. Today, he's not even looking at Elizabeth. C'mon, he says to me, I want you to meet him.

The baby's on the top floor, which surprises me. I would've expected to find Henry beside James's bed, if the kid didn't spend nights right in his father's arms. But the room has pretty light, wainscoting James told me he painted himself, antique blue walls. There's so much shit; I didn't realize babies have so much shit. Books and toys and some sort of lopsided dresser... I barely have time to take in the enormity of the transformation before James beckons me to a little basket beside a single bed under the eaves.

He's small, smaller than I expected, and I realize if Henry's this tiny at three months old, he must have really snagged James's heart when he was born. One fist curls beside Henry's cheek, but otherwise, he's all wrapped up in some kind of cocoon with a fitted cap on his head, so I can't tell if he has any more hair than he did in the photos James has been relentlessly emailing. I wouldn't call my experience with babies robust, but even I know he's some kind of miracle, and when I turn to James, he's staring at his son with such awe my breath catches in my throat.

Isn't he beautiful? he whispers. I nod, glad we're supposed to be quiet. I think if I had to speak, I'd end up crying. James has been waiting for this for such a long time, and after the year I've just been through, I'm happy to witness something so perfect. Without thinking, I wrap my arms around my friend in congratulations. His breath moves through me, all that sweet relief.

Only when she steps beside me, do I remember Elizabeth. She must have followed us upstairs, and as I drop my arms, she stares down at her son with an expression nothing like her husband's. I'm still trying to interpret what I'm seeing—anger? Confusion?—when she reaches into the basket. What're you doing? James asks in a low voice as she tries to work a pacifier into Henry's puckered mouth, You'll wake him.

Sure enough, the baby starts to squall, his little face screwing up so tightly I brace myself for the sound. But he mews in pitiful fits and starts like he's still learning how to cry. I'd pick him up myself, but James already has him in his arms. Jesus Christ, Lizzie, he mutters, and I make a move in the direction of the doorway, thinking I'll let them hash this shit out on their own. James gives me a furious glance, which I think might be displaced. I take a quick look around me, stalling on the single bed across from the crib.

He's not letting Henry sleep alone. He's sleeping up here with him.

Give me the pacifier, James says to Elizabeth, but she flees, her sandals clattering on the stairs. Jaw set, he goes over to the dresser and yanks open a drawer, then holds a fresh pacifier steady between Henry's lips even though the kid's wailing around it. James doesn't rock the baby, doesn't hush him the way anyone else would, and it takes a while for me to realize he's being so careful because Henry can't handle anything more.

Finally, the baby quiets. James sits gently in the rocking chair beside the bed, motioning for me to take a seat. I watch him gaze at his son like he's filling up for a lifetime away from him.

So this is what he looks like in love.

James / Chicago / May 2007

We're almost home and so far I haven't fucked up again, probably since we've been singing along to that *Cheesy Rap* CD like we're still in college. Put a six-pack between us and a cigarette in my hand and I might think I was behind the wheel of Joel's BMW convertible instead of my safety-conscious Volvo. I'm sort of sorry we're almost home even though I'm ready for Joel to see my son. I haven't felt this relaxed in *years*.

We belt out the last lines of Ice Cube's "It Was a Good Day" as I exit off Midway and into my neighborhood and the second the song ends Joel gets right down to business. So Henry probably still takes a bottle…, he starts.

I work on keeping my cringe to myself. Of course Henry's still taking a bottle, he's *one* and there's no breast to take anyway, that's for damn sure. He's not walking yet? Joel asks and I tell him Henry just started cruising. Joel smirks.

I'm a little concerned. Despite how much I need his help right now, despite how much I could use his company Joel's not exactly savvy about childcare and I've got a fickle little boy who won't go to anyone except his babysitter, a student of mine who told me last weekend she got a better paying gig. Now I have Joel, who can't get past the sexual connotations of the word *cruising*, stepping in as my sitter's surrogate. *Cruisin'*, I explain, keeping my tone even so we don't get crossways again, Means— I'm not an idiot, James, he says flatly, Jesus.

Got it.

Henry's hanging onto the coffee table when I open the front door, his cute little butt swathed in a Huggie. When he sees me he smiles and teeters, falling backward with a *plop*. I scoop him up, inhaling his sweet scent— cereal and lavender and diaper cream—my nose pressed to his neck. Then Joel comes up behind me. I wait for my son's face to crumple especially when Joel makes the mistake of holding out his arms. But to my amazement Henry goes cooing right to him, grabbing a handful of Joel's hair.

Henry's sitter and I exchange stunned glances. What? Joel says, looking over at us, You thought he wouldn't like me? He touches the back of Henry's head, which is covered with soft downy brown hair on the verge of needing its first cut. My son gazes at him with a solemnity fitting a god.

I feel a bizarre rush of gratitude toward my wife. If she hadn't left, Joel wouldn't be here.

Joel / Austin / October 2006

The day's warm when I hit the pavement. We haven't had a good cold front yet, but the temperature's supposed to drop tonight. For the moment, I'm more than fine in shorts and a tee shirt, my hair pulled into a ponytail at the nape of my neck.

I sent Adam an email. I wrote it, laced up my running shoes, and got the hell out of the house so I wouldn't sit around waiting to see if he'd write back.

I know he will. The next time I open my laptop, I'll find his name in my inbox.

I concentrate on my stride. Usually, I'm a good runner, light and easy. I like running alone, prefer the night or the very early morning when even a passing car feels like an intrusion. I could train for something substantial if I could get past the idea of traveling in a pack. The only cadence I could ever accommodate belonged to James. We used to run together in college; I remember dragging him out one afternoon in a freezing rain. He bitched his way through the first five minutes, but when he finally shut up, we settled into a rhythm that carried us six miles. That might have been the farthest we ever ran together, and as we slowed to a walk turning onto Pearl Street, rain-soaked and breathless, we looked at each other and grinned.

He'd kill me if he knew I sent that email, no matter how innocuous the language. And I kept it casual, believe me. I'm feeling Adam out, just looking to see how he'll respond. I'm not interested in some kind of reconciliation. Contact: that's all I want right now. Nine months since Adam told me he was moving to Seattle seems long enough for everything to have settled. There's no reason we can't be civil.

Miles melt beneath me, and with every step, I leave behind more of my anxiety. Adam will email, or he won't; we'll reconnect, or we won't. I have as little attachment to the outcome as I did to the hum of the refrigerator. *Bullshit*, James says in my head.

Rounding Chicon, I come down hard off the curb and tweak my ankle, just enough to make me wince and that's preemptive: early in my relationship with Adam, I bolted from his bedroom in a fit of pathos and stumbled halfway down the stairs, turning my ankle along the way. If my shoes aren't tight enough, I don't get the support I need and end up having to ice, even all these years later. After I cross the street, I stop and retie my laces, my quads shimmying in protest. Straightening, I find myself face to face with the guy from Central Market.

Endorphins have me high enough to think I've imagined him, and it takes spotting his Aston Martin in the driveway of the house on the corner before I realize he's more than a mirage. College friend, he reminds me after I pull out my earphones. I wipe the sweat from my face with the back of my arm. My shoelace was loose, I tell him, and he looks down at my running shoes, easily the most expensive item in my wardrobe. We can't have you tripping, he says, not realizing the irony of his statement. He caught me in the middle of a run, and my tongue feels thick, my head high. Do you live close by? he asks. Off Oak Springs, I say, Near Airport.

He nods as if he spends time there when in reality, that DB9 has likely made the trip across I-35 only a handful of times. Chicon has been heavily gentrified, but I'm even farther east, and most of the houses on my street have bars on the windows. This guy looks like he just drove over from a photo shoot with *L Style/G Style*. Flat-front khaki shorts, white V-neck shirt, brown leather sandals, and a blue- and orange-striped belt that would make me laugh if I didn't have a good idea of how much he paid for it. That's a Rolex he's wearing, and I bet he didn't snag those tortoise-shell aviators he's twirling by the stem from the lost and found at Deep Eddy this past summer.

Juxtaposed against the backdrop of Chicon with that DB9 parked in front of his friend's shitty house—though it's admittedly a nicer house than mine—he makes a provocative picture. And the way the light's slanting... In the haze of my high, I want to sketch him, and it's only after he laughs that I realize he asked a question I didn't even hear. I'm Brice, he says. I give him my name and shake his hand, though mine's sweaty. He has a touch like I'd expect, confident and sure. Why don't you come to my friend's party tonight? he suggests, and as if to punctuate the point, the front door of the house on the corner opens. Brice smiles at the woman who wanders barefoot across the yard. Now *she* belongs here, with her hippie skirt and long, curly hair. Celeste, Brice says when she reaches us, Tell Joel he should come to your party tonight.

Celeste smiles. She has a minuscule nose piercing, a gem of some kind that catches the sunlight. We're celebrating, she tells me. Celeste throws pottery, Brice explains, A few of her pieces were just highlighted in a magazine. Congratulations, I say, I know that's a good feeling. Oh! Celeste exclaims, brightening, Are you an artist, too? I nod, catching the lift in Brice's eyebrows. I tell her I have a show in DC in the spring, my first real exposure outside of Austin. Celeste brings the palms of her hands together like she just finished her yoga practice. I swear I almost mirror her movement. Come tonight, she says, I'll show you my studio, and you can tell me about your work.

I glance at Brice, who smiles back. Maybe I will, I say, and I ease back into my run. A quick look over my shoulder shows them walking into Celeste's house with their arms around each other. Brice raises his hand long enough to wave.

James / Austin / September 1991

Joel and I moved off campus to this little house on Pearl and some of my fraternity brothers are *pissed*. I'm pledge captain this year and I've been working my ass off but I guess that's not enough for them. They want me living in the frat house, not with my potluck freshman roommate. Parker— he's my big brother and kind of a dick—told me a few of the guys have been grumbling that I'm not around when they need me. That's bullshit, man, I said, I'm here every goddamn day. He backed off but somehow I've ended up with more work. Like this bouncy castle I had to rent. Party supplies don't fall under my job description but I was the one who had to make the call then show up early this morning to meet the guy who delivered it. He told me not to let more than six people jump at a time but at least eight girls and a couple guys have crammed themselves in there. Whatever, they're not my problem. I'm not a watchdog. There's a big ass sign right by the entrance and these idiots can read. Presumably.

Joel's here somewhere. Usually I can't convince him to go to these parties but he just shrugged this afternoon and told me he'd drink our free beer. Like he's got to worry about money. I took one look at his side of our dorm room the day I met him—at his CD player and computer and more clothes than he could fit in that closet of ours—and thought *fuck me, he's loaded.* But whatever, I'm happy to have him here tonight. We rent the same house but I'm never home.

Nice castle, Shelton says, stepping beside me and squeezing my shoulder. I thank him but I'm not smiling. I don't like Shelton, who's probably responsible for the extra work I've been getting. He's given me more shit than anyone else about where I'm living and that's not all. People are talking, Parker told me a little while ago and I would've bet my grade point by *people* he meant *Shelton.* Yeah? I said, slow sipping my beer, About what? Your roommate, he said and even though I felt a maw open up in my belly I made sure to beat him to the punch. Shelton have a thing for him or somethin'? I asked and Parker looked all grim like he'd caught me digging a grave I didn't realize was mine. You didn't do yourself any favors by bringing him here tonight, he told me. You've got friends outside the fraternity, I reminded him. Not fags, he said.

It wasn't the word that annoyed the crap out of me but Parker's bland-ass inflection. Keep an eye on him, James, he warned. I shifted my gaze over to the bouncy castle, which looked like it had about as much chance of making it through the night as a trailer in a tornado. Will do, I mumbled.

I've been looking around for Joel since then but I haven't seen him and I'm not about to ask Shelton. You bring a date? Shelton asks and I give him a sharp look since I know he saw me walk in with Joel. He smirks so I figure I'll fuck with him. I came with a friend, I tell him, But I'm looking at that girl over there. I tilt my plastic cup near the back door right at Kim Cunningham and watch Shelton's fist clench around his beer. I've heard him brag about nailing her but I'm sure as shit he hasn't. She's out of your league, he tells me and I keep my tone nice and mild. You think? I say like I'd ever give any credence to a word coming out of his mouth. Stick with your own kind, Fielding, he says, clapping my shoulder and I follow his eyes and see Joel standing near the bouncy castle with one of our pledge brothers. By the time I turn back, Shelton's halfway across the yard headed right for Kim. Whatever. I don't really want her anyway and I guess I've got my hands full with what's happening in front of me. I've figured for a while

Joel's into Carson and looking at him now there's not a helluva lot of doubt. I know his tell.

I tramp on across the yard and they both look up at me, Joel and Carson, Joel eclipsing his irritation so quick I'm impressed especially since he's probably six beers in. Y'all havin' fun? I ask. Sure, Carson says but Joel just drags on his cigarette like he's bored with the question. Beside us the bouncy castle lists to one side. I peer through the netting for a body count. You rented a death trap, Joel tells me and I say, It's not *my* fault these people can't count. I think we should give it a try, Carson admits. I start to shake my head then realize *fuck* he isn't asking me. He's talking to Joel. You in? Carson asks and Joel drops his cigarette. Why not, he says.

Joel / Austin / October 2006

I wouldn't have expected to be able to slide into a rhythm again after a run interrupted, but I had no trouble losing myself after saying goodbye to Brice. You don't know your limitations, Adam told me once when I went for a quick run before bed and came home a couple of hours later to find him furious. I always figure I could cave to worse addictions. I have in the past.

Adam. I've almost managed to let him slip from my mind, and now I stand in front of my laptop, catching my breath and trying to decide if I should check my email now or after I've showered. But the pull of that laptop suddenly feels magnetic, and I can't wait any longer.

There's his name, right in my inbox next to a subject line I didn't know how to write. I'd finally typed what was in my head. *Thinking of you.* That didn't have to mean anything other than that he was on my mind, and once he read my message, he'd see I wasn't trying to do anything other than make a benign connection.

What a crock of shit, I can hear James drawling. Well, maybe he's right, but I made sure the language of my email didn't reflect the depth of my emotion. I didn't tell Adam that even though it's been thirteen months since we broke up, I still have nights when I cry myself to sleep. I didn't tell him I can't bring myself to date, that aside from one drug-induced night this past summer, I've turned to a life of celibacy. I might have indicated that I miss him, but I certainly didn't come right out and say the words.

Adam hasn't shown the same restraint. I stare at the screen, sentences striking one after the other like I've stumbled into a sea of serpents. *I've wanted to reach out to you so many times, Joel... Tell me you're ready to give us another chance... One word from you and I'll book a flight to Austin... I've never stopped loving you...*

Every emotion I've worked my way through over the past year rushes to the surface, as if I've spent most of my time avoiding my therapist's office instead of huddled there in tears—until I couldn't afford her anymore. I don't know what I was expecting, but it wasn't this mind dump of regret or this whirlwind of entreaty. I knew Adam would write back, but I thought he'd be intentional. I thought he'd be deliberate. I stand up so quickly I knock over my chair. *Can I call you tonight? I need to hear your voice.* Is he kidding? Is he fucking *kidding?*

I quit my job, sold my house, moved in with him and made myself available in every way I could for *years.* I traveled with him to Kentucky to help take care of his father, considered adopting a *kid* with him, made excuse after excuse for his lies, and what I got in return was a half-assed confession that he was sleeping with one of his colleagues.

I start pacing, thinking about my truck parked outside, the brake job it needs, the way I buy gas five dollars at a time. I think about how much I stress over my rent every month, how often I debate the benefits of a fresh tube of paint over a week's worth of groceries. I think about how I feel when the class I occasionally teach at Laguna Gloria doesn't make.

I thought I'd gotten to a place where I could at least understand the motivation for Adam's affair. After we broke up, after his father died, I went with him to Kentucky, made love to him in his childhood bed. By then, I knew I wouldn't go back to him, but I wanted to give him that much because of everything he'd given me for so many years, because I knew that whatever he'd gone through with Bobby—his partner who died of AIDS in '93—had corrupted him in a way that was impossible for me to judge. I thought when we said goodbye that we did so on a compassionate note.

But there's no mercy in this email. *I've never stopped loving you.* Really? Even when you were lying to me night after night? Even when you were fucking someone else? All that time you were loving me? *I'll quit my job, sell my house...*

I will not go through this again.

James / Chicago / September 2005

I'm sound ass asleep when the phone pulls me awake, alarming me the way everything does now that Lizzie's pregnant. One unexpected sound and I'm skittering like a tree rat. Sometimes I feel like I'm the only one who can keep this baby of mine safe.

James? Joel says when I answer. What, I mutter, squinting at the clock and for a second he's so quiet I figure we got disconnected. When I realize he's crying I bolt right up. Beside me Lizzie sits up too. She's already feeling sick just a few weeks into her first trimester and I put my hand on her shoulder to try to ease her back down. Who is it? she whispers. I can barely mouth Joel's name. He's bawling and I stumble out of bed, murmuring *hey hey hey* as I make my way downstairs.

I finally quiet his crying enough to hear what's going on. Adam's having an affair. He confessed this past weekend while they were celebrating their anniversary. That *prick*, I hiss. I can't stay with him, Joel says, I can't even *look* at him. What're you gonna *do*? I ask. I don't know! he wails, But I can't stay!

Man, he needs me. He needs me there in Austin to help him figure this out. He needs me to help him move. Hell, he might need money too because what Joel brings in with his paintings isn't enough for him to live on. At the very least he needs me to put him on a plane to Chicago so he can get a little distance. But I can't leave Lizzie and I don't think she can handle the stress of having Joel in our home. We can't take any chances with the baby. Joel— I mumble. I know, he says but the fact that he understands makes me feel like an even shittier friend.

Friend. Like that paltry word can even begin to describe everything we are to each other.

I guess that's why I start talking, why I start telling him how much he means to me and always has, why I can't stand hearing him so upset, why I'd do anything for him, anything, I just can't leave Lizzie alone, not right now. I wanna help, I say but the words I should probably be keeping to myself—this situation's about him, not me—just make him cry harder. Joel, I plead, Baby, please.

The word slips out before I know what I'm saying and falls into the space between us whether it's welcome or not. At the same time I hear a sharp inhale and turn to find my wife standing at the bottom of the stairs. Here I am, caught in the worst possible place, between Joel and Lizzie, my past and my present, my heart so torn I don't know who to apologize to first.

My wife wins though if I'm honest with myself the baby gives her the edge. I hurry Joel off the phone then break the news about Adam's affair. Don't tell me you're going to him, she warns and even though that's exactly what I'd be doing if she weren't a handful of weeks pregnant I shake my head. Joel can take care of himself, I tell her but the words roll over and over in my belly. I'm not sure I believe them and even if they're true I don't want him to have to muscle his way through this alone.

By the time I call him back he's in his studio. I try to pick up where we left off, try to explain why I hung up so fast. You have a wife, James, he says, I'm not your problem.

I'll never forgive myself. I'll never forgive myself for so much.

Joel / Chicago / July 2006

I knew we weren't going to spend the same kind of time together we've spent in the past. James has a baby. I understand that. I wasn't expecting to bar hop. I wasn't thinking pot. But I don't know who's more attached to whom: that kid does not like to be out of his father's arms, and James isn't particularly interested in putting him down.

I might be annoyed if it weren't so clear that I'm privy to something special. I feel like I'm witnessing something deepen here, and so far, I haven't tired of watching the two of them together. I keep thinking of the birthday James and I spent under Barton Springs Road back in '96 by the train tracks at Zilker Park, and I don't care how many diapers I have to watch him change. I'm just glad he made it out the other side.

Elizabeth, on the other hand, could march me right into the mouth of madness. At first, I think she isn't letting us out of her sight because Henry's always with James, and she wants to be with her baby. That makes sense, even though the few times I've gotten James on the phone lately he told me Elizabeth isn't bonding with Henry the way he expected. I assume that's changing; I'm bonding with the kid, and he's not even mine. But the longer I'm here, the more I'm starting to think that I'm the reason she's following us around, and I know for sure that's the case when Henry falls asleep on my second night in town, and Elizabeth trails us onto the back porch. James has a bottle of wine, as well as the baby monitor, and he gives Elizabeth an odd look over his shoulder when she steps out behind us.

He's not rude. Let me get an extra glass, he offers, going back inside, and for a moment—the first since I've arrived, possibly for the first time since the night we met—Elizabeth and I find ourselves alone. She doesn't look delighted by the prospect. In fact, she's trembling, her arms crossed over a blouse that's probably too thin even in July for a girl who grew up in Houston. I'm trying to think of the best way to get in her good graces, and I finally say after a beat too long, You have a beautiful son, Elizabeth.

I don't think she's going to accept the compliment, and I'm not sure why. Because she didn't hear me? Because she doesn't agree? Because it's coming from me and I'm the enemy? Thank you, she finally says, and James swings open the door, holding a crystal glass that was likely a wedding gift. Taking in the tension, he pauses. I have a feeling he's remembering the last time he left us alone. I'll pour, I say, reaching for the wine.

I drink a little more than I usually do these days and probably more than I should. When I'm with James, every hold I have loosens. That's not necessarily a negative; sometimes I need the escape, that bottle of beer, a hit from a joint. But that's not what's going on here. I'm caught between James and his wife in a way that's getting worse with every visit. She alludes to their life together; James tries to pull me in; I drink. We're creating some seriously fucked up energy, and I pour my second glass of wine way too soon.

James / Chicago / May 2007

Joel and I are camped out on the single bed I bought after Henry was born when Lizzie put her foot down about letting him sleep in our room and I needed hourly reassurance that our baby was still breathing. Henry's propped in my lap, working away at his pacifier, sleepy-eyed in a pair of footed pajamas. We've had the sweetest, slowest night we've had in a long while with a walk to the park and takeout from the Italian restaurant a few blocks over and plenty of time for a bath. A half a dozen times I handed Henry over to Joel to see if my boy would start squawking but not one time has he made a peep. A little while ago I watched Joel put a fresh Huggie on him, my arms folded across my chest. I figured Joel would get the thing on backwards, assuming Henry stayed still long enough for Joel to fasten the tags but that kid of mine just sucked his fingers as Joel told him some story about the cat we saw out front. Man, you're some kinda magic, I said when Joel scooped Henry into his arms. You're just now figuring that out? he asked.

Every night before my son goes to bed we read. He likes books about animals and I've got plenty of them, board books with thick pages and bright colors. This has always been our time, partly because Lizzie's so done in by the end of the day but mostly because I'm pretty reluctant to go downstairs and leave Henry all the way up here by himself. So I usually turn in early, read in bed or finish up some grading. That way I'm close in case anything happens.

Tonight we're reading a book about an octopus and Henry blinks at its shiny tentacles. 'Night, buddy, Joel says when I finally finish and something about the way he touches Henry's cheek with the tip of his finger brings the tears I shut down at the airport earlier today right back into my eyes. After Joel's gone I rock my son the way I have every night for the past year even when I was tired as shit myself, even when Lizzie tried to tell me Henry would never learn to get to sleep on his own if I did the work for him. I'm not gonna let him cry it out, I told her. I found it hard enough to shift from the rocker to the crib every night, heart-breaking to sleep across an entire room from him. You're spoiling him, Lizzie told me that first night we brought him home after I flew out of bed the second I heard him on the monitor. I don't care, I said and the next day I bought the single bed.

I don't see how she didn't go to him herself. We should've lost him, coming as early as he did and after seeing him in NICU for weeks without being able to hold him close we finally had him home. I wanted him as near as I could get him and my wife just wanted a good night's sleep. Whatever, I know this sounds callous but I swear sometimes I think Henry wasn't born so much as he escaped.

When he's sound asleep I lower him into his crib. Henry sucks once, twice on his pacifier.

How that woman could leave him I will never understand.

Joel / Austin / October 2006

I'm still seething from Adam's email, and I yank open the back door and step into my scrappy backyard. The kids next door give me gleeful waves because I'm always friendly when I see them. Watch me, watch me! one of the little girls hollers, clambering into the tree house her dad built for her. He works construction, speaks rough English. His wife brought me tamales when I first moved in, and I'd thanked her, though I couldn't eat them since I'm vegetarian. She asked if I have a girlfriend. Boyfriend, I corrected her, and she tittered, one warm, brown hand clapped over her mouth. I think I make her husband uncomfortable.

I take a deep breath because it's not this little girl's fault Adam's an ass. Look at you, I say, walking to the edge of the yard. Do you want to come up? she asks, and her invitation makes me smile. I do, I say, But maybe another time, okay? She nods, throwing a black braid over her shoulder. Her little sister climbs up behind her, their younger brother toddling around the backyard in a Superman costume a week and a half before Halloween. They have a dog too, a scruffy mongrel that wakes me with his howling on bright nights. Looks like he's the babysitter, but believe me, there's no judgment in that observation. The kids' mother cleans houses even on the weekends. Your dad around today? I ask Isabella, the girl who offered up her tree house. He's at work, she tells me. I glance again at the little boy. Pablo, I think they call him. He has the dog by the collar, a sippy cup in his free hand. I know his sisters will watch him; they're responsible kids, for their ages.

Y'all have lunch yet? I ask, sounding more like James than myself. I'm hungry, the younger girl pipes up, like she's been waiting for someone to ask. Isabella shushes her. Want to go to Tito's? I ask them, referring to the taco truck around the corner. Isabella's sister squeals, jumping up and down hard enough to shake the tree. We're not supposed to leave the house, Isabella tells me. Does your mom have a cell phone? I ask.

I have to carry Pablo because if he's not in my arms, he's in the middle of the street. He's surprisingly docile once I pick him up; I'd expected a fight. Isabella walks beside me, but her little sister, Rosalinda, runs ahead of us. I still haven't showered, but my blood pressure's dropping. Isabella's talking about school and her friends and her dream of being an astronaut when she grows up. I want to see Earth from space, she says, Don't you? Pablo swings a chubby arm around my neck. The day's getting warmer, and fresh sweat makes our skin stick. Isabella managed to convince him to take off his Superman costume, but he's still wearing the cape.

We've missed the lunch rush at Tito's, and after we get our tacos, we carry them to the park around the corner. Isabella had to tell her mother three times that I was paying. I have a feeling I'll be getting tamales as a thank you. Now we sit at one of the picnic tables chained to the tree overlooking the swings.

Adam and I came here once. We were on the verge of a cold front that night, too.

Isabella eats one taco, Rosalinda two before she runs to the slide. Pablo sits beside me with his mouth full of tortilla. Taking her time with her lemonade, Isabella tells me in between sips about the trip she wants to take to Fiesta, Texas for her eleventh birthday next summer. I imagine that's a big vacation for her family. Hell, San Antonio would be a big deal for me at this point. My trip to Chicago in July decimated my checking account.

And that was before I tacked a hotel room on the end.

Do you like roller coasters? Isabella asks. Of course, I say, and she tells me she wants to ride on the kind that go upside down. She thinks they'll be good training for her future gig as an astronaut. You're smart to prepare now, I tell her, You'll have a competitive edge. She looks pleased. I can do a back flip from the monkey bars, she announces. Show me, I say, and she untangles her legs and runs off after her sister, checking over her shoulder to make sure I'm watching. Pablo climbs into my lap like he's known me all his life.

I used to hold Adam's niece, Grace, like this. Rye too, though Lindsey was already five by the time I met her and even as a baby didn't let anyone get too close.

I loved those kids. Sucks that losing Adam meant losing them too.

James / Chicago / April 2007

The only thing that calms my wife is distance from our son. For the past year I've watched her panic when she holds him. He retaliates by screaming something fierce every time she gets near him. I've told her if she just takes a breath or two, if she just relaxes he'll stop crying. She tells me she can't stand the way I hover over the two of them like I'm convinced she's going to do something wrong. So I try to leave them alone and let her manage without me. Listening in on the monitor makes me nuts. She just doesn't know how to talk to him, how to *be* with him.

I'm starting to think she's not mother material.

I want to throw Henry a birthday party. Everything we've gone through, the miracle he's shown himself to be every single day since he showed up last year six weeks ahead of schedule and Lizzie can't wrap her head around the fact that maybe that's something to celebrate. I just don't think I can handle a party right now, she keeps saying and I finally tell her all she has to do is show up.

I keep my word. I don't even ask for her input. I make all the decisions myself, plan everything from the presents to the party favors to the cake that looks like Mr. Boo, that funky stuffed bug Henry loves. The morning of the party I shoo her away with strict instructions to relax. A massage, a nice lunch, maybe a little shopping. When she gets home she'll be able to enjoy the party.

She never shows. That afternoon I've got a houseful of guests and Henry in my arms and I'm making one bullshit excuse after another to explain why she's not standing beside me. At first I'm pissed. Then I'm terrified. No one, not even Lizzie would miss her only child's birthday party and I keep ducking into the kitchen to check the phone, thinking she'll leave a message. I must call her cell a dozen different times but I cannot get my wife to pick up.

Monica finally brings her home hours after the party's over. Monica, Lizzie's best friend who didn't bother to answer when I called her this afternoon. Where the hell have you been? I ask.

Then I take a closer look at my wife. She's drunk and I'm so stunned I just let Monica maneuver her through the doorway. My wife weeps her way upstairs and into our room—her room since I haven't spent the night in here for almost a year—and tumbles onto the bed. I help her sit up long enough to take off her coat. Lizzie, I say as Monica unwinds her scarf, What the hell *happened*? But my wife's eyes stay shut.

The second I close the bedroom door behind us Monica lights into me. Am I seriously too stupid to realize that when Lizzie tells me she can't handle a party she means what she says? Can't I see what's happening right in front of me? Lizzie's *drowning* and I'm so obsessed with that baby I can't hear her even when she tells me explicitly what she needs. If anything happens to her Monica will hold me responsible, personally fucking responsible. She jabs her finger into my chest with that last threat and I grab her wrist. You going to hurt me too? she asks. I've never hurt Lizzie, I hiss, letting go. She smirks like she knows better and I actually *want* to hit her, Monica with her empty accusations and her borderline homophobia. Instead I lift my hands and step away from her.

I don't think she'll hear the *bitch* that makes it past my lips as I turn toward the stairs but the shove that sends me stumbling down the first couple steps tells me I'm wrong. After I catch myself I stare at her in disbelief. She looks horrified, I'll give her that. But I'm not taking any chances. After you, I say, gesturing for her to take the lead. I'll admit I savor her hesitation and I'll admit when she finally moves in front of me I think about how I'd feel kicking her ass right down that flight of stairs. But I keep my arms and legs—and verbal insults—to myself. In the living room I nod at Henry crashed out in his Pack 'n Play. Don't wake him, I warn and that mouth of hers stays shut until the front door closes behind her.

The next morning Lizzie apologizes. Profusely. Like our marriage and her entire relationship with our son depend on it. Somethin's gotta change, Lizzie, I tell her and she draws her knees up to her chest—we're sitting on her bed while Henry naps in my arms—and lets her hair spill over her legs. She looks like the girl I married and I cup her cheek in the palm of my hand.

That's the last tender moment we share. Two weeks later I watch her pack her bags. Henry's at the park with his babysitter. Lizzie doesn't wait around to say goodbye.

Joel / Austin / October 2006

Pablo's asleep against my chest by the time I get the kids back to their house, and I offer to put him down in his crib. Isabella opens the front door and leads me through a living room scattered with toys, then into one of the two bedrooms. All three kids must share this space. I step around a dollhouse—I'm guessing it's handmade and probably by the kids' father—then catch my reflection in the mirror. Pablo's sacked out, his lips pursed, his fingers clutching my sleeve. Gently, I unhook his hand from my shirt and take off his cape. Does he need a blanket? I whisper, and Isabella nods. You should be a dad, she adds as I lower him into his crib.

When we reach the living room, the front door opens. *Papá!* Rosalinda cries. Her father catches her in his arms, frowning when he sees me. *Joel nos llevo a comer tacos,* Isabella tells him. *Joel took us out for tacos,* and he instantly looks suspicious. *Mi momma dijo que estaba bien,* Rosalinda adds as she catches her father's expression. *Mommy said it was okay.* Where? he asks me. Tito's, I say, and he reaches into his back pocket for his wallet. I hold up my hand to stop him. No, no, I protest, My treat.

I can see him trying to compute that, why the guy next door would take his kids out for tacos. I'm not sure I'm going to like his conclusion. Meanwhile, he's counting out bills like he doesn't want to be beholden. *Espere,* I say. *Wait,* and he looks up, surprised I know even that much Spanish. I'm not fluent, but I can pick my way through a conversation. *Ayuda para mi?* I ask, trying to ask for help and probably butchering the language. *Que tipo de trabajo?* he asks. *What kind of work,* and I cast around for *bed frame* in Spanish. *Mi cama,* I say, *Abajo…* He's nodding, opening the door like we're going to take a look at my bed right now. I start to correct him, then realize this is probably one debt he wants to work off immediately. Shrugging, I wave goodbye to the girls. *Gracias,* they chorus without having to be told. Anytime, I say.

I follow their father out the front door, trying to remember his name. Fernando? He keeps his expression impassive until we make it to my bedroom, but once I show him the problem—the base of my bed has started to splinter, and if I drop down in the wrong way, the mattress sags—he finds his stride. He tells me what's wrong, speaking so fast I just nod and assume he knows what he's doing. *Comprende?* he finally asks. Enough, I admit, and he chuckles, the first time I've seen the guy crack a smile. *Mañana,* he tells me. *Muchas gracias,* I say, and he shakes my hand.

Disaster averted, I shut the door behind him. Now I'll get the damn bed fixed. Not a bad afternoon, given where I was after reading Adam's email a couple of hours ago, and I consider that much-needed shower. Instead, I find myself in my studio. I'd rather give this relief a chance to deepen, and there's no likelier way for that to happen than with a brush in my hand.

But the second I touch the canvas, I start crying. My anger has segued right into grief, my emotions complicated by Pablo's arms around me and Isabella's comment about me making a good dad. I never should've emailed Adam. I've been managing just fine. I've been painting. I've been running; I've been meditating. Now our breakup seems like yesterday instead of last year, and I'm sitting on the floor of my studio with my head in my hands. What was I thinking?

I don't even have to close my eyes to feel Adam's arms around me; shut, I can get there even faster. I can see him, too, that slow smile he saved just for me. His eyes were the same blue as the Caribbean where the ocean meets the shore and every bit as warm. He had long legs and calves I'd knead in the middle of the night because he'd wake up with cramps from not stretching well enough after he cycled. His hair had just started receding when I met him, and over the years, he grew more and more self-conscious; I never teased him. I didn't care. He looked at me like he couldn't get enough, like he'd take everything I was willing to give him.

When I concentrate on the ways he hurt me, when I think about the lies he told, when I picture him with the guy from his office, I'm so overcome with rage that I can't imagine ever wanting to hear his voice again. I hang on to ire because I know forgiveness will make me vulnerable. He still loves me. He still wants me. I knew that even before I opened his email this afternoon. I could so easily go back to him.

If I did, I don't think I could live with myself. Returning to Adam would mean accepting what he did to me, the way I've accepted every other deception I've been fed in my life. My father, my mother, James… I'm tired of assuming that everyone I love will hurt me. I expected more from my partner.

Adam might be sincere when he tells me he'll never make the same mistakes again. I'm just tired of feeling like a man betrayed.

James / Austin / September 1991

I'm not even sure how it happened but Joel's got a basketball game going in the bouncy castle. The one I ordered has hoops at either end and came with a ball so Joel divided people into teams. They're four on four: Joel, Carson and two girls on one side versus three of my pledge brothers and Kim Cunningham on the other. I've been recruited as the referee even though I tried to tell them we shouldn't all be in the bouncy castle at the same time. There's a weight limit, I insisted and two of the girls got all weird like I was calling them fat or something. Relax, man, Joel told me and I wanted to remind him he was the one who just a few minutes ago called the bouncy castle a death trap. But he wouldn't have heard me anyway. He's got his eyes all over Carson and fuck if Carson isn't giving him something back: half a smile, a shoulder bump and when they're huddled in a circle talking strategy a hand on Joel's waist that seems a little too close to his ass. If Shelton sees this shit I'm screwed.

Joel's team has four points on Kim's but they've struggled for every one. They're kind of at a disadvantage with two girls and right quick Kim's team gets a three pointer and the foul. Joel shakes his head like the call pegs me as disloyal and I tell him to keep his hands to himself. There's a double meaning there I'm hoping he'll hear but he's already following the ball. He gets most of the rebounds and this one he passes to a girl who turns right around and gives it away like she's decided to switch teams or something. Joel and Carson pound across the castle and when the ball goes up so do they, reaching in the same space and coming down hard together. They take their sweet-ass time untangling themselves and I end up missing the next call. Fielding! someone shouts, Where the fuck are you?

Refereeing two games, that's where.

Another twenty minutes and we're finally close to finishing. Kim's team has six points on Joel's and Joel calls a time out. I watch his team move toward each other, sweaty and out of breath, arms touching. The vibe in this castle's spinning me out and I gulp the beer in my hand even though I'm the one who told everyone we shouldn't be drinking in here. Kim raises her arms to straighten her ponytail and her teammates step closer without even realizing what they're doing. Across the tent Carson's nodding at Joel, who's talking like he knows how to score. Maybe he does. I guessed from the beginning but I've never seen his game in action. I actually think Carson might follow him out of here.

Two points then four. Another two and the game's tied. Kim has the ball and Joel gets the rebound then storms off across the castle. At the last second Brandon trips into him and the ball flies from Joel's hand. I call the foul and Joel flips Carson a smile so careless I cringe. I'm not the only one to catch it either. Everyone does and for just a second I hold my breath. Then Joel has the ball and he's balancing the best he can and *whoosh* right through the net. They're down by just one point and I get the ball back to him and there's quiet in the castle like something's really riding on this game then *whoosh* right through the net.

Now Brandon has the ball and he gets it to Kim who loops it overhead in this crazy pass and one of the girls on Joel's team almost, *almost* catches it. Todd grabs it instead and passes it back to Kim and when Joel goes up to block the shot Carson comes from the side and gets the ball like they had the whole thing planned from the start. But Brandon's on him and Carson makes a desperate pass to one of the girls and no one can believe it but she *scores*. Did I just win? she asks in disbelief. That's the game, I tell her, and Joel and Carson lift her up in some kind of victory parade that lasts all of five seconds before they're tumbling down. Dumb luck, Brandon says, helping her to her feet and I look at Joel sprawled next to Carson. They don't seem like they're in much of a hurry to get up and as I watch, Joel leans closer and puts his hand on Carson's arm.

If Joel's into guys whatever, that's his business but I do not need him hitting on my fraternity brothers. He should *know* better and I bolt a pissed glance over my shoulder for Parker or Shelton because Brandon's already kissing the girl who scored the winning shot and the other girl from Joel's team is on the receiving end of a hug I'm thinking her daddy wouldn't much like and with Joel and Carson looking like they're about to blow each other who knows what's next?

Kim Cunningham, that's what. Nice assist, she says to Carson, who squints past the sweat in his eyes to look up at her. Thanks, he says and she holds out a hand to help him up. Before he's all the way on his feet she's kissing him and he stumbles back until they're pressed up against the castle wall. For just a second his arms hang limp at his sides and then they're up and around her so tight her tank top rides above her jeans. I turn to Joel and man, the look on his face like Carson just kicked him in the balls *undoes* me. Hey, I blurt out before I can stop myself and Joel's expression changes quicker than the weather in South Texas. Good game, he says.

Joel / Chicago / July 2006

We're still sitting on the back porch, still drinking wine, still listening for

Henry on the monitor. Elizabeth shivers in the cooling air but seems reluctant to leave us long enough to get a sweater, and James isn't paying attention. He's drinking and animated, and he keeps trying to bring me along for the ride. I want to go with him, but I'm holding myself back out of respect for his wife and how wildly uncomfortable she seems, simply because I'm sitting here talking to her husband with a half-empty glass of wine in my hand. I don't even want to make eye contact with James because of how that might be misconstrued.

I'm thinking of taking a vacation, I finally tell them, just to be saying something.

I don't have the money for a vacation; the airfare to Chicago knocked the balance in my checking account below $100, and I had to let go of an etching I wasn't quite ready to sell just to buy groceries last week. That grant I was awarded helps to pay my rent, but living in Austin isn't cheap, even on the east side. I'm still getting used to managing by myself.

A vacation? James repeats, frowning, Where? Buenos Aires? I say, taking a guess. You're going to Buenos Aires? he asks, confused.

Well, of course that sounds ridiculous. He knows my financial situation. He even offered to pay for my ticket up here, in an ironic twist from our college days. It's just an idea, I mumble. You should go to the beach, he tells me, When was the last time you went scuba diving?

October 2004. Adam and I flew to Belize for a week and stayed at a resort one of our friends had recommended. I made him get certified to dive before we left—he'd been putting it off for years—and in Belize, we dove every day. In the evening, we'd watch the sun fall into the ocean, then make love with the doors to the veranda open wide. Tell me we don't have to leave, I murmured at the end of the week, coiled in a canopied bed beside him, and he kissed the palm of my hand.

Too long, I admit, and James turns to Elizabeth. Did I ever tell you about the time we went to Mexico when we were in college? he asks.

She shakes her head, already looking displeased. Why wouldn't she? The last thing she's going to want to hear about is a trip I took with her husband. And of course she doesn't already know. James didn't tell her much at the beginning, and he clearly hasn't filled in all of the gaps. I give him an irritated look of my own, but he ignores me.

His story falls flat. He should know better; he can't possibly come off well here. Does he honestly think Elizabeth wants to hear I fucked some girl on the balcony of her hotel while James made out with her friend on the other side of the sliding glass door? And his panic attack he had in the pool... Elizabeth's looking at him like she's wondering why she married him. You were fine once we got to the drop, I remind him, and he shrugs, missing the lifeline I've just thrown him. I didn't have a choice, he says, I wasn't about to let you dive without me.

I give up and let him bury himself, which he does quickly and efficiently. Joel was *cruising* the dive master, he tells Elizabeth, enunciating the word like it's some kind of secret, like he's part of a clique his wife can't possibly understand, let alone join. I know what *cruising* means, she says in a tight voice, and though she's been nothing but cold to me since I got here, I offer her a sympathetic smile. She doesn't reciprocate. James gazes at me over the rim of his wineglass, careless the way he usually is when he's had a drink or two. I give my head a quick shake to try to stop him from saying whatever he has on his tongue, but he just winks.

I know your tell, he says.

James / Fort Worth / March 2006

I don't realize how bad I need to see Joel until he gets out of his truck, this piece of shit that puts the pieces of shit I drove in college to shame. How'd you even get that thing here? I ask and he laughs. He's wearing sunglasses that hide his eyes but I know he's still hurting. I take him in a hug, our first since he and Adam split up—our first since that phone call last Christmas—then let go when Lizzie shows up behind me.

My spring quarter's just about to start but we managed to schedule in a baby shower first and I know the past couple days have just about put my wife over the edge. We flew to Houston on Thursday to stay two nights with my in-laws then flew up to Forth Worth yesterday afternoon so Lizzie would have a little time to rest for the shower today. The small talk has gotten to her and I'm guessing she's not thrilled about spending the rest of our time here with Joel, who drove up from Austin to see us. I wasn't about to tell him not to come. I haven't seen him since I visited him in Austin last summer and given everything he's been through since then—breaking up with Adam and moving out on his own—I wouldn't have dreamed of blowing him off this weekend no matter how much Lizzie doesn't like him.

Well, and I needed to be damn sure last Christmas wasn't going to be a problem for us. The longer we went without seeing each other the weirder we'd feel when we finally got together. I figured my eyes would be skittering all over the place when he pulled up just now but man, I cannot get enough of him. I give him a grin like we're still in college and he smiles back like he can't help himself. Sixty seconds and the weight of the past seven months just drops away.

My folks haven't seen too much of Joel since my wedding and dinner reminds me of Thanksgivings in college when Joel and I would make the trip north. I wish my sister could've been here too but at least she made it to the shower Lizzie's friends threw her last week in Chicago, pulling me aside when it was over to tell me my wife had three glasses of champagne before they'd even cut the cake and making me mad all over again that I hadn't been invited so I could keep an eye on her. Whatever, I get that most guys would be happy to leave the baby showers to their wives but that never did make sense to me. I want in on the action. Lizzie's not doing a great job of showing up for her pregnancy anyway. Someone's got to look out for that baby.

Lizzie knows better than to drink in front of my parents, not when she's pregnant, and without a glass of wine as a lubricant she sits so quiet during dinner that a couple times my mom leans over and asks if there's anything she needs. Each time Lizzie says no and the second we finish eating she excuses herself. I jump right up and trail her into my old bedroom, asking if she's okay, if there's anything I can get her. I don't care that she was borderline rude at dinner. She's pregnant, she gets a pass. I just want to make sure she's all right. Please, she says, skirting away from me when I try to smooth her blouse over her belly, Stop hovering.

I need to be understanding. I get that she wants her body back, I know her hormones are all over the place. But sometimes I get so tired of her tongue. I'm just tryin' to help, I tell her. You can start by leaving me alone, she says.

Well, that'll work since I've got plans with Joel anyway. You're sure you're okay? I say. I'm *fine*, she insists and I tell her I won't be late. Her brow crinkles. Where are you going? she asks. To grab a beer, I remind her. Just the two of you? she says and maybe it's last Christmas that makes me bristle. It's a beer, Lizzie, I tell her, Not a blowjob.

Her pretty blue eyes widen right up. Why did you say that? she asks, Why would you say that? Jesus, Lizzie, I moan, You're actin' like I'm goin' out to cheat on you. Are you? she asks. Of course not! I say. Then why are you leaving me here alone? she wails. You're gonna be asleep in an hour anyway, Lizzie! I say, And he drove all the way up from Austin to see me! So *what*? she cries, I'm carrying your fucking baby!

She might've had me without that expletive.

The windows in Joel's truck are old school and I crank mine down before he can even start the engine. I know he heard Lizzie and me arguing and I finally admit that she's pissed, that she doesn't want me to go anywhere tonight. She doesn't want you to go anywhere? he says, Or she doesn't want you to go anywhere with me? What's the difference, I mutter. I don't want to make trouble, he says. You're always gonna be the trouble between us, Joel, I inform him and he gives me a long look. I shake my head. Whatever, I mumble, I'm tired of apologizing for something that happened a year before I even met her.

I tell him to drive way the hell north of the city past the suburban sprawl and the racetrack but first I make him stop at a convenience store for a six-pack and some Marlboros. Then we head west along a road I haven't traveled since high school. I know of a cemetery out here and we speed right past its wrought iron gate before I realize we've missed it. A cemetery? Joel asks in the middle of a three-point turn, shaking his head. Historic, I say and he rolls his eyes.

When he shuts off the engine the night takes us in. Man, will you listen to that? I murmur, opening the door and setting one foot on the ground. Together we amble to the front of the truck and lean back against the hood. Beer? I ask, offering him a bottle and he takes it but shakes his head when I open the cigarettes. Sometimes, I admit, lighting up, A fresh pack of Marlboros feels like my new best friend. Thanks, he says and I laugh. I blame you for this habit, you know, I add. I'm taking a lot of blame tonight, he acknowledges. You're a bad influence, I agree. Let's just fuck and be done with it, he says.

Whatever, I like our banter, the *what if* we trade like we're sharing a cigarette. I like the tension between us and that we've managed to get it back after fucking ourselves ten years ago. So we crossed the line last Christmas, so what. Look at us now, standing here easy as ever. That's testament to something.

That's testament to us.

Joel / Austin / October 2006

My studio's well past dark by the time I stop crying. I couldn't paint right now if I tried, and I deliberate for only half a second before I reach for the phone. James and I haven't spoken much since I hung up on him after my trip to Chicago in July, and even when we've talked, we've kept our conversations brief, as if we want to make sure we don't linger so long we end up arguing. Now I just want to hear his voice.

You caught me at a good time, he says, I just got Henry to sleep. He starts talking about his son's appointment with the pediatrician, how often he's eating, how much he's sleeping. I can't bring myself to ask about Elizabeth, but James tells me that she's taking anti-depressants, and they're not helping. I've been researching postpartum depression for months, he says, And I promise you this disconnect between Lizzie and Henry was there before she even delivered. He tells me he doesn't know how he's managing; he has piles of grading; he was so fed up earlier today that he insisted Elizabeth make plans with a friend for the evening, just to get her out of the house. I haven't gotten more than four hours of sleep in a row since Henry was born, he tells me, but I can feel his relief. He would've agreed to four hours of sleep a night forever if it meant the difference between a life with Henry and a life without him.

So what's up with you? he finally asks, and I hesitate. He knows me well enough to notice; maybe that's why I called him. Out with it, he demands, and I admit that I sent Adam an email. True to form, he starts swearing. What the *fuck*, Joel? he says, Why would you do that? I don't know, I confess, I guess I just wanted to see how he'd respond. Don't be a dumbass, he says, He's going to think you want him back. I was innocuous, I mumble, realizing the word probably doesn't exist when it comes to how I feel about Adam. Sure you were, he agrees, What'd you say? I don't know, I sigh, Something about missing our deck and the sunset... Well, shit, Joel, he snorts, Why didn't you just invite him on down for a hand job? I wasn't that obvious, I insist. Whatever, he says, You were so fucked up last year, remember? Of course I remember, I tell him. Well, do you want to go through that again? he asks, All the lies and betrayal and deceit? Don't *yell* at me, James, I say. You're walking a masochistic line, Joel, he warns, and something about the way he's refusing to acknowledge my heartbreak or why I might have felt the need to reach out to Adam in light of how alone I've been feeling reawakens my anger from earlier. I guess you're here to make sure I don't cross any lines, I tell him.

Now he's pissed. You called me for advice, he says. I don't remember asking for your advice, I say, And a lecture's the last thing I need from you right now! I'm trying to *help*, he says. By calling me a masochist? I ask. Joel, he insists, He *hurt* you. So did you, James, I remind him, And yet here you are, front and fucking center!

That shuts him up long enough for me to take a deep breath. I don't want to end this call with me throwing my phone across the room, the way I did when I got back from Chicago in July. Look— I start. Adam did you in, Joel, he says, Adam did you in.

He's right. For months, I didn't know if I'd ever be able to follow my own advice and move on. If it hadn't been for my work, I might not have made it out the other side. A year later, I'm still walking around with an open wound. Even so, I'm trying. I could've gone so many different ways, but instead, I live clean. I don't sleep around, I rarely drink, I've succumbed one time, and one time only, to a little Ecstasy. Every day I run, no matter what the weather. I paint like it's my religion. I'm holding everything together in spite of what I've been through in the past year, in my lifetime. I'm not even jaded.

But Christ, I don't need to be berated for one moment of weakness, for reaching out to a man who loved me once and loves me still. I know Adam did me in. So did James, and if he had a modicum of self-awareness, he'd be able to see that.

Look, I start again in a low voice, I'm doing my best here without a lot of help. What's that supposed to mean? James asks, turning my words around so they're all about him, I'm on the phone with you right now, Joel! Yeah, thanks for taking my call, I tell him, and he groans. Could we have one conversation where you don't tell me all the ways I'm not giving you enough? he asks. Could we have one conversation where you're not a colossal disappointment? I retort. If you don't like what I have to offer, he says, Hang the fuck up. I'm *alone*, James! I cry, I'm alone down here, and you're in Chicago with your baby and your demented fucking wife!

We both hold our breaths. My demented fucking wife, he finally repeats. All right, I concede, That was... Out of line? he finishes, Un-fucking-called for? I said I was sorry, I tell him. No, he says, You didn't. Well, maybe I'm not, I mutter, and he lets out an incredulous laugh that gives me an idea of the groveling I'll have to do if I ever want to make this right. You know, Joel, he says, I have a responsibility to my son right now, and to my job and to my marriage. Believe me, I say, hating the way this conversation's devolving, I'm well aware I'm no longer part of the equation. I can't do this, he tells me, I don't have the time to negotiate your insecurity. Well, maybe if you didn't pull me in and push me away, I'd know where I fucking stood! I shout.

This time, he's the one who hangs up on me. Dropping my phone, I get to my feet, then slam my way into the bathroom, where I turn on the shower and rip off the clothes I wore for my run.

There's no way Celeste's party has already ended.

James / Chicago / May 2007

So what happened? Joel asks. He's sitting on the couch, one scuffed boot propped on the coffee table in a way that would make Lizzie nuts if she could see it. I'm sitting across from him in the recliner. The second glass of wine I've drunk has started to bottom out. There's so much shit pending: the last couple weeks of classes, grading, commencement, turning in what I need for tenure... Lizzie left right now for a reason. If Joel hadn't agreed to help I don't know where I would've turned.

I reach for the wine. Joel shakes his head when I wave what's left in his direction. He shook his head when I first opened the bottle too. You're not really gonna make me drink alone, I said, Are you? Now he turns a half-empty glass around and around as I take the last of the wine. I'll be sorry tomorrow when Henry wakes me up at six, when I get to my office and have to face a stack of papers but right now I just want to relax.

What do you think she'll say when she finds out I'm here? he asks. She *left*, I remind him and he shakes his head. He's probably thinking about his last trip here when Lizzie and I had that fantastic fight and he ended up leaving a day early. She didn't want him, Joel, I say in a low voice, Right from the start she didn't want him.

Whatever, he's going to fight me on that. He'll tell me she wouldn't have gone along with the fertility drugs or the shots I had to inject into her stomach or sex that got so monotonous we couldn't stand to even look at each other. But I'm thinking of the fights we had before Henry was born, about whether or not she should breastfeed (she didn't want to) or how much maternity leave she should take (she thought six weeks was plenty). Just lay off until after you get pregnant, I said once when I saw her with a cocktail. What if I don't ever get pregnant? she asked, Am I supposed to be held hostage for the rest of my *life*?

He's so beautiful, you know? I say and Joel nods, lifting his arms above his head and giving them a stretch. I figure he's just humoring me with that nod but then he adds, Kind of hard not to fall in love with him. Tell that to Lizzie, I mutter and he hesitates like he doesn't want to get caught saying the wrong thing. I wave my hand so he knows he has carte blanche. How much worse could it get? he asks.

For a year I've been managing everything on my own, trying to give Lizzie the space she needed to come back from her pregnancy and all those years of IVF. However hard that stretch of time had been for me I knew Lizzie had it worse. I might've gotten tired of jerking off into a cup but my wife had to deal with all the tests, all the procedures, the physical trauma of that miscarriage. Her body had to recuperate then go through everything all over again. The medications threw her off and with her hormones all over the place I could hardly expect her to settle right into motherhood.

I tried to get her help. I researched postpartum depression—which she swore wasn't the issue—scheduled appointments, picked up prescriptions. I told her we should pay out of pocket for a therapist her friend recommended since the guy wasn't on our insurance. I took every middle-of-the-night feeding, changed every diaper. I did all the grocery shopping, all the cooking, all the laundry. For a year I've done every goddamn thing so she could get back to feeling like herself.

What kind of a mother just leaves? I ask but that's not something anyone—and least of all Joel—can answer. He swallows the last of his wine; noted. I'll have to be careful about how I phrase this shit moving forward.

Have I thanked you yet for comin'? I ask. Once or twice, he says. You're gonna have your hands full, I warn. I can handle it, he tells me.

Man, I hope I can believe him. I don't doubt his intention to help but he has no idea how vigilant I have to be every second that kid's awake. You gotta be on him all the time, Joel, I say, You can't let him outta your sight. So I shouldn't leave him alone in the bathtub, he confirms. You're not makin' me feel better, I mutter and he sighs and leans forward to pull off his boots. Honey, he says, You're going to have to relax and let me do what I came here to do.

He throws that *honey* my way like I've earned it when in reality I've given him nothing but shit for almost two years. I've got the same feeling I had in the car on our way home from the airport like I've been holding my breath and now I'm finally letting it out.

You think you can do that? he asks. I can try, I mumble and he says, Well, that's a start.

Joel / Austin / October 2006

Celeste's party must be in full force because I have to park my truck a block away from her house. I'm grateful; I'd really rather not walk into an intimate gathering after what I've been through today. Nodding a greeting to a few people lingering on the lawn, I skirt through the open front door. There's a crowd, all right, and I duck into the kitchen, where I'm bound to find some alcohol.

I'm taking my first swallow of a surprisingly well-rounded Malbec when Brice meets my eye from across the room. He sure as hell doesn't fit in with the rest of Celeste's friends, not with those Seven for All Mankind jeans and Fiorentini Baker boots. This is a guy I could actually bring home to my father and not run the risk of rejection. Why the smirk? he asks when I reach him. C'mon, I say, You know you belong in Pemberton Heights. I live in Old Enfield, he tells me. Even better, I say.

Celeste approaches with a smile. I'm so glad you came! she exclaims. She's wearing a different hippie skirt, necklaces so long they reach her waist. Well, you have reason to celebrate, I remind her, and she claps her hands together. I do! she tells me, And I'm so thankful you've come to share my joy!

I'd laugh if I didn't find her so delightful. Come see my studio, she cajoles, reaching for my hand, and Brice lets me go.

Her studio's every bit as small as mine, but the energy instantly calms me. I make a slow circle of the shelves lining her walls. She's talented; there's no question about that. How long have you been throwing? I ask. Five years? she says, Brice bought me lessons one Christmas, and I was hooked. She trails a ringed finger along the pottery wheel. Do you want to try? she asks, looking up at me. Seriously? I say, and she invites me into the chair, showing me how to hold the wheel in between my knees, telling me to lock my elbows. Everything has to be dry, she explains, The clay, your hands... I touch my foot to the pedal. You're going to get messy, she warns, a fraction of a second too late.

Five minutes later, I'm covered with clay, and the hum of the machine has a couple of party guests pausing in the doorway. I let the wheel slow, resisting the urge to wipe my fingers on my jeans. I should probably stick with paint, I admit, looking at what I've thrown, and she laughs. Let me see if I can find a shirt for you, she says, and after I wash my hands, I follow her into her bedroom, all incense and candles and crystals. I still can't get my head around her friendship with Brice. He won't care? I ask when she offers me a shirt that obviously came from his closet. How could he? she says as I pull it over my head, When you look so nice?

She reaches for my hands; I let her take them. You have a turbulent energy, Joel, she murmurs, and I get the uncomfortable feeling she's reading my thoughts about Adam or maybe James. I unwind my fingers from hers, but she touches my arm, and before I know what I'm doing, I'm sitting on the edge of her bed. I'm barely aware of whatever's going on outside of her room, the music that bleeds around the doorframe, a medley of voices that might be drunk or high or some combination of the two. She touches my back until I stop crying. Her hair smells like patchouli.

When I finally raise my head, I feel as if I've been excavated and exposed to the sun. Adam lingers, but on the periphery, and I slip the rubber band from my ponytail and let my hair fall forward. She curls a lock around my ear. No more wine, she cautions. I make my way to my feet, apologizing for hijacking her party. I don't clear without permission, Joel, she adds.

I'm not even sure I consciously realized that's what she was doing. She looks angelic, her eyes vast and wide. I run a slow hand through my hair, watching as she picks up one crystal, then another from an altar in front of her window. She finally settles on something orange and vaguely phallic. When she presses it into my palm, my entire hand warms. Citrine, she says. I gaze down at the crystal shimmering in the light of the votives. You need sleep, she affirms, directing me toward the back door. What about Brice? I ask, realizing I haven't said goodbye, and she laughs. Sit in your car for five minutes before you leave, she tells me.

I do what she says. I feel like I'm dreaming, and when I hear a rap on the window, my eyes blink as if they weigh more than they should. The crystal Celeste gave me throbs on the dashboard. I crank open the window, letting in a rush of cold air. Celeste got to you, huh? Brice says. She did something, I agree, and he walks around the front of my truck. I lean over and unlock the door for him. *That shitty pickup*, I hear Adam say, but the words sound faint and so far away. Still, I hear them, and once Brice gets in beside me, I tell him I don't know what I'm up for. Tonight? he asks, Or in general? In general, I admit.

He stares through the crack in the windshield. That Rolex he's wearing would pay for this truck five times over, and I ache again to sketch him the way I did early this afternoon when I saw him standing in front of Celeste's house. He doesn't belong in this truck any more than he belongs on Chicon, but he owns whatever space he occupies. My father's the same way.

I just got out of a relationship, I add. How long were you together? he asks. Five years, I say, We broke up last September. He cocks his head. *Last*

September, he confirms, A year ago. I nod, and he turns more fully in my direction, his back pressed against the door. And you haven't been out with anyone for a year, he says. Should I be fucking my way through the calendar? I ask, annoyed. Fucking isn't the same thing, he tells me.

With the introduction of that word, the air in my truck electrifies. I think if I touched him, I'd feel a charge, and instead of debating my next move, I reach for him. He opens right up, like I'm exactly what he expected. He smells like privilege, like clothes tailor-made, and up this close, subtly of cologne. Everything about his kiss entitles me, and the windows collect condensate as my fingers follow his black button-down lower. Nipples hard, abs flat, and the buckle of his jeans slips right through its clasp until he stops me. Not here, he says. My place, I murmur, and he laughs. I pull away, the windows opaque from our breath. Nice shirt, by the way, he adds. Celeste said you wouldn't mind, I mumble as he rubs the sleeve in between his thumb and forefinger. Meet me for wine this week, he suggests. So I can return your shirt? I ask, and he smiles. So I can get to know you better, he says.

I palm the citrine Celeste gave me, feeling its heft in my hand. Somewhere in the distance, Adam calls my name. You have to have a first date sometime, Brice says, and Adam's echo gets lost in the reminder.

It's not that I've forgotten about Adam. It's not that I won't have to work shit out with James. But my drive home feels so much smoother than the drive I made to Celeste's a couple of hours ago. I pull into my driveway under the carport. There's a light on next door; now I know I'm looking at the kids' room, and I wonder if Pablo's up or one of the girls had a nightmare. Their dad will be coming over in the morning to work on my bed, and Celeste told me I should get some rest, but for now, I sit on my front steps and take in the night.

James / Austin / September 1991

I can't find Joel, who told me after we crawled out of the bouncy castle that he needed to take a piss. I followed him into the frat house but got waylaid by one of my pledge brothers and now I'm wandering around downstairs looking for Joel like we're playing some late-night version of hide-and-seek. Everyone's drunk or high or both and I'm kind of sick of the entire scene and just want to go home. This right here is why I jumped all over Joel's suggestion to rent a house together. If I lived here I'd be dealing with this shit all the time. I've got a grade point to maintain. I'm not in Austin just to spend my parents' money though I guess I've been doing a damn good job so far. I could've had a free ride at TCU since my dad's an American Studies professor there but man, I did not want to go to college where my dad's teaching.

I'm still trying to figure out if pledging this fraternity was smart. On a night like tonight I'm thinking not so much. I shake off a freshman who looks like she's about to hurl then duck around the corner into the kitchen and there's Joel finally over by the keg. He's downing a beer like it's water and I guess that means I'm driving which is fine by me. He has a badass Ford Explorer and he's generous with the keys. Hell, he's generous in general. I've got to be careful not to take advantage.

I start to head on over to him but then I see Shelton and I pull up short same as I did a few years back when I went fishing down along the coast and found a big old 'gator under the dock. Shelton's talking to Joel all friendly-like but I know that's a bunch of bullshit because Parker told me what he's been saying. I stay where I'm standing so I can figure out what I'm up against and that's when Shelton claps his hand on Joel's shoulder. I watch as his grip tightens and man, there's no *way* Joel's going to put up with that shit, not after what happened in the bouncy castle. Instead he gets this look that kicks me back to the day I met his dad.

His parents weren't supposed to come into town for Parents' Weekend last year. Joel hadn't invited them. But a week before the big day he heard me talking on the phone to my folks and I could hear him thinking that maybe he'd made a mistake cutting his own mom and dad out of his plans. Next thing I knew they were driving up from Houston and Joel was making his bed for the first time since August.

I didn't meet them until Sunday afternoon. I had my own shit going on that weekend with my parents and my little sister in town and the football game and I was already back in the dorm when Joel showed up with his folks. His dad didn't waste any time introducing himself or asking me about my classes and the fraternity I'd just pledged. His mom sat on the edge of Joel's bed like she knew better than to interrupt and after a minute I heard her ask Joel if he'd been working. *Working?* I wanted to laugh. I hadn't seen Joel open a book all semester and he sure as shit didn't need a job with all the cash he left laying around. But Joel started saying something about trying to work with oil paints and I realized what she meant. If by *working* she meant *drawing* then yeah. He was working.

They were talking in these real hushed voices I could barely make out but I guess his dad heard them same as I did since he gave his head a shake and told Joel he was wasting his time. Joel's mom bit her lip. His dad gave him a loose smile that didn't stand a chance at fooling me. I don't have to tell you what happens if you don't make the grades, he said to Joel and fuck if Joel didn't bite his lip just like his momma.

Saying goodbye his dad was all charm and I shook his hand and told him I was happy to meet him. I wasn't about to cause any problems. But after his parents left I turned to Joel like *what the hell was that?* I guess I expected him to rail a little on his dad, maybe agree with me when I hinted around that the guy was a prick. Instead Joel got this weary expression like I'd told him he was going to live to be a hundred and he'd just as soon be done with it.

He has the same look right now and man, that's all I need to get moving. I don't know what Shelton's saying but there's no way it's good and I reach them just in time to hear Shelton growl, You hear me, faggot? Joel starts to nod but then he sees me and I don't know, maybe me showing up was all he needed since here's what I expected of him, right here in this fake smile. His hand goes around the back of Shelton's neck like they're the best of friends and Shelton doesn't move. He just stares at Joel staring at him and for the first time I wonder if maybe there isn't a reason Shelton's being such a dick. Joel's tone isn't anything I've ever heard not ever. Slow and sweet as syrup but with an edge I feel all along my skin. Ohhh, he says, I hear you.

I watch Shelton's mouth open. Hell, I can feel my own lips parting but before anything else can happen Joel drops his hand and turns to me like I was his plan all along, Where've you been? he asks and I shake my head, mute maybe for the first time in my life. He slings an arm around me and even though I know that's for show I throw a smirk I guess I shouldn't over my shoulder.

Man, I'm gonna pay for that later.

The second we're out the door Joel's bravado disappears. We're quiet walking to his Explorer and he hands me the keys. I want to say something so bad, tell him I'm sorry about what happened with Carson or admit he's got bigger balls than I do but of course I can't say a damn thing. We don't talk about who he wants. We don't talk about who he is. The best I can do is repeat what he said earlier. *Good game.*

Joel / Chicago / July 2006

James never treats me with single-minded purpose in front of his wife, but tonight on his back deck, he's leaning toward me, caught up in our trip to Cancun the summer after our sophomore year in college. His wife keeps waving away the smoke from his cigarette, but he's not paying attention. He's focused on my tell. My tell, I repeat, and he winks again. I glance at Elizabeth, who looks even angrier than she did when James was telling her about the girls in Mexico. I don't have a tell, I inform him. Yeah, you do, he says with a laugh.

I'm curious in spite of myself. For years, I had to hide what I was feeling: from the guy in my high school history class who never would've let me borrow his notes if he knew I was gay; from Carson, James's fraternity brother; from James himself. I thought I had a mask no one could penetrate, and I shake my head, sure the wine has gone to James's own. I don't believe you, I shrug, and he smiles. I've known for years, he says, *Years*.

I'm suddenly not so sure I like what he's saying. How many years? I ask, my voice sharper than I intend, but just then, Henry snuffles. Everyone's eyes fly to the monitor as we wait for movement from the third floor. When silence follows, we let out a collective breath; Elizabeth speaks before James can get started again. You never wanted children, Joel, she says, Did you?

I throw a look at James to see if he ever told her that Adam wanted to adopt. He's glowering: he told her plenty, apparently, so I don't have to wonder what made her ask the question. That dig was intentional.

I want to let it go. All of it. The lack of privacy, the way she's trailing us, this undercurrent of animosity and jealousy I'm sick of navigating. I want to be the better person here, step up and recognize she's only three months in to eighteen years of raising a child, and that's on the heels of a miscarriage and one failed attempt at pregnancy after another. I want to acknowledge that she thinks I'm a threat to her marriage. I want to admit—because I know this deep down—that James has a belligerence when it comes to our friendship that most wives would never tolerate, given the context.

But I've had a really shitty year.

I'm loaded like my mother's .38 when Henry wails. James bolts from the porch, and the words I had ready to fire—*I guess that makes two of us*—I swallow with the last of my wine.

I don't need to hurt Elizabeth. She's already crushed; that's easy enough to see, and I'm part of the reason she's unhappy.

James / Fort Worth / March 2006

The night has no right to be so warm. A breeze blows from the south over the cemetery like the ocean might be right over the hill and I lift the latch on the rusty gate, the hinges singing in protest. Gate's cryin', I say. You're drunk, Joel tells me. I'm only on my second beer, I protest and he reminds me that I took down most of a bottle of wine at dinner. I look up from the gate. You keepin' tabs? I ask. Please, he says, You know better than that.

I swing the gate again, cocking my head at the sound. You hear it? I ask him. I hear it, he says. I beckon him farther into the cemetery. Are you looking for something in particular? he asks, following me.

I don't answer him. Back in high school I'd come out here with friends and we'd drink and talk and claim we'd bring a Ouija board the next time.

We were full of shit. None of us wanted to tempt the spirits in this cemetery, especially the two little girls who died within three days of each other just before Christmas in 1879 and who supposedly haunt this spot. I stumble to a stop in front of their graves like I'm paying them respect but what I'm remembering is the baby who died in 1993. By now he'd be twelve years old—if he'd turned out to be a *he*. That wasn't something they told us or maybe they couldn't tell. When Lizzie had her miscarriage we knew we'd lost a boy and now we're getting ready for Henry so I'm assuming. I could be wrong.

I've been wrong about plenty.

Man, I can still hear the hum of the aspirator and feel the weakness in my knees just before I passed out. Next thing I knew I was sitting in the waiting room by myself. I wasn't even there when it ended. I don't know what they did with... with...

What're you doing? Joel suddenly asks like he's onto me or something. Nothin', I say. You're punishing yourself, he tells me. Bullshit, I mutter. Yeah? he says, Then why the hell are we out here? I study cemeteries, Joel, I remind him, taking a stubborn swallow of beer and he says, In ancient Greece! I shrug like six-a-one. Your baby's going to pick up on this energy, James, he says and I snort. You gonna tell me my aura's off next? I ask. Go ahead and make fun if you want, he tells me, But we're standing in a cemetery in the middle of the night, looking at a grave for two girls who died more than a century ago. What's your point? I ask. Let it *go*, he says.

Well shit, how can I? How can I when Lizzie miscarried last time around? Even if she does carry Henry to term I've got years and years of parenting ahead of me. I can't be with my son every second of every day. What if something happens?

I'm not saying anything but Joel knows what I'm thinking same as always and he pulls me down to the ground then sits beside me and takes a sip of beer like we're in the middle of a maudlin picnic. I use a grave marker as a coaster and light a cigarette, careful to blow the smoke away from Joel. The nicotine steadies my hands and I take another drag, flicking ash onto the ground behind me. I don't get how something that's polluting my lungs makes me think I can breathe but that's exactly how I feel.

I'm afraid I'm gonna fall in love with him, I admit. That sounds about right, Joel tells me but I shake my head. I fucked up, I whisper, Junior year... I fucked that up. Shut up, he says. I could've fought her, I tell him, I could've... You were twenty-one years old, James, he reminds me. Old enough to know better, I point out, Old enough to take responsibility. Who says you weren't taking responsibility? he asks. C'mon, Joel, I mumble and he shakes his head. You told her what you wanted, he says, And when she told you she'd already made a decision, you went with her to get it done.

I did go with her. I did. And I paid for it too in cash I made from tips that summer waiting tables at a Mexican restaurant that left me stinking of refried beans and stale beer. Counting out bills the morning of my girlfriend's abortion I'd almost hurled. *My responsibility.*

You're the only one keeping score here, Joel tells me.

I have never cried in front of my wife or any other girl. Not with my college girlfriend when she told me she was pregnant or the day she had the abortion. Not with Lizzie even when she had the miscarriage. That night I held myself together until I got Joel on the phone. I don't think I've broken down in front of anyone else since I was a kid.

The harder I cry the harder I cry until Joel just pulls me into his arms. I bawl all over him and he holds on tight and when I'm empty I stay there a while longer instead of making up a reason to leave. I guess he's not in a hurry either since he's not moving. For a while there's nothing wrong with where we are or what we're doing, the two of us sitting in front of a century-old grave in the middle of the night with our arms around each other.

I don't know how long we stay there, me with my head buried in his shoulder and his hand running through my hair like some kind of mantra. I just know we're there a while. Our foreheads together, my eyes closed. I'm taking something from him and I don't even know what all it is but it's good. I can feel it's good and I finally open my eyes. He's looking right at me.

Joel / Austin / October 2006

The morning after Celeste's party, I wake up crying. I've had energy work in the past; I know there's no way to predict my emotions in the hours or even days following a session. Just because I felt calm and quiet when I left Brice last night, I had no guarantee I'd open my eyes today in a state of grace. As angry as I was after reading Adam's email yesterday, I should probably be grateful I'm lying here weeping. I could be hurling insults at James or inventing new ways to hurt myself. I could've crafted an email to Adam so cruel I'd never hear from him again.

I reach for my cell. In ten seconds, I could be hearing his voice. By tonight, I could have him in my arms. I could fall asleep listening to him tell me how much he loves me. With one phone call, I could change both of our lives, and I scroll through my contacts until I find his number. Not that I won't remember it always. I remember everything about him, every intimacy we shared, every kiss.

Every maddening moment of the last months we spent together until I found out about his affair.

Sometimes I have to remind myself that leaving Adam wasn't an act of self-sabotage, but self-preservation.

By Tuesday night, when I've agreed to meet Brice for a glass of wine, I think I'll be back to normal, even though these days, *normal* doesn't necessarily mean *up*. Despite a good hard run and an hour-long meditation, however, despite taking a restorative yoga class at a studio I like but definitely can't afford, I'm still walking into a wine bar, thinking I'd rather be just about anywhere other than on my first real date in years. I try picturing that moment in my truck on Saturday night: Brice's mouth, my hands on a chest I know he sculpted under the tutelage of a personal trainer. The way he smelled, like he'd been bred on trust funds. *Better.*

I've had the good sense to put on a sweater I bought the winter before Adam and I broke up, pants even my father would like, though if he saw the damp ponytail, he'd have a coronary. I'm not wearing my Redwings, which I've held onto since college and almost reached for tonight until I realized what I was doing. Seeing Brice, I still feel underdressed. I look at his jeans and blue gingham dress shirt, his navy blazer. I have a feeling he has a close relationship with his tailor. Do you work? I ask, knowing the question's impertinent, and he raises his eyebrows. Yeah, I work, he says, I'm a lobbyist.

I'm afraid to ask for which party.

Do you prefer red or white? he asks once we're seated, and I look over the menu and tell him I'm thinking of the 2003 *Domain Houchart cotes de Provence.* Is that a shot in the dark? he asks, Or do you know wine? I can make my way around a list, I admit, thinking of that job I had at Granite Café when Adam and I first got back together. If I hadn't been familiar with wine, the manager never would've hired me. *Thanks, Dad.*

You look nice, Brice says after we've ordered. You look like a card-carrying member of the Republican party, I tell him, and he laughs. If you Google me, you'll find out pretty quickly, he says. I knew I should've done my research, I tell him, and he says, Not even a cursory search? Why do I have a feeling you had me followed? I ask. You can never be too careful, he assures me, and I get the impression he's only halfway joking.

An hour passes faster than I expect, but that could be the wine I'm drinking. I'm having a difficult time getting past Brice's politics. He's fiscally conservative. He doesn't believe in universal health care. He doesn't think the government has the right to legislate what he does behind closed doors but feels that pushing for marriage equality creates more division than cohesion. Certain factions of the gay rights movement he doesn't understand. What factions? I ask, and he says he prefers subtlety. I make a mental note not to introduce him to Kyle. Not that we're going to get that far. I don't consider myself political, but I also don't like most of what I'm hearing, and I'm not bothering to hide it.

You seem agitated, he finally says. I don't understand how you can reconcile your politics with an equality agenda, I confess. It's entirely possible to work that agenda within the Republican party, he tells me. Does that mean you'll feel comfortable taking me to your next event? I say. I'm not sure I want to take you, he admits. Because it's too inflammatory, I conclude. No, he says, Because you're being kind of a prick.

He's smiling, but I'm still irritated. You wouldn't by any chance be intentionally trying to sabotage our date, he says, Would you? By questioning your politics? I ask. We don't have to talk politics, he tells me. Kind of hard to avoid any discussion of how you spend your days, I point out, and he reminds me what he told me earlier, that state lobbyists aren't aligned with a particular political party. You could also try being open-minded, he suggests. Like you? I say. Sure, he agrees, and something about the way he folds his hands together narrows my eyes. You're not religious, are you? I ask. Is that where you draw the line? he says. Look, I'm happy to fuck you even if you're not in alignment with my political beliefs, I tell him, But you told me yourself that fucking and dating aren't the same thing.

He takes that in while I wait to see if he laughs or gets pissed. My money's on the latter, and I watch him ruminate, wishing I didn't find him so attractive. Those cheekbones could have been carved by a river. Can we start over? he asks.

We talk about my work. I tell him about my upcoming show in DC, what I've been painting lately—circles, circles, circles—but he can sense the way I'm holding back. Part of that's my natural reticence; James says I'm not the type to open up. But I'm also sitting across from this guy, wondering what I'm doing here. The hole Adam left in my heart gapes.

At the end of another hour, I have a headache, and I'm regretting that second glass of wine. When Brice starts telling me about the new updates to his kitchen, I assume he's going to follow up with an invitation. *Finally.* I throw a lot of parties, he adds, Especially around the holidays. Maybe you could throw a private party tonight, I suggest. Sounds great, he says, For a third date. I almost groan. Maybe you should bend the rules once in a while, I tell him, knowing that if we part ways now, I'm not going to be able to gear myself up to go through this again. Is that what you're doing? he asks, Bending the rules? What do you think? I mutter, and he frowns. As tempting as I find you, he says, I have a feeling that if you come home with me tonight, you're going to decline a second date. Do you want one? I ask, and he's self-effacing enough to smile. Am I so boring? he asks. You'd be perfect for a younger, gay version of my father, I tell him.

He doesn't laugh, probably because thirty minutes ago, I told him I don't think much of my father. Instead, he catches our server's eye and makes a motion to close out our check. When I offer to split the bill, he shuts me right down, sliding a platinum American Express from a single-fold wallet (black, leather, Ferragamo. *Jesus.*). How do you and Celeste even work? I ask as he hands his card to our server without glancing at the bill. She's capable of withholding judgment, he says.

I sit back as he touches his thumb and forefinger to the button on his blazer. I'm behaving badly, I admit, and he shrugs. You're not interested, he says, And I'm not going to keep trying to convince you otherwise. Are *you* interested? I ask. I asked you out, didn't I? he says. But now that you've gotten to know me..., I prompt. I learned more from Google, he tells me, draining the last of his wine.

That means he saw some of my work online. I wonder what he thought and figure it's unfair of me to ask under the circumstances. I'm not very good at opening up, I tell him. I noticed, he says.

Outside, he hands his ticket to the valet. Where's your truck? he asks, Or did you take the bus? I give him a sharp look. Can your truck even make it all the way across town? he asks, and I start laughing. He nods. I wondered if a smart-ass remark would better get your attention, he says. Good call, I tell him. Too bad I didn't figure that out a couple of hours ago, he says. Our whole evening might have changed, I point out. I can keep going, he offers, We have sixty seconds before my car arrives. You want to give me shit about last season's loafers? I ask, looking down at my shoes, and he says, When I can focus on that wet hair? I pull it loose from the rubber band. Dry, I claim, and he steps toward me and slides his fingers around the back of my neck, where my hair's still damp. Liar, he whispers. You allowed to touch me in public? I murmur. As long as the governor doesn't find out, he says.

His car pulls to the curb, and he lets go. Maybe I'll see you running, he says. Seems likely, I agree. I watch him walk around the front of his car. At the last second, he looks over at me, one hand on the roof of that gleaming DB9.

Get in, he says.

James/ Chicago / July 2006

For two days Lizzie has been shadowing us. I should be thrilled. Here she's finally paying our son the attention she should've given him from the beginning. But I know why she won't leave us alone. She's jealous of Joel. I've been telling her for years that I've moved past what happened between us and she might've believed me when Joel was living with Adam. Now that he's single she's not so sure. Most of the time I can empathize and I go out of my way to downplay our relationship. I almost never take his calls when I'm with her. I don't even drop his name into the conversation. That way she doesn't have to think about him.

Today I'm tired and I've spent the past forty-eight hours maneuvering their dynamic. I just want to spend time with my friend and instead I'm getting a glass for my wife because she won't let us sit in the backyard by ourselves. Fuck it, I thought last night, if she wants to be part of the conversation so bad I'll include her. But that backfired before we could finish our wine. When she asked Joel if she was remembering right about him not wanting kids I almost told her to shut up. I might've if Henry hadn't started squalling. Instead I ran upstairs to get him then stumbled back down worried Joel might've told her to shut up himself. I found them sitting in a silence so miserable I knew he hadn't said a word.

I'm lucky Joel's being cool. He's got to be bored out of his mind. He's not really into kids and it's not like we're getting any time to ourselves. I can't even suggest going out for dinner tonight partly because I don't think Lizzie can manage Henry alone but also because at this point I don't think she'd let us leave without her. We've got no privacy and that's what my wife wants. Gritting my teeth, I reach for a beer even though it's early in the afternoon. Should you be drinking while you're putting Henry down for his nap? Lizzie asks. Did you want to put him down yourself? I say, giving her an innocent look when I know full well Henry will never fall asleep for her. She glares at me then catches Joel's expression. He's gazing at her like he's the one responsible for this shit. C'mon, I bark at him, handing him my beer, You're comin' with me.

She follows us upstairs. Not right away; she waits a few minutes so we can settle in. She wants to overhear us or catch us or something and fuck if she almost doesn't.

At first we're not even talking. Henry takes his bottle and Joel watches us same as he's been doing for pretty much every feeding since he got here. Holding my son and looking into his eyes I start to calm down. I'm sorry, I say after a minute and Joel shrugs. I shake my head. Seriously, man, I say, I knew this wouldn't be easy but— Does she know? he asks.

I don't have to ask what he means. No, I say. Are you sure? he asks. She's jealous in general, Joel, I tell him, She doesn't need a reason.

Henry's eyes are getting heavier but he keeps on sucking. I lift him long enough to give him a good burp then wipe a little formula from his chin. She doesn't trust me, Joel says. She knows I slept with you, I remind him. Ten years ago, he scoffs, It's not like that option's still on the table.

Man, I get so pissed when he says shit like that. I know we're not going to hook up again. I'm married, I have a kid, he's still in love with Adam, whatever. I get it. He doesn't have to act like he's disgusted by the thought.

I swap a pacifier for the bottle, my teeth set a little too hard. I'm tired of dealin' with this crap, I mutter. I shouldn't have come, he laments. That's not a solution, Joel, I tell him, Never seein' each other is *not* a solution. Are you sure she doesn't know? he asks. Jesus! I say, Give it a rest!

Henry whimpers and I jostle him a little. Across from me Joel doesn't say a word. It was one time, I mumble, It was one time and you were so trashed. So were you, he reminds me but I've just heard a noise on the stairs and I motion for him to be quiet. Anyway, I say, changing my voice right up, That was one helluva party.

Lizzie opens the door. He's asleep, I tell her and she nods. I shoot a glance at Joel, who looks like he doesn't much like me right now.

Whatever. Like he wasn't the one who dropped into that *fuck me* voice last Christmas.

Joel / Austin / October 2006

Brice lives in the heart of Old Enfield, his house a testament to subtlety and refinement, right down to the kitchen's top-of-the-line appliances and handmade cabinetry. This redesign could be featured in a magazine and probably will be in the next few months. He already has interest and a photo shoot scheduled for later this week. Let me get you a drink, he says, pulling open the sub-zero refrigerator. Water's fine, I tell him, and he reaches for a bottle of Pellegrino. Why'd you change your mind? I asked him on the way here, and he said, Because from the beginning, you've been the only one willing to bend the rules.

I take a sip from my glass of Pellegrino and look him over. I can be as slow and deliberate as I want; he closed this deal the second he invited me into his car. If I want to linger, I have that option. I can do so without regret. I'm not trying to forget, the way I was last July during that terrible trip to Chicago. I haven't just slipped a tablet of Ecstasy under my tongue. I'm not here under duress.

I might be lying. All night, I've been thinking about Adam; even now, there's a part of me that wants to reach for my phone to be sure I haven't missed a message. I don't understand why he hasn't called. Though I'm relieved—hearing his voice might make me cave—I'm also confused. I didn't expect him to take my silence so seriously. If he hadn't been profuse in his email, I could come to the conclusion that his feelings for me have changed. Given what he wrote, I can't imagine that's true.

He must have reread his own words and realized how I'd perceive them. He's desperate, and I'm angry. He's beseeching, and I'm hesitant. He's in love, and I'm afraid.

Where are you right now? Brice asks, and I pull myself back to the present, to the man standing in front of me. I've come so far over the past year, and right now, I can take another step forward. I don't even have to try that hard. He's not Adam, but in another time, I would've gone for a guy like Brice. That hair, highlighted by a Texas sun. Eyes somnolent and seductive, lips like I've caught him on the edge of a kiss. In another time...

This time.

He crushes my headache. I had a feeling he might; he knows what he's doing, and I stretch out in his four-poster bed and let him take over. *Polished.* That's the word that comes to me as he closes his fingers around my hips, his mouth on my ear. He's polished, from his pumiced skin to his technique to the words he's murmuring. When he finally pulls away and falls beside me, his head resting on folded arms, the curvature of his back golden in the light of the bedside lamp, I'm content enough to stay. Whatever I was still holding onto from Celeste's energy work has vanished. I let the feeling move through me, grateful for the release, grateful, frankly, that Brice gave in. You comfortable? he murmurs without opening his eyes. I let my fingers trace his lower back by way of reply, dip into the grooves on either side of his spine. The Pellegrino has fallen flat, but for now this is enough.

James / Chicago / May 2007

I find a student waiting for me when I get to campus. She's leaning against the wall outside my office, wearing impractical shoes and a snug-fitting top. I'm unimpressed because I know why she's here. She's one of my freshmen and she's flunking my Greek Mythology class. I haven't graded your paper yet, I warn her, unlocking my door and she pouts in a way that would mesmerize me if I didn't know better. Sheer beauty doesn't make up for an appalling indifference in the classroom. That I learned a long time ago. The girls who could captivate me at the beginning of the quarter are inevitably the ones who show up at my office right before finals trying to squeeze a higher grade from their poorly written essays or their half-assed exams.

Could you maybe grade my paper now? she suggests, following me into my office. Why should I give you preferential treatment? I ask, sitting behind my desk and waving a hand in the direction of a free chair. She slips into the seat like she'd slide into a warm bath. Well, since I'm here..., she says.

I gaze across the desk. I can shoo her away and close the door behind her and dive into the abyss of grading I have ahead of me. Or I can give in, find her paper and grade it while she watches, which might get her off my back if she managed to write something stellar—unlikely—but either way will find me looking at an afternoon with a line of students outside my door. I'm sorry, I say, But you'll have to wait just like everyone else.

Her expression reminds me of the student who sat across from me last week and told me his parents aren't paying for him to get B's. Now I try the same tone I used with him, one that stretches the last little bit of my patience. If there's nothin' else, I say.

She stares at me like she's either giving me the chance to change my mind or memorize this moment for future reference once her parents have contacted the chair of my department and suggested my termination. For all I know they've got the clout. Then she shrugs, flipping her hair over her shoulder. I'll check in later, she announces like that was her plan all along.

Once she's gone I grimace at the stack of papers on my desk. Man, I've got a sledgehammer of a headache and a major fucking problem. I have no idea how I can maneuver an eight-week excavation in Greece—and a baby—without my wife.

Scholarship is everything to me. I revel in its toil with thirteen years of study and seven years' worth of fieldwork encompassing the breadth and depth of my experience. The past two summers I've had to bow out of excavations, first because of Lizzie's fertility treatments and then because of Henry. This year I'm aching to get my hands in the dirt again and I've had to fight Lizzie every step of the way. I'm not willing to spend an entire summer away from my boy but she started telling me back in January that she doesn't want to take time off to come with me. She works for the city organizing different cultural events and while I get her need for autonomy I really needed her to come along. She swore she couldn't swing a two-month sabbatical.

I think she was lying. I've seen colleagues of hers finagle different arrangements over the past few years. You've got to talk to 'em Lizzie, I said not long after Henry's birthday party, We're gettin' down to the wire. I'm already going with you for the first two weeks, she snapped, What more do you want from me?

Here I am on the cusp of some of the most important research of my career—I specialize in classical funerary practices, representations of the Greek afterlife and the general death discourse—and I might have to back out of some incredible fieldwork excavating a necropolis on the island of Crete all because my wife won't come with me. I can't go six weeks without Henry, I told her, keeping the emphasis on my limitations instead of hers. Why remind her she'd never be able to handle Henry on her own in Chicago, right? But she floored me so completely I almost died. What do you mean? she said, I'm not bringing him home with *me*.

Here I was willing to abandon the entire project in order to be with my son and Lizzie didn't have any trouble leaving him behind for half the summer.

My expression gave me away. I can't take this anymore, Lizzie, I said and that's when she packed her bags.

At this rate I'll never finish grading these papers and I reach for the first one, getting about halfway through a mediocre answer to what I thought was an easy question about the influence of classical mythology on Western literature before I pick up the phone. We're good, Joel assures me when I grill him, We're thinking about a snack. Bananas are fine, I tell him, And those organic Cheerios but you gotta watch him since he could choke. And that would be bad, Joel guesses. I'm just worried, I mumble and he says, Thanks for the confidence.

Whatever, I don't want to hurt his feelings but he isn't used to kids. Part of the reason he and Adam started having trouble was because Adam wanted to adopt and Joel didn't. Oh, he'll let me ramble on about Henry but that doesn't mean he knows what he's doing and I feel compelled to remind him again of everything I told him this morning, most of which I've typed out for him and stuck under a magnet on the fridge. Don't forget Mr. Boo if you go to the park, I warn. James, he says, If you don't hang up the phone, I'm going to cut Mr. Boo's wings off myself.

Fine. I've got a graduate seminar in twenty minutes anyway. Two of my students, Kayla and Justin, have been taking an independent study with me this quarter and neither of them has ever taken part in field work. They're my youngest students and also my most promising. They need to get to Greece so I can see what they'll do outside the classroom.

One way or another I've got to figure this out.

Joel / Austin / October 2006

A creamy sunlight frames the dark wooden blinds, and I take my first conscious breath of the morning, already reluctant to peel back the duvet. Brice's bed feels deep and rich and warm, utterly unlike my own. When Adam and I split, I bought the cheapest bed I could find, which explains Fernando's presence in my bedroom a couple of days ago, as well as why I haven't had a decent night's sleep in months. Well, that and a grief so pervasive my emotional set point has an entirely new baseline. Brice's bed, on the other hand, seems like an indulgence. At one time, I wouldn't have allowed myself the luxury of lingering. Now I relax under the weight of his duvet and inhale the scent of his pillow, which smells light and posh, like the spa at that resort in Belize.

Good morning, Brice says, and I roll over. He's up, already wearing a suit, its drape sublime. Did you dress up just for me? I ask, and he laughs, adjusting a cuff link. Can you convince a Democratic senator to lend his support on a bill? he asks, opening the watch box on his bureau. He has a small fortune in there, and he takes his time selecting the right accompaniment. I'm meeting someone in forty-five minutes, he adds, And I have to stop by Rick's office first. The *governor*? I confirm. He nods. Rick care that you speak about him so familiarly? I ask, and he says, I'll ask him at lunch.

Sitting up, I pull my hair into a ponytail, then let it unwind when I can't find my rubber band. You don't have to leave right this second, Brice tells me as I throw back the duvet. I have to get my truck, I remind him. And I have to get moving, he apologizes, reaching for his wallet, You'll have to call a cab. You're not paying for my cab, Brice, I mutter, Jesus. Of course I'm paying, he says, leaving cash on the nightstand, If I didn't have an early meeting, I'd drive you myself.

I get to my feet and turn a half-circle, looking for my clothes. Relax, he says, Just because I'm leaving doesn't mean you can't have breakfast. I'm really getting your full service here, I tell him, Breakfast, cab fare, *and* a fuck. Don't forget the wine last night, he adds. Guess I'll have to make it up to you, I say.

There's that charge again, crackling the space between us. He drops his eyes to my dick, which jumps right to attention. Why don't you postpone that meeting? I suggest. Why don't you come to dinner with me tonight? he says. Tonight seems a little soon, I tell him.

For a moment, we're quiet. Brice touches the knot in his tie, glancing at his reflection, then meets my gaze in the mirror. Neither of us moves; I find this tableau every bit as provocative as that afternoon on Chicon, and I let the moment settle so I can remember the details if I want to use them some day. If I had a pencil, I'd start right now. Glint of sunlight on glass, his immaculate suit, the pale wash of my body, and the tangled fall of my hair: I'd immortalize this all.

I have to go, he says, Why don't you walk me out, and I can show you how to set the alarm.

I have only the most meager recollection of navigating these stairs last night, probably because by the time we got to them, I had Brice halfway undressed. Sure enough, he pauses at the bottom to pick up his shirt from the marble floor and lay it over the banister. The look he gives me over his shoulder, sheepish and coy, makes me laugh. I can't be late, he reminds me when I try to hold him back. I shrug like it's his loss and follow him through the kitchen, which streams with so much sunlight I'd need shades if I hadn't declined that third glass of wine last night.

Leave through the front door, he instructs, leading me into a laundry room off the kitchen, But set the alarm in here. He flips open the panel. Hit *arm,* then *enter,* he tells me, You have sixty seconds before the alarm sounds. What about a key? I ask, To lock the door behind me? Locks automatically, he says.

Once he's gone, I walk back into the kitchen, hesitating, then open the refrigerator. Brice could throw a dinner party for the entire Legislature without making a trip to the store, and I pluck a fresh bottle of Pellegrino from the door and fill a glass with ice. Drink in hand, I wander through the downstairs, feeling a bit like a voyeur but too curious to stop myself. His house presents even better in the light of day, and I stand for a minute in the foyer, gazing up at a chandelier that probably costs more than my house. And even the houses as far east as Oak Springs aren't that cheap anymore.

I wander into the living room with its long, low sofas. Through the front windows, I can see a slope of meticulous lawn and a spray of water from the automatic sprinklers. A Range Rover cruises past the property; I can barely make out the sound of its engine. Sipping my Pellegrino, I turn back to the interior.

Brice has conservative taste in art. But expensive; I recognize more than one of these artists. Again, I wonder what he thought when he saw my work online, and I feel an old, familiar tug of insecurity that I shake away with a quick reminder of my upcoming show in DC, the piece I sold yesterday that would've paid for my wine if Brice hadn't insisted on covering the check. I have a feeling I'm not his type. Not at all, really, which makes me question his motivation. Sex I can understand. But dating?

I've made my way into the dining room, a massive space with a table that could easily seat sixteen. An antique tapestry stretches the length of one wall. I have a feeling Rick Perry has been a guest here more than once.

I give the rest of the downstairs a quick look. Media room, bedroom with adjoining bath, and a home office so reminiscent of my father's that I take an immediate step back. All that mahogany and the mirror across from the desk: *Jesus*. Palm to chest, I force myself to go inside. Once I'm in there, the similarities dissipate, and I swallow the last of my Pellegrino, then leave the office and climb the stairs. Three more bedrooms, two bathrooms, an alcove perfect for a kid who needs to hide from his father... I think it's time to go, and I pick my cell phone from my pants, which I left on the floor last night, then realize I need an address for the cab.

It was Adam who upgraded my phone last year, wanting an easy way to stay in touch with me if he was in meetings. Since we split up, I rarely use the text feature, but now I'm grateful I don't have to interrupt Brice's meeting with a call. *Where am I?* I type.

Brice's response comes faster than I expect, like he was staring at his phone when my message came through. *The hot tub?*

Hot tub? I part the blinds. A magnificent pool sprawls below me, the hot tub foaming at one end, wisps of steam rising from its surface. I'm suddenly craving a latte or at least a coffee, and my stomach rumbles. I turn in the direction of the stairs, typing as I go. *I need your address.*

His response comes back as I'm opening the refrigerator again. Greek yogurt, raspberries and blackberries even though they're not in season. He has avocados in a bowl on the counter, a fresh loaf of Rudi's bread in the cupboard, some kind of granola in a box so pretty that I hesitate for just a second before tearing off the top.

I haven't seen this much food in one house since I lived with Adam.

James / Chicago / July 2006

The thought of spending the rest of my weekend wrangling my wife for thirty minutes alone with Joel has me wound so tight I yank open the fridge for another beer even though I've probably had enough, especially since I've got no idea how long Henry will nap. Just because I got him down easy doesn't mean he won't wake up in thirty minutes. Whatever, I'm fine with that. I love my boy. Joel knew what he was getting into when he agreed to come up here. He's not expecting to be entertained but he sure as shit thought we'd be able to share a beer without Lizzie hanging all over us. I'm good, he says, shaking his head when I offer him a bottle. You'll be good when you've had another drink, I tell him, pressing the beer into his hand.

Lizzie chews on her bottom lip and watches us for indiscretions. If I had any compassion left I'd kiss her pale lips, rub her thin shoulders. I'd reassure her because truthfully I want us to work. I want us to be a family. I want Henry to grow up in a happy home. And I used to love her. I did. I could get that feeling back maybe. I just need her to meet me halfway.

Joel's nursing his beer like he thinks I might've slipped a Rufie in the bottle. What's your problem? I hiss when Lizzie disappears for a shower I can tell she doesn't want to leave us long enough to take. He looks at me like he has about a thousand different answers before picking the same *I have a headache* excuse he used all morning. That beer might help if you gave it a chance, I tell him. This beer will make everything worse, he says.

Man, what happened to the weekend I had planned for us? I knew we weren't going to party like we did in college but shit. A couple beers on the back deck seems reasonable. I didn't think a conversation without Lizzie listening in would be too much to ask. I watch Joel kneading his neck with his knuckles. We're grinding it out here and when can I expect to see him again? Over the holidays if Lizzie and I make it to Fort Worth? Next summer? I can't accept that. I won't accept that.

C'mere, I say and Joel looks wary. Why? he asks. I'll rub your neck, I tell him and he automatically glances in the direction of the stairs. That's how self-conscious Lizzie has made us. We're afraid to go near each other. Well, I've worked too damn hard to get back to a point where my hand on Joel's neck for sixty fucking seconds doesn't have to mean anything. Will it help your headache? I ask. Probably, he admits. It's not like I'm offerin' to suck your dick, I tell him. Did you ever? he mumbles and I grimace.

Whatever, maybe this isn't just about Lizzie. Maybe I'm testing myself. We've only been alone one other time since last Christmas and that was when Joel met me in Fort Worth the week before Henry was born. I had my hands on him that night all right but only because I was crying in his arms, scared as shit about the baby and worrying over whether he'd come out okay. I think there was a part of me that had almost been afraid to see Joel that trip to Texas, afraid meeting up in person would prove that our phone call over the holiday had spoiled us for good. Instead I felt *more* connected to him like we had this whole history together and that phone call was just one more stratum. But this here weekend has kicked us in the crotch and who knows when we're going to see each other again?

Sit, I say, pointing to the floor in front of the couch. Make it quick, he mutters and man, that annoys the crap out of me. *Make it quick.* What if I don't want to make it quick? What if I don't want to be looking over my shoulder for my wife because she can't handle a friendship I've had for more than fifteen years? I haven't asked for anything from her this weekend, not one goddamn thing and I've spent about thirty minutes alone with my friend.

Fuck this shit. If I want to rub a crick out of Joel's neck I can damn well do so.

Joel / Chicago / July 2006

Elizabeth looks like a valentine on fire, heart-shaped face flushed, eyes flaming. To be honest, I'm glad she's angry. Sobbing I don't think I could handle. I knew better than to let James touch me with his wife right upstairs. I've seen her expression when he throws his arm around me. I caught the look on her face when he was talking about our trip to Mexico. I don't know what I was thinking.

I know what I was thinking. I was thinking I shouldn't have to be punished for Elizabeth's insecurities. I was thinking I spent money I didn't have on the plane ticket up here so I could meet Henry. I was thinking I had to get through my breakup with Adam alone because James couldn't leave Elizabeth long enough to help me. I was thinking I deserved to have some time with my best friend without his wife assuming I was out to seduce him.

I had a headache. He offered to rub my neck.

I'd also waited too long. I haven't slept with anyone, haven't even kissed anyone since Adam and I broke up. I can't afford massages. My skin forgot what it felt like to be touched, and the second James put his hands on me, I lost inhibition. I'm not saying something would have happened if Elizabeth hadn't found us. I'm saying I was so caught up that I didn't hear her whisper-thin steps on the stairs. I don't even know how long she watched us; my eyes were closed. By the time she spoke, James had both hands under my shirt, his mouth near my ear. Too much? he asked, digging deeper into my lats, and I might have groaned.

What's going on? Elizabeth cried, and even though we weren't doing anything wrong—we weren't—we sprang away from each other like she'd caught us with our shorts around our ankles. Nothing's going on, James protested, He has a headache. Then he can take a Tylenol! she told him like I wasn't even there. I don't like to take Tylenol, I muttered at the same time James said *he won't take Tylenol,* and that's when she got so angry, as if the fact that he knew me so well bothered her more than anything else.

You're making too much of this, James tells her now, and she says, *You're* not making enough of it! Elizabeth— I start, and she spins to face me. I'm not talking to you, she says, You... you... Lizzie, *stop,* James warns before she can fill in the blank with *cocksucker* or *fag* or whatever else she has ready on her lips. You don't even *want* me here! she wails to James, and I can see it coming, whatever he's going to say that will fuck us so hard I'll have to pack my bags. He's sick of the subtext, and three months of waiting for her to fall in love with their baby get the better of him. You know what? he says, You're *right.*

James / Austin / May 1998

Joel and I, we've been trying to get back to where we were for the longest time and we just can't. I hate pretending like we're something we're not and I'm tired of hiding my girlfriend and when he tells me he's heading to Houston for the weekend to see his dad I jump all over a grungy garage apartment with a window unit. Lizzie offers to help me move but I say no and tell her packing won't take me long and instead I work my ass off so Joel doesn't catch me halfway finished. Untangling seven years isn't easy even though I'm leaving just about everything behind, the furniture he bought the fall of our senior year, the television he had delivered when we lost the remote to the old one, the crappy smoker in the backyard we used through more than a few football seasons. But the rest of my shit is everywhere, including his bedroom.

I can't move my furniture all by myself and I get one of my undergraduate students to help. That's how much I want out. I'm ready to pay money I do not have for some guy to load his pickup when I could easily ask one of my friends from school. But everyone knows just a little too much about Joel and me and I don't need any more gossip.

What I'm doing is wrong. All these years we've lived together and I'm leaving without a word. But I can't think about anything other than getting out before Joel makes it back from Houston and when I hand $100 over to my student and shut the door of that garage apartment behind him I feel a relief I haven't experienced since before Joel and I started sleeping together.

I've escaped. Finally, finally I can move on and that night with Lizzie in my new place, her dress fluttering around her thighs I tell her for the first time that I love her.

My plan is to get back to the house tomorrow afternoon well before Joel comes home so I can tell him in person. When I find his Explorer already in the driveway I know I'm screwed. I try to backtrack and tell him a professor of mine had a garage apartment to lease and I wanted to take it before someone else did but no way is Joel believing that shit. Did your girlfriend help you move? he asks.

I don't know how he found out about Lizzie since I've been working real hard to keep her quiet. She's not my girlfriend, I lie and he says, You're fucking her, aren't you?

The girl I love, the one with the delicate eyes and skin so soft I feel like I'm living a dream isn't a *fuck*. *Fucking* was what Joel and I used to do. I worship Lizzie the way I would any goddess who'd saved me and man, do I want to take a swing at Joel. My hand *aches* to take a swing at him. You know what? I say, I feel sorry for you.

A fist Joel could understand. Muttering a congratulations for the bang up job he's doing with his life and suddenly I'm the one sprawled on the floor with a bloody lip.

Your mouth, your poor mouth! Lizzie cries that night in my shitty apartment. I've cleaned off the blood and pressed an ice pack against my lip. I tell her Joel's volatile and that he was probably high and as I lie to my future wife I know the freedom I felt as I was holding her in my arms last night isn't coming back. Years and years will pass and that feeling won't ever come back.

Joel / Austin / October 2006

I'm still in Brice's kitchen, happily toasting slices of Rudi's bread and spreading it with avocado, drizzling honey over a bowl of yogurt with berries and granola. I've figured out how to use the coffee maker, and I brew myself a pot, my first in a long time. I drink it black, the way I used to in college. When I'm finished, I go back for more of everything.

I'm on my second cup of coffee, standing in front of the French doors that open onto the veranda, when I feel inspired to check out that hot tub. Why not? Brice basically invited me with his text. I look at my phone to be sure I'm right, then unlock the door. The air feels like fall, bright and chilly with just enough sun to coax me toward the hot tub. I dip my foot in the water. Just one step, but the warmth invites me deeper until I'm almost fully submerged.

God, this feels good. If I lived here, I'd start every day this way. Adam and I had a pool, and in the summer, I spent plenty of time just floating. The water was too tempting, the sun the perfect prescription for my cold nature, and I learned early on that some of my best work came to me when I was doing absolutely nothing. Adam never understood. I could see the irritation in his expression when he'd come home from work and find me on one of the pool loungers, my eyes shut and my skin dark. But I was always working. Even then, I was working.

I linger a while longer, realizing as I stand that I don't have a towel. I'm going to leave puddles all over Brice's marble floor. Shaking myself off, I drip until I can't stand the cold any longer. Then I scoop up my phone and skitter across the veranda to the French doors.

They're locked.

Disbelieving, I turn the handle again, harder this time. *Locks automatically*, I hear Brice saying, and I groan. Surely, he meant the front door. Who would make the doors to their backyard lock automatically? *Someone who has a hundred thousand dollars' worth of watches in a box beside his bed*, I think. Cupping my hand over my eyes, I peer through one of the panes. Like it's going to do any good at all to see from this vantage point the mess I've left in the kitchen.

Okay, he has to have a key out here. It's not like I enabled the alarm or something. I'll find the key—he *must* have a spare key—and I'll be out of here in… I look at my phone. Jesus Christ. I've been screwing around for more than three hours. I have to get out of here before Brice realizes I've appropriated his house for the entire morning.

But I can't find a key. I look under planters, I lift the doormat, I run my hand along the ledge above the door. Nothing. I'm actually going to have to text this guy and tell him I'm locked out of his house.

Locked myself out, I type, already cringing. *Key under ceramic spider*, he shoots right back, nice enough not to point out that I've overstayed my welcome by several hours. I look around frantically for a spider. I have a feeling it's in full view of his front door. *I'm out back*, I type, and there's a pause, during which I swear I can feel him puzzling out whether I'm a total dumbass. *Gate on west side should be open*, he finally types. *Naked*, I type back.

This time, I have to wait a good sixty seconds before he responds. I don't even want to imagine what he's thinking. When my cell chimes again, I'm almost afraid to read his text. *Can't get there before noon.*

Well, what choice do I have? I'm just about to type *fine* when I get a follow up. *Unless you want me to send my assistant.*

That has to be facetious. *Noon works*, I type. He doesn't text back, and I don't blame him. He has lunch with the *governor* today. Shivering, I eye the hot tub again. I'm going to have to get back in there if I want to stay warm, and after I shift from side to side, contemplating my options, I set my cell on the lip of the hot tub and lower myself back into the water.

God, this feels good.

James / Chicago / Christmas 2005

For the first time in my life I won't be in Texas for the holiday. I really wanted to go home but I wasn't willing to take any chances with the baby, not after what happened last time. Luckily Lizzie's doctor agreed with me. At first I figured Lizzie would fight me but Joel sealed the deal. She knows if we head south I'll end up inviting him to my folks' place for the holiday since he's all alone this year. Since I made my last trip to Austin right before Joel and Adam broke up, Lizzie has quit pretending. She doesn't like Joel and she hasn't since I sat across from her the day after he tried to kill himself seven years ago and told her just how well I knew him. I'm still not sure how I convinced her to marry me.

Joel got home from Adam's dad's funeral a few days ago. Grief can be an awful powerful cement and I thought there was a good chance they'd end up back together but Joel called me on his way back to Texas. It's done, he said and when I asked if he was okay he took such a long time answering I started to worry. I will be, he finally admitted.

Man, his holiday's going to suck some serious ass.

Meanwhile I'm trying to get my wife to eat. Maybe a few crackers, I suggest since dinner won't be ready for another couple hours. I'm making food I know she likes, roast beef with parsley potatoes and carrots. Right now she's guzzling wine. It's Christmas, James, she says when I try to take the glass from her hand, Will you give it a rest?

The alcohol does not seem worth the risk to me. Nothing seems worth the risk. If I could lock my wife in our bedroom I swear to God I would. Because I think she's lying when she tells me she has to work late. I think she's going to the gym. I think she's getting her heart rate too high for a woman in her second trimester. I've pulled her friend aside and told her to help me out but Monica looked at me like she'd cut my balls off herself if it meant sparing Lizzie this pregnancy.

I touch my wife's arm and try not to take it personally when she winces. Please eat a little somethin', Lizzie, I beg and she shakes her head like the ultimate faux pas would find her answering the door with a mouthful of food. Monica and Chad will be here any minute, she reminds me.

Chad. Man, I hate that guy. But when Lizzie realized we were stuck in Chicago for Christmas she insisted on inviting her friends for dinner. The only reason I agreed is because she's pregnant and unhappy and I need her to chill.

Now I have just enough time to call Joel before they get here and I reach for my phone, Lizzie rolling her eyes. I'll just be a second, I tell her and I walk into the living room wanting privacy but not wanting to go so far out of earshot she thinks I've got something to hide.

You leave for Kyle's yet? I ask when Joel answers. In a few minutes, he says, How's Elizabeth? Starvin' herself, I grumble. She'll eat that dinner you're cooking, he reminds me and I say, Sure 'nough.

I can hear him moving around, getting dressed or whatever he's doing. He's only been in his new place for a couple months but I still don't like that I can't place him. So who's gonna be there tonight? I ask. I don't know, he says, Kyle swears we'll be low-key. I snort. Your guests coming soon? he asks. Yeah, I mumble. You'll be fine, he assures me, There's a reason you're doing this, remember?

He sounds good, better than he should and that worries me. Joel— I start and he sighs like he knows what I'm going to say. Hell, he probably does. How bad is it? I ask. Pretty fucking bad, he admits. Have you talked to Adam? I ask, steeling myself for his answer. No, he says, But it's taking everything I have not to pick up the phone. Don't call him, Joel, I warn. I'm not that stupid, he assures me.

But we both know it isn't a question of stupidity. Love will take us all down at some point or another.

Joel / Chicago / July 2006

My hands feel cold, and I rub them together as I take a last look in the mirror, trying not to think about the original plan I had for this evening: dinner with James, quiet conversation, maybe a glass of wine as I watched James put Henry to sleep. Instead, I've spent the afternoon in a hotel room I had to charge to my credit card, the one that's supposed to be for emergency use only. Though if this doesn't constitute an emergency, I'm not sure what does. I left James's house this afternoon in a cab bound for the airport, then thought about the effort I'd need to expend trying to finagle an earlier flight and leaned forward in my seat. Take me to Boystown instead, I said.

So far, I've killed a few hours in front of the television, then walked down the block and into a specialty shop, where I charged a gray button-down and a new pair of jeans so far out of my price range that I'm probably already close to my credit card's meager limit. Worth it, I think, ruminating over my reflection. I'm sick of looking like a jilted lover, and I need to do something to shake that away, no matter what the cost.

I try two clubs before I hit on the one I want. The night's young, but that's not going to matter. I'm strategic about the bar stool I select, the drink I order. By the time I have a Grey Goose and soda in front of me, I've already assessed and rejected the options at my disposal. But I won't have to wait long. I know this from experience, even if my experience takes me back to my twenties. I sip my drink and don't meet anyone's eye for longer than half a second. For years, I cultivated a look of boredom. The ease with which that expression comes back could chill me if I let it.

Three men approach over the course of the next hour. They're rebuffed politely and monosyllabically. My gaze never leaves the dance floor or the rim of my drink. As the night gathers steam, the crowd thickens. I keep my headache at bay with an occasional breath deep enough to fill my lungs and permeate my muscles. Another? the bartender asks when I have an inch left in my glass, and I shake my head.

I see him just before eleven, slipping onto a stool on the opposite side of the bar, wearing a look every bit as indifferent as mine. But more recently practiced; I'm sure of that. *Good.* I give myself just enough time to be sure, then turn my eyes back to the dance floor.

Even when I feel his gaze, I don't reciprocate, not until the last possible second, until I can sense he's on the verge of turning his attention elsewhere. Then he has all of me, and I watch him concede, laughing into his drink. His reward comes as the barest of smiles, and sixty seconds later, he's standing beside me. You're new here, he observes. I'm from out of town, I tell him. Fancy that, he says. I tilt my glass to the side so he can see it's empty. Texas, I add as he gestures to the bartender for a refill. You have a horse, cowboy? he asks, and I swallow the last of my drink. I ride okay, I admit. He leans against the bar, relishing an innuendo that was every bit intentional. He's darker than I usually go for, his hair thick and almost black. I'm guessing he doesn't wax.

You here for business or pleasure? he asks, and I welcome my second vodka and soda with a longer swallow than I've taken so far tonight. Neither, I say, keeping my voice even, As it turns out. He looks at me just long enough to empathize. I shrug. Maybe my luck's about to change, I tell him. Maybe you're right, he agrees.

For the ten-minute drive and the ride up to the seventeenth floor of his apartment building, we don't touch, not even when the elevator doors close and we're alone. Nor do we talk. In his apartment, he follows me to the bank of windows overlooking the city. What are you after tonight? he asks, and even though his question isn't anything new, even though he must have asked it dozens of times, the words bring tears to my eyes. I'm careful to swallow them before I speak. I want to forget, I say.

For six years, I've kissed no one but Adam. Now I lean in and in until the man in front of me pulls back. On the tip of his finger, he has one blue tablet. My groan sounds more like a whimper. His finger sways like something hypnotic.

I nod. He drops the tablet under my tongue and smiles.

James / Chicago / May 2007

I get home from campus worried about what I'm going to find. I'd planned to check in with Joel at least one more time this afternoon but I had so much work and so many students trying to convince me to grade their papers while they watched that when I finally looked up I realized I'd be getting home later than I'd promised. Hello? I call, slamming the front door and Joel's voice comes back to me from Lizzie's bedroom—Joel's room for the next month. Dropping my bag on the couch I head upstairs. Hi, I say in the doorway and Joel and Henry look up at me and smile. I take Henry in my arms and plant a kiss on his cheek. He sucks on his fingers then swivels his head in Joel's direction like he's checking to make sure his new friend hasn't bailed. I sit on the edge of the bed and Henry crawls out of my arms, rolling back on his bottom and patting one of those puffy books my sister sent him for his birthday.

How was your day? Joel asks, his voice nice and bright like a 1950's housewife. Funny, I grunt, rubbing my neck. I have dinner in the oven, he adds. Really? I say. Fuck no, he laughs, You're buying me dinner. You didn't fall in love with him today? I sulk. Love has nothing to do with it, he tells me, This shit is work. But he touches the top of Henry's head in a way that says he was happy to do it. I probably shouldn't swear around him, huh? he adds and I shrug. So what'd you do today? I ask. We got to know each other, Joel says.

He could be so pissed. He could've told me I haven't been there for him much the past couple years and he's got plenty to keep him busy in Austin without diving into my drama. He could've refused to come. But the second I told him what I needed he bought a plane ticket. He wouldn't even let me pay. And today instead of working in his studio he's changing diapers and reading puffy books.

What I've been through the past year—since before Henry was born, maybe even since before Lizzie got pregnant—catches up to me all at once and I look around at the dresser that still holds some of Lizzie's clothes, this bed we bought together... C'mon, Joel says, reaching for Henry like he understands the tears in my eyes, Let's figure out what we're doing for dinner.

While Joel's ripping into a bunch of spinach he and Henry bought from the corner store—he offered to throw something together after all—I stretch out on the living room floor and watch Henry shake Mr. Boo. I miss this kid during the day. I would've been happy to go out to dinner tonight but I have to admit I like just lying here with my boy. I read so many papers this afternoon I don't think I could read a menu anyway.

Everythin' all right in there? I call, hearing Joel smacking cabinets closed in the kitchen. I need a skillet, he tells me, appearing in the doorway with a dishtowel over his shoulder. To the left of the oven, I say.

Man, I hope he's not making something weird. Every so often I think about the way he used to eat in college, all that pizza, breakfast tacos every damn day. Beer 'round the clock. Now he's no more likely to eat a burger than he is to drink a margarita.

Joel might be militant about what he eats but he looks a hell of a lot better than I do that's for sure. He still runs but he doesn't have arms this defined from logging miles. He told me last night he takes some kind of yoga where the temperature locks in at one hundred five degrees. Doesn't that make you sick? I asked and he admitted that once in a while someone ends up puking or passing out. But you know me, he said, I'm hard-core.

Hard-core enough to have badass triceps at thirty-five, I think grudgingly, catching a glimpse of him through the doorway. Flat abs too, I bet and my eyes lift that shirt he's wearing.

This happens when I'm with him at least once every visit. Most of the time we're who we always were before I fucked up. But every so often I feel a jolt of *holy shit I slept with him* and I have to reconcile who we were with what we did and who we've become as a result. What? he said, catching my expression a few years ago when I was still stuck in the middle and I flubbed an excuse that left him raising his eyebrows.

Right now my mind has hold of his abs. I remember the first time I took them in—I mean really took them in. It was 1996 and we were just a few days into that whole mess we'd created. Every second I was sober was a second I wanted to rewind what we'd started. I'd lit a joint before he was even awake one morning and I stole a couple tokes on the back porch since I knew what he'd be expecting soon as he opened his eyes. The thought made my teeth chatter and I tried to tamp down my boner at the same time. A hit or two from that joint softened everything just enough that when I went back in the house I headed right for my bedroom. He was still asleep but he'd kicked off enough of the covers that I might've thought he'd staged the bed if I didn't know him better. From the waist down I couldn't see a thing but I knew he wasn't wearing anything because I'd taken his jeans off of him myself. His belly was flat and white and *cut* and I stared down at him, my breath high and sharp in my chest.

Just before I touched him his eyes flew open. His reaction wasn't like a lover's, I know that now. Back then I was too self-conscious about my own response, my hand caught mid-air, a hard-on I kept trying to make sense of and never could seem to figure out. What he didn't say was *Morning.* What he didn't do was smile. Instead he pulled right on into himself like whatever part of him had been laid out for me to admire—if that was what he intended, if that was what I was doing—was done and gone. I held out the joint and as he inhaled I unbuttoned my shorts.

Man, I do not need to be thinking about this right now.

I reach for a couple of wooden blocks then a couple more so I can knock them over and make Henry laugh. Five minutes, Joel says from the doorway and I look up. What'd you make? I ask, afraid of the answer. Frittata, he says, Eggs, goat cheese, peppers... I had goat cheese? I ask. No, he says, You owe me fifty bucks for the groceries. Terrific, I mutter, getting to my feet and pulling Henry up with me. Spinach salad, Joel adds, With pine nuts. You found pine nuts at the store around the corner? I ask and he says, I brought my own.

He's fucking with me. God, that feels good and I follow him into the kitchen carrying my son. Joel has the table set, a big bowl of salad in the center. The frittata or whatever the hell it's called smells excellent. I'm legitimately hungry for the first time since Lizzie left and I plunk Henry in his high chair and snap the tray in place, suddenly feeling cheerful.

A few minutes later I've mowed through half the food on my plate. Henry's cramming frittata in his mouth like he hasn't eaten in a week. I try to ease him back a bit and he glowers at me. Joel holds a glass of wine that's mostly for show. What time do you have to be on campus tomorrow? he asks. Nine-thirty, I say, my mouth full, But I gotta get Henry to preschool first.

Always dicey, that drop-off. That's why I hired a sitter. But even she couldn't be available every day and sometimes I've got no choice. It's a decent preschool and Henry doesn't go more than a handful of hours a week. I still don't like leaving him there. I also can't expect Joel to spend all day every day with my kid. He's already been asking about the closest yoga studio and if I expect him to stick around for another twenty-some days I need to make sure I give him plenty of time to himself.

There's no reason to send him to school, Joel tells me, That's why I'm here. What about yoga? I ask and he says he'll work it in. I reach for the wine and pour myself a second glass. Maybe I can even convince you to join me for a class, he adds. Is that a prerequisite for your help? I grumble and he grins.

Joel / Austin / October 2006

By the time the French doors open a little after noon, all the moisture has leached from my skin, and I've made the mistake—twice—of standing too quickly and feeling a head rush so intense that both times I almost passed out. Only the determination not to have Brice find me drowned in his hot tub kept me lucid. How's the water? he asks now, so deadpan I can't tell if he's pissed. I think I've had enough, I admit. He holds out a towel, and I straighten, shaking the haze from my eyes. I didn't expect the door to lock, I say. I told you the doors lock automatically, he reminds me. I thought you meant the front door, I mumble.

Too late, I realize what I've left for him in the kitchen: the remnants of my avocado toast, the container of Greek yogurt spoiling on the counter. I don't know what happened, I confess. Looks like you had breakfast, he surmises, surveying the damage. Then he looks me up and down. Naked, he adds. I'll clean up, I tell him. Let's just get you dressed, he suggests, So I can drive you back to your truck.

I guess he's not going to trust me to call a cab this time.

Once I'm dressed, I follow him outside. His DB9 winks in the sunlight. I feel like the worst kind of trick, the guy who can't even find his own way home. My first date in more than six years and I'm a disaster. Those French doors might have locked behind me, but I shouldn't have been checking out the hot tub in the first place, any more than I should have treated myself to a leisurely breakfast. Brice was probably thinking I'd grab an apple or a glass of juice while I waited for the cab that I should've called the second he pulled out of the garage this morning. I picture the way I was wandering around his house earlier, snacking on avocado toast as I looked over his art, and cringe.

Silently, I get in the passenger seat, and we crawl through the neighborhood, coming to a full, responsible stop as we hit Enfield. Then we're flying down the hill and curling around Twelfth. I give him a grin I can't help, and he slides a smile my way. He's still being nice; I appreciate that. Under the circumstances, he could've told me he was just going to drop me off on the corner. Instead, he's whipping us past the Capitol. Listen, I start, I'm sorry about... Everything? he finishes when I trail off. Well, maybe not everything, I admit. Just ransacking my kitchen and locking yourself out of my house, he concludes. Don't forget what a prick I was last night, I remind him, and he says, I haven't.

Perfect.

He takes me to the parking garage, where I expect him to stop at the curb. Instead, he takes me to my truck, door-to-door service, and as he idles behind my Toyota, I'm blindsided by a wave of emotion I'm not sure how to interpret. Since that moment in his kitchen last night, I haven't thought about Adam. I've been distracted. I've been having sex, sober sex, for the first time in more than a year. I've been eating gourmet granola and lounging in a hot tub under a cool October sky. I feel like I've been on vacation. Now I'm going home, where no one waits for me. No wonder I'm hesitating, and I look over at Brice, who hasn't said a word since he pulled up to my truck. At least his foot isn't poised over the accelerator. Listen, I start, but I don't know how to continue. I run a self-conscious hand through my hair, the tips of which are still wet from spending the morning in his hot tub. I'm probably leaving stains on his rich, leather interior. Thanks for the ride, I finally finish. No problem, he says, but I still don't make a move for the door handle. He raises his eyebrows. I can't be late to lunch with the governor, Joel, he says.

At his words, I spring into action. Scrambling out of his car, I fumble for my keys as I yammer another thank you. Before I can unlock my truck, he's gone, and I drop into the driver's seat with a groan. My movement releases a musty scent I swear I've never noticed.

James / Austin / April 1995

Joel's on the front porch with Kyle and I'm in the living room with a book open on my lap but I'm listening to them talk about where they're going tonight. I know it's stupid to feel left out but whatever. Ever since he met Kyle, Joel's been busy. He comes home later and later, smelling like the lake or drunk on champagne. He doesn't invite me along either. I know they're just friends—soon as I met Kyle I knew Joel was telling the truth—but that makes the time he's spending with him that much more irritating. What does Kyle have that I don't?

A trust fund and a weakness for cock, that's what.

I put my book down and get to my feet. I'm not eavesdropping, not really. I can't help that the windows are open.

Turns out they're talking about going dancing and that does it. I smack the screen door wide. Joel's sitting in the swing and Kyle's leaning against the railing, buffing nails he keeps so long they creep me out. I'm goin' too, I announce and Kyle rolls his eyes. Honey, he says, You're what we mean when we say *cock block*. I let the screen door bang shut behind me and step onto the porch, the wood dusty under my bare feet, the spring air fresh against my skin. If you come with us tonight, he goes on, examining his nails, You won't let your roommate here out of your sight.

I glance over at Joel, who gazes back without comment. Fuck you, I finally mumble, dropping my eyes. That's the problem, Roomie, Kyle croons, You won't sleep with us, so we have to look elsewhere. Yeah, sorry I can't accommodate, I mutter and Kyle looks me up and down like he can see right through the grubby shorts I'm wearing. Oh, I'm sure you could accommodate, he says.

Squirming I lift the baseball cap I'm wearing and rake my hand through my hair then settle my cap back on my head all without finding a retort. Kyle's looking like he'd let me bend him right over the porch railing and I finally send a silent plea in Joel's direction *c'mon, help me out here*. Kyle, he says flatly and that's enough for Kyle to quit. My lips tug into a smirk and man, I can tell Kyle does not like the way Joel jumped in to save me. You told me you wanted to get laid tonight, he says to Joel like I'm not even here.

Well, of course Joel wants to get laid. We all do. At this point I've clean forgotten what it feels like and even though Joel sleeps around plenty that doesn't mean he doesn't want more. So why does Kyle's comment piss me off? And why do I feel like I did the night before bid day? Like I'd probably get called back but maybe the fraternity would cut me loose instead and then what? Scowling I squint at a pickup across the street. When I look back at Joel he says, You really want to come with us? I shrug like I couldn't care either way and for a second I think he's going to leave me to my bullshit indifference. Yeah, I mumble, Please. Brace yourself, he says.

Joel / Austin / October 2006

Oh *my*, Kyle says, looking me up and down, You finally got laid.

I mumble something about energy work, stepping past him into his foyer. I've seen you after energy work, honey! he trills, I know better! Are you going to offer me something to drink? I ask, ignoring him, and he trails after me into the kitchen, popping a chocolate truffle in his mouth along the way. I shake my head when he offers me the box. Kyle has a sweet tooth so fierce he'd fight me over the last one.

I know where he keeps the tea, and I open the canister and sift through the teabags until I find chamomile. I'm going to have to tell him what I've done; I suppose I knew if I came here right from last night's parking garage, he'd find me out. Who knows? Maybe that's part of the reason why I came. Sometimes I get tired of keeping everything to myself, and I learned a long time ago that there's only so much I can share with James.

I turn on Kyle's electric kettle and reach for a mug. Girlfriend, he insists, *Dish*. His name's Brice, I confess. Kyle stops with a truffle halfway to his mouth. Brice *Whitman?* he breathes, and I groan. Tell me you didn't sleep with him, I plead. Oh honey, he says, Brice would never have me. He takes a thoughtful bite of his truffle, his head cocked to the side. I'm a little surprised he slept with *you*, he admits. Thanks, I say, and he waves his hand at what I'm wearing, as if that explains everything.

The day's warming, and I follow him onto his deck, where I pull a chair into a sunny spot as he adjusts an umbrella over our table. So are you going to tell me what you think of him? I ask, and Kyle brushes imaginary lint from his shirt. He's pretty enough, he decides. Kyle, I say, C'mon. How'd you meet him? he asks, sidestepping my question, and I tell him about my trek to Central Market. Squeezing the melons? he simpers.

I give him the rest of the story, how I'd turned down Brice's invitation to join him for champagne, the email I sent to Adam, the way I'd stepped off that curb on Chicon and straightened to find Brice right in front of me. By this time, Kyle's eating one truffle after another, like he's at the movies and I'm the entertainment. At this rate, he's going to gain back all that weight he lost last year. Have you heard from him? I ask, trying to sound nonchalant and failing. Adam? he says, and the casual articulation of a name so long cherished brings tears to my eyes. Have you? I ask. Of course we have, he tells me. What did he say? I ask. What you'd expect, he answers, licking his fingers, He loves you, he misses you, blah blah blah.

I'm shot with a despair so deep I don't know how I'm not burying my face in my hands. What did you tell him? I ask. That you've been doing just fine without him, he affirms. Then he looks at me from under his lashes. And that you've met somebody new, he admits.

Well, if Adam thinks I've met someone, that explains why he hasn't called.

You lied to him, I say, and Kyle shrugs. I might've lied about that once or twice already, he says.

My tea has cooled, and I take a sip, looking out over the lake. This view was my salvation last year when Adam and I split up. A few days after he told me about his affair, I packed my belongings, unsure where I was going or even what I could afford. Kyle was the one who insisted I stay with him until I could make a decision. I was here for almost a month, crying most of the time, refusing to leave the house except for restorative yoga classes Scott convinced me I needed. I'd go at noon, then come back here and spend the afternoon on this deck. The lake was usually empty, and I'd stare at the opposite shore, where I could see Mount Bonnell. James would call to check in, and hearing his voice, I could almost picture us there in college, passing a bottle of Bacardi back and forth. One afternoon, when I admitted I hadn't been working, he told me to go inside and get my sketchpad. I'm not really in the mood, I told him. That's like saying you're not in the mood for sex, Joel, he snorted, Get a goddamn pencil in your hand.

The first sketch came with James's voice in my ear. Literally; he stayed on the phone with me, rambling on about the classes he was teaching as I teased the first line from the tip of my pencil. You good? he asked after a few minutes. Keep talking, I murmured, and at the end of an hour, I had one of the drawings that would end up at that show in DC. Call me anytime you want to work, he said, but after he got me started, I didn't need the crutch.

I told James that I emailed Adam, I confess. A given, Kyle sighs, reaching for the last truffle. He wasn't happy, I add, and Kyle rolls his eyes. James doesn't want you for himself, sweetheart, he reminds me, But he never likes the idea of someone else having you either.

There might be some truth there, but my argument with James over the weekend wasn't only about jealousy. James liked Adam before the affair. He wants me to be happy, but like Kyle and Scott, he knows the way I've suffered. *Adam did you in, Joel.* Those words hurt because they resonated so soundly. They're the reason I haven't caved, haven't answered Adam's email, haven't dialed his number just so I can hear his voice.

Adam did me in, and I can't do that to myself again.

James / Chicago / Christmas 2005

I watch my wife, a whirl of skirt and scarf. No one would ever even guess she's pregnant. She lights the candles, nixes the holiday music I've got ready to go, passes *hors d'oeuvres* with a smile I haven't seen for months. Her mood doesn't have anything to do with me. She's just happy to have Monica here, tolerates Chad's racist jokes with a mild laugh that makes me want to smack her. What did the Mexican kid get for Christmas? Chad asks. I don't answer but that doesn't stop him from delivering the punch line. My bike! he crows.

The company sucks but the food looks like something from Charlie Trotter. We sit around the dining room table where Chad grunts over the roast I carve. I hope he chokes on the goddamn potatoes. Lizzie, I protest under my breath, watching her pour another glass of wine. Oh, give it a rest, James, she says, keeping her voice light since we have company, It's Christmas!

I don't think the baby knows the difference.

I wonder how Joel's doing at Kyle's party. I wish he could've come up here instead. I think the trip would've done him good and I'm getting more and more pissed I couldn't give him the option. I'm grateful Lizzie's pregnant but in an ideal world she'd be pregnant and Joel would be here with me.

I console myself with the thought that I won't have to spend next Christmas with these idiots. Henry will be here. He'll be seven months old, just about to crawl. Next year we'll probably have to hang the Christmas ornaments out of his reach. We'll be able to travel and even if we end up spending the holiday in Houston with Lizzie's family I won't be with this douche bag, who's knocking back wine as quick as my wife.

Lizzie's wearing the necklace I gave her last night, the one with Henry's birthstone. Whatever, maybe I shouldn't have gone with May. He could always come late. I just wanted this pregnancy to feel more real for Lizzie. She thanked me at first but when I fastened the clasp around her neck and turned her to face me she looked at me like I'd given her a dog collar. I had to remind her to wear it today.

Is that new? Monica asks, seeing Lizzie fidget with the chain. My wife nods. It's the baby's birthstone, I say proudly and Chad gets this look that tells me he thinks I'm being premature. I look at Lizzie and rein myself in. I've got a job here and that's making everything as easy as I can for her so this baby can thrive.

I just wish she'd put down that glass of wine. Her doctor would agree with me. I know because I called her myself a few days ago. She hemmed and hawed about talking to me all right but she was there for the miscarriage. Fifteen weeks in and I got home from campus to find Lizzie on our bathroom floor in a pool of blood. I cannot go through that again and that's exactly what I told her doctor. She finally agreed to have a heart-to-heart with Lizzie after the holiday. In the meantime I'm supposed to make sure she's getting plenty of fluids.

I nudge Lizzie's foot under the table and tilt my head at her water glass. I'm not trying to call her out but she's got to dilute that wine. She rewards me with the tiniest sip like she can't bear to tear herself from the conversation long enough to swallow. Like anyone gives a shit about the guy from Chad's office. He's an excellent analyst, Chad's saying, And a genius when it comes to evaluating risk.

I take a sip of water with a pointed glance at my wife, who pays me zero attention. She's staring at Chad like he's saying something fascinating. Definitely my go-to guy for portfolio construction, he's telling us and I excuse myself so I can bring in the Bûche de Noël. Joel would never touch this dessert. When I saw him last August I had to beg him to drink a margarita. Too much sugar, he told me. Didn't you make it through college on Lucky Charms and Rice Krispies? I asked. Well, whatever, he's missing out. So is Lizzie, who turns her nose up at this beautiful dessert I picked up especially for her. Fine. I hack off a slice for myself.

He's gay, Monica says as I'm taking my first bite and I look up. What? I ask and Chad looks annoyed like maybe he expected me to listen to his stupid story. I've been talking about one of the members of my investment team, he says, He's an asset, but he's gay. What do you mean, *but*? I ask and Lizzie frowns. I ignore her same as she ignored me when I told her to drink some water. I can't have him in front of our clients, Chad explains. Because he's gay? I ask incredulously. He's not exactly understated, Monica tells us. Honey, Chad laughs, He's *flaming*.

Am I really supposed to keep my mouth shut? In my own home?

Flamin', I repeat. You know what I mean, he confides. Would anyone like more wine? Lizzie asks and Monica holds out her glass. You know how they can be, Chad continues. How who can be? I ask. Fags, he says.

I can't believe I'm spending the holiday with this guy. *This* guy with his bald head and wire-rimmed spectacles and a gut he's got to be targeting for a New Year's resolution. I'm sharing my Christmas dinner with *this* guy because Lizzie can't handle the fact that nine years ago Joel and I slept together.

How many fags does it take to screw in a light bulb? Chad asks. Seriously, man, I mutter, shaking my head. Two, he announces, One to screw it in and the other to say *fabulous*.

He even lets his hand go limp. For just a second he reminds me of Kyle and *that* pisses me off so much I forget I've never liked Kyle or understood what Joel sees in him. You look a little defensive, Chad says, taking in my scowl with a big old grin, You have anything you want to tell us?

I shoot Lizzie a look and her eyes widen.

Wait, Monica says, Am I missing something? You mean other than that your husband's an asshole? I ask.

Chad sits up so straight his chair rocks back on its legs. Then Monica whispers something in his ear that has him glancing at Lizzie. My wife's pregnancy doesn't make you any less of a prick, I assure him.

I'm still bleeding when Lizzie shuts the door behind them and glares at me. What? I mumble and my wife folds her arms across her chest without seeming to care too much about the ice pack I've got pressed against the bridge of my nose. You just had to go there, didn't you? she asks. Go where, Lizzie? I say, He's a fuckin' homophobe. He's allowed to have an *opinion*, she tells me. He's not allowed to have *that* opinion in *my* house, I inform her. It's my house too, she reminds me. You can't tell me you don't find him offensive, I say. He was talking about one of his colleagues, she reminds me, Why are you making this personal? Because it *is* personal, Lizzie, I growl and that right there kills Christmas.

Joel / Chicago / July 2006

We're sitting on the sofa, a cushion apart, letting the Ecstasy take effect. We're sipping from bottles of water, and there's a pack of gum on the table. I realize the irony of reaching forward to examine the label for impurities, given that I've just taken a drug which always leaves me with a headache so intense that suicide seems a viable option. Every so often, I feel a flicker of exhilaration, but nothing's sticking yet. A glance at my phone reminds me that I've known the guy beside me for approximately fifty-five minutes.

James has called twice. I haven't responded. As I stare at the screen of my cell phone, he calls again. Laughter bubbles up from my chest and spurts from my nose. The guy beside me eases into a smile. You feeling it? he asks, edging toward me. What's your name? I ask, and his smile widens. Trey, he says. The word slips from his lips, and I catch it on my tongue, tell him my own between breaths. They're coming faster, and his mouth warms. My tongue feels electric and I pull his shirt over his head. He straddles my lap and I unbuckle his belt and close my eyes when my phone rings. My hands know where they want to go and they go and they go.

We're in Trey's bedroom and everything's fine, I could call James right now because everything's fine. Nothing separates my skin from Trey's and we're laughing and breathing and Trey's mouth my mouth we're sharing. I get to my knees and he pulls me down again and my cell phone keeps crying but I'm not, this time I'm not. I start at Trey's ankles and run my hands all the way up legs, abdomen, chest, into all that thick hair, my teeth pulling his lip, his dick sheathed and my eyes closed, open, closed.

We split the next tablet and climb a little higher, sprawled on his bedroom floor, stained cement cold under my ass. We're both sweating and he goes back for more water and dribbles some on my torso. I watch his tongue and orbit the ceiling fan and he spits his gum into my mouth because I'm grinding. I haven't been this high in so fucking long and I missed it, miss it, *miss you*. My name over and over and I say yes and his moan spirals me up and up and up we go.

In the shower I'm kneeling between his legs. He leans against the subway tile with his hands on my head and the water pours over us like from a font. I'm holding him up, my hands cradling his ass and he rocks. Then I'm the one against the tile and he glides one finger from the tip of my spine down. Condom, I manage to croak because I'm just crossing into the other side of my high, and he groans but suits up. You feeling it? he murmurs, and I moan. I've waited just a little too long.

James / Chicago / May 2007

By the end of the weekend I own a jogging stroller and I've experienced downward dog firsthand. This morning on my poor excuse for a run I stopped and collapsed on a bench but Joel kept going, reappearing twenty minutes later and telling me to suck it up. Tonight my glutes hurt so bad I can barely sit down to take a shit. Why I let Joel convince me that now's a good time to get back in shape I do not understand and after I get Henry to bed and Joel's in the shower I hobble down the stairs. I need a cigarette so bad and I dig around in the kitchen drawer and come up with half a pack of Marlboros and a lighter. Slipping out the back door I take that smoke right into my lungs.

God, what a *relief*. I give myself another drag, holding out my hand so I can see if it's shaking. My shoulders have gone into crisis mode. You can do a restorative class tomorrow, Joel told me when he heard me bitching about the pain. Sure 'nough, I mumbled but no way am I falling for that shit. I'm too sore. Anyway I've got grading to do.

I flick my ash into the yard and glance over my shoulder. I wouldn't mind slowing down some and savoring this moment but Joel will probably kick my ass if he finds me out here. I don't really want him to take up the habit again but I wouldn't mind sharing a cigarette. We've smoked together since we were sophomores and every time I inhale I picture us in that swing on our front porch of that house on Pearl. I spent many happy moments there and I suppose some not so happy ones. That swing connected us and smoking did too.

I keep expecting Lizzie to call. She's been gone for almost three weeks now and there's a part of me that's waiting for her to open the front door and tell me she's home. I keep watching Henry for signs that he misses her but he hasn't cried out for her, not once. I'm trying to figure out whether or not I miss her myself and I'm afraid of the answer. Seven years of marriage should leave me with something other than a fear she's going to fuck up the flow I've been feeling since Joel got here. I want her in Henry's life and for that reason I hope she calls but not if that means sending Joel home.

Now I just have to figure out how I can pull off field work as intensive as what I'm anticipating with a baby in tow. I need to keep money in mind too. When Lizzie left us she took her salary with her. I massage my quad up close to my knee where my muscle feels like it's on fire. Restorative yoga my ass. I'll be lucky if I can crawl out of bed tomorrow.

Why do I feel like I'm cheating on Joel with every inhale?

I glance over my shoulder and there he is, standing right in the doorway. Aw shit, I mutter, holding my cigarette below the table like maybe he missed the unmistakable stench of burning nicotine or the haze of smoke hovering around me. I brace myself but he just comes on out and leans against the railing of the deck. He's wearing flannel pajama bottoms like he's somewhere cold. You don't have to tell me I shouldn't be smokin', I say and he shrugs. If there was any way I could stop at one, he tells me, I'd ask if you had another.

Well, that makes me feel a little less guilty and I take one last drag then crush the butt under my shoe. At least Lizzie's not here to see, I add. She'd probably just blame me, he says. She blamed you for a lot, I admit and he says, You ever think she might be right?

I finger the crushed butt of my Marlboro mostly so I don't have to look at him. You never told her? he asks and I know he's talking about the Christmas before last. I shake my head. Could she have found out some other way? he asks. Like how, Joel? I say, irritated, You think I went around tellin' people?

That smile of his might as well be a scythe. I'm *married*, I remind him because I know what he's thinking and it's got nothing to do with Lizzie. Right, he says softly. C'mon man, I mumble, Don't... Allude to the past? he guesses, Talk about that phone call? You didn't break us up, I insist and he says, I sure didn't help.

Whatever, I can't argue with him there. From the get-go Joel's been in the middle of my marriage. I can't even count all the times Lizzie and I fought about my trips to Austin or Joel coming up here and that's without her knowing what happened on Christmas in 2005. I never told her, Joel, I repeat. All right, he shrugs. I didn't, I say and he raises his eyebrows like maybe my conviction has him wondering.

Flicking a flame from my lighter I fire up another Marlboro. My next words will come easier with smoke. For what it's worth, I say, exhaling, I don't have any regrets.

Maybe my lungs let loose a prism because that quick he's a rainbow of emotion, twitching every which-a-way like he can't figure out what to feel. He finally turns from me and looks out over the yard. With his arms crossed over his chest and the wind in his hair I sure feel like we've been here before. Joel— I start and he gives me a quick smile. You should probably tell me what you need from me tomorrow, he says.

Now who doesn't want to talk about that phone call?

Joel / Austin / October 2006

I call James as soon as I get home from Kyle's house, trying his cell phone first, then his office when the line rolls to voicemail. He answers sounding preoccupied and professorial. Sometimes I think about how long we've known each other, that he's been a part of my life since 1990, when graduate school wasn't anything more for him than a far-flung fantasy. Now he's sitting in an office in Chicago, a year away from tenure.

I get right to the reason I'm calling. I crossed a line the other night, I say, and he's quiet. He's probably replaying my crack about Elizabeth and coming to terms all over again with the memory. *Your demented fucking wife.* I'm sorry, I add, and he sighs. I don't know, Joel, he confesses, I wasn't a very good friend.

Well, I'm not going to argue with that. Let's just move on, I mumble. Done, he tells me, and I offer up a *happy birthday*, not wanting him to think I've forgotten. Do you—? I ask as he says, Remember—? There's relief in our laughter and magnanimity as we each tell the other to speak first. I was thinking about the time we spent my birthday at Zilker Park, he says. All that freedom to do whatever we wanted, I remind him, And you insisted on drinking a Cakebread in a train tunnel. We always had wine, he remembers. And cigarettes, I add. Pot too, he says, God, when was the last time you smoked a joint? The last time you came to Austin, I admit, The night Adam was arrested.

That shuts us down long enough to remind us why we haven't spoken over the past few days. I guess you've been in touch with him, he sulks, and I tell him that Adam wrote back within the hour. But honestly, I say, I just couldn't... Thank *god*, he bursts out as soon as he understands what I mean, I do not want to see you go through that again, Joel. *You weren't here to see me the first time around*, I almost tell him. But he's the one who got me painting last year, and I know when I take a step away from the situation that he couldn't be there for Elizabeth and me at the same time. He couldn't in good conscience choose me over his wife. Well, I haven't called him, I say. So what've you been doing the past few days? James asks, Besides avoiding me? I've been distracted, I say, and I swear I can feel him stiffen.

Clarity comes like a shot of adrenaline. I can't mention Brice. Not after what happened in July, not after our fight on Saturday night. Not after saying the word *distraction* like we've never used it ourselves. If I tell James about Brice, we'll just spiral right down again. I can't do that. Not today.

I had energy work, I tell him. That's why I haven't heard from you? he asks, sounding suspicious. I've been pretty raw, I say, But I didn't want to miss your birthday. Yeah, I might've held that against you, he agrees. Well, you can rest easy, I assure him, You've gotten a phone call *and* an apology. It's no Cakebread, he says, But I'll take what I can get.

James / Chicago / Christmas 2005

I thought Lizzie might forgive me for brawling over Christmas dinner but I guess she wasn't kidding when she told me to sleep on the couch. There's not even a hint of light under our bedroom door and that's good for the baby sure enough but I'm *pissed*. I don't see why I'm being punished and I track down Joel at Kyle's party and tell him what happened, the way Chad goaded me. Your whole intention for the evening was to get your wife to relax, he reminds me. I tried, I insist and whatever, I can almost see Joel rolling his eyes. *Like it wasn't him I was trying to defend.* What're you doin' right now anyway? I ask, changing the subject. Trying not to drink, he tells me. How's that goin'? I wonder. I'm on my second glass of wine, he admits, And it's almost gone.

For him that's a lot. You sound all right, I tell him and he says, Yeah, the anger's keeping me nice and tight. You wanna talk about it? I ask. You know I don't, he says. Then we'll talk about somethin' else, I suggest and he tells me he's supposed to be socializing.

I might be selfish but I don't want him to hang up and leave me sitting here all by myself on Christmas. You know if you get off the phone you're just gonna get another glass of wine, I tell him. I'll probably drink one either way, he says, sounding grim. Then I'll join you, I decide, getting off the couch and going into the kitchen. I pull a cork from the bottle of Bordeaux we didn't get a chance to finish at dinner. On the other end of the line I can hear him pouring a glass of his own. James, he says, his voice muffled. Yeah? I say and suddenly I'm talking to Kyle.

Happy holidays, Roomie, he simpers and even though there's probably a dig in there somewhere I choose to overlook it. After all, if it weren't for him Joel might be alone tonight and I couldn't stomach that. Merry Christmas, Kyle, I grumble. You celebrating with that pretty wife of yours? he asks and I say, Somethin' like that. Mm-hmm, he says like he's already heard I fucked up my celebration. Then he drops his voice. Hey, are you coming down here any time soon? he asks. No, I say, Why? Joel could use a friend right now, he tells me, And you know how bad he must be if I'm asking for *you*.

Well shit, he's right about that. But I can't trust Lizzie to behave herself if I'm gone. She'll try a kickbox class after work then meet Monica for martinis. The baby's not worth the risk.

Talk to him, at least, Kyle says and he passes the phone off to Joel again. Listen— Joel starts. Don't bail on me now, man, I interrupt, I just poured a glass of wine. Like you wouldn't drink alone, he tells me. Not as much fun, I point out. All right, he sighs, Give me a minute so I can find someplace quiet.

I sit my ass down on the couch and turn off the lamp, savoring the lights from the Christmas tree. I put it up myself this year since Lizzie's been so tired but she bitches about it every goddamn day. We've always had white lights but this year two of the strands were shot and I ended up replacing them with colored ones. I don't like them, she proclaimed, They look like something a kindergartener would choose. You're *pregnant*, I reminded her. I think she would've taken the whole tree apart and set it up again if she had the energy but instead she scrutinized my work then sent me back up the ladder to adjust the star. When I was finished she gave her head a little shake like she wasn't happy but was too resigned to do anything about it.

I like the colored lights and not just because Lizzie's probably right and they do seem better for a kid. Growing up I always had colored lights and one year I wrapped a strand around the front porch railing of that house Joel and I lived in when we were in college. Though maybe that was after college by a couple years. I don't know. That whole time we lived together blurs.

I'm back, Joel tells me. Where're you now? I ask. Guest bedroom, he says. You spendin' the night there? I ask. Yeah, I don't know, he hesitates, I really… What? I prod. I don't want to wake up alone, he admits.

God this sucks. He needs some serious support here and the best I can offer him is this phone call. I'm glad he had enough sense to go to Kyle's tonight but I know Kyle and he's the life of every party especially his own. No wonder he's asking for my help.

Maybe you need a distraction, I say, You got your eye on anyone there? You want me to get *laid*? he says. It's not the worst idea, I mumble. You've had better, he tells me, I just left Adam a week ago. You left him almost four months ago, I remind him, You're the one who decided to go to

Kentucky last week. His dad *died*, he says, The man was basically my father-in-law. Well, I don't like the idea of you being alone, I tell him. Why don't you come down here then? he asks, You have some time off. Joel, I protest, pissed that he's making me say the words out loud, You know I can't leave Lizzie right now. So you're trying to pawn me off on someone else, he says.

All right, this isn't cool. I'm supposed to be making him feel better, not worse.

Let's not fight, all right? I say, C'mon, man, it's Christmas.

There's something in the words that takes me back to another holiday but I can't remember which one. I've been through so many with him and sometimes the timelines get crossed, the year I left Fort Worth early after he had a fight with his dad jumbled with the year he told me about the scars on his arms mixed up with the year we were sleeping together.

Remember the Christmas lights we had on our front porch? I ask. Yeah, I remember, he mutters and I say, Sometimes I wish we were still in college.

He's quiet for so long I think I've fucked up again. Man, I'm just shitting all over this conversation and I try to think of something I can say that won't make him even sadder. I miss him, he finally ventures, booting us there himself. I make some kind of noise he can take for sympathy if he's desperate enough. Whatever, I liked Adam fine for a while but the shit that man has pulled over the past year makes me wish I had a shotgun. I'm going to call him, Joel decides. The fuck you are, I retort, sitting right up. I can't stand this anymore, James, he says, I can't... Listen to me, I tell him, leaning forward like he's sitting right in front of me instead of a thousand miles away, Adam cheated on you and lied to you and bought a *car* with the guy he was fuckin'. I know, he whispers, I know. Stop makin' excuses for him, I insist and he says, How can I not when I know what he went through with Bobby?

I don't know what it's like to watch someone you love die. I'm sure losing Bobby to AIDS fucked Adam up good. But I can't stand hearing Joel justify betrayal after betrayal. Adam doesn't get a pass just because Bobby died. Joel's dad burned the shit out of Joel's arms. His mom shot herself our sophomore year. It took a while but Joel got himself together. He was good to Adam. He didn't deserve what he got.

I tell him what I'm thinking, being careful with my words since I don't want to bring him down even more and after a while he takes the kind of breath that tells me he's starting to settle. Look, I'm not tryin' to demonize the guy, I say, I know you had something good for a while. We really did, he admits and I say, Sometimes things just end, Joel.

I can hear him taking another breath and I'm glad for it. How you doin'? I ask. I'm drunk, he mumbles. You wanna get back to your party? I ask. Not really, he says.

Well, I'm glad to hear that since I'm not ready to let him go. I sit back, taking my wine with me. For a few minutes we're quiet like maybe we're sitting in that old swing on our front porch and we don't need to say anything to recognize we're there for each other. Are you drunk? he asks. Not even close, I say, glancing at my wine. You better catch up, he tells me, his words soft and slurry. You better pace yourself, I warn. Why? he says, You worried you'll end up my distraction?

His question holds me fast. I know better, I finally manage, untangling myself but he's already talking again, something about missing sex. I grunt because I don't know how to explain the sex I've been having the past few years, how something that started with such intensity could turn so routinized that by the time Lizzie got pregnant I didn't want to go near her. Her hair, her skin, the perfume she wore that early on had made me tripping with desire… I had to get past that shit just to get hard. The only thing that kept me going was thinking of the result, that at the end of everything we'd have a baby. Now that she's pregnant there's no need to touch her.

You don't have to tell me that's seriously fucked up, I mutter, apparently having decided to unburden myself. And here I thought I was bad off, he says, Six days and I'm feeling it.

The lights on the Christmas tree wink. I rub my eyes. Six *days*? Wasn't he in Kentucky with Adam six days ago? Six *days*? I repeat and he says, Well. You wanna tell me how that happened? I ask and his voice gets all thick like he's thinking of crying again. I don't know, James, he says, I was up there for the funeral, and I knew I wasn't going to take him back, but I wanted… I needed…

Aw hell. I don't want to have to coax him out of another crying jag but what the fuck. I thought he was going to that funeral for moral support only.

We'd been out a couple of times, he explains, And a few nights before his dad died… You slept with him, I say flatly. Of course you're pissed, he mutters. You told me you were gonna meet him one night for a *drink*, I remind him and he says, Yeah, well, I let him fuck me too.

Bam. The image bleeds through the Christmas lights like one of his paintings, wet and bright with color. Once, just one time since we stopped sleeping together have I let myself linger over how it felt to be with him and I'm still struggling to admit that he was the one I had in mind the time that took. Now I have him giving shape to whatever I had in my head that morning last August before Lizzie's last insemination.

Why do you care so much anyway? he asks and what am I supposed to say? I just want you to be happy, I mumble and that's the truth even if it's buried in bullshit. I know, he sighs, I know you do. Why else would I be sittin' in the dark on Christmas, I tell him, Talkin' to you? I guess you're my distraction after all, he says.

Joel / Chicago / July 2006

Trey never bothered to close the blinds, and a dirty dawn crawls over the edge of the windowsill. I'm already starting to shake, and I zip my jeans with trembling fingers. I could use a Xanax, but Trey doesn't offer and doesn't seem to need one himself. From his bed, he watches me fumble with the buttons on my shirt. I've lost my gum, and I step into my shoes, drinking the dregs from one of the bottles of water on the dresser. Let me call you a cab, he says without making a move for his phone. I'm fine, I tell him, and he shrugs.

This part I don't miss.

Trey follows me out to the living room while I hunt around for my cell, my headache still in the flirtation stage. I can't bring myself to look at my missed calls. Any chance I could get another water? I ask, and he trudges into the kitchen to get me a bottle. You have everything? he asks, like he can't get rid of me fast enough.

There won't be a lingering kiss goodbye with this guy, not that I want one. I haven't even called for a cab yet, but I'd rather wait downstairs. Where am I again? I ask, and he gives me the address and shuts the door behind me.

By the time the cab arrives, my headache has dropped the seduction and decided to drill me. I fall into the backseat, mumbling the name of my hotel. As the cab moves forward, I look at my phone. I have four missed calls and three voicemails from James, all saying the same thing. He's sorry the weekend didn't work out like he'd planned; we'll try again another time. Nothing changes the end result. He's at home with his wife and infant son, and I'm in a cab, barreling down from a high that's going to leave a serious fucking mark.

I wish I'd never left Austin.

James / Austin / April 1995

The second we step foot in the club I see why Joel told me to brace myself. He fits right in and that throws me as hard as the trip we made to Mexico a few summers ago when he made me go scuba diving. I'd been a lifeguard for years but I dropped under the water with a tank and had a panic attack so serious I had to sit on the edge of the pool where we were practicing, my head between my knees. Joel tried to convince me we didn't need to go through with that dive but I knew I didn't have a choice.

Now in this gay bar I'm being sized up no matter which way I look. The researcher in me wonders if this is what women feel every day of their lives and I sidle instinctively a little closer to Joel. We don't even have a cocktail,

Kyle says to him when Joel puts a reassuring arm around me, Don't kill your chances yet.

Thirty minutes later I've guzzled two drinks and I don't know what to do with my eyes. And I'm *pissed*. Guys keep coming up to Joel and he pulls them into hugs, kisses their cheeks, slides an arm around their waists. I guess these are his friends and I can feel anger curling tighter and tighter in my belly, anger mixed with a shot of confusion because what kind of friend am I if I've got to have him all to myself? He has something here that feels entirely separate from what we share. Here we've had all these crazy years together—that drive to Houston after his mom killed herself, the way I dropped my fraternity out of some kind of acknowledgment of his grief, the way I ditched my family last Christmas when I found out Joel was heading back to Austin early after a shitty holiday with his dad—and anyone looking at us tonight would assume he barely knows me.

Meanwhile I don't know where to look, how to stand. I let Joel decide what I should wear tonight and I yank at the collar of a shirt that feels too tight. I want a cigarette but I don't have any with me and when I turn to ask Joel for one I see him farther on down the bar. He's not looking at me and he's laughing.

As I swallow the last of my drink and think about another one some guy slides into the space next to me. Aren't you something special, he murmurs, looking me over and I can feel my mouth open then close without a sound. I wouldn't be able to pick him out of a lineup. All I can see is *guy flirting*. Why don't we get you another drink, he suggests, gesturing for the bartender. I'm here with my boyfriend, I burst out, my eyes widening at my own lie. Oh yeah? he says, Who's that? I find Joel down the bar, his arm around someone I don't even recognize. For all I know he's on the verge of bailing on me. My new friend takes him in and gives me a smile I've probably given dozens of girls in my lifetime. Nice, he says, But he has nothing on you.

The bartender sticks a drink in front of me and I reach for the glass and knock it back, feeling the fire in my throat and then my belly. What am I drinkin'? I ask my new friend. That's a Moscow mule, he says, You like it? I force myself to look at him. He's got ten years on me, lines on either side of his mouth. His body smells hot and I'm not happy to notice.

You should tell me your name, he says. James, I mumble, which only makes him inch closer and give me a slow scan that makes me feel like I'm still standing on my front porch with Kyle. He moves his mouth to my ear. I'm Larry, he whispers.

Who's your friend, sweetheart? Joel suddenly asks beside me and I'm so happy to see him I about collapse into his arms. This is Larry, I say, gesturing with my glass and spilling Moscow mule all over my shirt. I'm drunker than I thought and I lick my lips. He bought me a drink, I add and

Joel says so flatly I'm instantly gratified, Wasn't that nice of him. Hey, Larry protests, raising his hands, I'm not trying to interfere. Joel looks him up and down. No problem, he finally decides. He glances back at me and I try to focus. You're drunk, baby, he says and I wrestle with the word, trying to figure out where I want it to land. Maybe, I finally admit and he cups his hand around the back of my neck in a way that tugs at something so deep inside me I barely recognize myself. You wanted to dance, right? he asks. Somehow I nod. Sorry, he says to Larry, But he's spoken for.

After everything I've seen tonight I feel like I've been invited into something that up until now Joel's been denying me. We skirt the dance floor, the music thick and loud and pounding. He's got hold of my hand and hold of my smile and I'm stupid with wanting something I never knew I wanted. Then he smirks. I knew you'd be in over your head, he says and man, I do not like his tone like I'm the butt of some kind of joke. It's not a big deal, I slur and he stops, the disco ball throwing rainbows around us. I fold my arms across my chest, drunk and stubborn. Not a big deal, I insist. Then I'll leave you to it, he says.

He turns to walk away and I watch him for half a beat before I leap after him. He slides his eyes in my direction, so bored and suave I panic. Don't leave me, I blurt out and he glances back at the bar. Larry's watching us like he can't wait to see what happens next. And… thanks, I mumble, staring down at my boots. Thanks? he repeats and I blow a sigh through my cheeks. For helpin' me out back there, I say. I thought you were fine, he reminds me. Yeah, I grumble, kicking at the floor, Well. Larry's still watching, you know, he says and I shoot a glance toward the bar.

The movement makes me dizzy and Joel steps closer and curls his fingers around my arms. After the past few hours his hands feel like relief. You're *drunk*, he says. Yeah, I concede and his smile spools so long he has his hands on my waist before it ends. I spend half a minute on his gaze before I realize we're moving. I don't recognize the song but the beat's all that matters. What're we doin'? I murmur and he pulls me closer, one hand on my neck like he had on Shelton's. We're dancing, he says, his breath slipping into my ear. His fingers scroll through my hair, firm and really fucking sure. My eyes flicker shut but not before I catch sight of Larry turning away from us. My senses have crystallized to one sharp point under my ear where Joel's pressing his thumb just hard enough to cut through my buzz. He could close his fingers around my neck and I swear to God I wouldn't care.

May I cut in? someone asks and my eyes fly open. Joel shifts away from me as Kyle steps into his place, sliding an unwelcome arm around my waist. I didn't know you were such a good dancer, Roomie, he says, his tone soft and syrupy. I know bullshit when I hear it, I tell him and he laughs. I glance at Joel who already has his arms around some other guy. I wouldn't be able to slide a c-note between them.

Why'd you come out with us tonight, Roomie? Kyle asks. He has to lean close so I can hear him over the music. His cologne makes my head hurt. I told you, I mumble, I wanted to go dancin'. He smiles. In the light from the disco ball I've got a feeling his teeth are capped. Just like you, sweetheart, he says, I know bullshit when I hear it.

I try to pull away from him but he holds me fast. He's stronger than he looks and I glance at Joel who's not looking at me. You ready to see this through? Kyle asks. I don't understand, I slur and he says all nice and pleasant like we're shooting the shit on my front porch, You know goddamn well what I mean.

Up until now we've been moving, dancing and arguing at the same time. Now I stop, drunk enough to take a step closer. Well, aren't you all big and brawny, Kyle breathes, giving one of my arms a squeeze. Don't threaten me, man, I say and that's when I lose him. I don't like you, Roomie, he declares. You don't even know me, I scoff. I know your type, he informs me and I roll my eyes. You've known me for two months, I tell him. Believe me, he says, I've seen everything I need to see.

I almost hit him. I'm drunk enough and pissed enough but just then Joel slides over to me. If Kyle won't dance with you..., he says, wrapping his arms around me again.

I look at Kyle over Joel's shoulder and smile.

Kyle's pissed, I tell Joel when we get home but he just laughs. I'll handle Kyle, he assures me. He's stripping off his jeans so he can shower and when he drops his boxers I realize that whatever we went through on the dance floor tonight doesn't mean shit. I'd felt a part of something I hadn't even known existed this morning. Fuck Joel's two-month relationship with Kyle. I knew Joel when it counted.

Now I feel a real rejection I want to excise, something that started as a pang the night Joel met Kyle and has been metastasizing ever since. I've crossed over into an alternate reality where Joel calls me *sweetheart* and *baby* and dances pressed up against me. But that doesn't mean he wants me. That doesn't mean he would've asked me onto the back deck when Kyle threw his party.

Man, I need to get laid. I need to suck it up and ask out that girl in my Ancient Mediterranean World class, the one with the braid all the way down her back. I'm spending way too much time wondering what Joel does with the guys he's picking up on the nights he's not with me.

You want the shower first? he asks, leaning over to turn on the water. I avert my eyes from his balls. Nah, I'm good, I say and he steps into the tub and slams the curtain shut.

Joel / Austin / November 2006

In the past two weeks, I've seen Brice four times, a ridiculous number of dates given that he spent the past few days in Dallas. I try to console myself with the thought that I can't really consider Celeste's party a date since Brice and I spent no more than fifteen minutes alone together. We kissed; big deal. I've done far more in half that amount of time and never defined the encounter a date. Why, then, do those fifteen minutes feel so monumental?

Maybe they wouldn't if I hadn't come right from Celeste's bedroom. Maybe they wouldn't if I'd experienced anything more than one intoxicated evening with a stranger since I left Adam. Maybe they wouldn't if I hadn't heard from Adam mere hours before Brice opened the door of my truck.

Those fifteen minutes count.

Then we met up at that wine bar downtown. When he drove away from me the next morning, I assumed I wouldn't see him again. I'd told him as much when he suggested we get together for dinner. *Tonight seems a little soon,* I'd said, and though in the moment, I meant the words, I ended up regretting them. A few days later, I woke up on the edge of a memory: arguing with Adam about the Christmas party for his office, way back in '99. I shouldn't have to beg to spend time with you, he'd complained, and suddenly I had the uncomfortable feeling I might be making the same mistake with Brice. He'd offered to share that Veuve Cliquot; I'd declined. I'd shown up at Celeste's party but pulled back when he suggested we meet later in the week for wine instead of heading right over to my place. On our first date, I denigrated his politics, then told him he was a better match for my father. Still he'd invited me into his car and then his bed. The next morning, he asked me to dinner.

Tonight seems a little soon.

He dropped me off at my truck, and I knew I wouldn't hear from him. I hoped, maybe. Or maybe I just needed something to divert me from the overwhelming impulse to call Adam. Don't you dare, girlfriend, Kyle warned, and even though Scott was more judicious when I confessed the temptation, I could tell what he was thinking. Scott likes Adam. He's friends with Adam. That doesn't mean he wants to see me backsliding.

So I committed myself to the paint, which worked until I woke up with Adam's Christmas party in mind. That night, I caved. I kept thinking back to my time in Brice's bed: the feel of his sheets against my skin, the Pellegrino I'd drunk, an artful fuck that told me I had no interest in another celibate year. I could have waited until the morning, or better yet, sometime Monday—contact on a Friday evening Brice would no doubt interpret as boredom, or worse, desperation—but by nine o'clock that night, I was so keyed up I didn't care.

He answered his phone, which surprised me. Guess where I am, he said as if he heard from me every day of his life. Rick Perry's house? I wondered, and he laughed. I'm in my hot tub, he told me. Yeah? I mused, What's that like?

We met for dinner two nights later. I insisted on paying; I had to use my credit card. Want to come back to my place for a Pellegrino? he asked as we left the restaurant, and the next morning, he drove me back to my truck.

The day after that, he called with an invitation so bizarre I had to accept. Come over tomorrow tonight, and help me give candy to the trick-or-treaters, he said, so I showed up at six under the misguided assumption that his doorbell might ring a dozen times over the course of the next few hours. Instead, we'd barely sat down. Apparently, kids from all over Austin show up in Brice's neighborhood on Halloween, and I half-expected to see Isabella and Rosalinda, Pablo in his father's arms. I have to kick you out now, he apologized, citing an early morning after we'd shut the door behind the last of the trick-or-treaters. Not so fast, I said, and he smiled.

Now I'm listening to a voicemail from him, asking me to dinner tomorrow night. I know the restaurant he's suggesting, and if he's not paying, I'll have to work off the debt in the kitchen. I just saw him on Tuesday. Do I really want to spend Saturday night with him?

Five dates in two weeks...

I think about the alternative. I can decline and spend tomorrow night working. I can crash at Kyle and Scott's—again. I can call James and hope he has time to talk (unlikely, given his six-month-old son, not to mention his wife). I can lament the demise of my relationship with Adam and my entire way of life.

Or, I can get dressed in the jeans I bought in Boystown this past summer, meet Brice for a two hundred dollar dinner, then go back to his place for sex.

Right.

James / Chicago / June 2007

I've still got a few days of classes and finals but I should be able to wrap up my tenure documents by the end of the weekend and after working my ass off for years and worrying about conferences and articles and book proposals I'm finally just about *done*. We're gettin' Henry to bed tonight, I told Joel this morning, And we're havin' ourselves a party.

He's finishing Henry's bath and I'm sending off an email assuring my colleague that I'll see her in just a couple weeks—one way or another I'm spending my summer in Greece—then go into the bathroom right as Joel's hauling my naked kid out of the tub. Man, this tag teaming shit *works*. I can't believe how much I've been doing by myself for the past year. I'm feeling caught up and ready for story time and I grab a towel and dry off my boy, stopping to play peek-a-boo. Joel leans against the sink watching us. This isn't something Lizzie ever did and I grin up at Joel, realizing as I do that I've started thinking about my wife in past tense.

After I put Henry to bed I meet up with Joel on the back porch and I feel good, like I deserve the cigarette I'm about to smoke. Startin' without me? I ask when I see the bottle of wine I picked up on the way home from campus but he shakes his head. I sit down beside him, scrubbing my hand through my hair and lighting up as he opens the wine for us. He probably needs the glass more than I do. He's the one who's been with Henry all day. I barely gave him thirty minutes for a run before he got dinner together then gave that boy of mine a bath. I've thanked you for comin' up here, right? I ask. Happy to help, he says, shrugging like losing four weeks of work doesn't mean shit. I give him a once-over. He doesn't look as tired as he could and he's not even bitter. Instead he's telling me he's grateful he's getting to know my kid. I hit the jackpot when I invited him up here and since I'm congratulating myself I almost don't hear him say he needed the distance. From what? I ask, tuning back in and he shrugs. Austin, he says, Brice. Brice? I repeat, What does he have to do with anything? We broke up, he says, Right before I went to DC last month. I didn't even know you'd gotten back together, I tell him and he gives me a look like I'm either a complete idiot or a total asshole. You knew we went to Hawaii, he reminds me. Well yeah, I say, I figured that was a one-shot deal. No, he says, That wasn't a one-shot deal.

Joel and I have talked since December, right? He's been living here for the past couple weeks.

Why didn't you tell me? I ask. Why didn't you ask? he says.

So I guess I'm a total asshole.

You should've said somethin', Joel, I say, taking a pissed off swig of wine. Well, now you know, he mutters.

We sit in silence and I start thinking that maybe I deserve this after what happened last fall. Even in the dark I can feel my face flushing when I think about making that phone call. I can still hear the wind outside my office window as I stared at Brice's photo, my grip on the phone tightening when his voice came on the line. And the fight I had with Joel as a result, the miserable weeks that followed when he shut me out so completely I figured we were as good as dead.

I miss Adam, Joel says, the words spoken in such a low voice I think for a second I didn't hear him right. Are you kiddin' me? I say, What the fuck is wrong with you? He saved my life, Joel reminds me and I grimace thinking how close I came to losing Joel forever. Adam showing up at the house on Pearl that day in '98 was a fluke. Letting himself in and finding Joel bleeding out in the bathtub was nothing short of a miracle and a big old reminder that I wasn't where I should've been that night. I'd fucked Joel over and he came so close to dying that nine years later I've got to light another cigarette to stop my hands from shaking. Tell me you haven't talked to him, I say through my smoke and Joel shakes his head.

Well, that's something. Last fall when he told me he'd sent that email I about lost my mind. I said he was stupid for reaching out to Adam after all that time and he made that crack about Lizzie and before I knew it I was hanging up on him. We fought a lot last fall I guess. Whatever, we've fought a lot since his last trip here. Sometimes I wonder what might've happened if Lizzie hadn't followed us around that weekend. I bet Joel wouldn't have left early. And if he hadn't left early he wouldn't have ended up in Boystown and we wouldn't have had that first fight, the one that seemed to start a domino effect that lasted phone call after phone call until he finally just cut me off.

Now he's staring off in the distance with such a faraway look in his eyes that I don't figure he'd hear me if I told him what I was thinking. I watch him remember Adam and I remember him looking lovesick at me and at least this time I can help. What can I do? I ask. Stop yelling at me, he suggests, Stop maligning Adam. I'm not gonna sing his praises, Joel, I inform him. So keep your mouth shut, he says, And for once in your life, just listen.

I do what he tells me. I don't say a word or whatever, I don't say much. I just listen to him and even though I don't like hearing how much he misses Adam or how many times he's thought about calling him, even though I'm plenty pissed at the hold Adam has on Joel I zip my lip and let him talk. I get an earful too. About Adam and Brice and the fight Joel and Brice had when Joel told him he wanted to make the trip to DC alone. About the work he's been doing down in Austin, the circles he's been painting. He talks and I listen and when he's finally quiet I don't jump in with something of my own. He lets out his breath like he's been holding it a real long time.

Joel / Austin / July 2006

I tried to sleep on the flight home from Chicago and couldn't, which means I've been awake for something like thirty-six hours. I'm so amped up my eyes can't close, and my pulse rate hasn't been this high since I used cocaine. I can feel the remnants of that Ecstasy spinning through my system like a cyclone ensnared, and—smart enough to know I shouldn't be alone right now—I drive right from the airport to Kyle and Scott's. They knew I was going to Chicago. They'll hear me out if I feel like talking.

They'll brew me tea and let me spend the night if I don't.

The second he sees me, Kyle starts clucking, and I trail him into the living room, where Scott looks up from his laptop and frowns. I like Scott, despite the fact that he kept Adam's affair a secret for months. I know he was hoping Adam would cut it off, remember the way he helped me the night Adam confessed and I fled the bed and breakfast where we were supposedly celebrating our anniversary. Desperate, I called Kyle, and when Scott answered Kyle's phone, I told him I needed a ride. He pulled up looking so grim the first words out of my mouth were: *You know.* He didn't bother making excuses. I guess I've always respected him for that.

Kyle, he suggests now, Why don't you get Joel a glass of water? Kyle flies into the kitchen, his dressing gown swirling around him as Scott tells me to sit. If you can, he adds. Long weekend, I admit, doing my best to oblige and putting a hand on my knee to stop my leg from jiggling. Scott just nods. He's good about giving people a chance to figure out what they want to say or if they want to say anything at all. He'd make an excellent therapist, unlike Kyle, who's already sweeping back into the living room like he's afraid I've given away something crucial in his absence. He hands me a tumbler of water, then sits down across from me, swinging one silk pajama-clad leg over the other. Tell us *all* about it, he says, ready for whatever gossip I'm willing to dish out. If you're not up for talking, Joel— Scott starts, and Kyle emits a shriek of protest. That's why he's here, love! he cries.

Their banter isn't helping my headache, and after I take a sip of water, I press my fingers to my temples. Was it really just yesterday that James had his hand on my neck?

Hard trip, I mumble, and Scott nods, giving me space to decide if I want to tell them why. Kyle merely looks impatient; I try not to hold that against him. He thrives on drama, and Scott keeps him on a short leash. Elizabeth didn't want me there, I explain, She wouldn't leave us alone, and James... Closing my eyes, I take a breath, the kind my therapist told me to try years ago. They had a fight, I say, Yesterday they had this crazy fucking fight right in front of me.

Kyle smacks his lips like he just swallowed a morsel of something delicious, and for the first time, I can feel myself getting angry with him. From the beginning, he hasn't liked James. He never forgave him for sleeping with me or me for falling in love with him. And he certainly can't understand why we've worked so hard to rebuild our relationship, why our loyalty to each other remains so staunch. Kyle, Scott says in a low voice, sensing my irritation, Stop treating Joel's life like a reality show. Kyle looks momentarily chastened but perks right up when my cell phone rings and my expression turns grievous. *Not his fault*, I remind myself, looking down at James's name on my caller ID. *What happened this weekend wasn't his fault.*

Well, at least I know you're not dead, James says when I answer.

Scott motions for Kyle to give me some privacy, but Kyle shakes him off, then bitch slaps his arm when Scott tries to pull him to his feet. Scott throws me an apologetic glance I'd wave aside if I hadn't been capsized by the sound of James's voice. Yeah, sorry, I mumble, finding my own, I've been...

High out of my mind. Preoccupied. *Distracted.*

I just got in, I admit. From Chicago? he asks in disbelief, Don't tell me you couldn't get an earlier flight!

I think about lying but ultimately don't have the energy. I didn't even try, I confess. You paid for a hotel? he groans. That's what credit cards are for, I sigh. Well, I'm sending you a check, he informs me, and when I tell him not to be ridiculous, he cuts me off. His insistence reeks of my father: all those gifts I took from him over the years, all that money. I'm not a fucking commodity.

Look, I'm really sorry, man, James says, Lizzie's just... *A bitch?* I almost say, but suddenly I can feel his hands on my back, his mouth next to my ear. He knew what he was doing. He knew the risk he was running, offering up a massage with his wife in the shower. Why does he always have to push the edge?

Is Elizabeth still speaking to you? I ask, trying to be magnanimous. He's not entirely at fault. I didn't have to sit down between his legs. I didn't have to let him touch me. I'm aware of what happened last Christmas. James has a wife, a relationship every bit as sacred as the one I had with Adam. I shouldn't have agreed.

She calmed down, he admits, After...

After you left. That's what he was going to say. She calmed down after I left, and I'm weary thinking about all of the future moments we'll have to mediate. I can never go back to Chicago. Elizabeth will never let James come down here without her. We're done, though I can't bring myself to say the words. I've known too much heartache in my life, too much loss. Now James will be one more casualty.

I went out for a drink last night, I tell him, surprising myself by sealing the deal. A drink, he repeats. Well, what did you think, James? I ask, my voice steeped in bitterness, That I'd check myself into a hotel room and lament the weekend?

Across from me, Kyle's mouth opens. Even Scott leans forward, and I give them both a macabre smile, like I've just been offered a glimpse of my own casket.

I ended up in Boystown, I add, even though James hasn't asked, and the memory of Trey fucking me in his shower supplants the feel of James's hands under my shirt. I welcome the reprieve. Boystown, James repeats, as if everything I'm telling him requires extra time to process. You've heard of

Boystown, I assure him. Well, yeah, he admits, I just didn't expect you to end up there last night. No, I agree, You expected me to go home to lick my wounds.

Kyle and Scott simultaneously shake their heads, offering me a pause I should consider. Nothing good can come of what I'm doing. C'mon, Joel, James mutters, sounding more annoyed than he has any right to sound, especially since I'm speaking the truth. C'mon, Joel, what? I ask, Don't you want to know what I did last night? You had a drink, he says flatly. Don't you want to know who I fucked? I say, Aren't you *curious*?

The word leaves my mouth like a kiss from the devil himself, and we all hold our breaths, every one of us: James, Kyle, Scott. All right, James says quietly, Let's stop before this shit gets out of hand. This shit's already out of hand, James! I cry, This shit was out of hand the day I fucking met you!

Then I'm spewing about the club, the alcohol, the tablet of Ecstasy I held under my tongue like I suddenly had possession of a whole other world. You didn't, James moans, Tell me you didn't. I did, you judgmental prick! I say, I got high, and I fucked some guy, and I know you're aching for every detail, so don't try to convince me otherwise! Jesus, Joel, he protests, What's wrong with you? What's wrong with me? I yell, What's *wrong*?

I hurl my phone so hard Scott ducks, though it lands without a scratch on the sofa beside him. Kyle scrambles to his feet. In Scott's arms, I cry out the last of the Ecstasy while Kyle handles James. *This isn't a good time, you're not hearing me, Roomie, he's not in a position to talk to you right now, for once could you give him some goddamn space.* Scott strokes my hair, whispers something soothing in my ear. I don't believe a word of what he says.

James / Chicago / August 2005

I never thought I'd get to the point where I'm sick of sex but I swear to God I'd rather jerk off in this cup than sleep with my wife one more time this month. I'm going to have to gear up anyway since her doctor wants us doing it as much as we can the day after her procedure but damn. Sometimes I feel like I'm getting nothing back from that woman. I've given up on the sugar talk. I can't remember the last time she came and I don't bother trying to get her there anymore. That sounds shitty but believe me I found out right quick she doesn't want me lingering. She just wants me to finish. In and out quick as I can. Keeping that hard-on of mine feels like a fucking miracle.

Right now my target's the cup. Lizzie left for work about thirty minutes ago even though she's got to be at the doctor's office in an hour. Deadlines, she claims and whatever, she probably just doesn't want to jerk me off. The last time we tried getting my sample that way—this was months ago—didn't end well. I was taking too long or some shit like that. What did she expect since we weren't allowed to use lube? You could go down on me, I suggested and she burst into tears. Let me tell you, there's nothing less sexy than your wife bawling over your limp dick.

I'm not doing much better on my own. I'm half-hard and half-hearted and the mediocre porn I have here isn't helping. I've got less than thirty minutes to get this done because the doctor needs my sample in enough time for Lizzie's appointment. At first I tried the donation rooms right there at the office but no way could I make anything happen with all those people sitting outside the door. I'll tell you one thing, it's a humbling experience cruising down the road with a warm cup of jizz between my legs. Every time I make that drive I pray I don't get pulled over.

I'm pretty demoralized here and I'm running out of time. In more ways than one: if Lizzie doesn't get pregnant today we're screwed. We're out of cash and out of options and I don't think our marriage will be able to handle all the guilt and anger and disappointment if this time doesn't take. Then what?

My phone rings like an answer and without letting go of my dick I crane my head to see who's calling. *Joel.* Well, I could use a break anyway. What's up? I ask, reaching for a tissue I don't need and Joel tells me he just got back from a run. I grunt because it's been years since I've run for anything other than the El. Believe me, he says, I needed it.

I don't doubt that. When I was down in Austin this past weekend Adam went and got himself in a bar fight then had some guy from his office bail him out of jail instead of calling Joel. I've known Adam for six years and I've always liked him but this last trip he was an absolute mess. His dad's sick and I know he's been spending time in Kentucky but Joel filled me in on some shit that sounds pretty fucking erratic. Like that Adam came home from work one day with a BMW he'd bought on his lunch hour.

I think Adam's fucking the guy who posted bail but I can't bring myself to tell Joel. I dropped a few hints last week, asked him if Adam has been coming home late and that kind of thing but Joel never has been able to find fault with the guy. Granted up until now Adam hasn't given him much reason. For years I've been grateful Adam showed up in Joel's life when he did. He was the one who found Joel with his arms all cut up and by the time they got together for good I was fixing to get married and move to Chicago. I was just glad Joel wouldn't be alone. Now he tells me he made reservations at a bed and breakfast for their anniversary. Man, he's trying everything he can to make this relationship work. Adam better get his shit together.

I'm just thinking those words when Joel says he has something else to tell me. Adam's charges got dropped. How'd you manage *that?* I ask because last I heard Adam had some pretty serious accusations against him, including clocking one of the cops who'd arrested him. Joel tells me the guy from Adam's office, the one who bailed him out of jail knows someone.

Aw man, if that guy's responsible for getting those charges dropped then Adam's sleeping with him for sure. I want to cry for my friend who's about to get his world blown the fuck apart but I keep my voice as hearty as a small town sheriff's. Super, I say but Joel gets real quiet like he knows I'm holding back.

Hell. Maybe I should just tell him what I'm thinking.

Joel / Austin / November 2006

I wait almost a month before I tell James about Brice, and I might have waited longer if he hadn't caught me on the phone tonight just as I was wrapping up some work in my studio. I'm supposed to meet Brice for dinner, someplace nice enough that I need to spend time getting ready. At first, I hedged my financial situation as more solvent than my truck would suggest, but I've maxed out my credit card. I finally had to come clean. He told me that moving forward, he'll pay the tab. I'm not sure I'm comfortable with that, I admitted. Then it's been nice knowing you, he said.

I'm a little pressed for time, but I'm feeling better than I've felt in a long while. I'm all over the circles that bottle of Dos Equis inspired last month. I have plans for Thanksgiving that feel both inclusive and healthy: two days with my father and his wife, then a weekend with Kyle and Scott. Brice gives me the illusion that money's flowing. He's fulfilling a lot of needs, actually, and not just financially. Not just sexually either, though I don't think I'd realized how much celibacy was affecting my creativity. I like this guy enough that I don't want to hide him any longer.

How's it going, man? James says, sounding as if he just downed a pot of coffee. I rinse the paint from my brushes, pressing my phone between my ear and shoulder. Like confetti, color speckles my forearms. I've been courting these colors all afternoon, plum and primrose and a sharp silver I mixed by mistake but had me barely breathing for a while, and I let my eyes linger before the water dilutes the color as James tells me he hired a new sitter, and he's trying her out. Just for a little while, he assures me, I'm supposed to go home in thirty minutes.

Well, no wonder he sounds manic. He doesn't like leaving Henry with anyone at all, including his wife. Where's Elizabeth? I ask. Kickbox class, he says, inhaling in a way that tells me he's taking in smoke, Every Monday, Tuesday, Wednesday, Thursday, Friday. Now that's dedication, I tell him, and he grunts like he doesn't agree but doesn't want to get into it. I shake off my brushes and squeeze the ends in an old towel.

So where are you anyway? I ask. Sitting in a swing at the park, he says. Nothing creepy about that, I assure him. Nah, I'm alone, he says, It's cold as fuck here. Here too, I say, though *cold* means something entirely different in Austin. I'm going to need a sweater tonight, and I go into my bedroom and pull a pair of jeans from my dresser. Years ago, I could make it a month without wearing the same thing. What I have in my closet these days I've cycled through so many times I don't have much left that impresses. I certainly don't have anything Brice hasn't seen.

I could go all out, wear a dress shirt and tie. I own both, though I haven't worn them since Adam's father's funeral. I hold the tie up to my reflection, James's voice in my ear. He's telling me about his own plans for the Thanksgiving holiday, what sounds like a full house. His parents and sister, as well as his in-laws, are all flying to Chicago. I just really didn't want to put Henry on a plane, you know? he confides. Uh-huh, I say, ditching the tie and pulling out the sweater I wore the first time I met Brice for wine.

Unless Kyle insists on treating me to a night out—which he does more often than makes me comfortable, given my inability to reciprocate—I don't eat at restaurants denoted by four forks in the *Austin Chronicle*. I suppose I'm lucky Brice wants to try this place, and I settle for the sweater and trade my jeans for the same pants I wore to that wine bar. Listen, I say, breaking into James's monologue about what constitutes the perfect pecan pie. *Pe*can, with the emphasis on the first syllable and a long e, in case I've forgotten that he has a definite opinion about the word's pronunciation. I have to go, I say. Why? he asks. I have a date, I say. Seriously? he says. I shuck off my jeans one-handed, then twist my way out of my shirt, trying to keep the phone to my ear. I've been seeing someone, I admit, crossing the hall to the bathroom. What? he says, Since when? A few weeks? I guess, that question mark at the end of my sentence intentional. Why didn't you say anything? he asks. There's not much to tell at this point, I say. Well, that's a load of crap, he says, The first guy you've dated since Adam and there's not much to tell?

He's irritated, all right, and I'm not sure if that's because I've kept Brice a secret or simply because Brice exists. What do you want to know, I sigh. Where'd you meet him, for starters, James asks. Central Market, I say. Central Market, he laughs, You go all William Carlos Williams on him?

I'm weary of the reference, but I'm not going to make the mistake of telling him. Instead, I hurry through a condensed version of how Brice and I met, how I stumbled upon him during a run and ended up at Celeste's party. So, what? he says, He's an artist? He's a lobbyist, I admit, turning on the shower. You're dating a *politician*? he groans, You going to tell me he's Republican next? We don't talk about politics, I inform him, sidestepping the question. You're dating a politician, but you don't talk about politics, he says, How does *that* work?

I'm about to tell him we've agreed to disagree, but he's already answering his own question. I'm not fucking his politics, he says in a voice that's supposed to be mine, though I can't for the life of me remember when I took that tone. Well, I'm not, I mutter, and he says, Holy shit, he's Republican, isn't he?

What's worse? To answer honestly or lie and have him discover the truth on his own? Jesus, Joel, he says before I can decide, What's his name? Brice Whitman I admit, resigning myself to the fact that James will probably Google him the second he gets home. Brice? he repeats with a snort of laughter, His name's Brice? Why are you being such a dick? I ask. C'mon, Joel, he says, *Brice?* What's wrong with *Brice?* I ask, and he says, *Brice* is the pretentious asshole who won't order tacos because he might get salsa on his Brooks Brothers shirt.

James could be happy for me or at least pretend. For almost fifteen months, I've been alone. Only twice in that time have I seen James, first when I drove up to Fort Worth when he and Elizabeth were in town for their baby shower, then again last summer when I ended up at that hotel in Boystown. I ask for so little, and for once, I could use some support.

This conversation is why I didn't tell you before now, I inform him. What, he says, You were intentionally keeping him from me? That's right, I tell him, and he says, Well, fuck you, too, Joel. Brice is taking care of that, I assure him. Jesus, he mutters, What's your problem? You are, James, I say, As usual.

James / Chicago / December 2006

I haven't heard from Joel in two weeks since I made fun of Brice. Whatever, the guy's clean, I know that for a fact. I've scoured the Internet and can't find anything more off-putting than his politics.

I still don't like him.

I need to remember that Joel's not going to be with this guy forever. We're talking rebound here made more appealing because Brice has a net worth that probably trumps that of the entire Classics department at U of C. I'm not saying Joel's dating him for his money but there's no way that hasn't come into play. I've seen that truck Joel drives. I know he barely makes rent.

I pull up Brice's profile again through his company website. I know Joel's type and this guy matches up: tall with a confident swagger I don't need to see in person to know he's got. Politically he makes no sense but Joel would tell me he's not fucking his politics. He said the same shit when I ragged him about that dumbass he was seeing the summer before we slept together. *I'm not fucking his brain.*

I link my fingers together and crack my knuckles. Chicago weather makes my bones ache and I glance away from my computer and out the window where the sky's fixing to dump a pile of powder. I should leave early but if I do this'll be the one time some straggler shows up to talk about his paper. I glance at my watch, the one Lizzie's parents gave me for my birthday last year and drum my fingers on the edge of my desk before I cave and pull up the other photos I found earlier. Brice Whitman, *summa cum laude* from SMU. Standing at the edge of a West Texas oil field. Shaking hands with Rick Perry. So this is the guy Joel's fucking. Well, good for him.

I scowl at my computer screen, annoyed that this guy's responsible for yet another argument between Joel and me. Yeah, I could've just congratulated Joel instead of giving him a hard time. But did he really expect me to pass up a name like *Brice*?

I wonder what the guy sounds like.

Thirty seconds later I'm talking to Brice's assistant. He's not in the office at the moment, she says and I have a hit-to-the-gut image of him in bed with Joel that I sure as shit don't need. I want the number for his cell, I say. She asks who's calling and I make up some stupid story about meeting Brice on the golf course a couple weeks ago and losing his business card. Which course? she asks and I bank on the guy's privilege. Austin Country Club, I say like she's a complete idiot. She comes right back with the number.

Brice sounds just like I figured he would. I can't even pick out his accent and I know he was born in Texas. Guess his parents shipped him off to prep school soon as he could start talking. I wonder what his colleagues would think of this little dalliance he's got going on with Joel. A lot I bet.

I keep a charade running just so I can get a sense of what he's like. Someone needs to look out for Joel, right? And since I'm not there to meet this guy in person I don't see another choice. Joel kept him from me for weeks. There's got to be something wrong with him.

Brice does such a good job of pretending he remembers meeting me I start to forget I'm lying. I've accessed my best drawl and I tell him I'm working with one of his districts and have some concerns about the regulations on jet fuel emissions. I didn't read up on this guy for nothing. Maybe we can get together in person, I say just so I can keep him on the phone while we negotiate our schedules. My assistant usually manages my time, he tells me, But let me check my calendar...

He suggests lunch and I swing him around to drinks one night instead. He agrees too quick and I wonder how Joel can possibly tell if this guy's being honest with him. Adam fucked him over. This guy could too. Lemme ask you somethin', I say. I'm going too far but I'm obviously not going to be able to meet Brice for drinks no matter how much time I've got in my fictional schedule. I need to know what this guy's really like and I need to know now. Are you seein' anyone? I ask.

He pauses long enough to tell me I've caught him off-guard.

Why do you ask? he says and I let my voice drop into full flirtation mode. He's either going to stiffen or cozy right on up to my suggestion. I like to know what I'm up against, I tell him. I hold my breath, my eyes on his photo. I'm terribly sorry, he says, I never mix business with pleasure. Maybe you should, I suggest in as seductive a tone as I've ever used with a girl. I'm flattered, he answers, But no, thank you. Look, if you're worried about that new boyfriend of yours findin' out, I say, grasping for anything that might make him cave, I'm discreet.

He's silent. *Finally,* I think. I've got him. Too late I wish I'd recorded this conversation on the off-chance Joel doesn't believe me. Then Brice speaks and I realize if he weren't so well-bred he'd come right through the phone to beat the shit out of me.

If you'd like to schedule a meeting related to business matters, you're welcome to contact my assistant, he says, Otherwise, we have nothing to discuss.

He hangs up and I drop my phone back on its cradle, pissed and well aware I've got no reason to be. If I'd been trying to catch Brice in a lie, if I wanted to tempt him I failed. That's *good* news.

I pull my gaze away from my computer. Jesus, what did I just do here? Did I carry on a conversation with that guy for ten minutes, pretending to be someone else? What the fuck is wrong with me?

Well, whatever. I've checked him out and he's obviously a good enough guy that he wasn't tempted. Joel doesn't have to know I've talked to him. Getting to my feet, I shrug into my coat then lean over to turn off my computer. Brice disappears as I pull on my gloves.

Some for reason I'm still pissed.

Joel / Austin / July 2006

In the light of day, I'm mortified by the way I unleashed on James last night, the way I transferred any blame at all for my behavior in Chicago right over to him, as if my fall from grace was his responsibility. Shit happens. I knew when I left town last Thursday that Elizabeth doesn't like me, that Henry would complicate matters, that everyone would be sleep-deprived and potentially on edge. I could've told James I didn't think it was a good time to meet his son. God knows I didn't have the money for the trip or much emotional wherewithal. But I went up there and put myself right in the middle of whatever drama James and Elizabeth were already creating, and even when I realized how much my presence was fucking everything up, I didn't tear myself away. Because I can't stand the ways we've changed either, or the ways we haven't.

I call him from Kyle's guest bedroom, where I've spent the night, and when he answers, I take a second to evaluate the timbre of his tone. You're on campus, I conclude. I'm in the library, he admits in a low voice. I'll call you later, I tell him, but he stops me. Hang on, he says, I'm stepping outside.

I run a hand through my hair as I wait for him to come back on the line. Closing my eyes, I can picture him on campus: plain-front khakis with a waist size an inch larger than he wore in college; a button-down that, by the end of the day, he'll be more than ready to pitch into the laundry because even in Chicago, July holds some weight; loafers appropriately collegiate. That watch with the brown leather strap that his in-laws gave him last year for his birthday. If he doesn't have a cigarette on him, he knows where he can find the nearest pack. I'm back, he says, and with the image I've conjured and his soft drawl in my ear, I halfway believe that if I open my eyes, I'll find him beside me.

I was out of control last night, I admit, and he murmurs what sounds like agreement. I try not to take offense; absent of Ecstasy, I might have responded to his phone call differently. I can't handle the drugs anymore, I add. You feel better this morning? he asks.

That he wants to know if I'm okay when he could be calling me on semantics—could I really *ever* handle the drugs?—reminds me how lucky I am that he's still in my life.

A couple Xanax and thirteen hours of sleep work wonders every time, I tell him, and he lets out a laugh that's mostly relief. In the mirror across from the bed, I catch myself smiling; my reflection hurts my heart. I guess I had unrealistic expectations for the weekend, I confess. I always do, Joel, he says.

Tears come to my eyes, Ecstasy's special afterglow. I let them fall as late morning sun filters through the curtains and colors the room with an amber light. I shouldn't have made the trip, I tell him. I can't never see you, Joel, he says, You're the best friend I've got.

I don't know how we'll move forward. I don't know how we'll find ways to see each other. I know he can't be everything to me; he told me so himself long ago. Still he's on the phone with me, even after that wreck of a weekend. My mother killed herself, my father remarried, my lover found another. Sixteen years after we met, James hasn't had enough of me.

We'll figure it out, he tells me, and because I can't imagine the alternative, I let myself believe him.

James / Chicago / June 2007

Joel might try to convince me he doesn't know much about kids but Henry has taken to him like he's been waiting for him pretty much forever. When I asked Joel to come up here I figured I was reaching. Neither of my parents can take that kind of time off work and I adore my sister but wouldn't trust her with a goldfish in a bowl. She's twenty-three and floundering her way through an undergraduate degree at Santa Cruz. Mostly she surfs and sleeps around, two activities about which she's equally passionate and unapologetically vocal. She makes my parents nuts.

So there really wasn't anyone to ask other than Joel. He's the only person I know with a schedule flexible enough to handle a month of last-minute childcare and since I've been wanting him to get to know Henry for the past year I figured what the hell.

That I've been missing Joel something fierce I probably factored in somewhere along the way too.

The past couple weeks have gone so much better than I expected. Not once has Henry cried when I've left for campus in the morning and though he's plenty happy to see me in the afternoon he keeps an eye on Joel, crawling back and forth from one of us to the other like he's reassuring himself. He ate lunch? I can't help asking, He spent time outside today? We went to the park, we ate lunch, he napped, Joel always says but last night he added, I wish you'd stop assuming I'm going to fuck this up.

I'm not really worried about that happening. I watch as Henry pulls himself up on Joel's leg. Hang on, Henry, Joel says. He's coring strawberries, slicing them and putting them in a little Thomas the Train bowl. Maybe if he had to fill this role on a permanent basis he'd get bored and bitter but he's such a natural I can see for the first time why Adam was resentful that Joel didn't want kids.

Probably best if I keep that to myself.

What are y'all doing today? I ask and Joel looks down at Henry. What do you think, sweetie? he asks my son, Should we go to the park? Can y'all pick up some wine while you're out? I ask, We finished that Chianti last night. *You* finished that Chianti, he corrects me.

Usually I stop myself at one or two beers but since Joel got here I've been drinking a little more, knowing I can count on him to help with Henry. Joel's happier with a glass of wine than a Shiner—some bullshit about the antioxidants—so whatever, that's what I've been drinking too. I still don't need him pointing out how much.

Maybe we should go *out* for wine, he suggests while I'm simmering. I don't have a sitter, I remind him. Find one, he says, reaching down and pulling my boy into his arms. Who am I supposed to call, Joel? I ask. I don't know, he says, One of your students?

Like I can leave Henry with just anyone. I don't want to put him through any unnecessary trauma right now. The thought of him waking up and finding someone he doesn't know, the thought of him crying when I'm not here... Look, if you need to get out of the house for a while— I start. I'm not the one who needs to get out of the house, James, Joel says.

I finish packing Henry's diaper bag so they can head to the park. Snacks, diapers, a couple changes of clothes, three pacifiers and Mr. Boo. I've got a blanket and diaper cream and a couple board books plus a few other odds and ends so Henry's not caught off-guard, so he's never caught off-guard.

You mean well, James, Joel says, But every so often you need to think about yourself. Henry, I start, stepping towards them as my son grabs onto Joel's hair but Joel pulls away from me. We're fine, he insists, Go to work.

I lift my bag over my shoulder. And find a sitter, he adds, Or I'll get one myself.

Joel / Austin / December 2006

I have to ring the doorbell twice before Brice answers, and when he finally appears, he barely glances up from his cell phone. Hey, he mouths, stepping back to let me inside. I follow him into the kitchen, where I open a bottle of Pellegrino and finish half a glass before he ends his call and gives me anything more than a distracted smile. That all you have in you? I ask. Parting his sport coat, I place my palms flat on his chest, then give myself the satisfaction of feeling my slow way down his hard-won abs. He catches my hands when I reach his belt buckle. Not now, he murmurs.

He's not in the habit of turning me down, and I take a step back, shrugging like I don't give a shit when in reality I'm already swirling with suspicion. I try to quiet the voice in my head telling me to take a look at his cell if he steps into the shower. Are you hungry? I ask, and he picks up his phone again.

If he doesn't want me and he's not interested in dinner—or even conversation—why am I here? I gulp my Pellegrino likes it's something substantial, watching as he pours himself wine with an absent expression, so used to me declining that he doesn't even offer me a glass. So what do you want to do? I say, If you're not hungry and you don't want to fuck? He raises his eyebrows at the edge in my voice, but when his cell phone rings, he snatches it right up like he was expecting a call. Give me a minute, he says over his shoulder, walking just far enough out of the room that I can't hear him. I edge a little closer and catch a low laugh.

Shit.

By the time he finishes his call and comes back into the kitchen, I'm convinced he's cheating on me. Never mind that we haven't agreed to anything exclusive. He's cheating on me. Are you fucking someone else? I ask, and he laughs, all the evidence against him I need. He's not even trying to deny the accusation. He's taking his calls in the next goddamn room. At least Adam had the decency to hide what he was doing. I'm serious, I say. Let me get you a brandy, he suggests. I don't want a *brandy*, I tell him, I want to know if you're fucking someone else!

His eyes on mine, his hands to himself: he knows how to manage me, and it's only been a little more than a month. Or maybe he's just this good. I think about my first night with him and the word that kept circling through my mind. *Polished.* He'd know just how to screw me over.

Sit down, he says, and I obey only because I'm shaking so hard I don't have a choice. With my head in my hands, I remind myself that he's not my boyfriend. I'm not in love with him. If he told me tonight that he didn't want to see me anymore, I'd be taken aback more than anything. I need to get myself under control.

Drink this, he commands, and I accept the glass he offers, taking the liquor like a shot. Under the influence, my chest warms. He sits beside me, his hands folded in his lap; he doesn't touch me, and for just a second, I wince. I remember the Halloween I had that dream about my mother; she knew that for most of my childhood, my father put out his cigars on my arm. Confiding in Adam, I was wild and sobbing, and he put his arms around me in spite of my exhortations to the contrary. He took care of me when no one else wanted the job. I brought myself back from the dead, and he left.

My ex had an affair, I say. Brice sits back, as if that explains everything. I'm textbook, all right; I probably would've bored my therapist if I hadn't hidden so much from her that I kept her guessing. I've been preoccupied, Brice realizes, combing through the events of the evening and recognizing what I might have misinterpreted as signs. You took your call in the other room, I add, You didn't want...

I gaze into my empty brandy glass. Without a word, Brice gets me another. How can I help? he asks, sitting down beside me again, and I take a breath and a slow sip of brandy. He could be turning tonight into an argument about my insecurities, of which I obviously have many. He could be reminding me that I have no claim on him and that he's free to fuck whomever he wants. Instead, he's listening. He's asking how he can help, and I falter over my next words, though my equivocation hardly matters. He makes a living negotiating hesitation.

I don't think..., I say, I don't want to... See me anymore? he finishes, but I have a feeling there's a smile under the deadpan expression I've learned he wears to hide his amusement. You read my mind, I tell him, letting my own mouth curl, and now, finally, he reaches for my hand. I don't know how to tell him I'm not in this for the long haul; I'm not even certain that would be fair. I'm not sure what I'm up for, I admit, circling back to the excuse I used the night of Celeste's party. He sees where I'm going, and his grin cracks the surface. Tonight? he says, Or in general?

If kissing him weren't so easy, I might not even be up for tonight. Instead, I let his mouth serve as solace for everything that's missing. I still can't get over his scent, that understated opulence he manages without cologne—I asked weeks ago, and he swears he doesn't wear any—and I pull him closer, my hands under that thousand-dollar sport coat. So, tonight's good for you, he murmurs. Maybe tomorrow too, I admit, Maybe next week. Sounds like we're something, he says as I unbutton his shirt. You better tell Rick, I agree, and he frowns. That's why I'm a little preoccupied, Joel, he says, Someone knows about us.

James / Chicago / December 2006

Henry's a squalling mess when I finally get back from campus. I've hired one of my undergrad students to help out and she's doing her best but looks like she's on the verge of telling me I don't pay her enough. He won't eat, she whines as he wails, Or sleep! Well, he doesn't do much else, I tell her, automatically feeling my son's diaper to see if he needs a change. I snag a blanket from the pile of clean laundry on the coffee table and sit down with Henry sobbing in my ear. I don't try to quiet him; I just hold him with one hand while I turn down the blanket with the other. Then I lay him in the center and wrap him like a burrito. He keeps crying but at least he's not flailing all over the place.

Lizzie's not home yet? I ask and my student gives me a blank look. I try to pop a pacifier in Henry's mouth but he's having none of it. My wife, I tell her. My student shakes her head and I fish in the pocket of my jeans for my wallet and flick one-handed through the bills. You'll be here at noon tomorrow? I confirm, passing her a couple twenties and she says yes but looks noncommittal enough to make me worry.

When she's gone I dim the lights and with Henry in my arms I go into the kitchen where I find a lukewarm bottle already fitted with the nipples I specifically told my rock star babysitter not to use. No wonder Henry's flipping out. I dump the bottle and start fresh, managing with one hand and no light other than the one above the stove so I don't have to put him down and he doesn't get any more overstimulated. Hang on, hang on, I murmur and when the formula's just warm enough I hold the bottle to his lips. He latches right on, sucking so hard and long I'm afraid he's going to choke. Not so fast, buddy, I caution but he keeps on sucking and every time I pull the bottle away long enough to burp him he starts crying again.

After five ounces he finally eases up and I wipe the corner of his mouth with the edge of the cloth I have draped over my shoulder. You want more? I ask, touching the nipple to his lips again and he opens up but without the mania.

Man, I'm going to have to figure something out, find someone who can handle him better. I've got so much grading right now and since I can't always rely on Lizzie to come home when she promises I have no choice but to find someone to take her place. Isn't that right, I whisper to Henry who has the half-glazed look of an addict, formula dripping down his chin. Twisting my arm, I glance at my watch. Seven-thirty. Lizzie's seriously late and I'm just looking around for my cell so I can call to find out why when I hear it ringing. Henry starts to whimper. Don't cry, don't cry, I plead, groping for my phone. What the *fuck*? Joel hisses in my ear.

Aw shit.

Hey, I mutter. Hey? he says, Did you say *hey*? I pinch the phone against my shoulder and spin around, looking for Henry's pacifier. Listen, I'm tryin' to get Henry to sleep— I start and he says, I don't give a *shit* what you're doing right now, James, do you fucking hear me? You're shoutin' loud enough, I mumble. Oh, I'm just getting *started*, he says as my fingers close on the pacifier. Sliding it in Henry's mouth I hold it in place while Joel tells me he knows I called Brice, he saw the number on Brice's phone, what the hell am I trying to do to him? Relax, I say, thinking my best bet might be to downplay what happened, I was just feelin' him out. You were *feeling* him *out*? he asks incredulously. How else was I supposed to get to know him? I ask. I don't know, James, he says, Get on a plane?

Henry breaks into sobs again. Yeah, I'm a little busy here, I say, bouncing my son up and down a few times, Kinda hard for me to get on a plane right now. Then you should've asked if we could come up there! Joel says. That didn't work so well last time around, I remind him and he says, Believe me, James, I remember. So what choice did I have? I ask, I wanted to know if he was a stand-up guy! And you thought *seducing* him was the best way to find out? he says. Gimme a break, Joel, I say, I didn't go that far. You called him pretending to be someone else! he shouts, You told him you'd be discreet!

Christ, do they tell each other everything? Dude, I was just lookin' out for you, I say, Okay? No, it's not okay! he cries, Jesus, James, don't you want me to be happy?

Now they're both sobbing, Henry in one ear and Joel in the other. I don't know who to turn my attention to first. Shh, I murmur, hoping that might cover my bases long enough for one of them to chill out, Shh. I need you to stop, Joel tells me, Just stop. Henry's cryin', man, I explain, You called at a bad time. No, he says, I mean, I need to not talk to you for a while.

His words yank me right into the phone. What? I say. I can't do this anymore, he tells me, Don't call, don't— Joel, what the fuck? I blurt, my chest flooding with alarm. I need a break, James, he says, I need a break from you.

Henry's crying so hard I have to put him down and walk away. What do you mean, you need a break from me? I ask, What does that even mean? Just leave me alone, he says. Joel, I protest but he's gone.

I stare at my phone in disbelief. That did *not* just happen. Joel? I say like he might still be on the line.

What's going on? Lizzie asks behind me and I turn to see her standing in the doorway, svelte in a tapered winter coat, her color so high she looks like a china doll, all that alabaster skin with two circles of red on her cheeks. She's so beautiful I want to hurt her. But Henry howls like something from another world and I leap toward him, Lizzie moving in the same direction. I reach him first and pluck him from the couch where I never should've left him. He could've rolled right off onto the floor. Who were you talking to just now? Lizzie asks. No one, I lie.

Stupid. She narrows her eyes as I try to force Henry's pacifier back into his mouth. Let me take him, she says and I yank away from her. I've *got* him, I insist but he's screaming like he's fixing to tell her otherwise. You didn't have him a minute ago, James! she says, You weren't even looking at him! You weren't even *here*, Lizzie, I accuse, You're never here! I was at work! she tells me, And I want to know who was on the phone! I try to turn away from her but she pulls me around, Henry sobbing between us. I want to know! she cries, I have a right to know! I was talkin' to Joel! I shout, Now back the fuck off so I can get my son to sleep!

She bursts into tears. Cupping Henry's head in the palm of my hand, I bring my lips to his ear. I'm shaking but I make my voice soft and easy. Shh, I say, Shh-shh. He cries and cries and I hold him close and shut my eyes. Tears fall from the corners.

Joel / Austin / December 2006

This is what I like about Brice:

His hair, his abs, his smile. He has a beautiful house and a flair for décor I find impressive, even if we don't share an aesthetic. He appreciates art. He listens when I talk. I've never seen him overindulge. He's generous; I haven't picked up a tab since the middle of November. He easily navigates my insecurities, which I rarely voice. He makes good on his promises. He knows how to fuck, and that's harder to come by than you'd think. He has a beautiful car.

This is what I don't like about Brice:

His clothes, his friends (other than Celeste, who I've seen exactly twice), his politics. Despite his generosity where I'm concerned, he's not even remotely philanthropic. I've never once heard him compliment my work. He doesn't recycle. He's fanatical about his furniture; he'd forego a fuck to save his sofa. He condescends to his housekeeper. He's exceptionally discreet about his orientation, and I've already spent enough time in the closet. He snores, albeit softly.

I try to focus on the positive. Everyone has faults, and I'm no exception. I think about the list Brice could write about me: poor as shit, duplicitous friends, work-obsessed. Skittish and reluctant to define our relationship. He's overlooking a lot, and I'm not giving him much in return.

He's not Adam.

Sometimes I wonder what might have happened if I hadn't run into Brice the same day I sent Adam that email. What if I'd fought with James but didn't have an invitation to Celeste's party? Absent of energy work, without Brice as a distraction, what might I have done in the days after I read Adam's response? Would my anger have dissipated enough to call him? Would I have felt compelled to tell him that Kyle lied, that I wasn't seeing someone new?

My name, Adam's voice… The thought makes me weep.

Then there's James, who'd obviously rather see me alone than happy. I'm still trying to come to terms with that phone call he made. Wait, wait, wait, I said after Brice told me about trying to track down the number on his caller ID, Are you sure the call came from Chicago? When he handed over his cell phone, my vision went gray.

James didn't even bother denying what he'd done. Instead, he acted like he was doing me a favor, like I should be thanking him. Dude, I'm just looking out for you, he claimed, so full of shit I started crying. All those years between us and he'd rather screw me over than come up with the truth. I can't do this anymore, I said, I need a break. I've blocked his number, tagged his email address as spam. If he's trying to contact me, I wouldn't know. Still I'm waiting to hear his boots on the front porch, even though he hasn't worn Redwings for years. I'm waiting for the grand gesture, the apology to beat all apologies, the declaration that will change everything.

Tonight, I'll go out with Brice. He'll pay for dinner, and we'll go back to his house in Old Enfield, slated for a magazine feature in the spring. I'll drink Pellegrino, then climb his marble staircase to his bedroom, where we'll have sex after he removes the duvet on his four-poster bed. He'll fall asleep first, and I'll listen to him snore and focus on the positive—his hair, his abs, his smile—for as long as I can.

James / Chicago / June 2007

I lie and tell Joel I couldn't come up with a new sitter but it doesn't do any good. He's already got one lined up by the time I get home from campus, some woman he and Henry met at the park. She could be anyone, dude, I tell him, I've got to vet her first. That's why we're going out *tomorrow* night, he explains, So you have time to call her references. I have too much gradin' tonight, I protest and he tells me I can use that excuse to get out of a run but not to get out of arranging for a sitter.

I'm irritated but I call every single one of the woman's references, figuring she won't check out anyway. She seems legit, which pisses me off. Now I've got no choice. What if Henry wakes up while we're gone? I ask Joel and he says all nice and patient like I'm the world's biggest idiot, That's why we're having her come early, so Henry can meet her before he goes to bed.

I don't feel vindicated when Henry sees her and bursts into tears. Go take a shower, Joel orders, plucking him right out of my arms. I don't think I can leave him like this, man, I tell him. Too bad, he says. I cast a semi-apologetic glance in the direction of the sitter who gives me a tight-lipped smile. You can't just bulldoze my authority, I hiss at Joel under my breath and he says, You mean the way you bulldozed my summer?

We stare at each other, Henry whimpering and Joel patting him on the back already looking hot as shit in a pair of jeans way more expensive than anything he can rightly afford and a gray shirt that matches his eyes. And fuck me for noticing. What am I supposed to even wear? I grouse and he says, I think you're missing the point.

But when I throw open the shower curtain ten minutes later Joel's leaning against the sink. Jesus, I mutter, snatching a towel from the hook. Does Elizabeth buy your clothes? he asks. Most of 'em, I admit, wrapping the towel around my waist and he says, his voice fading as he goes back into the bedroom, Well, she has terrible fucking taste.

I guess he finally decided to drop that filter.

While he ransacks my closet—I guess he's going to dress me tonight—I edge closer to the stairs so I can listen for my son. He's wailing and I look at Joel in dismay. He's upset, I say. He's adjusting, Joel tells me, whacking aside one hanger after another like there's nothing in my closet worth considering. I can't leave him like this, I insist and now he turns to me. Give him a few minutes before you pull the plug, James, he says wearily, All right? At least go get me a beer, I plead, Just so he can see that we're still home.

Joel sighs but disappears in the direction of the stairs, leaving me in peace to dry off and pull on a pair of khakis in case Henry quiets down enough for us to make it through the front door. No way would I wear jeans tonight, not with Joel looking like he might've spent a couple hundred on his own. I shrug into one of the shirts I usually wear to work and tuck it into my pants. Two weeks with Joel forcing me to run with him every other day and they're buttoning better than they have in a while. I take a look in the mirror, feeling pretty pleased with myself. I'm threading my belt through my pant loops when Joel comes back with my beer, groaning the second he sees me. Honey, you have to ditch those wrinkle-free khakis, he says, Just for one night.

It's stupid to feel hurt but I was kind of hoping he'd notice I've lost weight.

While I'm sulking Joel finds a pair of jeans at the back of my closet, a pair I haven't been able to wear for a good three years. Those are too tight, I tell him but he holds them up and squints like he maybe doesn't believe me. Try them, he finally says. Can you at least not watch me undress? I mumble and he rolls his eyes. I just saw everything you have to show me in the bathroom, he informs me.

Why do I have the feeling he's leaving off *and I'm not impressed*?

I grunt, stripping off the khakis and yanking the jeans over my boxers. They button as easily as they did when I bought them and I look up at him in surprise. I told you I'd whip you into shape, he reminds me, rummaging through my closet again. I take a swallow of beer, watching him come up with nothing. When we lived on Pearl I borrowed his clothes all the time. He had better taste and better clothes and he rarely took anything more from me than my old fraternity shirts. Now I'm not so sure I'd fit in his clothes and that's what I tell him when he gives up on my closet and opens the dresser where I cleared some space for him to unpack when he first got into town. He finally holds up a tee shirt I've never seen him wear. The color's weird, I tell him, hanging back. What do you mean? he asks. Look at it, Joel, I say and he humors me, holding it at arm's length. Seashell, he concludes like an artist, Barely ripe peach. It's not gonna fit, I warn. You won't know if you don't try, he points out. I groan. And take off the academic button-down, he adds, handing it over.

All right, so he has a good eye. The shirt fits better than anything I've worn in years. The material feels expensive so Joel either got it as a gift or has a knack for thrifting he never told me about. The color makes my eyes look real dark. I stare at my reflection, feeling what I used to feel back when going out for the night actually meant something.

Then I realize we're not going anywhere if Henry's still crying.

Taking the belt Joel hands me I listen from the top of the stairs. Henry's crying all right but it's that bullshit kind that means his heart's not really in it. Maybe Joel's right. Maybe Henry just needed a little time to settle down. Maybe if I make a big production out of leaving we'll never get out the door.

I suddenly really want to get out the door.

As Joel criticizes the shoes in my closet I fill the sink with water. The past few weeks I've taken a swipe or two across my face with an electric razor Lizzie bought me for Christmas, one I never thought I'd use but find works real well with my lazy shaving regimen. Tonight I figure I'll shave for real and I squirt some shaving cream into my palm then pat my cheeks. The second I pick up my razor Joel's yanking it from my hand. What're you *doing?* he says. I look sloppy, I protest, indicating my stubble. Sloppy was that gut of yours hanging over those wrinkle-free khakis, he assures me. Hey, I protest but he's not even listening. He's frowning at my hair. Where's your product? he asks. What product? I say, wiping my face as he searches through the cabinet. He gives me a *seriously?* look before he finally gives up and runs his hands through my hair. When he's finished I turn toward the mirror. I look good, I say and now he gives me the gratification I've been after. Yeah, he says, You do.

Joel / Austin / December 2000

Adam's going to leave me.

Granite Café is packed, filled with people celebrating the holiday, just a few days away. I have three four-tops and a demanding couple by the window, and the hostess just seated a table of six in my section. I don't even have time to breathe, let alone check my voicemail, but every so often, as I'm listing the specials or recommending a wine, I think about the argument Adam and I had this afternoon, and my nerves crackle with fear. Then I'll have an order up, and I'll forget for a while, until the thought comes to me again as I'm running someone's credit card.

Adam's going to leave me.

I've worked splits all week, a grueling schedule but one that pays well. I owe Marissa anyway; she took a chance on me this past summer, hiring me without experience. I've worked hard to prove my worth, and when I saw the schedule last week, I didn't say a word, even though I knew Adam would find fault. He has a corporate job with corporate hours and corporate pay, and he doesn't like that I'm usually working Friday and Saturday nights. For the past couple of months, he's been after me to quit and move in with him. At first, his invitation thrilled me. He loves me. He wants to be with me.

After a lifetime of taking money from my father, I know I have to make my own way.

Last night, I worked until close, and as exhausted as I was by the time I left work, I drove all the way out to Lakeway in the truck I bought last month, a red Toyota with a rusted bumper and a cracked windshield. I wait tables a couple of blocks from my house; I could've gotten away without buying a truck, not to mention the money I'm suddenly spending on gas and insurance. I just didn't want Adam to have to pick me up every time we made plans. So last night, when staying at my place would've made more sense because of my schedule, I told him I understood if he didn't want to make the drive to Pearl Street. He'd been making that drive for almost six months. I'd go to him.

I didn't expect him to wait up for me. After all the nights we'd spent apart, I just wanted to be near him. I wanted to sleep in the same bed, and he stirred long enough to pull me against him, then drift back into his dreams. I wasn't far behind, and this morning, I slept late, under the misconception that he'd be up early for a ride; he usually cycles on Saturdays. Instead, I came downstairs to find him sitting on the deck in the chilly sun. What're you doing out here? I asked, shivering, but he didn't answer my question. He wanted to know what time I was leaving. You're kicking me out already? I joked, but he didn't smile. He said he'd assumed I'd want to spend at least part of the day painting; was he right? I shrugged, though in truth, I hadn't expected to linger. Waiting tables generally gives me a flexible schedule. I can bring in money without having to sacrifice too much time or creative energy. Because of those splits, I hadn't painted much all week. I wanted to paint; I needed to paint.

What time do you have to be at work tonight? he asked. Six, I admitted, and he nodded. He wasn't looking at me; his eyes were on the lake, empty this late in the season, except for a few diehards. I reminded him that we'd have tomorrow and Monday all to ourselves, an intimate holiday we'd lucked into because Christmas falls on a Monday this year, and the restaurant's closed Sundays and Mondays. Too late, I remembered that Adam had wanted to take me to Kentucky for the holiday, a trip my schedule doesn't easily permit. Listen, I said, knowing I'd never be able to concentrate on the canvas if I went home with him angry at me, Why don't I stay?

I shouldn't have made the suggestion, and he shouldn't have agreed. We were fine for a while; sex on the floor in front of the fireplace will do that, and Adam made breakfast while I showered. We ate on the deck despite the wind, for the pleasure of coming back inside to warm ourselves in front of the fire. With his arms around me, I felt only a flicker of frustration.

By two, I was done. Adam wanted to watch a movie; I wanted to go home. I wanted a brush in my hand. I had color in my head and no promise of release. For a while, I consoled myself thinking about what I'd paint when I had the chance; when would I have the chance? I knew I'd be working splits this next week too, not every day but enough to make time seem scarce. The longer I sat beside Adam, the edgier I felt, and when he paused the movie to go to the bathroom, I foraged for a notebook and a pen, which leaked an inky, violent blue. Just doodling, I murmured as he sat down beside me again, but before long, I'd forgotten about the movie. Why are you even here? he finally asked, and maybe if I'd stopped scrawling long enough to answer, he wouldn't have told me to leave.

I apologized; I tried to make him understand. I'm not asking you to give up painting! he told me, I'm offering you time to work! He was shouting by this time; I wasn't used to seeing him so angry. What do you want me to do? I asked, Move in with you and let you fucking *support* me? Yes, he said, *Yes*. I can't do that, Adam, I insisted, I can't just let you *pay* for everything! You'll sell your work, he reminded me, and I told him there was no guarantee I'd sell enough to contribute much of anything. I made $5000 this year, I told him. So next year you'll make more, he said, And I might actually be able to spend time with you when you're not exhausted or completely disengaged. Adam, I protested, I can't just... Then we have a problem, he informed me, Because this isn't working.

Adam's going to leave me.

All the waiters at Granite Café smoke, and tonight, after my last table leaves and I'm counting out my tips, I bum a cigarette from one of the other servers. I haven't indulged for almost two years, since just after I tried to kill myself. I remember the last cigarette I smoked, outside the airport on my way to Mexico. I'd just been released from a recovery center, where I'd spent an intense three months analyzing what turned out to be the first layer of so much repression that I'm still coughing up memories a year later. Merry Christmas, Joel, Marissa says as I'm shrugging into my coat, and I give her a wave.

The night's cold, but my walk isn't long. I don't carry a lighter with me anymore, but Marissa lit my cigarette on my way out, and I take the smoke into my mouth, then lean back and exhale a cloud into the sky as I make my way home. Rounding the corner, I can see my lamp through the living room window, illuminating the front porch. I remember a Christmas long ago, driving home from Houston in my BMW convertible and finding James in that swing, a strand of colored lights around the railing. Tonight the swing's empty, but as I climb the steps, I crush out my cigarette and go inside for the phone. I step back onto the front porch as James answers; I don't need to tell him the story. He's been listening for months. You know what I'm gonna say, Joel, he tells me, and I close my eyes, the swing creaking beneath my weight. Somewhere in Chicago, he lights a cigarette, but he sounds like he's sitting right next to me. You love him, right? he asks. Yeah, I admit. Then you know what you need to do, he says.

James / Chicago / December 2006

A week before Christmas Lizzie and I still aren't speaking. Maybe if we were I wouldn't be missing Joel so much. Or maybe I'm just aware that he shut me out and even if I want to talk to him, even if I need him for some reason there's no way to get in touch with him. That pisses me off if I think about it for too long because what if I've got an emergency? Am I supposed to go through Kyle if I need to get Joel a message, if something happens to Henry?

Lizzie's working late tonight—or at the gym or having drinks with friends—and I've got Henry to myself. After eight months I've got his bedtime routine down pat and when he's asleep I go into the closet in my bedroom or what felt like my bedroom once upon a time. I've slept in Henry's room for so long now I can barely remember sleeping with Lizzie any more than I can remember making love to her. Sixteen months since our last unhappy fuck and what comes to mind when I think about sex with my wife is grim determination.

Somewhere in here I have a box leftover from college and I dig around until I find it then carry it downstairs along with the baby monitor. I need a cigarette and the farther away from the nursery I can smoke the better.

In the kitchen I crack the window above the sink and get myself a beer. Cigarette in hand I sift through the box with only a vague idea of what I'm trying to find. Ticket stubs and class schedules, the Longhorns football schedule from '93, pictures from the holidays and Spring Break until the photo I almost remembered drops from underneath a takeout menu from El Arroyo.

We're in the swing on the front porch of our house on Pearl. Joel's wearing one of my old fraternity shirts, the collar all torn and threadbare. He loved those shirts and even though he never told me why I'd bet he felt like he was giving those idiots I briefly called brothers the finger. He knew what they thought of him and what most of them called me since I lived with him even though back then he kept what he was doing nice and hushed. In the picture he's not smiling. Instead I'm the one with a big, goofy grin, my arm slung around his shoulders. I'm staring right at him but he's looking at the camera with eyes heavy-lidded. A cigarette hangs from his lip. We look young because we were. A friend of ours took the shot just before we graduated.

This is how I remember us, slouching in that swing with a couple Shiner Bocks and a pack of Marlboros. This is what I'm thinking about when I make stupid as shit decisions like the one I made a couple weeks ago. This guy, this friendship. This moment in time that had me gazing at Joel like he was the best fucking thing that'd ever happened to me.

I take a final drag from my cigarette and grind up the butt in the disposal then find the room freshener so I don't have to listen to Lizzie bitch about the smell. Hustling upstairs I snag a note card from my desk and scratch out a message before I can think twice about what I'm doing. The photo goes in the envelope right along with the card.

I'm not letting him go without a fight.

Joel / Austin / December 2006

I pull into my shitty driveway in my shitty pickup. I've just spent the past two hours trying to find a Christmas gift for Brice, and the experience has me so out of alignment I want to hit something. Adam, maybe, or an expensive bottle of scotch. I've come home empty-handed, too, so I'm going to have to go through this shit again tomorrow on Christmas Eve.

I hate the holidays.

I don't have much cash, for one thing. But there's also nothing I can get for Brice that he can't buy for himself, and that leaves me with what? Something personal. Exactly the kind of message I don't want to send, because despite liking Brice just fine and feeling good with our arrangement, I'm not so sure I'm interested in taking this much deeper. How can I, when I'm still thinking about Adam, when I'm still wondering what my life might be like right now if he hadn't spiraled out of control or if I'd opened up my heart enough to forgive him? We might be on our way to Kentucky. We might be getting our house ready for his family. My shopping trip today might have yielded more than irritation because I would have been picking out presents for his nieces and nephew. *My* nieces and nephew. Instead, I'm walking up to this piece of shit house with nothing to show for my efforts except an anger so intense I'm tempted to call Brice and break this off right now. I'm not sure I'm going to be able to fake my way through the next few days.

The holidays aren't easy for me. They never were, not even when I was a kid, and once my mother died, they loomed so large I started dreading them as soon as the weather turned in October. Adam made them easier, Adam and his family. I had something to focus on other than my past, and after a year or two, I might have even claimed to like Christmas, at least the morning itself. How could I not, when I got to see Lindsey and Grace and Rye tearing into their presents and sucking on peppermint sticks before breakfast? The only other times I'd come that close to a functional concept of family were those Thanksgivings I shared with James when we were still in college.

Of course, once we started sleeping together, we shut those holidays down.

So here I am, thirty-four years old, no money, no partner, no family to speak of other than my father and stepmother. And James: fuck him. I should be able to count on him at the very least, and instead, I've had to block his calls.

I'm going to have to do something to shake this perspective, and even *that* makes me mad. Sometimes I'd rather light a cigarette than psych myself up to make the healthy choice.

Slamming the door of my pickup, I turn toward the house just in time to see a long tail slither through a crack in the side. Well, that explains the skittering I hear above my ceiling at night. I never should've hauled in all of those pecans from the backyard. They're a bitch to shell, and now they've attracted the neighborhood rats.

Banging open the screen door, I reach into the mailbox. Nothing but shit that's going right into the recycling bin, and the electric bill. Once I'm inside, I drop the pile on the coffee table. From beneath the circulars, an envelope slides to the floor.

I want to open a Christmas card from James about as much as I want to open that electric bill. I can do without holiday greetings from the Fieldings tonight, and I leave the envelope where it fell.

James / Chicago / August 2005

I'm supposed to be working on that sample of mine—at this point I'll have to set some kind of record for fastest ejaculation under duress in order to get my cup to Lizzie's doctor on time—but I'm still on the phone with Joel, wondering if I should confess my suspicions.

Do you think maybe Adam's not bein' honest about that guy from his office? I ask, keeping my tone tentative and Joel's voice coils up tight as a cornered copperhead. He's not *cheating* on me, he insists, He's not capable of that. Everyone's capable of cheatin', I tell him, Under the right circumstances. Have you ever cheated on Elizabeth? he asks. I don't have anything left for anyone else, I say, Do you realize how much sex I'm havin'? Do you realize how much sex I'm *not* having? he asks.

Yeah, he mentioned that last week when I was in Austin. He's the one who should be jerking off in this cup. He'd have an easier time, that's for damn sure. I gotta go, I tell him, glancing at my watch. *Now?* he says, After you lobbed that accusation my way? I gotta get this sample to Lizzie's doctor, I explain. You're talking to me with a *cup* in your hand? he groans. I tell him the sample's still in my balls. Jesus, he moans, Why the hell did you answer the phone? Because I wasn't havin' any luck, I admit, I'm under a lot of pressure here. And you thought *I* could help? he asks. Can you? I say and he laughs. You're on your own, he tells me.

Whatever, maybe we needed some space from each other at first. No way would we have joked around like that a few years ago. For a long time we were friends and neither of us wanted to be the one who mentioned the weeks we were something more. Then time passed and anyone paying half attention could see how Joel felt about Adam and I don't know. One of us dropped a wink and suddenly we were back to where we'd always been, trading lines like we were making up for lost time. I guess Lizzie wouldn't be happy if she heard us but since I hardly ever see Joel she doesn't know. Or maybe I'm just careful when I'm around her. She doesn't like to be reminded that Joel and I were... well, whatever we were.

My eye catches his painting, the one I have to hide every time he comes up here. I don't know why I'm so secretive but I don't want him knowing I'm the one who bought it. That's why I sent one of my students to pick it up. I knew if I didn't buy it myself someone else would and even though I had to beg the gallery owner to wait until I had enough room on my credit card to take out a cash advance I finally scrounged up the money to pay for it. I bet it's worth a shit ton more now but I'm not going to risk trying to find out. I didn't buy it as an investment anyway. I bought it because he painted it right in the middle of us. I bought it because I can see my face in his shadow. I bought it because it's a fucking privilege to own it and the thought of anyone else having it makes me sick to my stomach. It's not even a good likeness, Lizzie says. Maybe not to her. But he saw something I still have a hard time admitting all these years later. He saw it and drew a red line through it and brought me to the other side. I almost killed him.

I haven't been back to that night for a long time but I still have his *you thought I could help?* in my ear. Man, I can see him, standing in front of his easel, paint all over his jeans. I held up the bag of pot and he took a shower and we sat in the living room to smoke, Beastie Boys on the stereo and cold bottles of beer in our hands. Before I knew it he was standing in front of me, his legs between my knees. That joint blurred all my inhibitions, which was exactly what I'd planned when I bought the pot. I was done dicking around. I wanted to *know*.

I'm good and hard now and if I was the husband I want to be I'd find my wife in my mind and make love to her like I should. Instead I'm thinking of the morning after Joel and I got high. I'd gotten the hell out of the house the second I opened my eyes but I went back pretty quick because I was thinking we should talk about what we'd done.

Whatever. I wanted more, okay? I wanted more and he backed me up against the front door like he was tired of waiting for me to come to my senses. I let him push me over to the couch and I let him pull off my jeans and I watched him go down on me like no girl ever has, not ever. Best blowjob of my life and it was Joel who gave it to me.

And Joel who's making me fumble for that cup because that's all it took. The memory of his mouth and a joke about getting me off.

Jesus is right.

Joel / Austin / Christmas 2006

I'm having a hard time reconciling where I am right now with where I was a couple of years ago. I know better than anyone how quickly life can change—if my childhood didn't teach me that, my mother certainly did the day she put a gun in her mouth—but I can't stop thinking about Adam and the holiday we shared a year before he told me he wanted to adopt, before his father was diagnosed with lung cancer, before he was passed over for that promotion. He knew I had a hard time with Christmas, and he told me we could stay in Austin, just the two of us. I said no. I said we should go to Kentucky so he could be with his family; I wasn't going to take that from him every year.

We flew up a few days before the holiday, went to a Christmas Eve service, woke up at dawn the next morning so we could watch his nieces and nephew open their gifts. His sister made sugar cookies in the shape of stars, and Grace, the youngest, ate so many she cried. I spent half the afternoon playing Nerf basketball with Rye. After everyone went to bed, Adam and I stood on the porch in the starlight. You know I love you, he said, Right? Tell me again, I whispered.

Now I'm standing in Brice's living room, dressed in a cashmere sweater, making small talk with someone from the Capitol. I'm drinking a specialty cocktail mixed by a bartender hired for the purpose. I just shook hands with Rick Perry, and I didn't get a good feeling.

I'm here as a favor to Brice, who's throwing a drinks party on Christmas Day for some senator he's trying to woo. Why do you want *me* there? I asked last week, and he told me the guy's wife has connections with an arts fellowship in South America. Buenos Aires, if I remember correctly, he said. Are you trying to get me to leave the country? I asked. I don't want her to get bored, he explained. So I'm supposed to entertain her, I concluded, and he took his time choosing his words. If she enjoys herself, he said, Her husband will be more likely to give me what I need. Why do I feel like a 1950's housewife? I asked. I'll buy you something pretty, he promised. I laughed, but this afternoon he gave me the cashmere.

I don't want to be here, but I don't have anywhere else to go. Kyle stayed in town for the holiday last year, but that was because of me, because Adam and I had just broken up. This year, he started hinting about the holidays just after Halloween, and I told him I didn't expect him to miss a vacation two years in a row. So he and Scott have flown to Aspen, and James and I aren't speaking. That leaves my father.

Stand Edward Grayson next to Rick Perry, and the choice seems pretty clear, even for me.

So here I am, trying not to get drunk in the middle of the afternoon on Christmas Day, prepared to chat up some senator's wife even though she's not here and if I had to guess, I'd say she's not coming. I know Brice well enough at this point to see when he's legitimately concerned, even if he looks like he's playing it cool, and he crossed that threshold about thirty minutes ago. He put a lot of thought into this party, and while he's certainly not about to let the rest of his guests know they're second tier, I can feel his tension rising.

I haven't had the best weekend, and I still have to get through tomorrow. You'd think that after fifteen years, I could let the day after Christmas pass without feeling like I'm about to get called in to my father's office and harassed about my grades, but that's not the case. Sometimes I feel like a day hasn't gone by.

When Brice gets down to his last dozen guests, I make myself scarce; I know he wants to keep our relationship unobtrusive. I'd probably count that against him if I weren't so ready to leave his living room. I've managed not to drink more than two cocktails, but the effort expended by not indulging has left me with a headache, and I weave around the caterers cleaning up in the kitchen so I can grab a Pellegrino. Brice has a chaise lounge beside his bed, and I head for it, drinking right from the bottle.

I feel lonelier than I should with my boyfriend downstairs. Maybe it's the holiday. Maybe it's James's absence, which makes my life feel on some levels like the coolest breath of air and on others like I'm drowning. Maybe it's that on this day more than most I either need space or someone's undivided attention. I don't need to be circulating a party. I don't need to be managing anyone else's mood.

I lean forward, elbows on my knees, and rub my neck. I have my hair pulled back, and I unwind the rubber band and let it fall, the motion automatically making me think of Adam. He liked my hair long, but I cut it before we got back together in '99, and I didn't start growing it out again until after we broke up last year. I wonder if that was subconscious manipulation on my part—I know he preferred my hair long—or simply a sincere need for change. Either way, I can still remember his hands in my hair. I can still remember the first night we spent together and the ways he moved me.

I reach again for the Pellegrino. Thinking about Adam makes me melancholy, and it's not as if Brice doesn't like my hair. He might not have loved that I showed up wet for our first date, but he slid his hand right up the back of my neck in front of that wine bar. He has no complaints, and as if I've conjured him, he appears in the doorway, loosening a tie my father might as well have chosen. I have glasses in the kitchen, Joel, he says when he sees the bottle in my hand.

So this is how we're going to start.

Didn't work out like you planned, I acknowledge, and he gives his head a short shake. I pat the chaise lounge beside me; he declines. You'll get him eventually, I venture. I wanted this wrapped up today, he tells me, Before the New Year. I know, I say, and he waves his hand impatiently, the assumption being that I just don't get it. I'm certain I don't, but that doesn't mean I can't commiserate, and what the fuck. I've just spent Christmas Day chatting up fifty of Austin's most Republican politicos. I'm sorry, he apologizes, seeing my expression, I'm not being fair, am I?

Pulling his tie from his collar, he opens the top drawer of his dresser and removes a small box wrapped in silver paper. Merry Christmas, he says.

Please don't let this be a Rolex.

But he's given me a sketchpad of inconsequential size, something I can easily tuck into my pocket or put in my backpack if I ever have the money to travel again. It's a token, a nod to whatever we're doing and nothing more. He knows me, he sees me; I have the proof in this gesture. It's more than enough, and I'm relieved and sincere when I thank him. You're going to need it, he warns me. Why? I ask, and he smiles.

James / Chicago / June 2007

Date night, Joel calls our time away from Henry. The first night we just walked a handful of blocks to a funky bistro I'd never noticed, probably because they don't cater to kids. A few days later Joel convinced me to try a movie. I'd spent the night checking my cell phone for updates from the sitter. Then he got me to try an open-air restaurant where we drank wine and ate *tapas* and he wouldn't let me talk about Henry at all. Date night, he reminded me when I slipped and said we needed to stop for Huggies on the way home. I'm goin' on an awful lot of dates for someone who never gets laid, I told him. Just like college, he reminded me.

Tonight we're going to a bar. To practice flirting for when you go on a real date, Joel told me this morning. I started having second thoughts before I even agreed. Dinner, a movie… I can handle those. But I'm way out of practice for this kind of scene and when we step through the doorway of some bar Joel promises I'm going to love—how the hell he even knows where to go I don't understand—I realize I'm a good eight or nine years past my last attempt at conversation with someone of the opposite sex unless we're talking parenting or academics. Joel says they don't count. C'mon, newbie, he laughs, pushing me forward when I hang back, You'll feel better with a drink in your hand.

After we've scored some barstools and I'm sipping a martini I take his advice and make a slow scan of the room, finding no one I feel capable of approaching even if I had the inclination. What I discover soon enough I find even more demoralizing: Joel's better at this shit than I am. We luck into talking to a couple girls (women? ladies? I don't even know what to call them.) who stand behind us trying to catch the bartender's attention and it's Joel who finally waves the guy over and offers the girls our seats, the invitation so subtle I barely notice. Within seconds he knows their names. Y'all come here often? I ask, fishing through time for the sort of opening line I used back in college. We're virgins, Andrea confides. We brought condoms, I assure them, going for a joke but they're quiet. Joel gives me a *what the fuck* look. You'll have to excuse my friend, he says, At this point in the quarter he's— Oh, you're at U of C? Andrea's friend interrupts and I can feel my chest swell. Whatever, I've got a right to be proud of what I've accomplished. He's an archaeologist, Joel brags.

Well, that's not exactly right even though I'm fixing to spend my summer doing field work but man, I like the way Andrea's eyes just widened. You some kind of Indiana Jones? she asks and I forget all about what happened when I mentioned those condoms thirty seconds ago and wink. You should see my bullwhip, I tell her.

Joel scatterguns his martini. I look from one of them to the other with an uneasy smile. I guess I don't need a background in psychology to read Andrea's body language. Oh man, Joel says under his breath as he flags down the bartender. He signs the tab, his hand clamped to my arm like I'm his dim-witted brother. Enjoy your evening, he says, dragging me away.

Once we're outside I shake him loose. I know what's coming when he grabs his crotch and I scowl when he leers at me. Ladies, he says, dropping into a lecherous voice I sure as shit didn't use. Whatever, man, I mumble as he breaks off into peals of laughter, You don't have to be such a dick. You didn't have to sound like a sex offender, he points out and I glare at him. I told you I wasn't ready for this, I say. Next time I'll believe you, he says.

I light a cigarette and take a long inhale then offer him a drag just to be mean. All right, he sighs, I'm sorry. I start walking. He falls into step beside me and we're quiet until he tells me he couldn't bring himself to go out for a long time after he and Adam broke up. Longer than a month, I remind him. Longer than a year, he admits and I almost correct him because that trip he made here last summer when he ended up in Boystown comes in at just under a year in my book. The guy he hooked up with that night he probably met at a bar. He probably danced with him the way he did with me the night I followed him to that club the year after we graduated. He probably—

Let's go dancin', I say. Dancing? he repeats, surprised. Why not? I ask. You know where to go? he says. I figured you'd know someplace, I admit and he stops walking. You want to go to a gay bar, he says flatly. Well…, I mumble. You're supposed to be flirting with *women*, he tells me. We did that already, I point out. That wasn't flirting, he informs me, That was harassment. I bet that line about my bullwhip would've gotten some attention in Boystown, I mutter and he gives me the same look he gave me when I didn't know what he meant by *product*. (Now I use Bumble & Bumble's semi-sumo, which Joel picked out for me. Kayla, my graduate student, came right out and told me she likes my new look.) Fine, I grumble, We don't have to go dancin'. Well, we're not going home, he tells me as we start walking again, We've only been gone an hour. And we're havin' such a good time, I say, sounding so shitty and bitter we both end up laughing. So what do we do now? Joel asks and I grin.

Joel / Austin / Christmas 2006

I'm still wearing the cashmere sweater Brice gave me, and I run my hand through my sweaty hair, the sheet beneath me slick and damp. I don't like the way I smell, like a wet animal. I don't like the way Brice just fucked me either, like he needed to work something out and figured I could take it. I think he's pissed that I didn't get him anything for Christmas. He tried to tell me he didn't care, but I'm guessing those tickets he bought for Hawaii don't feel as good to him now as they did a little while ago. Brice..., I protested when he told me where I'd be taking that sketchpad, and he interrupted me. Don't get hung up on the money, he said, We've been talking about going away, remember? I thought you meant a bed and breakfast in Wimberley, I told him, and he said, Wimberley, Oahu, what's the difference?

The difference seems pretty clear to me when I reach for my Pellegrino. Get a glass, Joel, he says. Why does it fucking matter? I ask. Because it's gauche to drink from the bottle, he explains, And why does every other word out of your mouth have to be *fuck*? I glance over at him, and he gives me a look like, *well?* Listen, I say, trying for patience, I know today didn't work out like you planned— In more ways than one, he mutters. Okay..., I say, Do you want to tell me what you mean? I keep waiting for you to at least pull out a card, he admits. Are you kidding? I say, I just spent my entire Christmas trying to help you! It's not like you had anywhere else to go, he points out.

For two months, he's been nothing but charming. So I should've gotten him a gift. So what? He should've bought me the sketch pad and left it at that. Hawaii was a risk, and he knew that. And now he's going to hit me where it hurts? Remind me of everyone I no longer have in my life?

I pull his sweater over my head. Keep your fucking cashmere, Brice, I say, and as soon as I get to my feet, he starts apologizing: he's had a long day, he's disappointed he couldn't corner his senator, he doesn't know how to interpret my failure to give him something for Christmas. I'm having an off day, he admits. An off day doesn't give you the right to treat me like shit, I say.

C'mon, Joel, he pleads, following me as I head for the stairs, It's Christmas.

I stop with one hand on the banister. I've heard that line more than once. I heard it last Christmas on the phone with James. We've always been a slippery slope, and that call just sent us sliding a little faster. Now I'm about to end the holiday without hearing his voice. The thought chokes me up, and I turn to the man who just a few minutes ago decided to remind me that James is missing. That's the point, Brice, I say, That's the *fucking* point.

James / Chicago / Christmas 2005

I guess you're my distraction after all, Joel says, dropping into the same voice I heard the night we went to my frat party and he got all up in Shelton's business. Just like that I can see him cupping the back of Shelton's neck and Shelton's mouth opening and how am I supposed to help the way my dick responds? Man, I can feel my breath catching same as it did at that party back in '91.

You still there? Joel asks when I don't say anything. Yeah, I mumble, I just... So far you're not much of a distraction, he tells me and when I'm quiet his interest fades like smoke from a dead cigarette. I should go, he says.

I feel like I'm standing in the middle of that club back in 1995. My Christmas tree might as well be a disco ball and Joel's bored with me all over again.

Maybe we both need a distraction, I blurt out, killing common sense. He laughs all soft and low like whatever game we're playing feels way better than anything else he's been dealing with lately. Are you going to be all talk, James? he asks, As usual?

Hell, he's *drunk*. He's more drunk than I've heard him in a long time. I need to rein this in before we get out of hand.

You think I'm all talk? I ask instead. You want to prove me wrong? he says and my hard-on suddenly feels like a threat.

Stop him, dumbass. He doesn't know what he's doing.

What'd you have in mind? I ask. Are you still drinking? he says and I look at my wine glass. *Not enough. Not nearly enough.* Yeah, I say and he lets go of the kind of sigh I never heard when we were sleeping together. I want to taste your mouth, he says.

The breath I've been holding comes out like a moan, booting me back to his bedroom on Pearl. I don't know what he was doing to me but I'm hearing myself in stereo, my moan married to some kind of plea for him not to stop.

That's what I wanted to hear, he tells me. Joel— I start but my protest's nothing more than a pant. Where's your hand? he asks and I know I'm fucked when I answer him. Where do you want it? I say. So I get to be in charge, he muses. Whatever you want, I say. Whatever I want, he murmurs, Whatever I want? Whatever you want, I repeat. What're you wearing? he asks and I look down at my pants, my dick straining against the material. I don't know, I say, Pants and a shirt. Belt? he asks. Yeah, I say and he says, Take it off.

You should not be letting him do this. Stop him right fucking now.

Now where's your hand? he asks. C'mon, man, I groan, Where do you think? I think it's on your dick, he says.

He's right. Like the morning I handed over my sample my hand's on my dick. *Lizzie.* I throw a look over my shoulder but I'm alone down here in the light from the Christmas tree and my hand feels like maybe it belongs to somebody else. *This is wrong,* I think. *This is really fucking wrong. You gotta stop.*

I know what you want, Joel tells me, his voice like a fucking marshmallow someone just dipped in fire. Yeah? I whisper, What do I want?

Even when we were sleeping together he didn't talk like this. He didn't say anything at all. Hell, half the time he was so quiet I had no idea what he was thinking and I couldn't bring myself to look into his eyes to read what I knew was likely there. Tonight he goes graphic on me and even though I know I should stop him, stop what we're doing, stop us from making this mistake, I can't. Man, I just can't.

My eyes slam shut and I let him take me where he's talking.

Somewhere in the back of my mind I keep thinking that everything's cool as long as I don't come. By the time I do I don't care. I grind out his name then wipe myself off with the throw from the back of the couch. What's he doing on the other end? Cleaning up?

I'm so drunk, he finally slurs. Yeah, me too, I say, lying to him on top of everything else. Your ceiling spinning up there in Chicago? he mumbles. Are you okay, Joel? I ask. I think I'm going to pass out, he admits. Yeah, I mutter, Okay. But hey, James? he says, Merry Christmas.

That's what makes me cry after he hangs up, that *Merry Christmas* delivered like I deserve it. The lights from the tree splinter and I press my fingers to my eyes. Even with them closed I can see those pretty colors.

Joel / Austin / Christmas 2006

I left Brice's house without the sweater I wore earlier today, and the time it took to walk to my truck in the cold night air—I'd parked around the corner to make room for the BMWs and Range Rovers his party guests drove—had me cranking up the heat as soon as I started the engine. Before I could cross I-35, the strain had burned out the unit, and after I banged on the dashboard like that was going to do any good, I resigned myself to a cold winter. There's no way I'll have the money to get my heater fixed.

By the time I get home, I'm freezing and wishing for cashmere. I head right into the shower, partly so I can warm up and partly so I can wash off the smell of that sex. Once I raise my body temperature, I pull on a pair of old pajama bottoms and make myself a mug of chamomile tea. I need to calm the fuck down because right now I feel like one step in the wrong direction could put me over the edge.

Christmas, and I'm alone. Forget Adam; forget James. I couldn't even make something work with Brice. Everyone has someone, and I'm here by myself. How the hell did that happen? Two years ago, I couldn't have been happier. I thought I had everything I'd ever want. Even last year, heartbroken from my split with Adam, at least I could depend on James.

I make my way into the living room, where my eyes fall right to his holiday card, still on the floor where it fell the day before yesterday. Well, there's the edge I've been avoiding. Christmas greetings from the Fieldings. Did he even bother to sign his name? Wrapping a blanket around me, I rip open the envelope.

I'm staring at myself. And James; we're both in the picture, sitting in the swing on our front porch on Pearl Street. We can't be much more than juniors or seniors in college. I'm wearing one of James's fraternity shirts, and a cigarette hangs from my mouth. James leans close, his arm slung over my shoulder.

God, we look young. I didn't know Adam. James hadn't met Elizabeth. We hadn't yet slept together. I might not have even officially come out to him, though he admitted long ago that he knew from the start. Could we legally buy beer? He's holding one, the bottle between loose fingers along with a cigarette. I've forgotten how good-looking he was back then, with all of that wavy hair and shoulders thick from swimming. And that smile, like he's seeing all of me and doesn't give a shit about the considerable imperfection. *Let me in,* he's written in the accompanying note, *and I'll keep my mouth shut.*

I just never have been good at telling him no.

I got your card, I say when he answers his phone. Man, he says, You've had me so freaked out, I'm looking at flights to Austin.

I appreciate the words, even though I'm not sure whether to believe them. I've been sitting on my phone all month, he adds, Waiting for you to call. I needed some space, I admit. You all good now? he asks. You crossed a line, I remind him. That's what we do, he points out, and I think about all the times we knew better and acted otherwise, including last Christmas. You could've cost me a boyfriend, I tell him. But I didn't, he concludes, and because I can sense how hard he's working to keep his tone even, because he hasn't balked at the word *boyfriend* when I'm still struggling with the term myself, I tell him I managed that all on my own. Aw, hell, he says, What happened?

I fill him in on how I spent the day, admit I hadn't gotten Brice a gift. Not even a Starbucks gift card? he asks. Brice has plenty of money, I mumble, He can buy whatever he wants. Haven't you ever heard the saying, *It's the thought that counts*? James asks. He got me tickets to Hawaii, I tell him, and he starts laughing. No wonder he was pissed, he says. I spent my day helping him, I protest. I'm sure he appreciated your help, Joel, he says, But isn't that what a boyfriend does?

If James thinks I've fucked up—James, who has always discouraged every guy I've dated, except Adam—then I have a feeling tomorrow will find me apologizing to Brice.

Think you'll make up? he asks, reading my mind. I don't know, I say, and he's quiet. Maybe he's hoping we won't; I wouldn't be surprised. There's a reason I've blocked James's calls. There's a reason we haven't been talking, and I have to look at the photograph in my hand to remember what made me dial his number tonight. We've been friends for a long time. Once, we were something more. We've worked hard to make our way back to a place of friendship, with only one slip. James's jealousy has been a constant.

I want you to be happy, Joel, he says, and tears come to my eyes. I wipe them away, suddenly glad that I called. What'd you get for Christmas? I ask, ready to change the subject. Stocking full of switches, he grumbles. Santa's one smart motherfucker, I tell him.

We're a thousand miles away from each other, but we might as well be in that swing.

James / Chicago / June 2007

Well, this is morbid, Joel says.

We're standing at the front of a cemetery under a watery moon. I bet it's nice and quiet in there, I tell him and he gives me an odd look. I should hope so, he says.

The gate swings open without a sound and the wind rustles the virgin leaves as I start down one of the paths, swinging the bottle of wine I insisted we pick up along the way. Isn't this trespassing? he asks. Probably, I admit but we keep walking until I pause under a tree that would've been perfect for climbing if it hadn't had the misfortune of growing in a graveyard. Here's good, I tell him, dropping to the grass and uncorking the wine. With a sigh Joel lowers himself to the ground beside me. Not what you had in mind tonight? I ask. I guess I should be used to your obsession with death, he says. Not death, I protest, Classical funerary practices, representations of the Greek afterlife and— The general death discourse, Joel finishes along with me, rolling his eyes.

All right, so maybe I already told him.

The Greeks, I announce like I'm at the front of a classroom, Stuck a coin called an *obol* in the mouths of their dead so they'd have money to pay Charon for ferryin' them to Hades. I think I knew that, Joel muses. Because I already told you? I ask and he laughs. Believe it or not, he says, I know a few things you didn't teach me.

Hell, more than a few.

I pass Joel the wine and lie down in front of the nearest tombstone, folding my arms across my chest like I'm already dead. Even if I put a coin between your teeth, Joel informs me, You'd be screwed. Thanks, man, I say, sitting up and he tells me he wouldn't fare much better. I give him a look to see if he's headed down some self-pitying path but he's just talking. What do you think will get you in the end? I ask, grabbing the wine, and he shrugs.

Riiight. Probably not the best conversation to have with someone whose answer could've been *my own damn hands*. I think about Joel swimming in his own blood in that house on Pearl and I've got to take a big old swallow of wine to make the picture disappear.

I'll go fast, he says at last, surprising me.

Man, how did he cut his arms and wait to die? Everyone talks about suicide being the pussy way out but sometimes I wonder.

I spend a lot of time thinking about death. Or whatever, I think about death in a certain context. I don't know why I gravitated toward my particular field of study but I guess I'd be lying if I said that Joel's mom's suicide and my girlfriend's decision to have an abortion didn't worm its way into my motivation. Maybe all I've been doing since college is trying to make sense of everything.

I worry about Henry, I admit. Henry's fine, Joel says and I shake my head. I worry about what'd happen to Henry, I explain, If somethin' happened to me.

One thing about Joel, he's not going to spout some bullshit about how nothing's ever going to happen. You counting up the number of cigarettes you smoked this week? he asks and I grunt. He gives me half a smile. Lizzie would probably rise to the occasion, he says. Lizzie's been gone for weeks, Joel, I remind him, adding that this is the shit that keeps me up at night, that after my mom's mastectomy a few years ago I don't feel like I can ask her for help and my sister's only twenty-three and Lizzie isn't capable of giving Henry what he needs... Will you take him? I ask, If somethin' happens to me, will you take him? Sure, he shrugs. Really? I say, You'll take him? What do you think? he says.

For just a second I can see us at that cemetery outside Fort Worth last year before Henry was born. I don't even have to close my eyes to bring back the feeling I had that night. Connection so strong I couldn't tear myself away, not when the beer was gone—Joel had two compared to my four—and not when I'd sucked down so many cigarettes my chest started aching. Twice he asked if we needed to leave and both times I shook my head even though I knew Lizzie would be pissed when we finally got back. We stayed out until four in the morning, the dark so deep. Days passed before the feeling faded.

I've missed him.

I'm allowed to fucking say that.

I've missed him.

Come to Greece with me, I say and he answers so quick I wonder what might've happened if I hadn't balked all those years ago when he came to me with the truth. Yeah, he says, Okay.

Part Two

Slow Burn

March 2008 - June 2009

James / Chicago

Every office on my floor has heat except for mine. I swear I can see my goddamn breath in here and the illusion of smoke has me patting the pockets of my coat—which I'm wearing by the way—for my Marlboros. I have a cigarette in my mouth but I can't smoke in the building and I glance outside where the snow's falling thick as cream gravy. Man, I'm tired of this cold. We've got weeks before the sun starts shining again. Or whatever, we'll get a day where I think I can walk outside in shorts and sandals like I'm still living in Austin until I open the door and my balls retract.

Kayla knocks as I'm pouring a cup of coffee from my single serving, piece of shit coffee pot. Do you have a minute? she asks and I wave her on in. She stops short a foot inside my office. Why's it so cold in here? she asks. You got me, I say, tearing open a packet of sweetener and dumping it in my coffee. I point to the chair across from my desk. Sit, I order and she does, pulling a scarf from her bag and winding it around her neck. The color—some kind of pink that Joel would probably call bubblegum or fuchsia or something—makes her eyes look as blue as the Aegean and my gaze falls automatically to the picture taped to my computer, Joel and Henry and me last summer. That photograph has raised a brow or two but whatever, I'm used to having my relationship with Joel misinterpreted. It's only when something's going on between us that I get spooked.

As he so kindly reminded me our last night in Greece.

Nice scarf, I say and Kayla lights right up. Shit, I need to be more careful. I don't want her thinking there's a chance something could happen here. I like her just fine but I do not need to be sleeping with my students even if they're twenty-six and interested. So what can I do for you? I ask, shifting to a more business-like tone and she gives me a crestfallen look before she admits she just wanted to chat.

I could use the company but I don't want to encourage her. That last night in Greece I had to pry her fingers from my arm and if it hadn't been for Meghan Porter, my colleague from California I would've had a hard time escaping. Of course if I hadn't escaped—if I'd gone ahead and slept with Kayla—I wouldn't have hiked up to the cemetery after Joel and Dmitri. I wouldn't have stumbled back to the party with blood oozing from my forehead. I wouldn't have shoved Joel into the shadows and we wouldn't be where we are now with me in Chicago and him almost six thousand miles away.

I take a scalding sip of coffee as Kayla toys with the end of her scarf and mumbles about possible dissertation topics. She's reaching and I know it but I'm grateful she's keeping our banter professional so I let her go on for a minute then give her some superficial feedback. She won't end up with any of these topics anyway. I just need to kill some time before my office hours end. I've been trying to finish a submission for publication; the deadline's next week. I thought I might make some headway this afternoon but with my office this cold I guess I'll be working tonight instead after Henry goes to bed. I've been waiting on Joel to call me back too. I left him a voicemail three days ago and I haven't heard a word from him. Six months after he left the country and I'm still thinking he's at home, throwing something together for dinner. I guess he's not feeling the same way.

How's Joel? Kayla asks like she's some kind of psychic, Have you heard from him? Yeah, I've heard from him, I say, irritated. So…, she presses me. He's fine, I mutter, glancing at my watch and stacking some papers on my desk to show her we're done. She gets the hint, sliding her bag over her shoulder. I'm going to warm up, she tells me, inclining her head toward the hallway. I give her a wave.

Well shit. Now I'm aggravated on top of everything else. How the hell am I supposed to know how Joel's doing? Since he left for Buenos Aires last September we've barely spoken. I call, he doesn't answer. A few days, sometimes a week later he calls back. Talking to him feels as dangerous as excavating that site last summer. One wrong step and I'll ruin everything.

I pick up the phone and stab in a number I've dialed enough times to know by heart. Four rings, five… I take a swallow of coffee and grimace at the temperature. That got cold in a hurry and I reach for the Marlboro I wanted earlier and light up. What're they going to do, fire me? I'm sitting in an ice box for my office hours. The least they can do is indulge my addiction.

There's Joel's voicemail. I drum my fingers as he tells me to leave a message. Look dickhead, I start but after the insult I don't know what to say. I don't have to think hard to remember lifting my head from that shitty pillow last summer, my mouth a sarcophagus. I had that shaky I-just-got-trashed feeling and I knew that once I got out of bed I'd look every one of my thirty-five years. Squinching my eyes, I tried to retrace my steps and came up with Kayla and Justin, Dmitri and the cemetery, the wine I was drinking. And Joel shoving me every bit as hard as I'd shoved him. I hadn't found him in the cemetery like I thought I would. I don't know who I found up there and when I started in on him…

I've left that *dickhead* hanging. Gimme a call, Joel, I mumble, Okay?

He used to need something from me. Sometimes I felt downright suffocated and I'd leave our house on Pearl and breathe like I wouldn't get another chance for days. Other times I felt favored. He had problems I couldn't even imagine and I was the one who got him through. What would he have done after his mom shot herself if I hadn't been on him about skipping classes, if I hadn't told him to get his ass painting again? Now he won't return my calls.

I hear my department chair in the hallway and crush my cigarette under the desk. Professor Fielding, she accuses, pausing in my doorway and sniffing the air like a bloodhound. Student just left, I tell her, She was smokin'. My chair looks me in the eye like she knows better. You'd think that by this time she'd consider me an equal but no such luck. Right from the get-go she didn't much like me and nothing's changed since I got tenure. I'll crack a window, I mutter and she gives me a nod.

Joel / Houston

My father didn't want me to visit when he was first diagnosed, and I'm fairly certain he doesn't want me here now. I come downstairs in the mornings and find him on his way out the door, if he hasn't left for his country club already. Don't get me wrong; I'm happy he's playing golf. I want him to feel healthy enough to do what he enjoys. I just expected to be included. You don't even play golf, Joel, his wife sighs, and it's the first time I can remember Catherine being short with me. She looks like a beauty queen with a hangover, and when I ask her what I can do to help, she shakes her head. There's nothing she hasn't already delegated.

I thought we'd at least have dinner together, anticipated the three of us sitting down every night to the kind of meal Catherine used to prepare when she and my father first got married. I've brought clothes to accommodate, mentally prepared myself for questions about what the hell I'm doing with my life. Instead, my father tells us he ate at the club, and since Catherine seems to be surviving on a steady diet of protein bars and stress, I end up eating by myself outside by the pool, where the sun feels warm and azaleas bloom along the perimeter. Why don't you join me? I ask my father, and he gives me an impatient look that makes me feel like I've never left his house. I take a centering breath, remind myself that I'm choosing to be here. No one asked me to come.

Maybe I should've paid more attention to the absence of an invitation.

I'm out of alignment. I've never been much good to anyone—including myself—when I'm not working, and I haven't touched my mosaic since I left Buenos Aires. I have a piece of glass in my pocket, a gem I found half-buried at the beach. My gaze has sharpened over the past few months, and my eye caught the glint of green midway through a run last week. I pulled up short and dropped to my knees, then pried what I saw from the sand. Softened by the sea, the glass glimmered in the sunlight. I can't pinpoint the color, though it's ordinary enough. It's the sparkle in the glass that beguiles me.

Still, it's not enough. I can finger glass, go for a morning run, disappear for a fifteen-minute meditation; nothing's strong enough to neutralize the energy at my father's house. I know this and still hope otherwise. That wasn't too bad, Adam said the last time we made the trip to Houston together years ago, and I burst into tears. He had to pull the car over to the side of the road as I folded myself over his lap and cried. My father hasn't threatened me since I was nineteen, but the second I see him, I expect him to light a cigar.

I could simply cut him off. Lydia Hernandez, my therapist back in Austin, told me that was perfectly within my rights, and Adam would've been thrilled if I severed ties. The first time they met, my father was in town on business and wanted to get together for dinner. I'd told him Adam and I were a package deal. My father relented; still, Adam had a hard time being civil. He couldn't charm you, huh? I joked on our way home. Joel, he's a master manipulator, he said, And I don't want you anywhere near him.

But he's my father, and I'm his son. You're nothing like him, Adam told me, so many times I lost count, *Nothing.* I'm not so sure, and even if Adam's right, my father's still a part of me. My relationship with him has had just as much of an impact on my life as my mother's suicide. My relationship with him has influenced my art. I don't know who I'd be without him, and that's not something I can easily throw away.

So I'm here, even though he might not want me. I'm here for the better part of a week. I'm here, and when I get a voicemail from James—the second one in three days—woe spreads throughout my body, along with a simultaneous, misguided shot of hope. If anyone understands me, it's James, and late that same night, I sit under the moon and dial his number.

James / Chicago

Henry's only been asleep for an hour and it's almost midnight. Man, I hate when he gives me grief about bedtime especially when I've got work ahead of me. Everything was moving along just fine until I shut him down after two books. I know better. Three books a night, that's our routine but I'm tired and feeling like a chump for thinking Joel's going to call when I'm pretty clearly the furthest thing from his mind and Henry's book about that panda named Stillwater takes twice as long to read as the others. So I said no and Henry threw a fit that lasted so long I had to walk out of the room so I wouldn't pop his little behind.

The thought of tackling a submission for publication sounds about as appealing as sex with my ex-wife but I'm sitting in front of my laptop anyway, trying to write a book review that doesn't completely discredit the colleague who offered me an advance copy. I've got a pack of Marlboros in front of me and I plan on rewarding myself the second I finish my work or the second it gets too late to concentrate, whichever comes first.

I'm betting on the latter.

Since I got tenure I've been slacking on the scholarship. I like writing papers but the past six months I've let everything slide. At first I thought I just missed Joel. I do, but I'd also gotten used to him helping with Henry. I realized midway through that first month he was here last summer that I felt better about leaving my son with Joel than I ever had with Lizzie and I didn't change my mind once we got to Greece. Every morning I climbed on that bus and headed to the site without worrying about what they'd be getting up to while I was gone. Maybe that's part of the reason I'm stinging right now. Joel and Henry bonded like nothing I could believe and I guess Joel's gone and forgotten all about their connection.

Anyway for months I didn't have to think about laundry. I didn't have to think about putting Henry down for his nap most days. Joel took care of everything and when we got back to Chicago and he took off for Buenos Aires I found out right quick just how much I'd been depending on him. That first week Henry and I ate nothing but takeout. I forgot to buy diapers and had to cart my bare-assed kid down to the corner store where he whizzed right through his pjs and my shirt. I was worse off than when he first came home from the hospital and that wasn't taking our moods into consideration. We were both hurting without Joel and not much has changed since.

I'm struggling to think of a diplomatic phrase for *limited conclusions* when I think I hear my cell phone. I cock my head and there it is, a muffled ring that tells me I left the damn thing in the living room. I know it's Joel and I catapult myself from the chair and down the stairs, snatching the phone and answering too late to disguise the urgency in my voice. Fuck Joel for making me feel desperate. Hey man, he says, sounding so cool I want to beat the shit out of him. Hey man? I repeat, *Hey man?* What? he says. It's about time you called, I say and he pauses long enough to remind me who's in charge here. Do me a favor, okay? he says, Don't be a dick.

Well, we're off to a rocking start.

I left you a voicemail, I tell him, dropping on the couch, Two voicemails. And I'm calling you back, he says.

Does he want me to thank him? Jesus.

My eyes automatically find *Crossing*. I moved his painting down here when we got back from Greece and he left for South America and I realized I wouldn't be seeing him for a long time. When I had it hanging in my office I'd have to turn sideways every time I wanted to look at it. Nowadays I catch myself glancing away from the TV to trace that line, the one he made right down the middle.

So, he says, How are you?

I'm pissed but I guess I can't tell him that or he'll hang up and it's taken three days and two voicemails just to get him to call me back. I'm fine, I mumble, Busy. How's Henry? he asks and I tell him about tonight's meltdown. I could've used a little of your magic, I admit. I'm not sure I have any in me right now, he confesses and before I can ask him why, he tells me to hang on. I wait, glancing again at the clock. Why the hell is he up so late anyway? It's almost three o'clock in the morning in Buenos Aires.

After his mom died he had nightmares. Half the time I'd find him in the swing on our front porch and I'd sit beside him as he smoked a shaky cigarette. The dreams got better after a while but I know he still has them and when he comes back on the phone I ask how he's sleeping. Fine, he says, Why? You're up late, I remind him. So are you, he points out and I tell him I'd probably be asleep by now if he hadn't called. Don't kid yourself, he snorts, You'd be on the back porch with a cigarette. Maybe I quit, I say. When you can smoke your way to an early grave? he asks, Please. I've known you to pick up a bad habit or two along the way, I point out and he says, You're the only bad habit I have left, James.

Ouch.

You workin' much? I ask, trying to change the subject. Some, he says. Some, I repeat and he says, Some, James, what do you want to know? What's your problem, Joel? I ask.

He doesn't answer me and for a second I think I've pushed him too far. Then he says, I'm in Houston. *Houston?* I repeat, sitting right up. I came to see my father, he adds. Why? I ask, What happened? He has cancer, James, he reminds me.

Thanks for treating me like a dumbass.

He worse or somethin'? I ask and he tells me his dad spent the day on the golf course.

Well, now I'm just confused. No way would Joel plan a trip to Houston without giving me a heads-up. His dad spent the day playing golf so that means he's doing fine enough. Joel plans on seeing me… right?

When're you comin' up here? I ask.

He doesn't say anything and a big old well of hurt opens up right in the center of my chest like I've taken a bullet from a shotgun at close range. My landscape has felt so bleak since we got back from Greece and I've gone ahead and convinced myself I'm not the reason Joel left. He needed to get back to work and who was I to stand in his way? He's dedicated and talented and he doesn't have the same responsibilities I have right now. Why would he stay in Chicago when he can experience South America? His leaving had nothing to do with me.

You sure you wanna be that far away from everythin', Joel? I asked him when he first told me about Buenos Aires and for a long time he didn't answer. I need the space, he finally said.

I need a break, James. I need a break from you.

I shake my head, blindsided by the realization that somewhere along the way we died without my knowing. Here I am, thinking it's only a matter of time before he cools down and comes home when in reality he's going out of his way to make sure that won't happen.

Why are we even talkin'? I ask. What do you mean? he says. Why are we talkin'? I insist, What's the point? The point of a conversation? he asks. The point of pretendin', I tell him.

He's quiet for so long I take the phone away from my ear to see if he hung up. My father's *sick,* James, he finally says. Remember when your mom died? I ask and he doesn't sound happy to be reminded. No, James, he says in a shitty voice, I've forgotten all about it. When your mom died, I tell him, You wanted me there. That was a long time ago, he mutters.

My lashes get thick with tears I'm not expecting and I think about ending this call right now because if he came to this country with no intention of seeing me there's nothing left to do but bury us anyway. You done? I say. Done? he repeats. With us, I say, impatient, Are you done with *us,* Joel. James, he sighs and in that hesitation I find me a pulse.

Joel

I almost said no. This past week hasn't been easy, and I'm still harboring hurt from Greece. Even a phone conversation with James felt like a stretch, but here I am, sitting in his living room like a trip to Chicago was my plan all along. There's not enough meditation in the world to anchor me right now, and with something that's starting to feel like instinct, I pull beach glass from my pocket. Henry toddles over to take a look. He hasn't let me out of his sight since I got here a few hours ago, and he's been crying off and on for the past fifteen minutes because James keeps telling him it's time for bed. I stroke the side of the glass, and Henry tests it for himself. What's that? James asks. Just a piece of glass, I answer, and he frowns, as if he thinks I'm foolish enough to give Henry something with a jagged edge. Before he can protest, I slip the glass back in my pocket. You want to read a book? I ask Henry, and he lets out a little squeal. Don't stay up there forever, James tells me.

In other words, my night's not over yet.

I remember where to look for the pacifier Henry still needs at night— for naps too, and sometimes solace—and he blisses right out, just like James with a Marlboro. What do you want to read? I ask, and he flings a few books to the floor, then hands me the one we read every day last summer, the one about the quiet cricket. I place a reflexive hand on my heart. He remembers, and we settle in the rocking chair in the corner and read the story together. I can smell his baby shampoo, and I take a deep inhale so I can come back to this moment when I'm in Buenos Aires next week. Something—the feel of this little boy in my arms, the memory of holding him just this way every night for more than three months last summer—brings tears to my eyes.

This is why I came back. For Henry, not for James. That last night we were in Greece, I'd leaned over the railing of Henry's crib, watching him sleep, his arms thrown open, his mouth puckered around his pacifier. His breathing brought my own back into balance. I was still trying to process what had happened earlier in the evening, trying to understand how much I was to blame. I'd agreed to make the trip to Greece. I'd treated Henry like my own son and James like my partner. The shift had been too easy; I was still used to behaving as part of a couple—because of Adam, because of Brice—and anyway, James and I have always been something other. I don't know what I was thinking, walking up to Dmitri like I might have been willing to cancel my flight out the next afternoon if he asked me to stay.

At the same time, I knew I wasn't doing anything wrong. All summer, I'd been taking care of Henry so James could dig in the dirt. I'd missed over three months of work to help him. Other than casual conversations with some of the graduate students, I talked to no one. James had my undivided attention except when I was with his son, and at the first indication that my interest might be elsewhere, he lost his mind. Do you want me? I asked that night when he stumbled back from the cemetery, and his eyes dropped right to my mouth. For just a second, I believed in the possibility of that kiss. Then he looked over his shoulder. *Oh, he wants you, honey,* I heard Kyle say, *Just not enough.*

I'm wanted, but not enough. Not enough for Adam to be faithful, for my father to respect me in spite of what I do and whom I love, for my mother to choose life over death. Not enough for James to tell me he doesn't care what anyone thinks.

But the way he looked at me when I took Henry from his arms this afternoon, like I'd just answered every prayer he prayed since I left... How many times am I going to ask him to apologize? I wanted space, and he's given it to me. What more am I going to ask from him?

Only yoga could have prepared me for the kind of balancing it takes to lift Henry from the rocking chair without waking him. I carry him to his crib and gently release him from my arms. Then I stand for a minute, looking down at him. Every so often, he gives that pacifier a suck. Like James with a Marlboro, I think, just as James himself steps beside me. You're some kind of magic, he whispers, and I give him half a smile.

James

At first I thought Joel was going to make up some bullshit story about not having the time or the money to come up here. I thought he'd tell me that the space he said he needed hasn't helped and he needs more. I had my arguments locked and loaded: he was 4500 miles closer to Chicago than usual; who knew when he'd make it back to the States; I'd pay for the damn ticket myself if he was short on cash. But I didn't even have to fire. Think Henry will recognize me? he asked and man, I coasted on that relief for the next three days. When he got here Henry went to him like a second hadn't passed, turning to give me a big old smile like this here was what he'd been missing since summer. Tears crawled into the corners of my eyes and I tamped them down but Joel saw them all right and tugged me toward him, his free hand on the back of my neck. His kiss on my forehead forgave everything and we stayed there like we were somewhere we belonged, Joel and Henry and me, the three of us, the way we used to be.

But that was when he first got here. Since then I've been fighting Henry for Joel's attention. I've let Henry stay home from preschool the past two days so he and Joel can spend some extra time together while I'm on campus but that just makes my kid want Joel all the more at night. I only get a couple hours with Joel before he tells me he's done. One look at him says he's not lying. So I send him off to bed and the next day we go through the same shit all over again.

I'm running out of time to make this right.

Lizzie has Henry two Friday nights a month. She can't handle more than that and she doesn't pretend she can. On those days I leave campus a little early so I can spend some time with Henry before she comes to pick him up. We've tried having me drop him off at her place but for some reason me leaving him seems to be more of a trigger than him leaving me so I just let her come to my place to get him. Henry spends the night with Lizzie, and I pick him up on Saturday at noon. Most of the time—even though I appreciate the chance to sleep in a bit—I'd rather be with my son.

This Friday for the first time I'm ready for the night off.

When the bell rings I open the door and beam a smile at my ex-wife. She's already brushing past me, making a big production of swooping toward our son who pulls right away from her. Well sure. This show is for Joel's benefit. Henry turns away from her, reaching for who he really wants. Let's give Joel a break, buddy, I say but Henry buries his face in Joel's shoulder.

Lizzie looks grim like she's used to being the outsider. That's what she told me on the phone the other day when I warned her she'd be seeing Joel at pickup. I'm used to being the outsider, she said and I sighed *oh Lizzie* even though whatever, she's right. Time to go, buddy, I say and here come the tears. Joel just rubs Henry's back in a slow circle, whispering in his ear. I don't know where a guy without kids gets his kind of patience.

Ten minutes later Henry's buckled into his car seat. He's clutching Mr.

Boo and sucking so hard on his pacifier we can all hear him. If I wasn't so ready for some time alone with Joel the sound could break my heart. See you tomorrow, Joel says and Lizzie gives us a tight smile. Who knows what she thinks we're getting up to tonight and I look at Joel standing there and wonder what my ex-wife's seeing, this guy with the paint-stained jeans and shit-kicker boots. Does she recognize that gray fleece he's wearing? She bought it for me a couple years ago in a size too small and never returned it. Fits him fine though and as I'm watching he brings his hands to his head and holds back his hair.

Bam. There it is, that moment I always get at least once every time I see him and sometimes way more and right quick I'm more than a decade gone. January's hurling cold rain against the windows in his bedroom in that house on Pearl and for once we're not stoned though I'm aching for something to soften everything because this here I can't handle, Joel catching his bed with the back of his knees and dropping back and me following him down, that kiss I give him on the side of his neck because no way can my mouth meet his sober. Then I'm pulling away and pulling off his jeans and as I'm shoving down my boxers he sits up. We aren't smiling, not either one of us. Back down he goes with his head against the pillow and I come right after him and then, right then he lifts his head and pulls back his hair. His eyes are closed and I'm propped on my palms and I start shaking so bad I can't hold myself up. I don't get why I want him. I don't get why him pinning his hair back with his eyes shut tight can make my belly feel like I've just crested the first hill of that giant roller coaster at Six Flags. Joel, I say in a voice so hoarse I sound like I've been smoking pot all morning and he opens his eyes.

I'm back in Chicago in 2008 and I guess I've let my gaze wander because when I lift my eyes I'm looking up from Joel's crotch. *Shit.* He saw that. I glance over at Lizzie to see if I'm fucked both ways but she's closing the door of her car. I give my son a little wave. Something on your mind, James? Joel asks. I give him a look so brief he's got to know I'm full of shit. No, I say and I call to Lizzie, Have a good time! I don't think she heard you, Joel tells me, his voice as dry as my mouth after our last night in Greece. I don't say anything as Lizzie's car pulls away from the curb. I just hold my breath because this could go one of two ways and I'm really hoping it's in the direction of *we should just fuck and be done with it* like I got at that cemetery outside Fort Worth the week before Henry was born.

Instead the front door of my brownstone slams shut.

Joel

I don't know what James thinks could happen tonight, but he let his eyes slide over me in front of his house like he has something in mind. I'm stone cold sober and have been since I got here at the beginning of the week, but that look of his triggered something so ancient I slam my way into his house and go right into the kitchen, where I get a beer from the refrigerator. I'm smart enough to hesitate with the bottle opener in my hand. I can go one of two ways here. I can keep my distance, and therefore my sanity, or I can walk into his smile and fuck myself in all kinds of ways. There's no middle ground anymore. Our last night in Greece took care of that.

Since I got here, I've been careful. I've spent most of my time with Henry, declined James's invitations to share a bottle of wine. You go ahead, I've said, and the past few nights, I've watched him drink without me. He loosens up until I cut him off and tell him I'm going to bed. He's still talking as I climb the stairs, and I shut the bedroom door and stand for a second in the dark, making sure I didn't leave too late. Enough wine and he could follow me. I really think he could.

The thought doesn't do for me what it did twelve years ago. Instead, I'm filled with dread, and when I hear his footsteps on the stairs, I hold my breath until he passes my door and takes the next flight to Henry's room. I'm hoarding the details from my trip to Houston, keeping quiet about the work I'm doing in Buenos Aires; so far, he hasn't noticed. He has too much he wants to tell me: about Henry, about the impact of his trip to Greece on his research, about the paper he just submitted for publication. Every so often, he'll say, *What about you, man?* and I'll just shrug and ask another question. Getting James to talk has never been a problem, and with a bottle of wine beside him, the past few nights have bled by. But then Elizabeth showed up a little while ago, and he looked so ready to be rid of his son that I would never have guessed this was the same guy who didn't want to let Henry stay with the babysitter I found last June.

He wants something from me, and he's impatient.

The front door creaks, and my beer opens with a sigh of relief. I get in a good swallow before he shows up looking wary. He knows what he did outside. He knows I could call him on his shit, if I want to go that route. I started in that direction a few minutes ago. Something on your mind? I asked as Elizabeth pulled away from the curb, and of course, he shook his head. Now he takes note of the bottle in my hand. You're starting early, he says. You want to join me? I ask, and there's the smile I expected.

James

Joel's pacing himself and I'm pissed. We're four hours in to our one free night together and he's just now opening his third beer and that's *after* he drank down a full glass of water. Whatever, I'm not trying to get him drunk but I've got a feeling that the bullshit underneath the surface here has to do with him not trusting me. What does he think I'm gonna do? One look at his crotch and he's assuming all kinds of shit that have nothing to do with my intention for tonight, which is to spend some goddamn time with him for once. I'm starting to feel like he came up here to see Henry and he's visiting with me out of some kind of obligation.

And he's not talking. I realized that last night. Since he got here I've been filling him in and I've barely heard a word from him. Did I imagine that moment the day he got here? Didn't we stand there all together like we did last summer, like we'd moved past whatever ways I fucked up?

Man, I'm not liking the way any of this feels and I root around in the drawer where I stash my Marlboros. You're going to smoke in the house? Joel asks when I light a cigarette. Henry's not here, I remind him. I'm here, he says. Sure you are, Joel, I mutter as I unlock the back door. I open it wide, letting in a wild wind. He winces at the weather like I've called it up to personally affront him. You really gonna send me out in this shit? I ask. He doesn't answer me and I smack the door closed, smoke streaming from my nose. You want a cigarette? I offer. You know I don't, he says. I think you do, I tell him, Just like I think you wanna drink that beer of yours a lot faster than you're drinkin'.

He doesn't say anything and I open a fresh one, my sixth. Maybe. I've got a feeling he's not just thinking about what happened outside. He's chewing on our last night in Greece and I lean against the kitchen counter and watch him relive that shit because I am too. There's nothing we can do to change what happened. He can't take back what he asked me and I can't take back the way I answered him with a look over my shoulder that fucked us so hard he moved to another country.

After eight weeks of work in Greece my team had accomplished more than we'd ever expected. For days we'd been digging and photographing and tagging and just like that I was going to have to leave everything behind. I wasn't ready. I didn't feel like going home to face a full schedule of classes and another Chicago winter. I wasn't ready for Joel to head back to Austin either and that's what I was afraid he was fixing to tell me the second our plane touched down. *An entire summer with you has been more than enough,* he'd say and then what?

But that last night in Greece something else had my attention. We were supposed to be celebrating, that's why we were outside with a bonfire and a keg and more wine than my students probably needed to be drinking and Joel was off to the side talking to the water delivery guy. I watched them exchange glances like they were passing notes in high school and man, that feeling I got in my gut the day I saw Joel on our front porch with the guy he picked up at the taco place near our house right after we graduated from college came creeping back. Joel must've felt my eyes on him because he glanced in my direction and smiled and the next thing I knew he was loping toward me. Let me tell you I did not appreciate how good he looked, his hair tied back with that leather band and his legs as lean and muscular as they'd been in college. He looked like he'd been hanging out in Greece all summer and easy as you please I let myself forget that I was the one who'd invited him in the first place.

You having fun? he asked when he caught up to me. I grunted, tipping my cup to my mouth. He was holding a cup too but that was just for show. All summer he'd been drinking water like he was afraid if he touched anything else he'd lose control or something. To see if I was right I took the cup from his hand. You're drinkin', I said, surprised to see the wine and he tore his gaze away from the water delivery guy with such reluctance every beer I'd slammed so far that night fired my face at the same second. What? he asked. You're *drinkin'*, I told him. Oh, he said, taking back the cup, Yeah, I guess. You guess? I repeated and he shrugged. I stared in the water delivery guy's direction. He looked like he'd just stepped out of a postcard, hair like an Adonis and deep-set eyes. *He couldn't have shown up next week? I* thought. *He couldn't have delivered water somewhere else? He had to show up here?*

And then he came over to us like the three minutes he'd spent away from Joel had just about done him in. Dmitri, Joel said and I gripped my cup so hard the plastic cracked, beer spilling over the sides. Uh-oh, Dmitri cooed, sounding just like Henry when he drops his sippy cup. I shook beer from my fingers and sucked the side of my hand. Joel wasn't even paying attention. Instead he was staring at Dmitri like some shred of decorum was the only thing stopping him from kneeling down right there in front of everyone. I took Joel's wine from his hand and drained the cup. I get you a drink? Dmitri asked Joel when I handed it back empty. Please, Joel said and Dmitri left us, letting his smile trail so long behind him I almost groaned.

We should take one last walk through the cemetery, I suggested once Joel and I were alone. Yeah, sure, Joel agreed but when I made a move in that direction he said, Not now, man. We're leavin' tomorrow afternoon, I reminded him. Yeah, but…, he said and I raised my eyebrows even though I knew damn well what was going to follow. He gave me a slip of a shrug I'd have to describe as pretty and I got pissed all over again for noticing.

I'd had too much beer. Way too much beer.

I apologized the next morning. I apologized for days but I can see standing across from him now that none of that stuck. He might be sitting at my kitchen table but his head's full of Greece.

Joel

James looks as grim as I feel, which means he's thinking about the same night I am. I watch him smoke, wishing for a cigarette of my own and placating myself with a beer I don't need. I should excuse myself, tell him I'm tired and want to go to bed. Never mind that it's barely ten o'clock. I need the distance. More and more, that's what I need. Distance from someone who used to be the only one I wanted. Last summer, the thought would've made me weep. Now I'm just on guard. Someone has to look out for me, and it's not going to be James.

But the way he's staring past me, beyond my shoulder and through the doorway, with an expression so wistful I want to close my eyes: he's craving what I miss almost more than my mother. I take a deep breath without the benefit of a cigarette. I can't seem to bring myself to shut this down, and I watch as he rubs his finger where for years he wore a wedding ring.

He was drinking that night in Greece, though he wasn't smoking. He couldn't find his Marlboros; I remember helping him look for them before we left for the party. I shouldn't be smoking anyway, he finally said, and I didn't disagree with him or tell him I'd just spotted them on the bookshelves. Maybe if I'd stopped him, we wouldn't have ended up here. Maybe those cigarettes would've slowed him down because he would've taken the time to inhale in between cups of beer.

When I caught James looking at me from across the campfire his graduate students had built, I gave him a smile. I felt benevolent, satiated from the summer. We hadn't talked about what would happen after we got back to the States, but I wouldn't have been opposed to staying in Chicago for a while. I knew he wanted me there and not just because of Henry. Whatever we'd been through over the past decade we'd managed to surmount. I think I felt a certain pride in that, in who we'd become, and I told Dmitri I'd be back in a minute and walked toward James to congratulate him on what he'd accomplished over the summer, what we'd both accomplished. I should've known when he grunted a reply that something wasn't right. Instead, I glanced over at Dmitri, who I'd met twenty minutes earlier delivering water and who didn't waste much time before he came our way and offered to get me a drink. Let's go to the cemetery, James said the second Dmitri turned his back. Sure, I agreed, but I told him I couldn't right then. Because of *Dmitri?* James asked, and before I could answer him, Kayla and Justin, James's top tier students, stumbled over, drunker than they should've been at that point in the evening. Are you having fun, Professor Fielding? Kayla asked, pulling up beside James, her words running all over each other. I guess, James said, and she gave him a big smile and leaned in close. Fun is good, she confided, reminding me of the Dr. Seuss books I'd been reading to Henry all summer. Go easy on the alcohol, Kayla, James told her, and she laughed, waving her hand so expansively she spilled half her wine. On our last night in Greece, she said, Anything goes!

Justin seemed to be taking her advice to heart. He edged closer to me, like I'd ended up on his radar for the first time all summer. I gave him a brotherly smile as James unhooked Kayla's fingers from his wrist. I've had such a good time with you, I heard her purr. At least he knew enough to disentangle himself, and I indulged Justin for a few minutes until Dmitri came striding back to us with a cup of wine for me and another for himself. *Efharisto',* I said, getting a big grin in return. Justin pawed at the ground with the toe of his sandal, and James barked at him, his voice so harsh that every single one of us gave him our attention. What? Justin asked, cowing just enough—to James's tone, to his authority—that I felt bad for the guy. C'mere, James slurred, grabbing the sleeve of Justin's shirt. He might as well have tacked *dumbass* on the end of that command, and I raised my eyebrows. The second they went up, James paused. I could see him trying to work something out, and he finally shook his head. I need a drink, he muttered, and Kayla stepped a little closer. Let's get one together, she suggested.

I cut my eyes in his direction, but he gave me a look that told me he had everything under control. I shrugged. I had something else on my mind anyway, and I nudged Dmitri. Let's go for a walk, I said.

By the time we got back, James was gone.

James

You sure you don't want a cigarette? I ask, lighting my second from the butt of my first and Joel rolls his eyes. Whatever, he's the one who got me hooked. I don't think you want to do this, James, he says when I remind him of that. Do what? I say without taking the cigarette from my mouth, Tell the truth? Is that what we're doing tonight? he asks. C'mon, Joel, I mutter, Lighten up.

It's the wrong thing to say because he takes a swallow of beer so Pavlovian I have to sit down. I'm supposed to be making this shit right and instead I'm tempting him with cigarettes and more beer than I've seen him drink in years. I guess this is what I do to him and I take a drag of my Marlboro, wishing for something a little stronger so maybe we really could lighten up. I'm not sure the truth's going to get us anywhere.

The truth is that I didn't hook up with Kayla our last night in Greece and every time I see her on campus I thank God for my colleague from San Diego who realized what was happening when Kayla dragged me over to the keg. The truth is that my colleague diverted her attention so I could make an escape. The truth is that the last cup of beer I'd downed had me pissed in every sense of the word.

I headed toward the cemetery, sure that's where Joel and Dmitri had ended up. The night was bursting with stars, giving me enough light to track my way up the hill and when I reached the fence I could hear them, Joel and Dmitri, low murmurs that reminded me what I was interrupting. Under my hand the gate cried out and I pictured them breaking apart at the sound. The image satisfied me like I could not believe. Stumbling forward I tripped over a loose stone but caught myself before I hit the ground. I peered into the dark, wondering if they could see me and furious by the thought that they were hiding. I fuckin' hear you, man! I shouted. Creeping up to one of the bigger headstones, I jumped around the back like I was playing some kind of macabre hide-and-seek. Nothing. Another headstone, another jump. Nothing. When I got to the statue of Thanatos I was sure I'd find them. I sprang around the corner and heard them crashing just past my field of vision, got the barest glimpse of Dmitri topping the hill. I see you! I screamed, flying after them but I didn't catch myself in time. I went down, whacking my head against an old broken stone. Blood gushed from the wound and I moaned, bringing my hand to my head.

Moonlight washed over me and I tracked its path through the craggy trees and around Thanatos who stared down at me with plenty of reproach. I stayed long enough for the blood on my head to get tacky, long enough for the shadows to shift. Then I hauled myself to my feet.

I had a long walk back and when I got to the bonfire I found Joel standing at the edge with Dmitri like nothing had happened. He saw me at the last second, his eyes widening at my bloody head. Palms on his chest I shoved him. He barely had a chance to stumble backwards before instinct kicked in and he was shoving me right back. I saw you, Joel! I shouted, I fuckin' saw you back there! What're you talking about? he said but I was all up in his shit, grabbing fistfuls of his shirt. Hey hey hey, Dmitri was saying, trying to wedge himself between us. I pushed him away. I *heard* you! I insisted, I *saw* you! What're you *talking* about? Joel said. I am your problem? Dmitri asked suddenly and I turned on him. Well, aren't you an intuitive cocksucker, I hissed. James, what the *fuck,* Joel breathed and I snarled. I should've known you'd follow your dick, I said.

His eyes narrowed and I felt a flame of triumph. I wanted him mad. I wanted him every bit as pissed off as I'd been sprawled out there in the cemetery under the eye of Thanatos. You had one job to do this summer, I said, stabbing my finger at him, One fuckin' job! Are you talking about *Henry?* he asked and I said, Well, I'm not talkin' about gettin' your dick sucked! Dick sucked? Dmitri repeated and I groaned. Why the hell are you still here, man? I asked him and the dumbass actually looked to Joel for a reply. Give us a minute, Joel said to Dmitri. You heard him, I growled when

Dmitri didn't move. Please, Joel said to him, Give us a minute.

Dmitri stepped away but I held my ground. You ready to apologize? I asked. For *what*? Joel said. For runnin' away from me back there, I reminded him. I have no idea what you're talking about, he told me and I said, You gonna tell me you weren't fuckin' Dmitri in the cemetery? I haven't been *near* the cemetery, he said, And the closest I've come to sex with Dmitri is this fucked up accusation. I saw you! I cried, I heard you! You're wrong, he said.

I got quiet. My head was starting to hurt and I touched a clump of hair, matted with blood. Joel didn't ask if I was okay. All summer, he said, I've been watching your kid. Whatever, I muttered. No, not whatever, James! he cried, All summer I've been watching your kid! I saw you, I insisted but the words didn't seem to have the same power they had a few minutes ago. So what if you did? he said.

For a second I thought he was going to 'fess up and my gut roiled in response. I did not want to think about him with Dmitri and once he put language to the image that'd been skidding through my skull ever since I'd heard that low laughter at the cemetery... I didn't care how much I shouldn't care. I just couldn't stand thinking about them together.

Do you want me? Joel asked and my eyes fell right to his mouth. Like a girl's, red and full and man, I couldn't help it. I thought about shoving him into the shadows and just letting go of this burden I'd been carrying since the first day I saw him. Then I stopped, suddenly aware of how we must look to my graduate students. My colleagues too. I snuck a glance behind me *who's watching, who can see* and when I turned back I might as well have been staring down at Joel on the floor of that bouncy castle at my fraternity party our sophomore year. Sometimes, James, he said, I wish I'd never met you.

You told me we were fine, I mumble now and he sighs. We're the same as always, he tells me. We're not the same as always, I say, This is *not* the same as always. What do you want from me, James? he asks, You asked me to come up here, and I came. You've spent the entire time with Henry, I remind him. Are you seriously jealous of the time I'm spending with your *son*? he asks. I wanna talk to you! I exclaim and he groans. Isn't that what you've been doing all week? he says, Talking? I want *you* to talk to *me*, I say. There's nothing to say, he insists, My father has cancer; I'm working with glass. You're breakin' my heart, I tell him.

For just a second I think I've got him but then he takes one of those deep breaths that makes me want to punch a hole through the wall. Whatever, I'm glad he finally learned how to calm himself down but right in this moment I want a reaction from him. I want him to acknowledge that we're not connecting because this distance scares the shit out of me. He's going to fly back to South America in thirty-six hours and when will I have another chance? I need something real from him before it's too late.

And I know how to get it.

Joel

I don't know what James is doing upstairs, but I can hear him banging around in his office. I'm on my third beer, though I'm taking cautious swallows, trying to be smart. He's on his seventh; I'm counting, though I don't need to number off the empty bottles to know he's drunk. The last words he spoke to me as he was leaving the kitchen gave me plenty of indication. You're breaking my heart, he said, and for a second, I thought I'd burst into tears.

Now he's upstairs looking for something, and I'm wishing I'd boarded a plane south when I had the chance. As happy as I've been to spend time with Henry, I'm not capable of negotiating James right now. How can I give him reassurance when I feel none myself? Of course I'm lying when I tell him we're the same as always. How could we possibly be the same?

I've gotten used to people hurting me. I always think James will be different.

Somewhere above me, he lets out a cry of triumph. I meet him at the bottom of the stairs as he's scrambling down, lugging a canvas. He turns the frame to face me, and as his image jumps from the paint, I stumble backward. That's what I thought! he says, hauling the painting over to the the sofa and folding his arms across his chest.

For the first time in a dozen years, I stand in front of *Crossing*, tracing that midnight border, the curve of his mouth, the scarlet line I slit across the canvas like I was ripping open a vein. I can still feel the paintbrush in my hand; I can almost catch the scent of pot. For years, I had no idea where *Crossing* ended up. All this time? I finally ask, and he says, Where else, Joel?

I lower myself to the floor. James follows me, leaning back on the palms of his hands. For once, he's quiet, and I think about the moves this painting has made, from our house on Pearl Street, to that gallery on 5th in Austin, to James's apartment, to the loft he and Elizabeth rented when they first moved to Chicago, to this brownstone. I think about where he's kept this painting hidden, and why. I think about everything I could say right now, about my time in Houston, the work I'm doing in Buenos Aires, the ways he disappoints me.

In the end, I don't say anything at all. I finish my beer, and he drinks another. After a while, I follow him into the kitchen and watch him eat cold macaroni and cheese from the container until I scramble some eggs. Do we have any salsa? he asks, and I get a jar from the refrigerator, my mouth full of tortilla.

I don't mind the *we*.

James

Lizzie wants to get together for lunch and I have to cancel my one o'clock class and hustle my ass across town to meet her. Trust my ex-wife to choose a place where we need a reservation for lunch on a Tuesday. Why we can't just meet up for a taco I don't understand. Sometimes I can't imagine what I saw in her.

Whatever, I know what I saw. The opposite of Joel.

Got any beer? I ask our server when I find Lizzie already waiting for me and he gives me the kind of choices that make me long for a Shiner Bock and that swing on my old front porch. I settle for coffee and smile at my ex-wife. We've met for lunch twice since she left, once to go over the paperwork my attorney laid out last September and once about a week after everything was final. I don't even know why I'm here today. How've you been? I ask. I'm doing well, she says, Thank you for asking.

Since September we've been so polite it's painful. A few days after I got back from Greece she came by without calling first. Joel was still in town and I hesitated before I waved her inside, checking over my shoulder for Henry. I could hear him in the kitchen with Joel and I said Lizzie's name nice and loud so Joel would catch on that I didn't want him coming into the living room. Where's Henry? she asked and right then Henry blew through the doorway. More than four months had passed since the last time she'd seen him and I scrutinized my son's face for signs of recognition. Sure enough, Henry cocked his head like he was trying to remember something and I felt broken-hearted and vindicated in the same awful moment. He's walking! she gasped, turning to me and I said in a mean-as-shit voice, He's seventeen months old, Lizzie.

She tried to coax him into her arms but Henry wiggled away from her and went to his walker, which played an obscene music the second he set the thing in motion. Dada! he exclaimed, making sure I was watching and I said his name the same way even though I wasn't feeling much enthusiasm. What else does he say? Lizzie asked. Ball, I admitted, not thrilled to be sharing, And cat and dog and bye-bye.

I didn't mention Joel's name and she didn't think to ask.

So why are you here? I demanded and she gave me a wide-eyed look like I might've missed that she'd abandoned us. I'm his mother, she said. You've been gone more than four months, I pointed out, And now you just show up? Do I honestly need an appointment? she asked. Do you honestly have to ask? I bit back. I didn't come here to fight, she told me, turning away and sitting down on the couch, one pretty leg crossed over the other. Man, I did not like the liberties she was taking like she still lived with us or something. She was wearing shoes I could mistake for ballet slippers, a thin skirt with a flounce along the hem. A few years back her beauty would've destroyed me and for a second I wondered if she'd shown up because she wanted to try again, if she'd worn her hair around her shoulders because she was trying to entice me. I was thrown by a wave of revulsion so fierce I almost staggered on my feet. I don't think I'd realized how far out of love I'd fallen.

Henry bonked the walker into the coffee table, music blaring. Does that have a volume control? Lizzie asked, cringing and even though Joel and I had wished the same thing a thousand times in the past few days I rolled my eyes. He likes it, I told her. Well, she said, speaking under her breath, You always did put him first. Of course I put him first, I snapped, I'm supposed to put him first. And what about me? she asked, Or did you already get what you wanted?

I looked over at Henry who was babbling to himself but with a tilt to his head like he knew something was up. Let's not do this in front of him, I told her. You don't want to have this conversation at all, she said, The last thing you want to admit is that you might have done something wrong. What exactly have I done wrong, Lizzie? I asked, I've been takin' care of him without your help since the day he was born.

She smiled a tiny smile like I'd gone and said what she expected. Henry swung past us and headed into the kitchen where he slammed the walker into the cabinet under the sink. Easy, I heard Joel say in a quiet voice and Lizzie flew to her feet like someone had lit a firecracker under her ass. What's *he* doing here? she cried. I needed the help, I told her. What happened to Henry's sitter? she asked and I started to laugh. Lizzie, I said as Henry bumbled back toward us, She's been gone almost as long as you have.

I'd insulted her and she tapped the toe of her slipper on the floor like a ballerina about to fly into a pirouette. How long has he been here? she demanded, and I was happy to tell her the truth. He came a couple weeks after you left, I informed her. Lizzie raised a shaking hand to her mouth. All this time, she said, It was never me you wanted.

Aw man, Joel was hearing that shit and as I winced she snagged my son. Where's his diaper bag? she asked as Henry started struggling. You're not takin' him *anywhere*, I warned but she just tightened her grip. I'm not going to stay *here*, she informed me and Henry started to cry. Then go, I said, But you're not takin' Henry. I'm his mother, she reminded me, raising her voice over Henry's screams. Then start actin' like one, Lizzie! I told her. I haven't seen him in *months*, she said, And I'm not going to spend time with him under *your* judgmental eye! You *left*! I yelled and then we were fighting, shouting and pulling him between us, Henry's wails and the music from that walker pretty much wrecking any chance we had of being reasonable until Joel grabbed hold of my shoulder. Look at your son, he said to me.

The second I realized what I was doing I let go. Lizzie stumbled and Joel, the only sane one out of all of us caught my boy. Shh, he whispered as Henry clung to him, choking his name, Shh. I led Lizzie to the couch where she cried until Henry's sobs turned to hiccups. Somewhere along the way Joel had found a pacifier and Henry sucked like there was something real on the other end of it, a fistful of Joel's hair in his hand. Every so often Joel met my eyes, waiting for me to tell him to leave but no way was that going to happen and we all stayed right where we were until Henry fell asleep, his head on Joel's shoulder. I still want to see him, Lizzie finally whispered, Sometimes.

Turns out *sometimes* means two nights a month. Whatever, I can handle that. Being a single parent is easier than being married to Lizzie and even though I wouldn't mind a little extra help I don't necessarily want the source to be my ex-wife. Now I brace myself, worried she's ready to announce that she's feeling better and she thinks she can handle seeing Henry more often.

Instead she tells me she's moving to Boston.

What? I say, What about *Henry*? I'll visit, she tells me, And when he gets a little older, he can come to see me.

It's a rare moment when I can't find words but I'm downright speechless. No one gets more than I do that Lizzie wasn't cut out for motherhood. I just never thought she'd cut and run entirely.

There's no need to berate me, she adds, I already know what you're thinking.

I guess she does. I don't think there's any way I could disguise it. I don't figure I can change her mind either. I might've been able to convince her we should buy the brownstone, I might've been able to persuade her to try a fifth round of IVF but she's moving to Boston, there's not a doubt in my mind.

Well, fuck me.

How's Joel? she asks as I'm paying the check and I shrug like I didn't just talk to him on the phone a couple nights ago. Lizzie waits until I've scrawled out my signature. I thought he'd be spending more time here, she muses after I've set down the pen. *You and me both,* I want to say but instead I mumble something about the opportunity he has in Buenos Aires. Still, she continues, I imagine having him live so far away must be hard for you. He's not my boyfriend, Lizzie, I say irritably and she gives me a Mona Lisa smile that makes me sorry I bought her lunch.

Joel / Buenos Aires

The beach glass won't be enough to finish my mosaic, and I end up buying some tiles ready-made: vitreous glass and metallic, both of which I have to cut myself. I try for a while with hand-held nippers, and that works for some of the smaller pieces, gives me the control I need, but I also purchase a tile-cutter with a wheel that scores a line in the glaze and allows me to just snap where I want. Either way, I have to wear goggles; the first time I tried the hand-held nippers, I shattered the glass and sliced my cheek, near enough to my eye to make me cautious.

The larger pieces—the ones that measure maybe a solid inch across—I can glue to the metal with my fingers. For some of the smaller bits, like the one I find outside a *minuta* not far from my studio, I have to work with tweezers. The precision I'm finding necessary for this project blows me away, and by the time I'm finished working every day, I have a headache unsurpassed by any I've experienced. Nothing helps unless I close my eyes, and I usually do, at an hour that would embarrass me if I didn't have such conviction in my vision.

I still can't see the end result. I often can't, but for some reason, maybe because I don't usually work on a painting for more than a few days before it's finished, I'm far more aware of intuiting my next step. I don't deliberate, never hold a piece of glass in one place, then another. Somehow, my fingers know where to go, and I trust in the process, certain that everything's falling into place exactly as it should.

Days pass, and the only time I touch glass might be the moment I stop mid-run to pick up a glint of something special from the street. I'm still painting, still sketching, still talking to Cameron, who curated my first show and updates me once a week with a new placement, a certain painting consigned. He wants me to send him my latest, and I take shots with a digital camera and email him attachments, then pack whatever he wants to see in person. My stipend barely covers the cost, but somehow, just when I'm looking at my account and wondering where I'm going to get the money for groceries, I hear that I've sold something else. There's talk of a show in Dallas, a show in Atlanta, another in DC. I try not to get caught up in the details. My work takes my focus, my mosaic most of all.

I spend a lot of time by myself and realize one day as I'm eating lunch alone that I haven't spoken to anyone other than my landlady in three days. Kyle sent me a picture of the dog he and Scott just adopted, but I have no social circle in Buenos Aries, and I haven't been on a date since I left Brice.

That doesn't mean I haven't found my way into someone's bed once or twice. The encounters aren't memorable, nothing I'll think about again. If I ran into these men on the street, I might not recall their faces. For a while, I believed that was exactly what I needed. Sitting down to another meal alone, I'm not so sure. I think about where I was three years ago, when *home* meant *Adam*. On a Friday afternoon in June, I might be in the pool. I might be in my studio with a paintbrush in my hand. We'd likely have plans for the evening, with friends or by ourselves. We were having a hard summer three years ago—that year marked the beginning of the end—but we were together.

I know what it's like to fuck someone, to get caught up in the moment and desire release. I don't remember what it's like to spend an evening with someone I want to see in the morning. Maybe that's why I gave that kiss credence last summer, that kiss that could have happened if James hadn't looked over his shoulder.

Sometimes I wonder if I should call Adam, whether he'd be happy to hear from me or so angry because I never responded to his email that he wouldn't bother to answer. What would I feel, sharing lunch with him, knowing we'd be spending the night together? What would my life be like if he hadn't cheated on me, if I'd never left? I look at my mosaic, beginning to fire its own light. I might not have been offered that show in DC. I wouldn't have spent last summer in Greece. I wouldn't be living in South America, and I certainly wouldn't be working with glass.

Without thinking, I reach for my phone. In ten seconds, I can hear his voice.

Then I go for a run, the way an addict would go to a meeting. A mile in and I'm out of danger, the moment past, the craving suppressed.

I don't love him any less. I don't hate him anymore.

James / Chicago

I keep trying to get Joel up here and he keeps telling me no. At first he says he doesn't have the money but when I offer to buy him a ticket he says he can't come to the States without going to see his dad. I get that and I also know that his last trip to Houston balled him up nice and tight. No way will he go through that again unless his dad gets a lot worse and that right there means I'm looking at a long time before I see him.

I'd feel guilty wishing his dad would get worse just so Joel can come to Chicago but I don't give a shit what happens to the guy. I had my suspicions freshman year but the night of Joel's mom's visitation I had to pick my friend off the floor after what his daddy said to him. I told Joel to quit school, told him he'd have a better shot waiting tables instead of handcuffing himself to whatever money the son of a bitch was using to buy him off. That was before Joel told me about the cigars. Once I found out why he had those scars on his arms I would've been happy to take a brick to his dad's skull. But I didn't see him until Joel tried to kill himself.

I got the call on New Year's Eve as Lizzie and I were driving to Fort Worth. We'd spent Christmas with her folks in Houston and we were trying to get back in enough time to have dinner with my family before we went out that night. Champagne, that's all I was thinking. I wanted to forget. For the first year since we'd known each other Joel and I hadn't said *Merry Christmas*. We weren't speaking and I needed to get rid of the guilt. I needed to celebrate the girl beside me who didn't know anything about what I'd done to Joel or with him.

I didn't recognize the number on my phone but looking at the area code I figured we'd left something behind at Lizzie's parents' house. Hello, I said, keeping my eyes on the road and for just a second I thought I was listening to Joel. Then I realized I had his dad on the line and my foot lost the accelerator. I knew before he told me why he was calling that I wasn't going to hear anything good.

Afterwards I found out how close we came to losing Joel. If Adam hadn't shown up without calling first. If Joel hadn't swallowed a handful of Xanax before he picked up that box cutter. If he'd been just a little more precise when he cut his left arm. I think about what had to line up in order for me to see him in a hospital bed instead of a casket and even all these years later—knowing all I've got to do if I want to hear his voice is pick up the phone—I have to grit my teeth so I won't start bawling.

The second his dad told me what happened I headed for Austin, driving faster even than I was driving Joel's convertible when I totaled it. At the hospital I met Catherine for the first time and Adam too. By that time we knew Joel would make it through but that didn't mean the waiting room felt like a celebration. Seventy-six stitches and a pumped stomach made us think Joel had a shit ton of therapy ahead of him and I listened to his dad talk to Catherine about treatment options and held Lizzie's hand, waiting until the nurse told us we could see him.

Joel's dad went in first and came out a few minutes later working his jaw like he'd just helped himself to a big old plug of tobacco. One jerk of his head in the direction of the elevators and Catherine was following him around the corner. Please, Adam said, holding me back as I got to my feet and I looked at the tears in his eyes and let him go on ahead of me. After all, he'd been the one to find Joel and as I waited I hunched forward, elbows on my knees, feeling like I'd sat this way before and remembering with a sickening sensation the day I took my college girlfriend to get an abortion.

I'd cried like a baby that day. Joel was the one who got me through.

Joel's dad still wasn't back when Adam sat down again beside me with his head in his hands. Are you going in? Lizzie asked when I didn't move. Yeah, I said but I sat there a second longer, thinking that once I saw Joel lying in that bed there'd be no turning back. However we moved forward was still on the other side of that door. He sedated? I asked Adam and he nodded. *Well, thank God for that,* I remember thinking. Because I didn't know what to say to him.

What does a guy look like twenty-four hours after he's dug a knife so deep in his arms he almost bled to death in his bathtub? Nothing like the guy who smoked with me on our front porch and tossed me the keys to his BMW and covered the cost of so many six-packs I probably owe him beer for the rest of my life. Whoever I found in that hospital bed couldn't have painted *Crossing*. I couldn't have slept with that guy, sober or not and that's when I started shaking. Where the fuck was *Joel?*

I don't know how long I sat beside his bed but I was there when he opened his eyes. Hey, I said, figuring out a way to smile. I reached for his arm and all that gauze wrapped around his wrist stopped me and my hand dropped to his shitty hospital blanket instead. The tears I'd managed to hold back burst from me all at once. I laid my head on my arms and cried for what he'd done and for what I'd done too. I'd made mistakes. I'd lied to Lizzie. I'd left out details, the kind of details that would change the way she looked at me forever if she knew them. I'd kept Joel a secret because I didn't want to lose her and instead I'd almost lost him. That right there, him with his arms stitched up tight and those fingers looking like they'd never painted a thing, that was my doing. That was my responsibility. I'm so sorry, I whispered. Get out, he said and I lifted my head. What? I gulped, wiping my eyes. Get *out!* he yelled and man, I flew out of there like he'd lit his own cigar.

Adam stood as soon as he saw me but I caught Joel's dad coming down the hallway and I went after him the way someone should've years ago. I don't know what all I was shouting but I got in a good hard punch and something about him being to blame before Adam pulled me off him. Catherine was crying and Lizzie too and I didn't wait around to make nice. I took off out of there and I haven't seen Joel's dad since.

Now he's sick and I don't much care except for how it affects Joel and I guess me since I'm the one who's missing out on Joel's company. So, what? I say the next time I've got Joel on the phone, Am I just not gonna see you unless there's an emergency or somethin'? Come to Buenos Aires, he suggests and I snort. Sure thing, I mutter, I'll be there in time for supper. Next month would be better for me, he admits. Yeah, I'll check my calendar, I tell him. I'm not joking, he says. I've got a kid, Joel, I remind him and he says, Bring him.

He's serious.

I'm leaving for Greece the first week in July, I tell him. So come the week before that, he says, And leave right from Argentina.

He's for real and I don't know which makes me happier, that he offered the invitation or the idea of seeing him. You mean it? I say. Would it make you feel better if I begged? he asks and for the first time since last summer innuendo doesn't seem like such a risk. Gimme what you got, I say. Get your ass down here, he tells me, And I will.

Joel / Buenos Aires

I'm in the habit of running in the mornings, but the weather's getting colder, and for five days in a row, I can't make myself get out of bed early. I leave the covers eventually, but by that time, I'm ready to work. *I'll run tomorrow,* I think every day, but the next morning feels colder than the last, and I sleep late, again. If I'm not careful, I'll kick myself right out of the habit, and that won't be any better for the glass than it will for my psyche, which has become so dependent on a daily endorphin rush that by the afternoon of that fifth day, I'm neglecting the glass in favor of grappa, the purchase of which I'm able to justify because of the weather. I sit in my studio with the bottle, annoyed with the light and myself for the slip. At least a few beers with James doesn't mean I'm drinking alone, and to make myself feel a little less guilty, I call him up. He's coming here at the end of next month. We can talk about his plans.

But he doesn't answer, and I leave him a message, realizing that my voice has the slightest slur. He'll catch it and worry, and I make an ass of myself trying to preempt his concern before I give up and glug some more wine. Rain slides in sheets down the windows. I'm thousands of miles from anyone I know.

My resistance might be low enough to make a mistake. There's a reason I don't drink like this anymore, and it's not just because the alcohol occludes my creativity. A glass of wine and I'm nostalgic; a bottle and I'm liable to dial phone numbers I shouldn't. I'm already opening the door of my closet and digging through the box on the shelf for photos I don't need to see.

This one, the summer we got back together. My hair's short, my smile wide. We're sitting on the deck at Hula Hut with a margarita apiece. Adam has his hand along the back of my chair in a gesture that manages to look subtle and proprietary at the same time. I ache now remembering the way that felt. To be so claimed, to know that whatever the events of the evening, we'd end up together... I got you, Adam said once, catching me from behind when I slipped climbing out of the pool, and those words enveloped me like the wings of an angel. With Adam, I always felt supported. That's why I denied the signs of his infidelity. I didn't believe he'd cheat on me.

Taking a sloppy sip of grappa, I drop the photo and shuffle through some others. In Kentucky with his family. In scuba gear during our vacation in Belize. Halloween a couple of years before we split up. We'd known better than to have our own celebration on Kyle's favorite holiday, but we always had fun at his party. That year, Adam wanted to go as pirates, an idea I liked just fine until he showed me the dress he'd found. I'm not going as your wench, I said. Why not? he asked, The costume's gorgeous. Then you wear it, I told him, and he pointed out that he'd never be able to fasten the bodice. Just try it on, he insisted, and so I did, to humor him. He stood behind me, looking at my reflection, then silently handed me a wig with black hair longer than I'd ever worn my own. Maybe some lipstick, he suggested, and I cut my eyes at him. You're lucky I look so good, I said.

Adam makes a convincing pirate, with that headscarf hiding the way he'd started losing his hair and that gold hoop earring. I look downright pretty, so close to *girl* someone could've read me as such, if they'd been able to discount the way I clomped around in my first pair of heels. Ditching those, my feet were a dead giveaway. Even so, I got hit on more that night than I had the entire previous summer. They know what's under your skirt, Kyle reminded me. My legendary dick? I asked, and we all laughed. That's when someone snapped this photo, and I stare at the three of us caught together, Kyle and Adam and me, and have to take another swallow of wine to rid myself of the taste of that lipstick.

I could say hello, right? What's wrong with saying hello? We shared more than five years together, spent weekends and summers and holidays with each other, slept every night in the same bed. If it weren't for Adam, I wouldn't have had the time and space to work the way I did. I wouldn't even be alive, and I stumble back to my desk, reaching for my phone just as it starts to ring.

Did I summon him? I lift my cell to my ear, too suspicious to speak.

Joel? James says, and tears gush from my eyes like they've been waiting all afternoon to fall. I take a shaky breath that sounds more like a sob. Dude, what's wrong? he asks, alarmed. Tilting the bottle of grappa, I'm dismayed by how little is left. I think..., I say, I might... You sound drunk, he accuses, Are you drunk?

I'm unwilling to commit to an answer; he's smart enough not to laugh. Why are you drunk in the middle of the afternoon, Joel? he asks. I missed my run, I say, The rain... You run in the rain, he reminds me.

He's right. I've run in the rain many times and once with James. Thirty-something degrees as the sky fell and we still made it six miles. My running shoes had ice in the laces by the time we climbed the steps to our front porch.

Talk to me, man, he says, and I retrace the day, telling him about the turn in the weather and buying that bottle of wine. I'm really close to calling him, I confess. Who? he asks, confused, and when I don't answer, he starts swearing. I listen to him, unable to tell if Adam's a motherfucker for

cheating on me or I am because I still love him. I lift the bottle of grappa to my lips, but for the first time in the past couple of hours, the scent of wine closes my throat. Caught up in his rant, James doesn't stop to ask if I'm okay. Three years! he cries, You left him almost three years ago! Doesn't that tell you something? I say, Because if after three years I still want him... Joel, James tells me, You're spending too much time *alone*.

My shoulders slump. He's saying the same thing I've been thinking over the past few weeks. This isn't about Adam; it's about isolation. Short periods of time to myself work miracles for my art. Months of solitude do not. The glass hasn't suffered yet; even now, drunk and distressed, I can run my eyes over what I've been playing with the past few months and feel my insides vibrate. But I can't live on my work alone, however appealing that sounds on the surface. I'm sliding here, and I can't run the risk of falling farther.

You're still coming here, right? I ask, and he tells me that he and Henry will see me in a matter of weeks. Not a long-term solution, he adds, and for just a second, I'm angry. A long-term solution would've involved moving to Chicago, a possibility I might have been willing to consider if James hadn't dicked me over our last night in Greece. Instead, I'm living in a different goddamn hemisphere. Sometimes I feel like everyone's trying to chase me away from them: my father, my mother, Adam, James. I get close; I get vulnerable; I get fucked. There's a lesson there somewhere, and it doesn't make me want to venture out in the Buenos Aires rain to try to find somebody to love.

You going to be okay? James asks. You know me, I mumble, and he tells me that's why he's asking. I don't want you hanging up and calling someone you shouldn't, he says. A phone call isn't a commitment, I sigh. Joel, he says, A phone call to Adam would be domino number one. I thought you were domino number one, I tell him, but he just laughs. Hang in there, Joel, he encourages, I'll see you in a few weeks.

I drain the last of the wine in the sink, then hold the empty bottle up to the light. Not my smartest purchase, but the color could be worse.

I'll smash the bottle and use the pieces.

James / Chicago

Man, the end of my quarter can't get here quick enough. I'm sick of my students, tired of office hours and aching to get my hands in the dirt again. I won't be going back to Crete. Instead I'll be working inland about three hundred miles from the coast. I've been invited by one of my professors from UT into work already in progress and I'm honored to be included. I don't know how I'll manage with Henry in tow but no way am I going to let this opportunity pass me by. Come with me, I said to Joel on the phone last month, figuring he had every right to kick the shit out of me for asking him after what happened last time around. I'll lose my stipend, he reminded me without taking time to get pissed and I guess I can't fault him for not wanting to take that risk. He's doing good work down there and he can't give up just because I want to go to Greece. So I've hired a babysitter to come along for the ride, an investment that pretty much cancels out the extra money I've been making since I was awarded tenure. She comes highly recommended despite a bleached strip shot through her ebony hair. Whatever, Henry seems fine with her. I guess I can get past her resemblance to a skunk.

First we're going to Buenos Aires just Henry and me. You ready to see Joel? I ask Henry and he gives his pacifier a good long suck. I need to wean him off that thing but I'm guessing right as we're about to embark on some hardcore international travel isn't the best time. I really hope Henry doesn't lose his shit midway through our flight. The last time I flew with a toddler I had someone helping me. I've got no idea what to expect once we're in South America either. Joel tells me his studio's about 750 square feet and filled with glass. I guess we can always stay in a hotel but that's not the point. We're going down there to see Joel.

I need to put my eyes on him. He left me a voicemail a few days ago that worried me and when I called him back I got him drunk and deliberating a phone call to Adam. What the fuck is wrong with you? I asked, which maybe wasn't the best way to handle him but come *on*. It's been three years since they split up! Adam fucked somebody else! For *months*. How Joel can think about the guy without *that* being uppermost in his mind I don't understand. Joel, I finally said, You're spending too much time alone.

I don't care how much satisfaction he gets from his art. I like my work too. But I can't spend all day every day on my own. I don't know what I'd do if it weren't for Henry. I get that having a kid isn't the same as having a partner but at least I'm seeing someone at the end of the day.

Joel needs to come home. Fuck his stipend. That money's not going to do him any good if he's drinking and depressed. I know him and I know what he needs. Human contact for one. Minimal alcohol for another. Put him alone in a room with a case of vodka for a week and he won't make it out alive, I don't care how many pieces of glass he collected on the beach. He's been down there nine months. He's not ready to leave yet?

I can't think about him being down there without missing him.

I can't think about him being down there without blaming myself.

Joel / Buenos Aires

I've been painting since the grappa, easing into what feels best to me, what comes most naturally. I have no intention of backsliding, mostly because of how shitty I felt after drinking that bottle of wine, but also because I can hear in James's voice what he's going to suggest when he gets here with Henry. He's going to try to convince me to move back to the States. He's going to tell me I need to be around people who know me— never mind that I don't know a soul in Chicago other than James—and I need to come home. He might even settle for Austin. I can hear his reasoning now. Kyle and Scott live there; I know the city as well as a friend; I'd be a mere two and a half hours by plane away from him.

I don't want to move back to Austin. I don't want to be reminded of the life I had there with James, with Adam. I know I spent time there without them. I know I did good work in that run-down house east of I-35. I miss the greenbelt and tacos and ordering a Shiner Bock without getting a blank stare in return. But my time there has ended; I know this as emphatically as I know my name. I might pass through there; I might make a visit to see Kyle and Scott. I won't live there again.

Chicago feels almost as wrong. James makes his home there, and it's true that he complicates everything. I love him in so many different ways I don't know if I'll ever get to the bottom of what he means to me. I like the idea of being close to him, and I love the thought of seeing Henry grow up. At the same time, I think moving in his direction—not in the direction of Chicago, but in the direction of James himself—might end up being a slower and more painful suicide than the first one I attempted. I can trust him with my life, but not with my heart.

I'm not done here either. I'm inspired by the city itself, by the beauty of its language, by the colorful buildings in my neighborhood, and especially by the street art that's becoming more and more prevalent. Working with the physical limitations of a public space requires a certain innovation, and while that doesn't mean I'm moved to make my own mark on the walls of this city, the absence of restrictions on graffiti gives Buenos Aires a feeling of artistic expression and freedom. Art and community intersect here in a way I never found in Austin.

Still, I'm not necessarily a part of that experience. I'm peripheral, focused on the glass and uncertain that I can replicate the space I need somewhere else. Give me a sketchpad, and I can get lost just about anywhere; my studio has always been inside of me. Something's different with the glass. I don't know if it's the 750 square feet I call my own or Buenos Aires itself, but I'm held here by a force unseen. I feel it when I'm running, let intuition guide my feet, inspiration choose what diverts me. With glass in my pockets, I head home.

James won't understand. James will shake his head and tell me I need to get over myself. He'll tell me I can recreate my studio anywhere; I've done that more than once. He'll tell me that if I'm getting sidelined by a thunderstorm and a bottle of wine, I'm farther down the path of self-destruction than I want to admit.

I've been proving him wrong every day since his phone call. The weather's cooler than it's been since I first arrived in Buenos Aires last September, so I've changed up my routine. I set an alarm to be sure I'm up early enough to take advantage of the light. I meditate; I choose a yoga pose that speaks to me; I eat a little breakfast. Then I work, just as the sun spills into my studio, illuminating my space like it's some kind of temple. The glass surrounds me, glinting with possibility, and I work until I'm ready to run. By the time I get back to my studio, the sun's low enough in the sky—we're on the cusp of winter here, after all—that I'm ready for a shower and a more substantial meal. Then I read or talk to James. When I sleep, I dream about glass.

The week before James arrives, I go for my run, grateful for the late afternoon sun. We've had several warmer days in a row, and I'm happy to squint against the light if that means I can make it through the next thirty minutes without sweat chilling my skin. I get into a good rhythm, but I'm keeping my eyes open for glass the way I've become accustomed. Today, nothing gets my attention until something makes me detour down an alley I've never noticed. Here the sun seems sparse, and I'm that much more appreciative for those moments when the light streams in between the back ends of the shops. I'm halfway down the alley when I stop. The glass shines as sharp as a winter wind. I gaze into its glare so long I'm hypnotized, and I have to shake my head to get my bearings.

That's when I see the bike.

It's old school, black with chrome handlebars and a worn leather seat I'm suddenly aching to straddle. I step closer without realizing what I'm doing. When I open my hand, blood drips onto the sidewalk; I've clenched my fingers around the glass hard enough to open the skin, and I wipe my palm on my shirt, startling when someone steps from the shadows, a cigarette pinched between his lips. *Ella es hermosa, no es cierto?* he asks. *She's beautiful, isn't she?* I nod. Without missing a beat, he hands me a towel. *Gracias,* I mumble, wiping the blood off my hand, and he gestures again to the bike. *Ella esta para la vente,* he confides. *She's for sale.*

My heart bucks for no reason I can see. *Cuanto vale?* I ask. *How much,* a ridiculous question given the number in my bank account, not to mention that I've never ridden a motorcycle in my life. *Cincuenta y cinco mil,* he says. *Fifty-five thousand.* Then he looks me up and down without a hint of provocation, taking in my sweaty hair and blood-stained shirt. *Pero para usted, el dice,* he says, *Cincuenta. But for you, fifty.*

That's almost $6000. I have it, but just barely. Still, I can't take my eyes off the bike, and when he invites me to try it out, I swing my leg over the seat like I've been riding it for years. *Se siente bien?* he asks. *Feels good?* Feels *right,* I murmur. I grip the handlebars, caressing the chrome with my fingers. He watches me, then takes the key from his pocket. *Dele una vuelta,* he says. *Take it for a ride,* and I shake my head. *Yo no...,* I say, *Yo nunca he...*

He dangles the key in front of me as if he doesn't understand.

I start the engine. He shows me how to pull in the clutch and put the bike in first, heels on the ground, toes up. When I let out the clutch and pick up my feet, the bike pulls forward. The second my heels hit the ground, I let in the clutch, then look at the guy beside me. He nods, indicating that I should try again. I do, twice. The fourth time, I roll back the throttle to pick up a little speed. Once I'm moving, I put my feet on the pegs. My ride wavers; I hit the brakes, and the guy grabs me before I lay the bike flat on the asphalt. *Hale el embrague,* he says. *Pull in the clutch.*

I don't know why he's being so nice, but I'm not going to argue with him. This time, I make it ten feet. *Vaya,* the guy says, gesturing at the alley up ahead, *Vaya.*

I go twenty yards, then fifty. When he catches up to me, I ask him how to turn, and he shows me how to press on the handlebar, roll the throttle, and slide through. The trick: look where I want to end up. If I keep my eyes straight, I don't make the turn. So I lean in the correct direction, rolling on the throttle to increase my speed just enough to complete the turn. To come out of the turn, I have to let off of both the throttle and the handlebar. Then I'm upright again.

Twice I lay the bike down, the second time hard enough to give me a little road rash. I can't imagine what fifty miles an hour would do to me if I'm bleeding from hitting the ground at ten, but I don't linger long with the thought. I want back up, and the guy—Santiago's his name—coaches me for an hour, until we have to turn on the headlight to see. The darkness gives me an extra thrill, and I let myself race to the end of the alley at forty miles an hour, then circle back and come to a stop that's nearly perfect. Feet on the ground, I play with the clutch and roll the bike forward and back.

Me compras mi moto, Santiago says. *Buy my bike,* and I don't know what the hell comes over me. *Si,* I say, *Perfectamente.*

James

I'm in Joel's shower trying to scrub off whatever I might've picked up on our flight down here. Henry's already been doused and Joel has him outside now. They're chatting with his landlady who lives next door and offered to watch Henry if Joel and I want to go out to dinner one night or something. I don't know, she seems nice enough. I've never been too keen on leaving Henry with someone I just met but I'm guessing before too long I'm going to want Joel to myself. He wasn't lying about his studio. He's living in the same space he works and we'll all have to cram in one bed when it's time to go to sleep tonight.

I wash my hair, my elbows just about touching the walls of the shower. After that drunken phone call a few weeks ago I didn't know what to expect when I got here but Joel seems to be doing just fine and that means I'm going to have a helluva time convincing him to leave. He has a good setup here and it's damn clear that he's as caught up with his mosaic as he's ever been with the paint. There's a wall of metal peppered with shards of glass he's picked up over the past few months and even though I can't figure out where the hell he's going with it I know enough to realize that's not the point. I get the same feeling here as I did in our house on Pearl. Don't get me wrong, I'm right glad to see how well he's doing. I'm just pissed that if I want to see him again one of us is going to have to get on an airplane.

I rinse off and bang my way out of the shower, reaching for the towel on Joel's bed. I can still hear them outside and after I get dressed I go on out there. Where's your landlady? I ask when I find Henry and Joel alone, and Joel tells me I'll meet her another time. Tomorrow, in fact, he says, She invited us to dinner.

Man, that sounds like its own kind of torture, trying to keep Henry appeased during a seated meal but whatever. I'll have to roll with the punches this summer so I shrug and watch as Henry leaves off the beetle he'd bent down to examine and wanders in the direction of a motorcycle parked at the edge of the courtyard. Whose bike? I ask and Joel says, Mine.

I give him a look to see if he's fucking with me. *Yours?* I ask. He nods. Yours, I repeat, You've got a motorcycle. I just bought it last week, he says. Are you shittin' me? I ask. Kind of an impulse buy, he admits as we walk over to see it. I scoop Henry into my arms before he can touch something he shouldn't.

Joel straddles the bike. I've got to admit he looks good on that seat and I watch him fish a key from his pocket and start the engine. Henry's eyes widen at the roar and I take a step back, patting my boy at the same time. Together we watch Joel roll forward and make a slow turn around the courtyard. How do you know how to ride already? I ask when he comes up beside us again and cuts the engine. I feel like I've been riding forever, he says, You want to try? I don't know how, I remind him and he tells me to sit down anyway. At least get the feel of it underneath you, he says, Remember the snowmobiles?

I pass Henry into Joel's arms and sit on the bike. Turn it on, Joel says and I do what he tells me but shake my head when he tries to get me to let out the clutch. I don't wanna freak him out, I say, looking at Henry suck his fingers. He's fine, Joel says, Don't be a pussy. Maybe don't call me a pussy in front of my son, I suggest and Joel looks at me like I'm being fussy. What does he expect? I remember the snowmobiles we rented in Heavenly the winter we were sleeping together. I hit a patch of ice and flew right over the handlebars and into a bank of snow. Nothing but luck kept me from breaking my neck. I could barely get my ass back on the damn thing to return it to the rental shop. Now I'm older and I'm not going to be able to handle this motorcycle any better than I could breathe underwater the summer we went to Mexico.

You got a license for this thing? I ask, cutting the engine. Not yet, he says. Insurance? I ask. He shakes his head. And you're ridin' it anyway? I say. Joel shrugs. Where's your helmet? I ask. Why are you giving me a hard time? he says. I'm not, I mumble and he raises his eyebrows. You want to sit on the bike, Henry? he asks, turning to my son and maybe it's my rapid-fire response that sets Henry off. Absolutely not, I declare and Henry collapses into tears. What's your problem? Joel asks me as my son wails. They're dangerous, Joel, I inform him. The engine's not even on, he points out and I say, taking Henry right from his arms, Yeah, well, I'm his dad so I get to fuckin' decide.

I go back into his studio where Henry sinks to the floor and sobs. As he cries I look through what passes for Joel's pantry. And here I thought *I* wasn't getting to the store often enough. I give up and settle for an apple— not Henry's favorite—but I can't find a knife. How the hell is Joel living like this? I take a bite and offer the apple to my kid who screws up his face and screams loud enough for the landlady to hear all the way across the courtyard. Henry! I bark but whatever, it's not his fault I've yanked him out of his schedule and into another time zone. He's tired and hungry and of course he wanted to sit on the motorcycle. It's a goddamn shiny *bike*.

I open the front door ready to wave the white flag and Joel looks over from where he's talking to some guy. They're laughing and speaking Spanish and all I can think is *great, this too*. I don't call out to him. I just stand there in his doorway, my kid crying behind me and my arms crossed over my chest and after a minute Joel wanders on over, taking his sweet-ass time, a glass container in his hand. Who was that? I ask and he tells me his landlady made empanadas. That was her son, he adds, but I've perked right up at the word *empanadas*, taking the container and prying open the lid. Damn, those look good. What kind? I ask. *Carne y humita,* he says, lapsing into Spanish as he reaches for Henry who throws his arms around Joel's neck like he's the only one who'll ever understand him. English, I remind Joel and he blinks. Meat in some, he says, Corn and red peppers in the others. Henry, I say, You want an empanada?

He's not listening to me. Joel's whispering in his ear and I catch the word *bike* and grimace. *Way to remind him of what he's missing* but Henry starts quieting down and when Joel picks up one of the empanadas Henry reaches right for it, which I guess was Joel's plan all along. I watch my kid shove half the pastry in his mouth. You sure you don't wanna come with us to Greece? I mutter but Joel's not as judicious as he was when I asked him last month. I think we do better a week at a time, he says and man, that rankles me for the rest of the goddamn night.

Joel

I shouldn't have assumed I could manage a two-year-old in my studio. I should have remembered the way I felt in the back room of that house on Pearl Street and the pains I took to keep pretty much anyone except for James out of there. Henry wants to touch everything, play with the brushes, run his fingers over the parts of the mosaic I've already finished—the parts he can reach. The second I turn my back, Henry's into something. *Watch your kid,* I want to say to James, but he barely stops talking long enough to pull Henry away from the canister of paintbrushes or pick up the canvas Henry knocks to the floor. I can't play with both of them at once, and I finally tell them I have to go to the store, just so I can escape. Can't we all walk there together? James asks, but I shake my head as I close the door, then fly out of the courtyard, the bike's engine thrumming like a heart on Ecstasy. You didn't take your helmet, James says flatly when I return, handing it over, and I groan. What can I say? I like the wind in my hair.

Sometimes I pull my hair back at the nape of my neck, but I'm just as likely to leave it loose. When I had that convertible after I graduated from UT, my hair was short. Even then I liked the way the wind felt, and I remember one Christmas when I drove with the top down most of the way back to Austin after visiting my father. With the bike, I'm even more exposed to the elements, and I press my icy nose to Henry's cheek and laugh when he squeals.

There's plenty in Buenos Aires to entice kids, and after the first couple of days, I start insisting we get out of my studio. Everything has to be carefully orchestrated because of Henry: what he eats, what time he naps, whether or not James can find Mr. Boo. James doesn't want to linger in La Boca, and in a way, I don't blame him, not with Henry in his arms. There's enough crime—petty and otherwise—that I could afford to be a little more careful myself, so instead, we walk a few blocks to Caminito, which reeks of tourism but has plenty of eye candy. One morning, we go to the zoo, where Henry claps his hands when he sees the tigers. At the beach, I freeze in the fifty-degree weather, but James strips to his shorts and plows through the water. Other than the *empanadas*—and the night we have dinner with my landlady—we have no choice but to eat our meals out, and more often than not, Henry falls asleep as we're making our way back to my studio after a late dinner. I'm ready to follow him to bed, but James beckons me around the corner, where we sit facing the sheet of metal I've fastened to the wall. Tell me what you're doing here, he says, gesturing at the glass, already halfway drunk from the wine we ordered at dinner. In a way, it's a relief to have someone to tell. Remember your studio on Pearl? James asks, and he sounds so wistful I'm taken aback. I remember you interrupting me for pizza money, I tell him, trying to blunt the moment, and he laughs, then says he's more than making up for all of those meals now. He's right; I've paid for little since his arrival, for which I'm exceptionally grateful. I still can't believe I bought a motorcycle, and the main reason I don't have the license isn't because I'm blasé about its importance. I just don't have the cash for the course.

For a week, I don't work, but I know my time will come, and once we establish something like a rhythm, I'm able to let myself sink into Henry's presence here and give in to James's loquacity. I haven't opened up to anyone since I saw him in Chicago, and even though we spend plenty of time bullshitting, we have a few serious moments, too. Too bad your excavation isn't in South America, I say his last night here, and he looks so happy I regret that dig when he first got here, about the two of us doing best when we keep our visits to a week.

We've been friends for a long time. I know his triggers.

I manage to get him on my motorcycle only once while he's here. My landlady has offered to watch Henry so James and I can have one dinner to ourselves, and though James gives a backward glance as we close the door behind us, he was able to leave Henry without a fuss. My landlady has a really sweet cat. Still, James mumbles, and I remind him that we'll be able to pick up his son that much sooner if we take my bike. He hesitates, looking across the courtyard. Fine, he finally says.

I tell him to hang on, cautious with the throttle since I've never had someone ride with me, then drive slowly out of the courtyard, making sure I'm comfortable with the extra weight. Then we're down the street like a shot, James's hands tightening on my waist. I shout a *you okay* over my shoulder, but I can't hear his answer, not with him wearing my helmet. As I slow for a turn, he leans instinctively with me, tilting toward the right. My handlebars glint in the setting sun.

I park on the street in Puerto Madero, near a restaurant I know he'll like, one that would've been out of the question if he hadn't agreed to get on my bike. Well? I ask when he steps onto the sidewalk and takes off the helmet that he's been giving me shit for not wearing myself. Cool, he says, shrugging like he doesn't want to admit the truth, and I hide my smile. I've seen that look before.

James / Corinthia

This trip's been a disaster from the start. We're underfunded and overworked and the farmer who came across the remnants of this temple when he plowed his field last summer lost his spirit of cooperation about the time we started digging up his farm. Whatever, I know we're more than a minor inconvenience but we're talking about a potentially magnificent discovery here—if we can come up with anything worthwhile. So far we've unearthed a whole lot of nothing and our farmer friend, without the bragging rights he expected wants his goddamn field back. We're moving as fast as we can but we've had two cases of theft so far and torrential rains we didn't expect. I'm living my life in the mud.

Henry's not any happier than his daddy. He's done with his sitter, done with the rain, done with never seeing me and when I get Joel on the phone—which I've managed twice in the past month—I don't feel so agreeable. I know it's not Joel's responsibility to watch my kid every summer and I know I'm the one who fucked us up last year. I still could've used the help, and hearing him go on and on about glass I lose my patience. Not at him—hell no. I'm not that stupid. I grit my teeth and grit my way through our call as Henry clings to my leg, screaming around that pacifier. His sitter's working out about as well as our excavation.

Then there's a day in the middle of August that dawns so bright and beautiful I remember why I wanted to come here. Something's going to happen today and when I get to the site my colleague, the one who invited me here, waves me on over. We're close, he says, keeping it simple and man, I feel it too. The air out here shimmers like something sacred. I'm ready to figure out what we've been missing.

I've been in the mud for over an hour when I feel air on my cheek, a kiss from the dead. I turn nice and slow like if I move too fast I'm going to find out I'm wrong. But there's the hole, right there in plain sight, about the size of my little finger. David, I say and he can tell by the sound of my voice I've got something.

We're in the room by the end of the week, pushing nightfall but fueled by what we've found. In the light of that setting sun I get a glimpse of the ground.

Looks like my summer has a mosaic too.

Joel / Houston

I'm not here just because I feel obligated.

This is what I tell myself as we sit in front of the television, my father propped on a sofa never intended for use as a sickbed. Saffron tassels sprout from the pillow that cradles his head, lending a jaundiced hue to his pallid complexion. Beneath a cashmere blanket, he crosses and uncrosses his stocking feet, unable to get comfortable; he's midway through a second round of chemotherapy, though the doctors haven't made any promises. Every few minutes, Catherine makes another offering: hot tea, vegetable soup from the next-door neighbor, a plate of cookies with a smattering of chocolate sprinkles. He meets every suggestion with scorn. I've stopped trying to convince him he'd be better off on a raw food diet, that maybe he should cease the chemo altogether. Privately, I give Catherine a dozen links she should read. Tonight, she talks about ice cream, which my father considers for half a second before he rejects.

I'm not here just because I feel obligated.

This is what I tell myself as I sit in an armchair beside my father, feigning interest in the political shows he watches with increasing frequency. He admires Barack Obama for his pluck, despises his ideology; I glean this information not because we have a conversation, but because I know my father. And he does not do sick well.

I catch him looking at me and feel like I should apologize for being in good health, for the length of my hair, for the strength in my arms when I help him toward the stairs. My second morning here, I went for a run, and when I returned, wiping the sweat from my face with the hem of my shirt, I had to shake the uncomfortable feeling that he'd rather this was happening to me.

I miss my mosaic. I miss the feel of glass running through my fingers like crystallized beads of water. I miss Elías—the guy I've been seeing for the past few weeks—though not enough to call him. Maybe I don't even miss him. Maybe I just feel nostalgic for my life in Buenos Aires, which I've abandoned in favor of this visit to my father, with whom I've always had a contentious relationship. For years, I felt like I had to hide from him. Literally—he's responsible for at least half of the scars on my arms—but also figuratively. I wasn't honest with him about my art, my sexual orientation, or my anger, which burned at such a steady rate for so many years that I didn't even realize how much a part of my life fury had become. I was twenty-eight before I finally stopped apologizing for who I am. Since then, we've shared mostly polite, if superficial, interactions. I'm not sure how much longer our father/son façade can hold up.

I'm not here just because I feel obligated, but I'm not sure I can explain why I left my work behind to make this trip. My father doesn't want me here. My presence does nothing except make him think he's going to die. That I've traveled five thousand miles to see him leaves him just as suspicious of my intentions as it leaves me.

If I'm not here for his money, I must be here for his love, and that's about as depressing as you can get.

James / Chicago

I pick Joel up from O'Hare and leave him alone. Whatever, it's hard as shit not to break into a monologue about the work I left behind a few weeks ago—I've been wanting to get him alone for more than a month to talk to him about that mosaic—but one look at him when I pull to the curb in front of the airport has me shutting my mouth. His last trip to Houston wound him up good and tight and I'm guessing this visit wasn't any better. We're not going to be belting out Ice Cube on the way home, not this time around. He drops into the passenger seat with a half-assed hello then stares out the window. Those circles under his eyes mean he hasn't slept much and the way he's drumming his fingers on his leg reminds me of a trip we made to Houston just after the holidays our sophomore year in college, a trip I wish I couldn't remember. Man, I don't even want to think about what happens when his dad dies.

I keep quiet all the way back to my brownstone but I can't help Henry's excitement and I brace myself as I open the front door, nodding at his new sitter. If I know my kid he'll come flying through the dining room on his tricycle—*my bike* he calls it thanks to Joel—and crash right into us. Sure enough, here he comes, bent over the handlebars like a miniature Hell's Angel. The second he sees Joel he pulls up short and lets go of a crooked little smile that makes us both laugh. Nice bike, Joel tells him. Henry climbs off and pats the seat with his hand. You gonna give Joel a hug? I ask but I should've known I didn't need to wonder. Joel's already swinging him into his arms. Can I have a ride? he asks Henry and my boy giggles. This right here I missed, watching the two of them together and I catch Joel's eye to make sure he's up for it. Got any beer? he asks covertly.

He drinks three of them, one right after the other. After a while his eyes lose the edge I saw when he first got in my Volvo and I make a quiet call for a pizza so he'll have something in his belly if he decides he isn't finished drinking. Dinner's on the way, I say and he gives me a slow nod from where he's sitting on the couch watching *Wow! Wow! Wubbzy!* with Henry. Get me another beer, would you? he says. You sure? I ask and he looks at me the way he used to when I grilled him about going to class those first few weeks after his mom died.

I get him a beer and pray for that pizza to come and when the car pulls up to the house I meet the delivery guy halfway down the front steps. Keep the change, I tell him, hustling back inside and turning off the television without giving Henry a countdown. He howls until I show him the pizza box. Then he clambers down from the couch and gets on his tricycle for the trip into the kitchen. You too, Joel, I order when it looks like he's not going to move and he drags ass same as he did back in college when he'd sleep for days and I'd finally tell him to shake it off at least long enough to eat. Now he slouches at the table, his head in his hand. I have to put the pizza on his plate for him. Eat, I say, kicking his foot.

He gets two slices in him and I guess I've got to be satisfied. Hell, he'd probably tell me I don't need the four slices I just mowed through like I hadn't eaten all week. You want any more, Henry? I ask my son but he's leaning over his booster seat dropping pieces of crust for the cat we just adopted. It's big and orange and charming as hell when it's hungry so the damn thing has doubled in size since we brought it home last week. Rufus doesn't need your dinner, I tell Henry.

Yeah, that's right. Rufus. My kid christened the family pet with a name he can't even pronounce. Wufus wants some, Henry whines and I touch his hand and look at Joel, hoping he'll give me a little help. He's staring off into space like Henry and I are background noise, some stupid sitcom he could just as easily put on mute. I'm guessing it's pointless to ask if he wants to give my kid a bath.

I handle everything myself same as I always do and when I get back downstairs after Henry's asleep I find Joel in front of the television with what I'm hoping is his fifth beer and not his sixth. You good? I ask, sitting down beside him and he takes a look at his bottle. Then, tilting his head back he looks up at *Crossing*. I crane around and find my own image under that line of red. James Fielding, age twenty-five, pre-PhD, pre-marriage, pre-kid and right smack in the middle of something I still don't understand. Long time ago, he says like he knows what I'm thinking. Hell, he probably does. No one knows me better than Joel. Twelve years, I say and he nods, running his hand through his hair.

We look back at the TV. I borrow his beer. I've got a shit ton of work I'm probably not going to start tonight. I don't even care.

Joel / Buenos Aires

I met Elías at a gas station, which wasn't as seedy as it sounds. He was at the pump next to mine, and he asked about my bike, which still feels—except for the glass—like the best thing that's happened to me since I moved to Buenos Aires. I've been riding now for almost four months, and some afternoons, I drive away from the city just for the feel of an open road and the wind in my hair. When I get back to my studio, I need to steep myself in the shower to get warm, and I'm reminded of my trip to Chicago last month. The first of the fall fronts blew through the night I arrived, and I'd shivered on the sofa in the living room. Henry had moved out of his crib, and with him sleeping in the single bed on the third floor, there was nowhere else for me to go. You're not sleeping on the couch, James informed me, but I didn't like the idea of spending the night in his bed without Henry between us. What do you think I'm going to do, he said, Grope you in your sleep?

Luckily, I laughed, which diffused some of the tension that seems to follow us from year to year, from country to country. He brought me some blankets and told me he'd see me in a little while; he wasn't lying. An hour and I was standing outside his bedroom door, shivering. Told you so, he said, without looking up from his reading. I got under his covers, so cold I couldn't care less how close he got. I slept well for the rest of the week.

The day I met Elías, the air felt like spring, but faintly, like the clouds could have a change of heart and chase away the sun. I still needed the leather jacket I'd picked up one day at a flea market a few blocks from my studio, and I had a mild regret shrugging my arms through the sleeves, not because the weather necessitated its wearing, but because I gave up cigarettes. The jacket makes me want a Marlboro, and that afternoon, I stopped at a gas station not so much to fill the motorcycle's tank as to buy a pack of gum, which I hoped would stave off my craving long enough to overcome it. I came out of the store unwrapping a piece and saw someone circling my bike. The guy looked up as I approached, and for some strange reason, I offered him a piece of gum. His eyebrows darted up like a pair of errant sparrows. *Extraño,* he said. *Weird.* But he took the gum as well as my number.

I've since discovered that Elías speaks a little English, but that first conversation we held in Spanish, a language I could barely navigate in my college class and now need, ironically, on a daily basis. Elías and I see each other a couple of times a week and talk even less. He's biding his time; I know the signs. For now, I don't feel like discouraging him. I've been lonely here, and the first time I let Elías into my studio, and then my bed, I feel a relief that rushes over into the rest of my day. After he leaves, I choose a 60 x 60 gallery-wrapped canvas and paint without wondering where I'm going, working so late I lose the light and have to finish with my studio lamp burning beside me. *Circles.* They bleed outward, reminding me of the tie-dye shirts I used to see for sale along the Drag back in college. James had one, garish in color, that he wore to Barton Springs when he didn't need his lifeguard whistle around his neck. I can see him now, barefoot on our back porch with a beer in his hand, his hair still wet from the pool. For my purposes, I've chosen a muted palette, and I give my attention to two simple circles that brush up against each other and spin off in different directions, then replicate with minor variations and sync up again. *Circles.*

Elías isn't my boyfriend, though he might disagree. We don't talk in specifics. *Cuantos años tienes?* I asked last night. *How old are you? Veintiseis,* he said. *Twenty-six,* and I thought about where I was at twenty-six, living in that house on Pearl Street, smoking cigarettes and spiraling. I'll be thirty-seven in a few months, and I suppose that's something to celebrate. I might not be here at all.

James / Chicago

I got roped into trick-or-treating with some of the parents from Henry's preschool and we've caravanned to the most kid-friendly neighborhood where my son, cute as a cowboy, bites a ballerina when she snags his stick horse and decapitates it with one swing. Henry shrieks like we're in a scene from *The Godfather* and goes on the attack. I'm mortified. He never bites, I say, sounding just like every other parent making the same claim and within two minutes we've been ostracized to the back of the group with the stragglers. I have a really hard time not smacking the shit out of my son and I try one of those deep breaths I've seen Joel take a thousand times and crouch down beside Henry, trying to ignore the dirty princess picking her nose right beside us. You got so mad, I say to my kid and even though he's sobbing he gives me a big old nod like yeah, I *did*. I nod back at him, giving my sympathy a little time to sink in before I tell him that even when we're pissed we don't go around biting people. My hoss got bwoked, he whines. *Bwoked.* I know, buddy, I say, That sucks. That sucks, he repeats darkly and I try not to look at the parents judging the profane little vampire I'm raising. *By myself,* I add silently because whatever, it's Halloween and who the hell knows where my ex-wife is tonight. You still wanna go trick-or-treatin'? I ask and he sniffles. Man, I'm almost hoping he says no and that makes me feel like the delinquent daddy I've been since we left for Greece in June.

After a summer in the dirt I came back to Chicago and threw myself right into the fall quarter. Every spare second I've got I've been writing up what we found outside Corinthia, submitting papers for publication and trying to line up as many conferences as I can. The only time I took a break was when Joel came here and that's because he showed up looking like he was the one with the shitty diagnosis and not his dad. More and more often I've been late picking up Henry from preschool and now that he moved into his big boy bed—he kept climbing out of his crib in the middle of the night and the first time I saw him standing beside my bed in the dark I almost had a heart attack—I don't even get nights with him. I don't think I realized how much I'd been counting that time as quality over the last couple years. Him too I guess, which might explain the way he went after the ballerina and the way he's still standing in front of me with tears running down his cheeks. I pull him into a hug until he stops crying. You ready to get some candy, buddy? I ask and he nods.

I scoop him up and hightail after our group, falling into step a minute later with the momma of that dirty princess. She squeezes out a tight-ass smile then looks away. Whatever, Henry's happy and I walk alongside him, thinking about Halloween my sophomore year in college and how I'd wandered down Sixth Street wearing a Dracula cape and fangs. Joel wasn't wearing a costume, he never wore a costume, not until he and Adam got together. One year they went as a police officer and prisoner, another year as a pirate and his wench. You're wearin' a *dress*? I asked in disbelief and he said, I look good in it. Or maybe he said, Adam likes it. Or maybe he said both and I just can't remember but a few nights later he emailed me a picture and I squinted at it a while before I caught on that this was *Joel* I was staring at in a corset and eye liner. And now hell, that's what's on my mind as I trudge down the windy street with Henry holding my hand, that picture and our phone call this afternoon. He's got a date with someone named Elías tonight and I'm betting he's the same guy I caught Joel talking to when he was here last month.

Whatever, I shouldn't say *caught* like Joel was doing something wrong.

I could hear him as soon as I closed the door of Henry's room at the top of the second flight of stairs, not the words but the laugh, the same laugh I remembered from that Christmas after he broke up with Adam. I caught that laugh and crept down the steps, keeping care to tread wide when I hit the one that creaked. Is that what you want to hear? Joel asked into the phone and I took another step, his voice kicking up all kinds of confusion. Why was I sneaking up on him like this? Tell me, he said like he was talking to me and only me except he wasn't and I knew it and I got pissed enough to forget why he'd ended up in Chicago in the first place. I took the last couple steps in a leap that made me think I might still be in that Cretan cemetery. Even then I thought it was bullshit the way he shoved his phone out of sight down between the cushions on the couch like maybe that'd mean I hadn't seen him. I could've let him off the hook and I probably should've, given what he'd left behind a few days earlier in Houston but instead I dropped down beside him and dug around until I found his phone. Anyone I know? I asked. I just met him, he said. You sounded awfully fuckin' familiar to me, I told him and he got real quiet. Am I supposed to apologize? he finally asked.

No way could I name everything going on in those eyes of his but I felt like I'd made a couple wrong turns and ended up on the shitty side of town. All that work making us right and I was going to end up having to start from scratch again—if he let me. Nah, man, I said, handing over his phone, You're supposed to tell me about him.

He didn't. He said there wasn't anything to tell, they'd just started hanging out and he'd be sure to give me a heads up once they set a date for the wedding. I grimaced and got us both a beer and we talked about what time he should pick up Henry from preschool the next day. Until this morning I'd shoved the memory from my mind but then Joel casually mentioned a date with some Elías dude earlier today and what the fuck ever, I've been thinking about it ever since.

I bet he's the same goddamn guy.

Henry and I follow the dirty ballerina up someone's front steps. Twick or tweat, Henry sings, holding out his jack-o'-lantern when I prod him. In go a couple Blow Pops and a Snickers bar. Thank you, Henry says solemnly, turning to show me his loot. Nice job, I say, You wanna try another house?

He holds out longer than I expect and I finally haul him back to the car as he sucks on a Blow Pop. I've got a feeling I'm going to be eating a shitload of candy over the next few days just so he doesn't eat all this himself and I buckle him in his car seat then glance at him in the rearview mirror as I start my Volvo. You have fun tonight, buddy? I ask but he's got that glassy look in his eyes that tells me he's too tired to answer and by the time I pull up in front of our brownstone he's sound asleep, his lips red and sticky. I sit there for a second, staring at my son and goddamn, it's not my ex-wife I wish were with me.

Joel / Buenos Aires

I drop my bike for the first time on a day I should've known better than to ride. We've had rain all morning, and though the clouds have parted, I look off to the left of my studio and have a feeling we're getting the last of the light. But I'm out of cement, and I'm getting close enough that I don't want to wait until tomorrow to work. I'm not finished with my mosaic, not yet, but I'm starting to see something take shape, and I want to know what happens next.

I'm two blocks from home when the rain comes. My first thought goes to the cement, a bag on either side of my bike. If they get wet, this whole excursion was for nothing, and I speed up, realizing too late that today would've been a good day to wear my helmet. Without that visor, rainwater stings my eyes and wrecks my visibility. I've been watching for rainbows on the road, keeping my bike upright, when I spot a manhole cover; the metal might as well be ice when it's wet. But it's the corner that kills me. I take it the way I always do, leaning into the curve, but suddenly the rear wheel loses traction and steps out so fast I'm skidding. I'm on the ground before I know what's happening, the bike sliding right past me. I'm lucky; there's no traffic, and I sit in the rain, jeans torn and leg bleeding, then stagger over to my bike. I'm the one with the scratches, though, and I breathe a little prayer of thanks. I wouldn't have been able to afford the repairs.

Elías croons over the rash on my thigh, the contusion on my elbow. I let him spend the night. After he drifts off, I take a closer look at my leg. The road ripped the hair right off, and I wish for my shaman back in Austin, who could probably recommend some kind of poultice to speed the healing. What did I give to Adam, back when we were together? He wiped out more than once, and I worried about him every time he cycled, especially if I didn't like the look of the weather.

I wonder if he's still cycling. I wonder if he has anyone to worry about him the way I have—

Who? Elías? He's...

Attractive, attentive, available. All of the above.

I limp to the other side of my studio for my phone, then slip outside into the damp courtyard. Under the Erythrina tree, I sit on my landlady's bench, stretching my injured leg out in front of me. My jeans will be wet, but I want to hear James's voice. Holy shit, he says when I tell him what happened. I glance at my motorcycle glistening in the gloom, tell him about wanting to make a run for the cement, about the rain, about the skid that stole my oldest pair of jeans. I burned the shit out of my leg, I say, But the gloves saved my hands. Were you wearing your helmet? he asks, and when I admit I wasn't, he says, Jesus, Joel. I know, I mumble, With the rain— Fuck the rain, he insists, You need to wear your helmet, period.

I'm probably wasting time if I argue with him, and I mutter something that might mean I agree, which he doesn't buy. Don't make me tell my kid you're dead, he says. How's Henry doing anyway? I ask, and that's all he needs to get off the subject. He talks about Thanksgiving, about their plans to go to Fort Worth, to take Henry to the zoo. Remember that time we snuck into the Botanic Gardens back in college? he asks. Vividly, I say. You sure you don't want to meet us up there? he asks. I'll see you after Christmas, I remind him.

I'm going to Houston for the holiday. My father isn't doing well, and though I'd never visit at that time of year, especially considering our history, Catherine intimated the last time we spoke that I should make the trip. I don't want to think too much about what her suggestion means, but I have a feeling I'm going to find out.

Henry misses you, man, James admits, I do too. I look across the courtyard at my studio, where Elías sleeps without me. Do me a favor, I say, Don't hang up yet.

James / Fort Worth

My sister's in town from Santa Cruz for the holiday and my folks don't know what to do with her. For the last three years they've given her ultimatums. If she can't get to her classes, if she can't make decent grades, they're not going to keep paying her tuition. Need I remind you, my dad has said to her more than once, You could be going to TCU for free. Ashley's always got the same answer. Fort Worth is hours away from the ocean. This surfer girl has no desire to be landlocked.

Ashley's exactly the sort of student I despise but she's my sister and I'm not grading her exams. Talk to her, my mom pleads the morning after I pick Ashley up at the airport. We've all been awake for hours except for my sister who sleeps with the same commitment she brings to surfing and sex. Nothing I can say she hasn't heard a thousand times, I tell my mom, pouring a third cup of coffee. She's never going to graduate, my mom says. So stop paying her tuition, I suggest and my mom gives her head a worried little shake like actually following through on their threat might be too harsh. Maybe you can take her out for lunch, she says.

I figure I'll do that anyway. Ashley always waits until Christmas Eve to do her shopping and my mom wants Henry's help decorating a gingerbread house. Like *Hansel and Gwetel!* he crowed when she showed him and I shook my head. Joel read him that damn story back in September, never mind how much I protested. I was concerned Henry would be scared but instead he's obsessed, leaving trails everywhere he goes. Do you want to help me decorate the gingerbread house? my mom asked my son but that's a no-brainer. Henry hasn't had candy since Halloween. He got one look at the peppermints and licorice sticks and his mouth opened in a cute little O. I still don't want to be around for the aftermath. You put Henry down for his nap this afternoon, I tell my mom, And I'll try to talk some sense into your daughter.

That's how I find myself at University Park Village on Christmas Eve. I've convinced my sister to walk—the weather's unseasonably warm and my parents live just a few blocks from campus—and Ashley pulls me toward Blue Mesa. Let's start with a drink, she says and somehow we end up sitting outside with margaritas. You got a list at least? I ask, Or an idea of what you need to buy? Where's the fun in a list? she laughs. I can't be gone too long, I warn her. Relax, she tells me, Mom's been dying to get some time alone with Henry.

I don't see how Ashley would know that since she just got here last night. Mom's worried about you, I say and she rolls her eyes. Mom needs to get out more, she tells me. Mom had a double mastectomy a few years ago, I remind her and she says, All the more reason for her to have a little fun.

My sister sounds kind of callous but she's right about our mom needing more fun, same as she's right about her wanting to spend time with Henry. You're still blowing through their money, Ashley, I mutter and she heaves a big old sigh and tells me they can stop paying when they're ready. Then what're you gonna do? I ask, Without a college degree? I'll figure it out, she says, shrugging. I wish I could be that nonchalant, I tell her. I bet you were, she sings, When you were my age!

Was I? For just a second I close my eyes and drop myself back in time to when I was around Ashley's age, to our house on Pearl after Joel broke up with Darryl, that guy who worked for UPS. I finally had Joel all to myself and we spent every night on the front porch or smoking in the backyard. The conversation we'd had over the summer, the one about Puritanism and repression and that lecture I'd heard about the Battle of Chaeronia left me trying to figure out what that had to do with the burning in my gut every time I thought about Joel with someone else. Maybe we were supposed to move forward. Maybe I was holding us back.

So I brought home a bag of pot. When we were good and stoned and I'd toked away my apprehension I stepped toward him. He tried to stop me, I'll give him that. He said some bullshit about not sleeping with his friends and I felt like he'd caught me on the chin, lumping me in with everyone else. I kissed him a second time, pissed and defiant. The hard line of his jaw and the flatness of his chest under my hand wasn't like any girl I'd ever touched and I shoved him into my bedroom. Is this really happening? he whispered. I was tempted to laugh but I didn't and I didn't answer him either.

I wasn't a good lover. I'd just turned twenty-five, first of all, and while multiple partners was a way of life for Joel it sure as shit wasn't for me. I was deep in grad school and girls seemed like their own kind of hell. I had plenty of friends who were girls but I didn't sleep with them and I didn't know what to do with Joel. Whatever, I knew what I wanted in the moment but when we were finished I just wanted to get away from him. I felt like Pandora: the box open, my curiosity satisfied and the winds of evil swirling around me.

So, no. *Nonchalant* wouldn't be the word I'd choose.

I open my eyes, convinced Ashley's going be staring at me with her eyebrows raised but she's doing that texting thing on her phone. Who pays for that bill? Our parents? You dating anyone out there in California? I ask. Sure, she says, shrugging without looking up from her phone. Anyone in particular? I ask and she laughs.

There's nothing wrong with my sister sleeping around but there's enough of the Texas boy left in me that doesn't want to think she's a slut. I squirm around in my seat until she looks up. You really have to get over yourself, she says. You're gonna do what you're gonna do, I mumble and she says, What about you? I try to flag our waiter, not sure if I'm fixing to ask for the check or another margarita. I don't have the time to date, I tell her. You have to get laid every once in a while, James, she advises. I do all right, I mutter and she gives me a look like she knows better. Hey, how's Joel? she asks. He's fine, I grumble, He's getting laid plenty.

Well, that came out sounding bitter as hell. I clear my throat as Ashley cozies up to the table like I'm about to let her in on the latest gossip. Jesus, Ashley, I say, irritated. Oh, you're *jealous*, she crows. I don't care who he fucks, I inform her and now her eyebrows shoot way the hell up. I meant because he's getting laid, she says, What did *you* think I meant? Nothin', I say, waving again at our waiter, Let's get another drink.

We get home later than we expected and drunk to boot. Those blue margaritas were strong as shit though I knew that going in and still ordered a second one. We blew through our shopping, stumbling through Barnes & Noble and Pottery Barn then walking back to our folks' house, where my mom takes one look at me and tells me I'm just as bad as my sister. I mumble an apology with one eye on the couch. *Can I sneak in a nap before Henry wakes up?* Don't even think about it, my mom says.

Joel / Houston

I've tried. I've made the trip—at Christmas no less, knowing the kind of trouble my father and I have around the holidays—and I've done my best to spend time with him, whatever time we have left. But it's clear he would've preferred if I hadn't come. I'm too much of a reminder of what he has lost, and while he might be able to cordially receive the few friends and colleagues he'll still allow to cross his threshold, the fact of the matter is that my presence here has been met with something just shy of animosity. We haven't quarreled; nothing outwardly hostile has been said. But there's a pervasive tension that runs between us like a current, undercutting every gesture I extend.

Then, on my last night in town, something softens. My father has a good day, and I think I surprise everyone, including myself, when I suggest that we spend the evening alone, without Catherine. After she leaves, when he asks if I'll pour us each a scotch, I change the subject and tell him we should go outside. Let's get some fresh air, I say. He agrees, and I maneuver him through the back door and onto the deck. There's a chill to the air beneath the humidity, and as he settles into a chair, staunchly refusing my help, I go inside for his cashmere throw. Coming back, just inside the door, I watch him, feeling a thickness in my throat at the thought that he'll likely not be here this time next year. He'll be lucky to make it to spring.

Outside, I hand him the throw, knowing he won't want me draping it over his shoulders. He crumples the cashmere in his lap as if my fuss isn't necessary, but I notice the way he adjusts his position, trying to maximize the blanket's warmth. Whatever we've held between us, I hate watching him suffer. I finally turn away, pretending to be absorbed in the quiet lapping of the pool. I've spent my share of time here the past few days; Catherine likes the water heated, and though there's a part of me that finds the expense outrageous, I also don't know that I would've made it through this visit without a pool for escape.

For a while, we're quiet, our proximity enough. Tilting my head back, I examine the sky, absent a moon and blurred with light reflected from the city. My last night here with him and how many more after that? Five? Ten? How many more greetings will we share, how many goodbyes? With my mother, I had no warning. She was here; she was gone. Without my father, I may feel far more alone than I anticipate.

There's a minute part of me, foolish and naïve, that wants to tell him what I'm thinking. I might even be optimistic enough to open my mouth, but then he speaks in a voice that sounds mildly annoyed, as if he can guess what I'm thinking and disapproves. Where's that scotch? he demands. Really, Dad, I start, and he says, Joel, pour me a fucking drink, or I'll have to go in there myself. I take note of the slight trembling of the hand that clutches his cashmere and sigh. Neat, he says as I move past him, as if I've never watched him make a drink, as if I don't know the way he likes it.

As if I've never made one of my own.

At the sideboard, I pour a drink for each of us. I've not had a scotch in years; I don't like the taste or the memories that accompany its aroma. But something—some authoritative note in my father's voice or some ancient desire to please him—makes me reach for two glasses. The pleasure he exudes when I return to him armed with two drinks awakens something deep in my gut. Without speaking, we clink glasses, then sip. I'm knocked backwards over years I'd rather forget.

A few swallows and the silence we share no longer feels companionable. I ponder my options, realizing with a slow dread that short of leaving him here alone, I don't have any. I glance at my father, who stares back with a malevolence I don't think I'm imagining. Then he smiles, and I'm suddenly not sure of anything. It's good to see you with a drink in your hand, he tells me. I nod, certain I'll say the wrong thing if I open my mouth. He reflects on his glass, like he's becoming reacquainted with an old friend. Catherine wouldn't approve, he confides, winking at me, and I feel—and simultaneously despise myself for feeling—flattered that he's including me in his transgression. I chase the emotion with a healthy dose of scotch, as if years in therapy taught me nothing.

As the liquor tightens its grip on my sanity, my father's tongue loosens. First, he tells me that he stashed some money overseas so the sons of bitches who indicted him two years ago for tax fraud can't get their hands on his money. He'd like to leave a little something for Catherine, even though she has her own money, but there's plenty left for me. We've never talked about what would happen after his death, and now he admits that he'd like to see me use some of what he's leaving behind. *In addition to a legacy of pain and humiliation?* I hear James asking as if he's right beside me, and when my father gives me a long, contemplative look, I worry I've spoken aloud. You're a lightweight, he snorts, with the same distaste he'd use if he declared me a pussy.

Right now, in this moment, I feel like I've never left his house.

Thirty minutes later, we're on our second drinks. In a moment of greater conviction, I would've refused to pour him another, wouldn't have indulged myself. Instead, I went inside as if I'd been born without a backbone, came back and sat beside him as he told me about the rat Catherine found drowned in the pool last week and the nest the exterminator found in the attic. I'm weepy at the thought and mull in silence about their little deaths until my father barks at me to snap out of it.

Our evening has deteriorated; I've given in to him with the same apprehensions and fear I've exhibited for most of my life. For a moment, I shut my eyes; what I want is to leave this house, and tomorrow's flight to Chicago doesn't feel soon enough. *Mephistopheles,* James called my father once, years ago, but I'm not laughing anymore.

When I open my eyes, I expect to find my father watching me. Instead, he's gazing off across the backyard. His despair feels so acute that I straighten, setting what's left of my drink on the table beside me. The motion catches his peripheral vision, and when he looks my way, I meet his eyes with none of the hesitance I feel. For the briefest moment, he looks frightened. When I speak, my voice quavers with a confusion and sorrow made more profound by alcohol I never should have poured. Dad, I say, I love you.

My father looks into my eyes, which feel so raw and naked with pleading I half-expect to shed tears of blood. Then he struggles to his feet and goes inside.

James / Chicago

I knew Joel would be done in from his trip to Houston but I figured he'd be all right after a day or so. Instead he holes up in my bedroom and starts sleeping, which was pretty much how he spent his time after his mom died. I'm worried about him and Henry's not making life easier, whining because Joel's not giving him any attention. My boy's tired anyway from our trip to Fort Worth over the holiday where he was overstimulated and overindulged same as always and even though by now he'd probably be mellowing some, having Joel here but catatonic has him tied up every which-a-way. I might as well be dealing with two kids here.

On Joel's third night in town I park my cranky son in front of the TV while Joel watches me clean up after a dinner he didn't eat. What the fuck *happened* down there, man? I finally ask and he has to get halfway through a six-pack before he can tell me. I'm so stunned I sit my ass down. That motherfucker, I say and Joel shrugs in a way that doesn't fool me for a second. He's dying, he mumbles. Don't do that, I hiss, Don't make excuses for him! You have to look at the context, James, he says. He burned holes in your arms! I remind him, You gonna justify that too?

Now he's looking at me like I'm the one who lit the damn cigars. Whatever, I might've gone a little too far but I don't need him to pull up his sleeves to see the scars he's carrying and I'm not just talking about what his dad did to him. I'm not the only one who drove Joel to pick up that box cutter ten years ago. You shouldn't have gone there for Christmas, I tell him. What was I supposed to do, James? he says, He's my father.

Well, that means a whole lot of nothing in my book. What matters is how Joel's being treated and one look at him slumped over the kitchen table tells me everything I need to know. I don't want you goin' back there, I order and he tells me I might just get my wish. He's dying, he admits and his voice splinters right in half.

Quick as I can I bring him in close, my mouth to his ear. I don't know what all I'm murmuring, something like *okay all right let it out* same as he did for me that night in the cemetery the week before Henry was born. He finally starts to settle down but I hold on tight until I think he's good and calm. My head..., he says when I pull back. You're taking a couple Advil whether you want to or not, I inform him, But you gotta lay off the beer.

I bring his Advil and take his Coors and after he closes his eyes on the couch I grab Henry so I can hustle him into the bath. I've tucked him under my arm like a giant football and he giggles as I run up the stairs. Man, those cigarettes haven't done me any favors. I do a little touchdown dance once we hit the bathroom then stand Henry up on the sink facing the mirror so I can raise his arms over his head. Hip hip..., I say and he shouts with that sweet lisp of his, Hooway! I pull his shirt over his head as I catch my breath. Nice job, buddy, I say, swinging him off the sink and plunking him on the floor in front of the tub. I tug his little socks off his feet and make a face so he laughs then wriggle his pants over his bottom. I've got to get this kid potty-trained but so far he's about as complacent as they come. You wanna try— I start but he's already digging around in his bucket of toys. I turn on the faucets, making sure the water's not too hot. Leaning over the tub, he drops an octopus and starfish in the water, adding a velociraptor from his dinosaur set. I put him in with the toys.

I should've brought Joel's Coors upstairs with me. If I could make it downstairs and back again without worrying that my kid would drown I would. I don't see how Joel stopped at three. If I'd just come off his holiday I'd be looking around for a shot glass and a bottle of tequila. No wonder he spent the past few days in bed.

Henry's leaving a trail of bubbles along the side of the tub and I hear him say something about the witch. *Hansel and Gretel* again. He's probably going to want Joel to read that to him before bed. I touch my boy's cheek. His skin's white and smooth, perfect except for one tiny scar where Lizzie scraped his leg on the underside of the kitchen counter when he was nine months old. As pissed as I got when she showed me I knew she hadn't acted out of malice. She'd had an accident and she felt bad about it. I can't imagine intentionally hurting my son and thinking about what Joel's dad did to him gives me my own damn headache.

I don't know Joel's scars like I could. I saw them from the start, not when we were living in the dorm but once I started lifeguarding at Barton Springs. Every time I worked, Joel would come along with me and swim and one day he pulled his shirt on just as I hopped down from the chair for my break. I might not have noticed if I hadn't caught him with his arms over his head. I almost said something but I stopped myself, intuition slamming my mouth shut the way those cigars must've shut his own. He finally told me about them one Christmas when we were sitting in the swing in the middle of the night. We were out there because he'd had a nightmare and given that he'd come back from Houston days ahead of schedule I figured that seeing his dad had triggered something. What do those dreams of yours have to do with him anyway? I asked and that's when he told me. I could hardly look at his arms even though he'd twisted one around to show me.

When we started sleeping together I didn't pay Joel's arms any more attention than I did the rest of him, which is to say that for the most part I closed my eyes and fucked him. But that's a whole other story. Or hell, maybe it's the same one. I don't even know anymore.

The scars on Joel's arms, the ones he made with that box cutter in '98 I try to ignore and that's partly because I don't think he wants me staring. The first time I saw them I almost broke down and wept. They were fresh then, less than a year old and I couldn't believe he'd cut into himself on purpose. Jesus, Joel, I'd said, *Jesus.* I couldn't take my eyes from them and that's when he blamed me for what happened and we went another couple months without speaking.

Co-dependent, one of our college friends called our relationship. *Wholly inappropriate* was my ex-wife's term. *A mind fuck*, Joel said our last night in Greece and hell, I guess not everyone's got a dynamic like ours. All I know is that from the first time I saw him in our dorm room I knew that what everyone else saw was bullshit compared to what he had going on under the surface. Maybe I could've pegged him for a poser but I never saw him that way. I just wanted to dig up the truth. I just wanted to know him.

Whatever. I still do.

Joel

I've never liked January. Approaching a new year, I can't always see the possibility in the days ahead of me. Maybe that's what happens when you have a childhood like mine. On the surface, my life seemed privileged. But from moment to moment, I never knew what might set my father off, and even though I tried my hardest not to upset him, I was bound to make mistakes. When I did, he let me know.

I've been doing my best over the past few days to forget what happened in Houston. Telling James might have helped; I can't decide. In the moment, I needed someone to hear me. Since then, I've been able to get out of bed. I'm eating. I can handle Henry, and that's important to me because soon enough, I'll be back in Buenos Aires, and who knows when I'll see him again?

When my father dies, most likely.

James couldn't be kinder, and maybe that's why there's a part of me that wishes I hadn't said a word. Ruminating about my father, I could convince myself that I was being melodramatic. I could make excuses. I could justify. Once the words left my mouth, once I saw James's expression, I knew I was fucked. James's deference toward me now is all the proof I need. You want me to open a bottle of wine? he asks, You feel like going to lunch? I try to choose the path of least resistance, but I stymie when James asks how I want to spend New Year's Eve. The thought of going out just about brings tears to my eyes. I know if I admit I'd just as soon skip the celebration, he'll tell me that's cool. He's not going to force me to party. But I can't imagine how far in advance he had to book his sitter. What'd you have in mind? I ask. We can keep it low-key, he shrugs, Dinner, drinks. Yeah, I say, Sounds good.

But I'm less capable of making it through the evening than I thought. Halfway through dinner, my hands start shaking. I hide the tremor under the table, but I'm not fooling anyone. You want to leave? James asks, setting his fork on his plate. I shake my head, determined not to make a scene, even the kind that simply calls for our check ahead of schedule. Listen, he says, We don't have to stay. Stop, I hiss, Stop being so nice to me.

The words feel familiar, and when he cocks his head like he's hearing an echo, I know I'm not saying them for the first time. I scratch through the dirt of my memory and come up with nothing. He has the moment pegged, though; I can tell by the way he's shifting his gaze.

Sometimes I hate how well he knows me.

You might as well tell me, I mutter. Tell you what? he asks. We're in a perpetual déjà vu, James, I say, Or haven't you noticed? He saws into his steak without answering, and I hold my glass steady with both hands the way Henry would, waiting for James to open up since he expects the same from me. He finally leans forward. Do you honestly want to talk about your mom's visitation? he asks.

That's all he has to say. Years drop away like I never lived them in the first place, and I stumble through the front doors of the funeral home and around the back of the building. The night hangs heavy and humid, James right behind me, and *Stop! Stop being so fucking nice to me!* I scream, because I think I'm the one to blame. He's wearing a suit and a tie he borrowed from my own closet, and I see him through my nineteen-year-old eyes. *Give me one goddamn minute to myself.* He walks away from me, and I crouch down at the back of the funeral home the night of my mother's visitation and cry.

Which makes for a better death? I ask, fast-forwarding eighteen years, Cancer or a gun to the head? Jesus, Joel, he mutters, and I remind him that not even a year and a half ago, he had me sprawled in a cemetery not far from this restaurant, talking about what would get us in the end. That was hypothetical, he says. And this isn't? I ask. I was trying to make sure you'd take Henry if something happened to me, he says, and I wink. Bet you're second guessing that request tonight, I tell him.

James

Well, that was a bust. I thought if I got Joel out of the house tonight he might lose the look he's been wearing since he got here, the one that reminds me of the construction paper Henry left on the back porch last summer. A few days in the sun and the color was done. I knew Joel wasn't up for a party but I figured he could handle sitting across from me at a restaurant with a bottle of wine. I'd made a reservation and arranged for a sitter weeks ago and even though he showed up here way worse than I expected I didn't see why we couldn't still find something to celebrate. A new year had to bring something good, right? We didn't have to talk about what happened in Houston. We didn't have to talk about his dad at all.

But halfway through dinner his hands started shaking. We can leave if you want, I finally said and he got pissed at me for giving him the kid-glove treatment. What was I supposed to do? Pretend like I didn't notice he was suffering? I've never been good at seeing him struggle. Not when his mom died, not when he broke up with Adam, not now.

I don't think I can let him leave on Sunday. I don't think he's doing well enough to go back to Buenos Aires alone. Who does he have there anyway? That guy who dances with the ballet? Élias doesn't know Joel. No way would Joel talk to him about his trip to Houston or what happened with his dad. What if Joel gets down there and can't get out of bed? Who's going to help him then?

Maybe you should stay here a while, I suggest on our way home. What do you mean? he asks and I shrug. Just for a week or two, I say, Just until you feel better. Why don't we stop off at the cemetery, he suggests. Now? I say, confused. Sounds like you think I'm going to end up there anyway, he points out, Might as well get the ball rolling. That's not funny, Joel, I mumble and he sighs like I'm being too sensitive about the wicked lines he cut into his arms. You're the one making it sound like I have a box cutter in my back pocket, he says.

I don't say anything but inside I'm crying. Minutes is all we're talking here. Minutes and Joel would be dead instead of sitting in the passenger seat of my Volvo. I keep my eyes on the road and try not to think about him opening his wrists in that bathroom on Pearl. I try not to think about how close he came to dying. I try not to think about how awful my life would be without him.

I'm sorry, he says, I'm not myself tonight.

Hell, I know that. I always know. That's what comes of a friendship that's twenty years gone.

What can I do? I ask but he doesn't have an answer.

Joel

I'm all over the place tonight, alternating between a serious frustration with James—just because he's being himself—and a fragility that makes me regret making that trip to Houston more than I've regretted just about anything in my life, ever. Part of me feels like screaming. Part of me wants to bury myself in James's bed and cry. I need the glass, my bike, a run.

Or a good, hard fuck. My eyes automatically drift toward James, the only potential object of attention here in Chicago, and that seems pretty masochistic, even for me. If I could get away with a phone call to Elías, I might try; he called a half a dozen times this week, and I've returned a call exactly once. You still seeing that guy? James asked my first night here, and when I shrugged, he grunted. He's jealous; surprise. Now I look him over like he's an option if I so choose.

We're watching reruns of *Friends*, a fairly depressing way to count down to the New Year, though I suppose it beats spending the holiday in the hospital with seventy-six fresh stitches in my arms, circa 1998. Could be worse, right? We're watching *Friends* and drinking wine, and I assess him from the corner of my eye, trying to be objective the way I would with any other hook-up and finding that impossible. Aside from the fact that he's not my type, I know him too well.

I shift my eyes back to the television as I take another sip of wine. I've had too much tonight, but at least I'm not shivering anymore. Instead, I jitter my leg, trying to diffuse the tension left in my body, tension I may have naturally been trying to eliminate with those tremors, and glance again at James. I haven't slept with him in almost twelve years, and most of the time I'm able to forget that we ever did. Only when he fucks up, like our last night in Greece or when he called Brice, does what happened between us hit me like I've belly flopped into a swimming hole.

Then there's the phone call the Christmas after I left Adam. But that hardly counts; I was plastered, and so was James. He never would've risked his marriage or Elizabeth's pregnancy, not if he wasn't drunk, and I know that somewhere in there, he thought he was doing me a favor. That whole conversation started out with him telling me I needed a distraction.

Which is exactly what he'd be right now. A distraction from what happened in Houston, from my father's inevitable demise, from the calls I keep getting from Elías, calls I want to want to answer but don't. From Adam, who must be thinking about me today, because how could he not? Ten years ago, he found me bleeding in my bathtub. I must be on his mind.

He's on mine. Now, still. I'm heading into another year without him, and nothing feels any easier. *Move on,* I told him in his parents' kitchen after his father's funeral, and here I stall. How can I not look back? I don't want to forget any part of us. I want to remember every moment. I want to remember the way he kissed me in Belize before breakfast as the sun blazed into our room. I want to remember his arms around me on our deck after a day spent in the pool. I want to remember the night I met him and the day he took me back—the second time. I want his hands, his mouth, his bed. I want him before he cheated.

I slide my eyes over James, taking liberties he's too naïve to notice. Even drunk, I know what I'm doing, and I stare at his messy head of hair. He yanked his shirt out from his jeans thirty minutes ago. I'm aware of the weight he's gained since he left Austin, since Henry was born. Big legs, muscular from doing a whole lot of nothing; I've told him more than once that running will streamline his quads, but he doesn't listen to me, swears he doesn't have the time. And his mouth… How did he kiss?

Like I was his nightmare. Like he couldn't let go. Like I was everything he wanted, and he was everything he feared.

So, that doesn't help. I reach for my wine, settling back closer than I was a moment ago, close enough to feel the heat from his body. He glances over at me, oblivious to the fact that right now, I'm this close to telling him what I need.

What I want? That's another story. What I want isn't in this room or this city. What I want disappeared the day I told Adam I wasn't cut out for kids. What I want I'm never getting back, not from Elías or anyone else I might find in Argentina.

What I need, however… What I need I can have with one well-placed hand. This isn't like the time I drove James to Padre a couple of years after we graduated from college, crushed by the weight of the love I felt for him and as terrified of him finding out as I was of never telling him at all. This is one friend helping another, because what I need right now he can give me, and it doesn't have to mean a thing. I know what he has under those pants, and though panache has never been James's forte—I know this for a fact—what I need isn't subtle. What I need isn't grace.

What I need is a good, hard fuck.

I lift my hand to touch him and never figure out where I would've landed. We both hear Henry on the stairs at the same moment. James jumps to his feet in alarm, and I squeeze my eyes shut. I'm saved and damned, and when James tells me over his shoulder not to go to sleep yet, I nod. No, I say, I won't.

James

On Joel's last full day before he heads back to Buenos Aires we take Henry ice skating. Neither one of us can skate for shit but we stumble across the ice anyway, Joel making more of an effort than he has all week and more than I expect given the way he's been feeling. I kind of thought he'd bag or at least sit on the sidelines. But he's trying with Henry for real and that night as I'm cleaning up the dinner dishes—on feet that make me feel for Achilles—I watch him flick a dishtowel back and forth, lost in thought. Henry wanders in and out of the kitchen, dragging a wooden pull-toy in the shape of a bunny rabbit. He keeps up a running monologue and even when he disappears through the doorway into the living room we can still hear him.

After eighteen years I'm used to Joel's silence but he's not thinking about his work right now. I'm not even sure he's chewing on what happened in Houston. Since New Year's Eve he's been weird with me. Don't go to sleep yet, I told him when Henry woke up but fuck if Joel wasn't sound ass asleep when I came back downstairs twenty minutes later. At first I couldn't even find him and figured he was on the back porch. Instead he'd gone to bed, lights out and everything. When's the last time you fell asleep before midnight on New Year's Eve? I asked the next morning and he gave me this real faint smile I haven't been able to stop thinking about since. He's not drinking either. Don't get me wrong, I'm not interested in the way he was drinking on New Year's Eve, swallowing one glass of wine after another the way he used to after his momma died but I like seeing him with a beer in his hand. Now he backs away when I offer to open a bottle. I figure I did something wrong somewhere along the way but I'm afraid to ask. I don't want to set him off, not when he's about to leave. I don't know when he's coming back to the States. I wouldn't blame him for keeping his distance even for the funeral.

Man, I hate the idea of going a long time without seeing him.

Washing the dishes I start thinking about the few friends I know from work. Every once in a while we go to see the Bulls, sitting in cheap seats and drinking beer, skimming the surface of anything more than departmental politics. Sometimes we grab a coffee in between classes and bitch about our students. But we never go any deeper. And what I'm finding the older I get is that none of the men I know do. Our wives supplanted whatever friendships we used to have, the ones held together by history and intimacy and the kind of freedom impossible to maintain with a mortgage and a car payment and kids. I'm not denigrating family. I wanted Henry years before he was born. A few of the men I know honestly love their wives. But somewhere along the way we've given something up and every so often I recognize how close I've come to losing the one person other than Henry who means the most to me.

Hey, I say but Joel doesn't look up. I need to get him out of wherever he's gone and without thinking I reach for the sprayer and squeeze the trigger. Water hits him square in the chest and he jumps back, his expression so shocked I can't tell which way he's going to go. What the hell? he says and I duck when he whips the dishtowel in my direction hard enough to sting. Taking a chance, I aim the sprayer again and he swivels, getting a shot on the back. Enough, he says, starting to laugh, Truce. Truce, I agree, happy to see him smiling again and when he turns back to me I drill him in the gut. He comes right at me, trying to wrestle the sprayer from my hand as I soak the front of his shirt, water all over the floor. I aim up, catching him right in the face. He lets go, wiping his eyes and laughing and the next thing I do comes with zero forethought.

I brace him against the sink, my fingers crawling through his hair and my body pressed so close I can feel the water from his shirt bleeding into mine. For five seconds I kiss him and for five seconds he's right there with me until suddenly he realizes what's happening and he shoves me away from him. What're you *doing?* he says. I-I don't know, I stammer.

Henry wanders through the doorway and I take my eyes from Joel even though I can still see him standing in front of me, water soaking his shirt and dripping from his hair. Before I can turn back he blows past me. Wait— I protest but he's gone.

Joel / Buenos Aires

By the time my plane hits the tarmac, I can't breathe. I struggle through customs, get my bag, and sink with a wheeze into the back of a cab. The driver eyes me over his shoulder like I'm something contagious. I'm hoping I'm not. I'm hoping I just need a good night's rest and a full day in my studio tomorrow.

Alma, my landlady, admires her Erythrina blooms in the light of a dying sun, smiling when my cab pulls up to the courtyard. Then she takes one look at the way I stumble from the back seat and releases a string of Spanish I'm not well enough to understand. As I pay the driver, she takes my bag, chastising me when I protest. I think she's saying, *Get yourself inside, fool.* I don't have the energy to argue. She follows me through the door and sets my bag beside the bed, then slaps her hand to my forehead and clucks her tongue when she feels the heat. *Cuanto tiempo?* she asks, patting her chest, *how long?* I tell her since this morning, and it's getting worse.

She orders me into the shower. I feel so awful I don't care that I'm about to strip down in front of my landlady. Sweater, shirt, jeans, boxer briefs: my skin stings in the air. She bundles the clothes I drop and shoves them into the laundry bag. *Agua muy caliente,* she says, *Por tanto tiempo com ousted pueda. Very hot water for as long as you can handle.*

I can't take more than a few minutes. I dry myself, pull on underwear. Alma's stripping my bed, and as soon as she gets the bottom sheet snug, I crawl on top. She fixes the bed around me, the way my mother did when I was small. The memory brings a sob to my throat, and I choke it back. *Gracias,* I say, *Gracias.*

She stays. I'm not sure what she's doing... my laundry, maybe? Something's humming, and for a moment, I think I hear James. The thought agitates, scrapes like sandpaper across my subconscious. Why am I irritated? I try to catch hold of the reason, but it's like a single breath from the muse. Ephemeral, with just enough tease to torment.

Sometime later, I slit my eyes like a snake. Alma's shaking a thermometer, but I don't see James. Did he already leave for campus? I turn my head on the pillow, trying to find his scent. I know he left it here. He left it here along with the Tag Heuer I bought him for his birthday: *It's a watch, James, not a commitment.* He left the watch, he left the cat, all my gifts strewn like pebbles, a trail in the moonlight to my heart. I came to Chicago and made him buy a jogging stroller, but we ended up in the cemetery with the god of death. I'll slide the coin between my father's teeth myself, dive into the Styx to claim my own invincibility since my mother's not here to hold my heel. I tried to sleep downstairs, but the cold sent me scrambling, and I stared down at him and took what I wanted. He was gone by the morning, left with the keys to my convertible, left me with an extra bedroom and a box cutter in my hand. *The wounds that hurt the most are the ones we self-inflict.* I breathe in the cigarette I'm holding, and my chest fights back. What's taking him so long anyway? Amanda brought the Thin Mints, and he likes those the best.

After the fact, I barely remember the emergency room. The doctor wants to admit me; I'm just coherent enough to refuse. I figure I know what I have—a double shot of pneumonia—and if I'm supposed to die, I'd rather be within reach of all of that gorgeous glass instead of in a hospital room. Alma seems to understand what I'm thinking because she packs me right back to my studio and props me up in bed with pillows from her own house. I fall asleep and lose three days.

Por favor, I whisper when I wake, shaking my head when Alma tries to give me chicken broth, and she acquiesces but only after I've agreed to a mouthful of water with turmeric and black pepper. *Mañana usted come,* she tells me. *Tomorrow you eat,* and she straightens the blankets and gets me a fresh glass of water.

I make it to the bathroom by myself, though Alma says she won't leave until I'm back in bed. A glance in the mirror tells me that I look every bit as hollow as I did right before I tried to kill myself, and I quiet the tremor that quivers up my spine. I'm not steady on my feet, but I wash my hands and run them through my hair. My toothbrush I never had time to unpack, and I make my shaky way into the bedroom and tell Alma what I need. She has me sit on the bed while she looks through my suitcase. I don't even know the day of the week. *Jueves,* she says, handing me my toothbrush. *Thursday.* She has heavy eyes, and I know that's because of me. I glance out the window, the long one near the ceiling. The sky wears a lavender cape. *Gracias,* I say, *Gracias,* Alma.

After I've brushed my teeth, I crawl into bed. *Mañana usted come,* Alma reminds me. She turns off the lamp on her way out, and the one left illuminated has such a low wattage I likely wouldn't be able to read by its light. On the other side of the wall, the room's lit, and I can imagine the glass catching its glow. I've created my own church in there, and I take a deep breath, grateful for the moment to be here, to be in this space once again. Why do I feel like it's been such a long time?

Chicago.

His hands wringing the water from my hair, his mouth so wild I opened right up before I realized what I was doing.

Somewhere in the midst of my fever, I forgot. After a dozen years of careful reconstruction, James kissed me, and when I asked him what he was doing, he couldn't come up with a reason. I don't know, he said, and I left the house with a shirt full of water. Has he even tried to call?

I look for my cell phone and find it in the front pocket of my suitcase, the battery long dead. Whimpering, I dig around for the charger, then plug it in and get back into bed.

I'm asleep before I have a charge, but my phone's the first thing I reach for when I open my eyes again. I have one *ya regreso, cariño?* voicemail from Elías—*you back yet, baby?*—and thirteen from James.

I guess he tried to reach me.

James / Chicago

I might've created this hell with that kiss but Joel sure as shit doesn't have any trouble fanning the flames. I fell all over myself his last night in town, apologizing even though the words felt as wrong to me as anything ever had like maybe I wasn't supposed to be saying them. Why was I claiming to be sorry for something that felt so good? That kiss felt good. I don't like admitting it for all kinds of reasons but *damn*. I can't stop thinking about those seconds I had him pinned against the sink and the way he just let me have at him. I haven't had a kiss like that in *years*.

I get it though. We went there once before and fucked ourselves so hard I never thought we'd make our way back. We'd be stupid to go down that road again. I don't blame him for being skittish and I didn't exactly pick the best time to seduce him if that's what I was intending. (And I *wasn't*. There was nothing premeditated about that kiss. Nothing I'd ever envisioned following through on anyway and I can hardly monitor every thought that makes its way into my head, *Jesus*.) After that trip he took to see his dad I had to go and take advantage of him.

So I apologized. That night when he finally stumbled home with ice in his hair then again after his shower and again the next morning as he was packing. I didn't want him leaving on such a sour note. The last time that happened a few months after Henry was born left us screaming at each other for months. I did not want to go through that again. Hey, I said, cornering him upstairs a few hours before his flight while Henry watched *Sesame Street*, I wanna make sure we're okay here. We're fine, he said but he wouldn't meet my eyes. I could feel myself starting to panic because I knew if he walked out that door and we didn't have a better resolution I'd be right where I am tonight. With a cell phone in my hand and a dozen voicemails already under my belt.

I haven't heard from him since he left. I dropped him off at the airport and for five days I've been the dumbass leaving voicemails that started off as casual as a first quarter pass and have pressed me into the Hail Mary I can tell I'm just about to leave him. All the anxiety I've been hauling around this first week of classes comes right on out. Jesus, Joel, I say in a *what the fuck* voice I'm hoping disguises the fear I'm feeling, Grow some balls and call me.

I guess I'm being kind of a dick but whatever. I'm tired of being punished.

I'm grousing through dinner a couple hours later when my phone rings. I open my cell even though I've tried to set a good example for Henry by not letting phone calls interrupt our mealtime. Glad to know you're alive, I tell him right off. I have pneumonia, he croaks.

Hell, he hasn't been avoiding me! He picked up pneumonia somewhere and I got him wet and sent him out of the house so upset he didn't stop long enough to grab his coat and now he's laid up a continent away from me sounding like someone took a knife to his vocal cords. Why aren't you in the *hospital?* I ask and he says, I'm better off here. Alone? I say, You're better off alone? Alma's checking on me, he mumbles. Joel! I cry, Pneumonia's really fuckin' serious!

I shoot Henry a look to see if he picked up on the *fuckin'* but he's busy dropping little bits of chicken on the floor for Rufus. This doesn't have to do with money, does it? I ask Joel and he moans, his breath as shallow as Barton Springs right where it meets the steps. Stop, he says, I'll call you when I feel better. I wanna talk to Alma, I demand. She doesn't speak English, he reminds me. I bet her son does, I say, remembering how cozy they looked out in the courtyard my first day in Buenos Aires and he gives up. I scribble the number on the back of the pizza menu. If you don't start feelin' better, get your ass to the hospital, I tell him.

I hang up catching Henry's eye. I've gotta make another call, buddy, I say, Okay? He drops a wedge of chicken, hanging so far over his booster it's a wonder he doesn't topple. Henry, I snap as I dial Alma's number, Keep your food on your plate.

I can't understand Alma but she hears the word *Joel* and passes me off to her son Mateo who remembers me from last summer. Joel's sick all right. Pneumonia in both lungs and a fever so high I want to sue the doctor who didn't insist on admitting him to the hospital. I can't believe Joel's down there by himself and I ask Mateo right out if I need to buy a plane ticket. He tells me his momma's checking on Joel every few hours. What about nights? I ask, I'll pay for someone to stay with him. He tells me there's no room in the studio, that they thought about moving him to their house but Joel's better off at home.

Home? When did Buenos Aires become *home?*

Mamá says he needs to be near the glass, Mateo says.

Yeah, that's when.

I tell him I understand, that I appreciate his mom checking on Joel and I give him my number so he can call me if Joel needs anything. Anything at all, I reiterate. Hanging up, I grimace at the thought of Joel by himself six thousand miles away from me with fucking *pneumonia*.

Enough. He's been gone long enough. Time to get him back to the

States. He can bring the goddamn glass with him.

Now Henry's dropping his peas on the floor one by one. Fucking *Hansel and Gretel*. I'm going to kill Joel. Rufus sniffs at Henry's peas then sits back and starts grooming himself. Henry, I sigh and my boy looks up at me all sweet and innocent like he hasn't just dumped half his dinner on the floor. I'm leaving a twail for Wufus, he says in a bright little voice, So he can find me! Rufus doesn't need a trail in order to find you, I tell him, But you need your vegetables to grow big and strong. Wufus needs to gwow big and stwong, too, Henry says, dribbling a few more peas from between his fingers.

If that cat gets any bigger we're going to have to walk it on a goddamn leash.

No more, I say, taking Henry's plate away from him and he howls like I've shoved him into the witch's oven myself.

Joel / Buenos Aires

I keep dreaming about James. Drunk dreams: that's what they feel like, the kind that seem so restless and real I open my eyes expecting to find him here with me instead of in Chicago. My fever burns so brightly that my eyes hurt, and I keep them shut as Alma lays cool cloths on my forehead. *Beba,* she says, holding a glass to my lips. *Drink,* and one time when I sip, it's Mateo who has his arm around me. *Su amigo llama,* he says. *Your friend calls,* and his phrasing suggests something that's happening on an hourly basis. *James,* I think. *El es su...,* he adds, leaving the sentence incomplete. *He's your...,* and I burst into tears. Mateo kisses the side of my head. Shh, shh, shh, he says, Shh, shh, shh.

I cry until I sleep, and dream about my bike. Behind me, James holds my waist, one finger threaded through my belt loop. I can feel his heartbeat, his breath on the back of my neck. Through the rain we ride, picking up speed when we pass campus. When I take a hard left onto Pearl Street, he leans with me, and I bump the bike across our front yard and up the steps. We're in the swing, and I rest my boot on the bike's seat. The motor thrums as James shakes a joint from a pack of Marlboros. You want some of this? he asks, lighting up, and when he holds out his hand, I grab his wrist and lick his fingers. They taste like paint.

Alma wakes me for turmeric water, forces me to cough until I want to spit. *Por favor,* I gasp, holding up a weak hand, but she tells me I cough again or we're going back to the hospital. I can taste something sharp and metallic, and suddenly, I have too much saliva in my mouth. I throw up right in the bed. Alma clucks like I've disappointed her, then hauls me into the shower while she changes my sheets. Though I'm shaky, I make it back into bed myself. Alma breaks out another round of turmeric water.

I collapse into my next dream. I'm in a cemetery, one that feels like Greece but looks nothing like where James and I used to roam. I can smell turpentine, and I'm holding Henry's hand. Where do you want to go? I ask him, and he chortles like a cherub. He's carrying a doughnut; it's not his first, because chocolate rings his mouth. To find the witch! he cries in a voice filled with glee. Glass rains down, soft as rain, and I laugh along with him. Where's your dad? I ask, and he breaks away from me and runs deeper into the cemetery. I can hear him, but every time I think I've found him, his giggle comes from another direction. Henry, I call, cupping my hands around my mouth, and his name rustles in the leaves of the pecans. I don't want him to get lost; he's never been east of I-35. Is he big enough to climb into Isabella's tree house? Hand over hand, I hoist myself up. Hi, Adam says when I reach the top, What took you so long?

My fever's gone the next time Alma comes to check on me, and I sip a cool glass of water, then cough obediently, this time without getting sick. James…, I say, unable to finish the sentence, and she tells me that Mateo will call him in the morning. I sink back into the pillows, grateful that Alma's willing to deal with him right now. I don't have the strength. *Su otro amigo…,* she says. *Your other friend…,* and I ask who she means, sure she's going to say Adam. I've been calling out to him in my sleep. I can still see him in my dream, standing in Isabella's tree house, the shirt I gave him for his last birthday open at his throat. She smiles and pats me on the head, like I'm her child or a pet. *El esperara por usted,* she says. *He will wait for you.* I can't quite figure out who she means.

James / Chicago

Man, I've been so jittery since I found out Joel's sick. There aren't enough cigarettes in the world to calm me down. I keep skipping out on my kid, slinking onto the back porch while he's playing or watching TV just so I can make it through a Marlboro. I've heard from Mateo, and Joel's fever came down but that doesn't make me worry any less. All the way up here in Chicago I can't do a damn thing to help him and finally I decide to call him myself, knowing I might be interrupting his rest but not much caring at this point. I just need to hear the guy's voice.

Hey, he says, answering the phone so soft and slow that relief rocks me on my feet. Jesus, I whisper, sinking into the nearest chair, Jesus, Joel. I know, he says, I've been pretty sick. *Pneumonia*, I say, swallowing the lump in my throat, I've been so fuckin' *worried*. I'm all right, he assures me, I'm just really tired. Maybe I should come down there, I suggest. Aren't you back on campus? he asks and I tell him that doesn't matter, that if he needs me to make the trip I'll be on the next plane.

He doesn't say anything and I realize *shit* he might not want me down there, not after what happened in my kitchen the night before he left. Hell, maybe he doesn't even want to talk to me at all. I know he's been sick but I've been getting every single update from Mateo. Joel couldn't pick up the phone for thirty seconds this whole time? And I'm the one who caved tonight. If I hadn't called him just now how long would I be waiting to hear from him? Maybe forever. Maybe he's done with me. Maybe him answering tonight is just a prelude to me getting dumped. Joel— I start but he's already telling me he's tired, that he doesn't have the energy for a conversation.

Fuck me. I *knew* it.

What are you reading? he asks. What do you mean? I say, confused. What are you reading right now? he asks. I look around me, my eyes falling on the copy of *The American Journal of Archaeology* I left sitting on the coffee table last night. Perfect, he mumbles when I tell him. Perfect? I repeat. Just read, he tells me. What, out loud? I ask. I'm too tired to talk tonight, he says, But I could really use the company.

I open the journal and scan the first couple paragraphs. I'm not so sure Joel's going to be interested in questions about who owns antiquity even if I think they're relevant but I start the book review from the beginning. Don't stop, he says when I pause.

I end up reading the entire review and the one after that on acquisition and exhibition. I've gotta be boring the shit outta you, I finally tell him. Not really, he says, It's good to hear your voice.

Joel / Buenos Aires

I have a couple of choices and plenty of time to think them over, now that my fever's gone. I feel better, not necessarily well enough to work— though I might cut a little glass this afternoon—but well enough that I can't spend the entire day sleeping. I've been out of commission for more than a week, and I've spent a good number of those days in a state of delirium, though this time I didn't smoke or drink anything to get there. I've had so many dreams about James I'm surprised I didn't manifest his knock at my door, had so many imaginary conversations with Adam I half-expect to find an email from him in my inbox. The only guy I haven't considered is Elías, who showed up here when I was fighting for breath and didn't appreciate being turned away. I've had to appease him with promises to see him once I'm feeling better.

Maybe I'll follow through. I can't figure out what I'm doing with James, calling him every night and letting him read me to sleep. Every time I think about what happened the night before I left Chicago, my breath vanishes. That's not the same as the flutter I feel in my chest when I think about seeing Adam in Isabella's tree house, though maybe I'm not being fair. They've both hurt me deeply. James just has dibs on the most recent wound, even if I don't include that kiss in his kitchen.

I'm not going to lie. That kiss was good. Maybe it shouldn't hold any weight; I might have guessed I'd like his lips, given what I'd been contemplating just a few days earlier. But I was drunk and agitated on New Year's Eve, and in his kitchen, we were one hundred percent sober. Sober, I would never have gone there, never. I wouldn't have thought James would either. He might zero in on my crotch, but he wouldn't make a move. Take that Christmas we spent on the phone. No way would he ever have let that happen unless he'd been drinking, and heavily.

So this kiss feels different. Unintentional, but lucid. For James, that's a first.

Which leaves me with two choices, maybe three. I can ignore what happened between us and assume we'll move on. I can broach the subject, the way I did when I realized I'd filled his ear with a full-on description of my very best blowjob, though this time around we don't have the excuse of inebriation, and anyway, a couple of weeks have passed since our kiss. The time for a conversation was the moment I came in out of the snow; at the latest, the morning after. Or I can settle in to what he might have meant, trust that he's not going to fuck me over, and tell him I'm... curious.

Now there's a word that's gotten us in trouble. I'm not even sure it's accurate. I'm not so much curious as confused. By my father's illness, by my lingering feelings for Adam, by the chemistry that underlies my relationship with James and has for so long I can't remember when it didn't. No wonder I want to spend all of my time with the glass. Nothing else makes sense anymore.

I sit in my studio, in the center of everything light, and think about those five seconds in James's kitchen. I responded like I'd been waiting for him. He kissed me like he meant every moment.

Hope has never felt more dangerous.

James / Chicago

I'm at the park with Henry, pushing him on the swing. Higha, Daddy, he calls and I give him a little extra. He isn't satisfied and he tries to kick his legs but he doesn't really know the right rhythm. I've got a feeling he's fixing to scream and when I pull back on the chains to slow him down some he opens his lungs. Henry, I say, stepping in front of him but he's full throttle now. The mommas over by the playscape, the ones who look like they could use a few carbs raise their eyebrows. I give the women a tight smile and squat down in front of my son, quick enough to catch the foot he kicks at my teeth. You wanna go really high, don't you? I say but I'm too late. He's in full meltdown mode and I haul him off the swing as he tries to whack me. Time to go home, I tell him and that *really* doesn't help.

He's thrashing so much I drop him. He runs off and I consider going after him then sit my ass down on one of the park benches instead. I can see him squatting inside a tunnel in the playscape. I should probably go over there and let him know he doesn't have the upper hand but I'm pretty damn tired from reading to Joel half the night. I'm not complaining, believe me. I'm just tired and the swings trigger me every time Henry and I come to the park. I shouldn't have brought him today but we were getting a little crazy inside the house and even though it's freezing and I had to knock a foot of snow off the swing Henry's always a little easier in the fresh air.

Sometimes I wonder what our lives would be like if I'd gotten tenure someplace warm.

I look at my phone. Nothing. I'm being obsessive, checking for voicemails every fifteen minutes. For the past five nights Joel and I have been on the phone for hours without really talking at all. I read from *The Journal of Archaeology* or give him something from what I've been writing lately—mostly about that mosaic from last summer—and he listens. I keep expecting him to shut me down but he has me going until almost eleven, two in the morning in Argentina. You're so far away, I told him at one point last night, thinking about all the land and water and air separating us and he said, I'm right here.

Why can't I stop thinking about that kiss? We've kissed plenty of times.

Except we haven't. Back when we were sleeping together we never kissed. That first night, sure. But after that? Hardly ever. I took what I wanted from him and gave him almost nothing back. And that's the truth.

I'm better off not thinking about what happened in '96. We're both better off. We've moved on, moved past, become something else. That kiss in my kitchen was a blip on the radar same as the phone call the Christmas after he broke up with Adam.

Henry peeks out from the tunnel. I give him a wave and he ducks back inside. At least he's giggling.

That night I wait around until I can't stand it anymore and call Joel myself. Hey, he says, sounding all drugged up. You workin'? I ask because I know that voice, I've heard it often enough over the years. I'm cutting glass, he admits. I thought you didn't answer the phone when you're workin', I tell him. I make exceptions for you, he says.

Man, I feel like a Friday night football field under a Texas sky and when I get a look at myself in the mirror by the front door I look high and bright like I'm the one with the damn fever. *What the hell?*

Was that too much for you? he asks since I'm not saying anything. I open my mouth but a whole lot of nothing comes out. Maybe I should rein myself in, he says.

Ever since he left Chicago I've wanted him on the phone and now that he's here and asking for something other than a reading I can't figure out what to say. I don't…, I start, What're you…? You're good at this, he tells me. You like that? I mumble, I got plenty. So give me something, he suggests.

I'm full of innuendo that can't make it past my lips and I can feel him taking a step back like I'm a colt he thought was ready to break until he got close. How's Henry? he asks, changing the subject and for the rest of our conversation—which is damn short, compared to every other call we've had this week—I can't bring us back. Listen, I'm pretty tired, he finally says and I mumble *get some rest* and just like that he's gone.

After he hangs up I grab myself a beer. I've got plenty of work I've been putting off but I can't concentrate for shit and I end up standing in front of *Crossing*, my eyes tracing the same line over and over. Man, nothing feels right about what just happened. He wanted something from me, something more than a bedtime story and I didn't deliver.

Whatever, maybe I didn't want to deliver. He lives in Buenos Aires, I live in Chicago, we're *friends*. We're not supposed to be anything else.

Then why the hell did you kiss him? Because you're the same prick you've always been, wanting to see how far you can get? Because you want his attention?

I might as well be twenty years old and saddled with diving gear.

Joel / Buenos Aires

I'm out with Elías. I knew if I stayed home, I'd end up calling James, and I wanted to see how I'd feel if I went a night without talking to him. The verdict: bored. I'm so fucking bored, and that's a problem because Elías, who hasn't seen me since before the holidays, has pulled out a stellar seduction: drinks, dinner, a rooftop exhibition in Barracas. He's invested, and I'm bored.

My head's somewhere else, taking that shot of water to the chest again and again, trying to figure out why when there's no answer sound enough to satisfy. I went along with that kiss for five seconds too long, and now I can't think about anything else. James might be similarly stuck. I can't let that matter. I know his limitations, and the couple of comments I've lobbed his way since I've been home have thrown him off so much that I've had to remind myself not to get pissed. There's only so much James can handle.

We're talking, of course. We talk every day. But we're not saying much of anything.

Elías runs his hand through my hair, leans in close with perfect lips. A month ago, his mouth might've been enough. Instead, I'm going through the motions. I could be kissing anyone at all, and I step away from him. *No aquí,* I say, *not here,* as if the crowd at this exhibition is my only concern. That's all the invitation he needs.

Ten minutes later, we're in a cab. I look down at our fingers entwined and feel nothing other than an arousal so faint I feel like I've swallowed a sedative. I'm not expecting divine inspiration, but I shouldn't have to gear myself up to sleep with him.

Maybe I'm just tired. The pneumonia did me in, stole my strength and enough weight that my jeans ride low on my hips, even with a belt. Why wouldn't my sex drive be lower than usual?

But it's not. If I close my eyes, I can get there so fast I'm terrified.

We can't go there again, James and I. We can't. That's why I'm here tonight with Elías. Elías, who's attractive and considerate and doesn't think anything of holding my hand in the back seat of a cab or kissing me in the middle of a gallery. Elías, who didn't fuck me over twelve years ago or leave me bleeding in a bathtub while he headed south to meet his girlfriend's parents.

What's wrong with me? I thought I'd buried this shit years ago, moved beyond the bitterness and resentment. Why am I trying on these emotions tonight like they're my favorite pair of jeans? One kiss shouldn't have this much power.

Esta lista? Elías asks as we pull up to his flat. *Sí,* I say, *Estoy lista.* He pays the driver, and we walk through the gate. *Espere,* I say, stopping him halfway up the stairs.

Nothing. I feel nothing at all when I kiss him, and my frustration makes me probe a little deeper. He mistakes my tongue for enthusiasm, pulls me closer.

Nothing.

Pissed, I follow him through his front door. *Algo de tomar?* he asks. *Something to drink?* and I shake my head. He smiles. *Te extrañe,* he says, stepping closer. *I missed you,* and I know I'm fucked when I can't bring myself to return the words. I don't have to mean them. I'm sure Elías enjoyed himself plenty while I was out of town; he has advantages as a dancer with Teatro Colón's Permanent Ballet. Tonight, I just have to play the game, and Elías brings the back of his hand to my forehead, checking to see if that pneumonia has a return trip planned.

Before I can reassure him, my phone rings. I pull it from my pocket: James. Who else? If I don't answer, if I let him roll to voicemail, he'll leave a message. How compelled will I feel to listen to it before I go home? How many times will he call if I don't try to reach him right away? If I don't get back to him at all tonight, what's he going to think? What do I *want* him to think?

I'm hesitating too long, and Elías raises his eyebrows. James, I tell him, From Chicago. *Conteste la llamada,* he says. *Answer the call,* and I do. He doesn't step away. Instead, he moves closer, one hand on my waist, his cologne as subtle as a scent imagined. Hey, I say into the phone, and James might as well be standing right next to me. You workin'? he asks.

Almost nine years since he left Texas and he still has that drawl, still leaves his *g* hanging, like he can't be bothered with the whole syllable, like enunciation might be fine for city folk, but he's too simple for that bullshit. That he grew up surrounded by professors and has tenure at a university just make his accent more enticing. No, I say, Not right now. Good, he sighs.

I want to have a beer with him. That's what I want tonight. I want to sit down with him and drink a slow beer. I want to be known, and no one knows me better than James.

No one except Adam. Between the two of them, they have the whole story, or as close to the whole story as any two people could. They're part of my mosaic, and I guess Elías has a place, too, because he's sealing the space between our hips, grazing the tips of his fingers along my neck. I tilt my head like a marionette.

I was thinking about camping, James says as Elías lowers his lips to my skin. Camping? I repeat, my breath taking the last half of the word, but he's already talking about the summer after our freshman year when we moved into the house on Pearl Street. We were dating girls from the pool; Melissa, Cathleen, and James were lifeguards at Deep Eddy, and I spent my days cultivating a tan that just about brought my ethnicity into question. From the pool, I watched James and Cathleen spin closer and closer, shrugged when James suggested I date Melissa so we could double. Melissa was a bitch and beautiful, with long hair and heavy tits that did nothing but remind me of what I wanted: the guy from my comp class who fucked me hard and kept it quiet. Melissa wanted James, I think, and James could've had her. But he never went for girls with curves, and Melissa had little else. So I became her consolation prize, and one week, when they all managed to score a day off at the same time, we decided to go camping.

I'd never been camping, ever. My father's taste leaves no room for anything rustic, and growing up, the closest I came was a catered cookout in full view of our backyard pool. But when James made the suggestion, I kept thinking about the late-night trek we'd made outside Austin city limits the previous fall, the same night we came home screaming, just for the release. We'd spent some time parked beside the road that night, drinking beer and staring up at the sky, the stars a handful of diamonds some god had strewn across the night. The thought of being in that space again... I liked the idea, and without hesitation, I blew a grand on backpacks and sleeping bags and an easy-to-assemble tent. What's my contribution? James sulked, brooding as usual about the disparity in our finances, and I gave him my best look of incredulity. The girls and the beer, man, I said, You're bringing the girls and the beer.

We had the equipment but not the expertise. With vague directions from one of James's fraternity brothers, a two-hour drive turned into three and a half. I was the only one with cash, which was typical but unfortunate since I had nothing but hundred dollar bills, one of which I had to cram into the permit box since we arrived after hours. A late start hiking meant we were stumbling up a poorly designated path as the sun was setting, scrambling for firewood after night had fully fallen. I followed James's lead, pretending like I knew what I was doing, like I'd pitched dozens of tents, built hundreds of campfires. Honestly, as long as we had access to beer, James and I were fine.

The girls were another story. Even Cathleen couldn't handle the mosquitoes, and by the time she started complaining about them, Melissa's voice had turned into one long whine. You're lucky she's hot, James muttered under his breath, and I wanted to tell him that no pussy was worth what we were hearing. Yeah, I said instead, No shit.

Our biggest mistake turned out to be delegating the food to the girls. We'd thought we were being logical. Girls cook, right? We'd bring the camping supplies and beer; they'd take care of the food. We probably should've realized they weren't lugging a cooler up the hill, but we didn't, and by the time we'd lit that fire and set up the tent, we were starving. I'm too hot to cook, Melissa complained from where she was sitting on top of a rock, winding her hair into a ponytail, and James looked like he wanted to backhand her. We pitched the tent, Melissa, I said. Opening our cooler, I dug out a couple of beers and tossed a can to James. He was wearing one of his fraternity shirts, and he lifted the hem to wipe his face, his stomach flat and tan, even in the dark. I caught Cathleen looking, or maybe she caught me.

That last thought, *maybe she caught me,* comes almost eighteen years after the fact, with James's voice in my ear. That summer night, west of Austin, there was nothing for Cathleen to catch. James meant nothing to me, nothing more than a friend. I wouldn't have thought twice about his abs, wouldn't have noticed his tan. I don't understand why I'm seeing him so clearly now. But I am, with accuracy. Like he's the one standing in front of me instead of Elías.

Elías, who unzips my jeans one slow notch at a time. I know where he's heading, and I rock on my feet as he slides my jeans over my hips. *Te extrañe,* he whispers. James could hear him if he'd give his monologue a rest, but he's still talking, asking if I remember what happened next, what the girls brought for dinner. I have to respond, and my words come hot and low, like he designed his story to seduce. Remind me, I say.

We'd gone camping in the middle of July in Texas. We didn't need a fire to stay warm. The hills were full of coyotes, but we didn't need the fire to keep them at bay. We'd built the fire because we needed to cook, and we stepped back from the flames, wiping the sweat from our foreheads, and told the girls to take over. Melissa let out a sigh and climbed to her feet as Cathleen dragged her backpack toward the fire. Y'all let us know if you need any help, James said like some Southern gentleman. They have it under control, I assured him, but it turned out they didn't. We watched in disbelief as they pulled out a box of macaroni and cheese, a sack of apples. Are you serious? James asked, That's all you brought? Of course not! Melissa said, We have M&Ms too.

James and I exchanged stupefied glances. We're *starving*, I told her, and Melissa gave a little huff like I was cramping her Queen of Bitches style. If you just *give* us a minute, she said, We'll get started. How're you going to cook that without *water*, Melissa? I asked. You brought water, she reminded me. We brought water to *drink*, I said, You want to hike to the river in the dark to get more for that macaroni? And you only brought one box, James added, How're you going to feed four of us with one box?

Cathleen blinked, then stared at the provisions like she was seeing them for the first time. I almost felt sorry for her. She wasn't usually the clueless type. I don't know what we were thinking, she admitted. They should've told us, Melissa said to her, and she turned in our direction, saying, You didn't *tell* us. Burgers and dogs! James cried, You go camping, you eat burgers and dogs!

Remember? he says in my ear. I open my eyes. Elías has drifted down, and I watch my dick disappear in his mouth. Yeah, I say, I remember. At least you got a blowjob that night, James tells me.

He's right. I did. We used our drinking water to boil the macaroni, ate three apples apiece, learned that M&Ms melt in your hands at ninety degrees. When we ran out of beer, we crawled into our tent, which warmed right up with our body heat. I knew James wouldn't get laid; he'd already let it slip that he and Cathleen weren't sleeping together, had mumbled something one night after a few tequila shots that she was a virgin and he didn't want to push her. But you and Melissa...? he'd asked, and I'd grinned like I couldn't get enough of her.

I was grateful for the sex. I was nineteen, and I was getting laid pretty much whenever I wanted. I could fuck Melissa, and when I really needed something else, I could hook up with the guy from my comp class. The sex with Melissa still counted as sex, and that night in the tent, mellowed from all of that beer, I pulled her on top of me. Her skin was damp and sweaty; she felt different than she usually did, smelled different. I kissed her, knowing that James and Cathleen were making out too. We'd separated our sleeping bags with my portable CD player, but I knew if I extended my arm, I could touch them, and the thought made me even harder. Under the sleeping bag, I wrapped Melissa's hand around my dick. One song faded— we were listening to Madonna's *Immaculate Collection* at the girls' insistence— and before another one started, I could hear Cathleen's whisper and James's breath.

I don't know who decided a hand job wasn't going to cut it, but at some point, Melissa had her head under the covers. It must've been sweltering down there, but I don't think it took me very long. Still, I'm surprised James knows. The night was dark, and Madonna was loud. I took care to be quiet, too; I mashed my mouth in my palm when I came.

I remember, I say, barely able to get the words out. Elías has his jeans unzipped, one hand on his hard-on, and my moan slips through my lips, so slight that if James hadn't stopped talking, he would've missed it altogether. Instead, he catches the sound, and his voice drops so low we might as well have crawled back to that Christmas after I broke up with Adam. I want to talk about that kiss in my kitchen, Joel, he says.

His hands in my hair, his mouth opening me up... I have Elías on his knees but James in my head, and I shove Elías away from me, my balls tightening in instant protest. I groan, Elías swearing a stream of Spanish. Then he clocks me.

I go right down. I'm still weak from the pneumonia, and the ache in my balls doesn't help. The second he sees me on the floor, he starts apologizing. I wave him off when he crouches down beside me, but he takes my jaw between his fingers, looking grim. *Usted esta sangrando,* he says. *You're bleeding,* and I swipe my mouth with the back of my hand, my focus on the phone that fell when I hit the ground. Elías scans the room. *Allí,* he says, reaching under the bookshelf. I take the phone and hold it gingerly to my ear, stopping James mid-sentence. —happening? he's asking. I'll call you back, I tell him.

Elías doesn't look any happier now that I've hung up. I think he already knows what I'm going to say.

He doesn't offer to drive me home, but he does get me an ice pack and call me a cab. Another guy I've lost because of James. I remember every one of them, Paul and Simon and Darryl and the guy who made reservations at Basil Café because I'd told him it was a favorite. What was his name? William. William, who was thoughtful and kind and so unassuming he didn't keep condoms on hand, who was probably the sort of boyfriend who'd leave love notes on my pillow. I bet he's in a healthy, functioning relationship right now. I bet he's so highly evolved he'd take my call if I tracked him down, even though I fucked him and never talked to him again.

I indulge in a mental rant all the way home. I figure I deserve it. My mouth tastes like blood, I've killed whatever chance I had with Elías, and now I'm going to have to either lie to James about how I spent my evening or tell him the awful truth.

Oh yeah. My father's dying.

I peel off the pesos I need for the fare, avoiding eye contact with the driver, who obviously wants to hear the story behind my swollen lip. Mumbling *gracias*, I trudge to my door. I'd like to go right to bed without stopping to do any more than rinse my mouth, but my cell phone weighs heavy with voicemails from James, and I go into my studio and open my phone. Across from me, a wall of glass shimmers in the dim light.

James picks up on the first ring. Dude, what happened? he asks, and I take a deep breath. Between my fingers, I roll a piece of just-buffed bottle glass the color of the moon. I had a date with Elías tonight, I start.

I expect him to say something, but he's quiet. Rolling the glass back and forth, I try to explain: I hadn't been out with Elías since my return to Buenos Aires, and I went out with him tonight because I've spent every evening lately on the phone. I needed to get out of the house, I say, but more than that, I needed to stop thinking about what happened my last night in Chicago.

We went to dinner, I tell James, and to an exhibition I wanted to see. There's no reason for me to add that Elías is attractive; that's a given, and I'm not trying to make James jealous. As the quintessential Scorpio, he already has that covered. After a month away from Elías, I say, I should've been happy to spend time with him. I should've been ready to sleep with him. Instead, I felt nothing.

We went back to his place, I continue, And you called. I tell him I didn't know whether or not to answer, until Elías said I should. I opened my phone, and Elías came closer. For the first time all night, I say, I felt something.

Again, I wait; again, James says nothing, his silence so uncharacteristic I look at my phone to be sure our call hasn't been disconnected. He's still there, and I take another breath because here's where this conversation gets hard.

At first, Elías was just... close, I say, Waiting for me to finish talking to you. I open my hand, and a sliver of moon glistens in my palm. I should've stopped him, I confess, closing my fingers around its shine, But you kept talking, and there was something about your voice...

I trail off, partly because I don't know how to tell him what I mean and partly because I do. For the first time maybe ever, he's not jumping in to finish my sentence. He's not saying anything at all, and I bring the moon to my mouth, as if the glass has healing properties. Maybe it does. I can't imagine trying to have this conversation anywhere else, and I draw strength from the work I'm doing in here, the coruscation of hundreds of pieces of glass. I'm right where I should be, and I decide that if I've been honest up to this point, I might as well trust that he can handle the truth. That kiss, I say, That kiss in your kitchen— Wait a second, he interrupts, Just… wait a second.

Why do I have the feeling he's about to flip out?

You had *sex* with Elías tonight? he says, While we were on the *phone*? We weren't…, I mumble, We didn't actually… He groans. You're not seriously going to try to make a case for semantics, he says, Are you? Look, I say, You called, I answered— And somehow Elías ended up with your dick in his mouth? he asks. I didn't intend for that to happen, I tell him. Well, I didn't intend to kiss you! he says, But I'm sure as shit paying for that now! We're both paying for that, I inform him, and he barks out an incredulous laugh. Fuck you, he says, That kiss was instinctual. Well, your instincts suck, I tell him, Otherwise, you might've taken what I want into consideration. Yeah, because that's what *you* were doing tonight, he says, Taking what *I* want into consideration.

He has me there. I think about how I'd feel if I were on the other end of this call, how I'd feel if James was telling me that some girl gave him a blowjob while we were on the phone tonight. He has every right to be angry.

You're always telling me what a disappointment I am to you, Joel, he says, just before he hangs up, Turns out you're the expert.

I close my phone, then lean back in my chair. In front of me, the wall glimmers.

My mouth really fucking hurts.

James / Chicago

Henry and I have such a nasty weekend that by Sunday night he's sobbing and I'm just about melting down alongside him. I've stuck him in the tub and that bought me some time but now he's asking for those goddamn crayons Ashley bought him so he can draw on the tile. I do *not* have the energy to clean that shit up tonight and instead of telling him we can color tomorrow but tonight we're going to cozy up with some books and a bedtime snack I'm stupid enough to say no. Just no without inflection or redirection. He loses his mind. Instead of commiserating I yank him squalling and squirming out of the tub.

Not one of my better parenting moments.

We'll both feel better after a good night's sleep, I promise as I pack him off to bed even though that seems unlikely since we started this morning the same damn way we ended last night. He's still crying and he hiccups himself to sleep. After I leave his room I check my cell phone. Nothing. *Nothing.* No voicemail, no email, no apology from Joel of any fucking kind.

I'm not saying I was right to kiss him. I probably should've held back. But *goddamn.* We've spent the past couple weeks on the phone. He had me reading to him for fuck's sake! And that first night we talked after he was feeling better: *I make exceptions for you.* What the hell was that? I mean *shit.* Here I was thinking that we…

That we what? Really, where am I going with that sentence?

I fix myself a drink, a strong one, flicking enough olive juice in my glass to tell myself I'm having a martini. Then I pry open the kitchen window since I can't stand the thought of smoking on the back porch in the cold.

Thirty minutes later I've smoked three cigarettes and I'm halfway through my second drink. I feel barely better. I've got our conversation from the other night playing on a loop and I grip my head in my hands, a just-lit cigarette between my fingers. What did he say the other night? *I know I should've stopped him… For the first time all night I felt something… There was something about your voice…*

There was something about your voice…

Did he ever finish that thought? I take a drag from my Marlboro, squinting like that's going to help me remember.

There was something about your voice…

Leaving my drink on the counter, I go looking for my phone. I guess I have to call his ass myself.

He doesn't answer. Three rings, four… He's not answering. He didn't have any problem talking to me the other night, did he? He was plenty busy with Elías and he still managed to pick up the phone. Son of a *bitch*, I say and as soon as I start cussing he answers. Hey, he murmurs, all quiet and open like he just finished meditating or spent his whole damn day in down dog. God, he pisses me off and I return his *hey* a little too loud. What were you talkin' about the other night? I ask, launching right in. What do you mean? he says and I take a fierce inhale on my cigarette. What do I mean? I repeat, What do I *mean?*

He doesn't say anything though that's typical Joel these days, taking a breath, setting an intention. Where the hell did I put my drink? You said there was somethin' about my voice, I tell him, heading back into the kitchen where I spot my glass near the sink. I swallow another mouthful of martini as he sighs. The sound, that soft explosion of breath in my ear, filters right on through the vodka. Lust and fury all bound up together, *awesome.* Are you alone? I ask and he waits so long to answer that my fist clenches. Yeah, he finally says, I'm alone.

Well, there's that at least though I'm not liking the way he sounds all sad and shit like I'm kicking him when he's down. Where's *Elías*? I ask, making sure I say the name with plenty of bitterness and he tells me he doesn't know. He wasn't too happy with me the other night, he admits. Why's that? I ask because seems to me Elías got exactly what he wanted. I cut him off, Joel tells me.

Does that mean they're through? They're not seeing each other anymore?

Kind of at a crucial point, he adds.

Jesus.

So that was it? I say, He didn't get his mouthful and he decided to end it? Can you be any more vulgar? he asks. Can you be any more hypocritical? I snap back.

If we were in the same room I'd be able to see his reaction. A continent away from him I've got to make assumptions and I take one last drag on my cigarette and grind it up in the disposal. He might be pissed enough to hang up.

All right, he says instead, You win.

Yeah, I don't much feel like I've won anything. I feel like I've been fucked over and I run my hand over the beginnings of a beard I've been too lazy to shave this weekend. Elías gave me a bloody mouth, he offers. *What?* I say. He apologized, Joel assures me, Right away, actually. Oh, well, if he apologized, I say sarcastically but Joel starts defending the guy. I shoved him away from me pretty hard, he confesses, I caught him off-guard. Are you makin' excuses for him? I say. I hit you once, he reminds me. I deserved it, I tell him and he says, Well, maybe I did, too.

We're quiet for a minute as I suck some more of that martini through my teeth. There's one thing I don't get, I finally tell him. What's that? he asks. Why'd you stop? I say. You mean, why didn't I just... finish? he asks. Seems kinda stupid, I point out. Stupid and painful, he agrees.

I feel a rush of anger and a simultaneous surge of desire that makes me light another cigarette. Sometimes it's easier if I can just tamp this shit down. Nothing's going to come of us anyway. But I can't help the way my mind brings up image after image like I'm running my memory along those mala beads I've seen in Joel's studio. I track them back in time *that kiss in my kitchen his bedroom in Buenos Aires the campfire on Crete* on back through to the night I started everything with that bag of pot and a single-minded purpose. But I don't have to stop there. I can go back even further to *the train tracks under Barton Springs Road the night he took delivery of his new Explorer the swing on our front porch that same night Darryl came looking for him.* Then all the way back past *Padre and that bong we made from a Diet Coke can the first gay bar I suggested the men I saw leaving his bedroom and the men I didn't* all the way back to the first moment I thought about him. Not because I suspected something, not because my girlfriend kept dropping hints, not because I felt some kind of idle curiosity about what the hell he saw in that guy at the dive shop in Cancun or the guy he told me was just a study partner. I'm going back to what I saw on our front porch the day before he left for Europe the summer after our senior year. The guy he'd picked up at that taco place in a thunderstorm while I was working that shitty job answering phones for a security company. The one who showed up in our living room dripping from a shower. I was reeling but I made damn sure I shook the dude's hand since Joel had never brought anyone home. Then Joel walked him out onto the front porch *the front porch the same fucking porch where we sat drinking beer in our swing* and for the first time I watched Joel slide right into a guy the way he slid into Melissa watched them kiss watched the way Joel gripped his arms like he was trying to memorize his triceps so he could think about them later. A proprietary *mine* shuddered through me like I'd been digging around the depths of our friendship and ended up hitting a fault line I didn't know existed. I've been dealing with the aftershocks ever since.

I stopped, Joel says, Because I realized what I was doing. The guy kneelin' between your legs didn't clue you in? I ask. I knew I was getting a blowjob, James, he tells me all patient-like, It just took me a while to realize you were the one getting me off.

Maybe I shouldn't have called him a few drinks in.

What'd he say?

I'm trying to be honest with you, he explains, I'm trying to be upfront. Upfront, I repeat in a daze because *what's* he saying? That my voice got him *off*? That's... that's...

Well, way fucking better than what I expected to hear, that's for damn sure. I've spent the past few days chewing on what he was doing during our last conversation. If I didn't like thinking about Elías four months ago when I first heard about him you can bet I haven't been pleased with what I've been picturing lately. For the first time in days I feel the space around me open up like maybe I'm not so screwed after all. Then right on the heels of that thought comes another one. *What the fuck do you think you're doing, Fielding?* and man, there's no hiding that from Joel. He knows me too well.

Why don't you tell me what you want, he says. What do you mean? I ask warily. What do you want from me, James, he says, What do you *want* from *me*?

I remember the first time I met Darryl, the UPS driver Joel dated the summer before we slept together. That guy's gonna bore the shit outta you the second he gets his pants back on, I told Joel and he laughed all right but the next time I poked fun at Darryl's IQ Joel kicked me out of his studio. *Can I help it if I want you all to myself?* I'd asked him earlier that summer and fuck if I don't almost repeat the same words tonight. *I want you all to myself* ready on my tongue like I've been waiting for him to ask but then I pull hard on the reins because hell, I don't even know what *I want you all to myself* means. What am I really saying? Am I fixing to invite him to move in with me or something? What the hell would that even look like?

I don't know, I finally mumble and he says, Then why are we talking?

The line goes dead. Hello? I say like a dumbass and just as I'm thinking I've fucked us over again thank *God* the phone starts ringing in my hand. I answer blurting out apologies until my sister's voice interrupts me. Oh good, she says, I could use a little drama tonight.

Joel / Buenos Aires

Well, that's done. I've laid every single one of my cards on the table, and James still can't commit. My twenty-five-year-old self would've been embarrassed by the way I've put myself out there, but I just feel wrung out. Thinking about how honest I've been with James the last two times we've talked, and realizing that he can't even admit that he might want to take us further, makes me want to put my head in my hands and cry.

I might know we're finished, but I'm still expecting him to call me back, and his failure to do so has me picking up my phone every few minutes to see whether or not I still have a charge. I hung up on him for good reason, but the James I remember wouldn't let me leave without a fight. A few days ago, he called wanting to talk about that kiss. How could one blowjob derail whatever he wanted to tell me? It's not as if I was cheating on him.

If that's how he's interpreting what happened, though... I know how that feels, to find out that the one you love has been sharing intimacies with someone else. The moment Adam told me about his affair will always have the distinction of being one of the worst of my life, vying with my mother's suicide for first place. If James made assumptions about us based on that kiss in his kitchen, he has every reason to feel betrayed. The thought sickens me, makes me reach again for my cell. Reason holds me back from calling him. We kissed once, weeks ago, and when I realized what we were doing, I shoved him away from me. He could hardly misinterpret the way I fled his brownstone. He might well have wanted to talk about what happened, but he couldn't have imagined I'd have anything good to say.

Of course, he tried to talk to me the night he kissed me. I'm the one who stood in his living room, wet and shivering, and told him I just wanted to take a hot shower and go to bed. I'm the one who refused to meet his eyes the following morning. I'm the one who left without letting us bring any resolution to the first line we've crossed in years. Why have I put off talking to him?

Fuck Adam. If he hadn't fallen apart, he'd be here for me right now. I wouldn't be on the verge of tears in a 750 square foot studio on a continent thousands of miles from my birth, trying to wrap my head around the clusterfuck that James and I have yet again managed to become. Adam never would have let me go to Houston over the holiday, not without him, and even if I'd confessed my feelings for my father and found myself utterly devastated by his response, Adam would have been there for me. He would have pulled me into his arms and told me that he, at least, would never leave me. He, at least, would never disappoint me. He, at least, would never betray me.

I want to tell him. I want him to know what he's done to me, the life he's stolen from me. I feel violated, tempted by redemption, then plunged into the depths of a hell I'm constantly trying to escape. I scroll through my contacts until I find Adam's name. My thumb slides across the screen, warm under my skin. I could call him right now, unleash the way I did years ago, the night I agreed to see him and caved to his kiss. He'd take it again, this wrath writhing within me. He took it then, and maybe that's what finally makes me set down my phone. Adam's aware of his wrongs. I don't need to remind him.

James still hasn't called, and I stand in my studio and stare at the mosaic taking shape in front of me. This is commitment. This is dedication. Every day, I give to the glass, and the glass gives to me. If I'm looking for loyalty, I don't have to look any further.

James / Chicago

I love my sister but sometimes she rubs me the wrong way. I'm still trying to figure out how she's on the other end of the line instead of Joel and here she's pleading with me to get down and dirty with her. Don't you have enough drama of your own? I ask. C'mon, she begs, You never tell me anything!

Well, there's reason enough for that. Ashley and I have a dozen years between us. She's my little sister. I'm supposed to take care of her, not ask her for advice.

Let me guess, she says when I keep quiet, You were talking to *Joel*. What makes you say that? I ask, caught off-guard. Who else? she laughs, You don't have a girlfriend. I could have a girlfriend, I mutter. You could, she sings, But you don't.

I light another cigarette. No smoke has ever seen the inside of my little sister's lungs. She doesn't even smoke pot, says she wants her oxygen at full capacity if a wave trips her up. When she was little she used to cry if she caught me smoking. God, did my parents give me shit about that. Think of the example you're setting for her, my mom used to tell me but all those Marlboros I smoked just made Ashley steer clear of them herself.

Are you smoking? she whines now. Don't start, Ashley, I bark and she sighs. I take an intentionally long inhale to piss her off. So? she wants to know. So what, I grumble. Why are you apologizing to Joel? she asks. It's complicated, I mumble and she says, So explain it to me.

I clonk a few ice cubes into my glass and pour what's left of the vodka over them. Ashley had a crush on Joel back when they first met and he didn't do a damn thing to dissuade her. Instead he bought her earrings and little purses and once when she was in fifth grade a Hello Kitty lip gloss kit that pretty much put the seal on her love for him forever. When she found out he likes guys she sulked for *days*. Thanks for leadin' her on, dude, I told him but he just laughed like a schoolgirl crush wasn't any big deal. Maybe that's why when that Girl Scout showed up on our doorstep a few weeks after his dad announced his remarriage Joel took her seriously. I guess Ashley got over him all right but that soft spot she has for him might as well be marshmallow.

Let me ask you something, she says, dropping her voice like I'm her best girlfriend, Have y'all ever… you know.

Man, sometimes I wish Ashley didn't speak her mind.

None of your damn business, I say, sure I don't want to tell my little sister about the night I brought home a bag of pot because I'd decided Joel and I needed to loosen up. Well, that's a yes, she laughs. I'm not talkin' about this with you, Ashley, I tell her. Oh please, she says, Are you afraid I'm going to tell Mom and Dad?

I feel a quick flash of anxiety like I've been caught crawling out my bedroom window in the middle of the night and I have to remind myself that I'm a thirty-fucking-seven-year-old man with tenure and a mortgage. What's *wrong* with me?

He was with you after Christmas, right? Ashley asks. So? I say. So what *happened*? she persists with the same tenacity a pit bull would sink its teeth into a toddler. Man, my sister's wasting time on the waves. Any law school would be happy to have her. What makes you think somethin' happened? I ask and she says, I smell bullshit.

Sugar and spice and everything nice, that's my little sister. You kiss anyone with that mouth of yours? I wonder. Sometimes, she admits, Sometimes I go right to the blowjob. Jesus, Ashley, I mutter and she tells me to grow up. I'm not your baby sister, she tells me. You'll *always* be my baby sister, I point out. That's sweet, she says, And antiquated. Whatever, Ashley, I mumble and she tells me that if I could get past this idea of her in pigtails she might be able to help. I've known Joel a long time, she says, I've seen this dance you do. What dance? I ask and she laughs. One step forward, she says, Two steps back.

Awesome. I swallow some more vodka and glance at the baby monitor. For once I wish that kid of mine would wake up.

He was with you after Christmas…, she prompts and I knock back the rest of my drink. Yeah, I admit. And…, she encourages.

Aw hell, maybe I should tell her. She might actually have something for me. I don't want to think too hard about this fact but it's likely she's seen more action in the past few years than I ever have, depressing as that sounds. Maybe she can help.

All right, I say, closing my eyes, I guess I kissed him. You guess? she laughs, Did he kiss you back?

For five seconds. For five seconds I kissed him and my hands took his hair and he opened right on up and kissed me back. For five seconds I stopped fucking *thinking*.

Yeah, I mumble. That's cool! she exclaims, Right? It's complicated, I remind her. Why? she says, Because he lives in Buenos Aires? Because we're *friends*, I tell her and she says, Shouldn't that just make everything better?

I almost tell her to stop being naïve but decide against it. She's got a point. Without our history that kiss wouldn't have felt half as good.

We've been down this road before, I tell her and she practically squeals. I knew it! she cries, When? A long time ago, I mutter, Twelve years. Damn, she says, taken aback.

For a second she soaks in what I've told her while I light another cigarette. At this point there's so much smoke in the kitchen—even with the window open—that my eyes are smarting.

Y'all slept together way back then? she asks. Yeah, I say. More than once? she asks and I nod because I'm not thinking about my sister or how she can't see me up here in Chicago. I'm thinking about Joel *the way he looked the way he smelled the way I wanted him and hated him and his expression after the last time the time in the dark after he found out he had a show his first-ever show and we went out to celebrate and I'd told myself told him I was done but on the back porch he touched me and I let him. I fucking let him and after I came when I told him I'd made a mistake he looked at me like I'd carved his heart out of his chest with the box cutter he ended up using himself two years later.*

I guess my sister knows me well enough that she's taking my silence for a *yes*. So that was a long time ago, she says, This could be different. In theory, I admit. Here we go, she sighs. What do you mean, *here we go?* I say. Why do you have to pick everything apart? she asks. That's what I *do*, I remind her, I'm trained in analysis, Ashley. Oh right, you have a *PhD*, she says, alluding to the shit I give her for being on a six-year undergraduate plan and I lose my fucking patience. What do you want from me? I ask, I've spent my life buried in excavation. Okay, she says, So what's at the bottom of this thing you've got with Joel? Love! I cry and man, everything inside me, everything I've wound up tight for so long, instantly unspools.

Holy *shit*.

Ashley's laughing and I guess if I weren't so thunderstruck myself I'd be congratulating her on unearthing the biggest discovery my life has ever *seen*. Instead I'm shaking all over. Man, no amount of vodka's going to calm this kind of quaking and I drop into a chair at the kitchen table, the buzz that started somewhere in my chest finding its way into my arms and legs and *tongue.*

What is it about him anyway? Ashley asks and I see my life with Joel flash before my eyes from the beginning. He's shaking my hand in the middle of our dorm room my eyes on his sketch pad his hands all over Melissa at Barton Springs we're sitting in the swing on our front porch driving to Houston after his mom died teetering at the top of Mount Bonnell his scuba gear his BMW I'm sitting in the barstool in our house on Pearl when his mouth hits mine my bedroom his bedroom his studio and Heavenly and the afternoon he realized I'd moved out without telling him first. The call I got from his dad. Working our careful way back over beers over dinners over the phone. Trip after trip, half of them punctuated by an argument. Cemeteries and Henry and our last night in Greece my hands around his waist as he opens the throttle on his motorcycle opens his mouth in my kitchen.

Everything, I say, It's everything.

Joel / Buenos Aires

I'm in a dream so vivid I believe it's real. My bike between my legs, the wind cold in my hair. His arms around me, *back where we started.* White flakes of snow fall from the sky, stick to my leather jacket. The motor thrums beneath me.

I know before I see the headlights. There's nothing, not a sound, no horn, no scream of brakes. Just the slow slide into the bike's front wheel, the lift, the wrench of his hands from my waist. I hit the ground, and a current courses through my body like some kind of electrocution.

As I rise from the dream, light scatters around me. I fumble for the phone. Joel, Catherine says.

James / Chicago

We're running late and I can't find my phone. I left it right here on my nightstand because when I woke up this morning the damn thing didn't have a charge. I wasn't planning on calling Joel before I left for campus or anything—the conversation I want to have with him needs to happen without interruptions, not in the middle of a drunken night, not when I'm trying to get my kid off to preschool—but I generally make an effort not to let my cell phone die since I got rid of the land line before my last trip to Greece and I'm not going to get any points for being a responsible parent if I need to call poison control and don't have a phone. I don't know what the hell I was thinking last night, forgetting to plug it in.

Well shit. I know what I was thinking. I was thinking about what I'll say to Joel when I finally get him on the phone. I was rehearsing lines I thought I might not say to anyone ever again and certainly not to Joel. I kept thinking I'd gotten this wrong, that the vodka and cigarettes had my head as cloudy as the Brazos River where it meets the Gulf. *This here is what you get, dumbass, for taking advice from your little sister.* But Henry climbed into bed with me this morning and the first thought that came to me as I woke up was *I've gotta talk to Joel.*

So I plugged in my phone and got in the shower and since then I've been running around getting Henry's breakfast and packing his lunch and I haven't touched my cell phone but it's not on the nightstand anymore. I pound down the stairs and find Henry in the kitchen peering under the table where the cat has its eyes narrowed. Have you seen my phone? I ask and Henry straightens right up and claps his hands. Hot and cold, hot and cold! he cries.

Aw hell, he's talking about that game Joel got him into last month, the one where he hides something and I have to dig it up while he shouts *warmer* and *colder* at me. You'd think this game would be right up my alley but Henry doesn't want to hide one of his toy cars or Mr. Boo. I've found animal cookies floating in the toilet and my car keys in the fridge and now he's got my cell phone God knows where. Henry, we're late, I tell him and his eyes look just like the cat's.

All right, all right. I squat down beside him so we're on the same level. You really like this game, I say, Don't you? So cold! he proclaims and what the fuck, I'm probably going to find my phone faster if I play the game with him. I give him a smile I don't so much mean but I want him to know I'm ready to look. Cold! he repeats. I get up and take a couple steps toward the living room. Wama, wama, wama! he says, jumping up and down, the word making barely any sense with that lisp of his.

I creep around the living room, following my son's enthusiastic instructions and coming up with nothing. Watch out, watch out! he shrieks when I lift the couch cushion, So hot! Henry, there's nothin' *here*, I say but he just giggles. Man, I'm losing my patience. If I'm not in the car in three minutes I'm going to have to haul this kid to campus with me. Are you sure it's in the livin' room? I ask. Hot, he insists and I take a big old breath. Henry, I say, We're late and we can play this game later but right now I need you to tell me where you hid my phone.

Henry gives me the kind of stubborn look that lets me know the trouble I'm going to have when he's a teenager.

Ten minutes later I'm driving too fast for my neighborhood, determined to get this kid to preschool even if that means I'm getting to campus a few minutes late. In the backseat he sings to himself about Rufus and a trail into the woods.

I still don't have my damn phone.

Joel / Bogota

I can't get on the plane. They're making the announcement for the second time, and I still can't move. I have my boarding pass in one hand, my cell phone in the other, and I keep pressing numbers, like that's going to change the fact that James won't answer his phone. A half a dozen voicemails… *Where the hell is he?* Maybe he turned his phone off last night—if that's the case, I'm going to be unbelievably angry, because he knows how tenuous my father's situation is right now—but I've been sitting in the Bogota airport since I landed at 11:30 this morning, and at this point, he's been awake and on campus for hours. I tried his office a couple of times, too, and I still can't get hold of him.

Beside me, a woman slides a bookmark between the pages of her paperback. All around me, people are getting in line. I watch them, knowing if I'm not right behind them, if I miss this flight, I might not see my father alive again. Catherine's expecting me, and my father's dying, and if I knew James would be at the other end of this flight, *I could get on the fucking plane.* This is what we agreed. This is what he promised. I get a call from Catherine, and he'll be on the next plane south. The logistics have been finalized, *but they don't fucking work if James doesn't answer his phone.* I know we argued last night. I know I hung up on him, but *come on.*

I try him one more time, listening to the first ring and the second and the third until I finally just hang up before I roll to voicemail again. What else can I possibly say?

Maybe I should fly right to Chicago, and James and I can make the trip to Houston together. Even if for some reason he's not answering his phone because he's pissed at me, once he sees me, he'll cave. And whether I see my father alive or not doesn't matter as much in this moment as not having to make the trip alone.

I go up to the information desk at the gate and explain my situation, that I'm supposed to be on this flight, but I've changed my mind and want to go to Chicago instead. The woman behind the counter eyes me with suspicion, then punches my information into her computer. I shift from one foot to the other, checking my cell. The soonest I can get you to Chicago is at noon tomorrow, she finally tells me, and those tears I've been beating back come to my eyes again. You have to have something sooner than tomorrow, I plead, but she shakes her head.

As her colleague makes the last announcement for my flight, I moan. Sir? the woman says. Okay, I say, Just… put me on a plane somewhere else.

Somewhere else, she repeats, and I say, *Anywhere.* She takes a long look at my face, then starts pecking on her computer. I glance again at my phone, shaking it like it's a magic 8 ball and has all the answers I need.

I have a plane leaving in thirty minutes, the woman says. Oh, that's good, I whisper, That's so great. I'm practically crying, and I hand over my credit card, watching as her colleague closes the door to the jet way. With the gate empty, a sort of serenity settles around me. I'll land somewhere else and make my way to James. From there, we'll go together to Houston. I gaze at the angel in front of me with tears in my eyes. Where am I going? I ask, and she gives me the brightest of smiles. Seattle, she says.

James / Chicago

I picked the wrong day to be late and I sure as shit picked the wrong day to be distracted. (Distracted, Jesus. Like I needed *that* one-two punch.) I'm head of the search committee for the Professor of Antiquities we're looking to hire and fuck if I haven't forgotten that the candidate I've been arguing for got here this morning from BU. Kayla picked her up at the airport and now Jenna, the new candidate, is standing in the hallway outside my office with my chair who gives me a look that'd make me swallow my cigarette if I hadn't just crushed the damn thing on the stairs. Whatever, at least I got Henry to preschool. If I'd spent any longer looking for my phone I'd have my kid in my arms right now and no way would that go over well. I turn on the good old boy charm, hoping that might appeal to Jenna who's originally from Mississippi. My chair wrinkles her nose like I've just crawled out from a south Texas bayou. Maybe she just doesn't like the smell of Marlboros.

I'm the one giving Jenna a tour today and that means I don't have time for the quiet cup of coffee I wanted before I've got to teach my Greek Art and Archaeology class. I need a few minutes to get myself focused because after last night I'm all over the place. I guess I could usher Jenna on into my office and brew something to tide me over but I have a feeling my chair won't appreciate the ashtray I left on my desk. Why don't we take a walk? I say, ignoring the phone ringing on the other side of my door and giving my chair a wave. *You can go now. I've got this under control.*

Sure I do. That's why I'm asking Jenna questions and drifting off when she answers. That's why I've got her hiking around campus in the middle of January. Head of the search committee with my number one candidate in front of me and I can't concentrate because I'm wondering if Joel's still pissed. I'm wondering what I'm going to say to him on the phone tonight. What makes me think he'll be happy anyway? Just because I'm ready doesn't mean he's feeling the same. *Tell me what you want from me,* he said before he hung up and I fumbled around for my balls and came up empty-handed as usual. What if I'd answered him? What if I'd said, *You. You're what I want.* Doesn't mean he would've been like, *Well, good, since I want you too.* Maybe he doesn't.

Man, that right there stops me in my tracks. Why have I been assuming he's into me? Just because once upon a time I caught that fishhook smile of his? We were kids, barely out of college. So we had phone sex a couple years ago. So what? He was drunk out of his mind and still so in love with Adam that I had to convince him not to reach out to the guy the same damn night. And that kiss in my kitchen… He pushed me away from him. He fled the fucking *house* then lit out for Buenos Aires and didn't call me for days. *He was sick,* I argue with myself. *He wanted you to read to him every night.* Riiight. Because nothing says *I love you* like asking someone to read a book review aloud from *The American Journal of Archaeology.*

By this time I'm muttering under my breath and Jenna who figures I'm saying something relevant to her presence here on this campus asks me to repeat myself. I blink at her then blurt out a question so inappropriate I want to die. Are you single? I ask and the second I realize what I've done I start stumbling all over an apology. Man, I hope she doesn't take this up with my chair. I'm at the beginnin' of somethin' with someone…, I confess and then I start shaking my head since Joel and I aren't at the beginning. We're in the middle. Hell, maybe we're at the fucking end.

But Jenna's nodding like she understands. *Thank you, Jesus.* Anyway, I mumble.

If I thought I could get away with a cigarette, you better believe I'd light right up and I clap my hands together to refocus. Jenna's shivering like she never did get used to Boston. Still got Mississippi in your blood, huh? I ask. Maybe a coffee? she pleads and I look at my watch and figure we've got just enough time to grab one before she's off to meet the dean.

You'd think after that debacle I'd get my shit together and I guess I teach my class without looking like a total idiot but probably not by much. Somehow I make it through the rest of the day. We have lunch with the graduate students, I teach a graduate seminar (while Jenna meets with the provost), I sit in on a sample Ancient Empires class that Jenna knocks out of the park. I sneak off for a cigarette before straggling into her lecture late in the afternoon in just enough time to wish her luck and pat my pocket for my cell phone before I remember what happened this morning. I hope Henry's sitter doesn't need to get in touch with me. She'll have her hands full since I forgot to remind Henry I wouldn't be the one picking him up from preschool but what am I supposed to do about that?

I want to listen to Jenna's presentation and I've got a question ready to lob her way when she's finished but my attention's worth shit. I might as well be one of my lazy undergraduates. I still can't believe I asked this woman if she was single and thinking about that has me fuming about the guy Joel's been seeing and why am I the one who's always jealous anyway? When's the last time Joel asked if I was dating anyone? I get laid plenty.

Well, whatever. Not plenty. Twice since Lizzie left, both one-night stands. The first woman I met at a conference and never saw again. The second woman I run into occasionally at the park. She's got a kid Henry's age. I don't even know how the hell we got off the ground. We saw each other at some kid's birthday party and I guess she was just as desperate as I was because suddenly I was suggesting we meet for a drink. She said she'd just bring a bottle of wine to my place and since Henry was going to be with his mom I said fine. That's about how the sex was too, *fine*. Don't get me wrong, I was glad to get what I got. This dry spell I've been working my way through over the past couple years borders on outright celibacy. Why doesn't Joel ask about that? The last time he took any interest at all in who I might be dating was when he came up to Chicago right after Lizzie left. Here I am getting all bent out of shape over that Elías guy and how much does Joel care about who *I'm* seeing?

Maybe he doesn't. Man, am I fixing to get myself rejected here? When was the last time I heard Joel say something other than *tell me what you want* or *do you want me?*

Heavenly, that's when. Nineteen ninety-fucking seven and we were sitting across from each other in a restaurant so posh I never would've been able to foot the bill. And as if that wasn't enough I'd flown off my snowmobile earlier in the day and just about broke my neck even though I was wearing my helmet. And there was Joel drinking wine and looking at me all moon-eyed and I knew, I fucking *knew* he was going to say the words that would bring us down. I was willing him to keep his mouth shut and he came out with *I'm in love with you* and by then I had my head hanging low because that was the end of us right there. No way could I keep sleeping with him after that though whatever, I did for a while.

Jenna's wrapping up and I'm still in Heavenly. I don't even know if she's done a good job and I shake myself out of '97 and look around at my colleagues. I can't get much of a read from my chair but Kayla's wearing a big old smile and Justin sends me a thumbs up over his shoulder so I guess what I missed wasn't so bad. I knew I made the right call, arguing to get Jenna out here and I tell her congratulations on our way to dinner.

Man, a single day has never lasted so long.

Joel / Seattle

Slouched in a chair in baggage claim, propelled by a force that feels like nothing I can explain, I call Adam. Before I left Bogota, when I was told I was heading to Seattle, I uttered a laugh I expected the ticket agent to return. Seattle? Please. But she'd cocked her head with a half-smile, and I realized I've somehow ended up on the butt end of a cosmic joke. For three years, I've been avoiding Adam, and suddenly his voice fills my ear, sleepy and so familiar I have trouble saying his name. In the stunned silence that follows, I add my own, as if he might not have recognized my voice. I know, he says. There's no judgment in his tone, just disbelief. Did I wake you? I ask. I wasn't sleeping, he admits. Oh, I say, Why not?

That's a question I shouldn't have asked. He could be with a lover, a boyfriend, a partner. I'm not thinking clearly. Still he answers, without a hint of hostility. I have trouble sleeping sometimes, he says, and I wonder if that's because of me, because of what happened to us, before I dismiss the notion as narcissistic. How are you? I ask, and he's quiet, as if he's trying to remember or hesitant to share. I have a nice view, he finally tells me. At the moment? I ask, Or in general? From my office, he says. Are you still with Microsoft? I ask, and he tells me he's been with them for three years, like maybe I've forgotten how long it's been since we broke up or why he moved in the first place. What about you? he asks, I hear you're in Argentina. I am, I say, Though my time's almost up.

There's a beat of silence I know exactly how to interpret. You're coming home? he asks, and we both balk at the word. *Home.* For years, I knew what that meant, first because of the space I shared with James on Pearl Street and then because of Adam. We lived together for more than four years, and I didn't ever imagine wanting anything else. I might have preferred living in a different sort of house in a different part of Austin, but the way I felt waking up next to Adam every morning was all I needed. Adam *was* home, and now I have to reorient myself to those 750 square feet where I've been working for the past year and a half.

I don't know what I'm doing, I confess. Are you still painting? he asks, and though I'm thousands of miles away from my studio, my mosaic clicks into place, my own personal kaleidoscope. I'm using glass, I tell him. What do you mean, glass? he asks, confused, and I change the subject and ask about his family.

He tells me that his sister was in Seattle just last month with her husband and children. His niece has started taking driver's ed. His mother had to sell the house, the ranch and horses in Kentucky. Did you ever consider going back? I ask, and he tells me he'd thought about the idea for weeks but ultimately didn't want to do it alone. He says the words matter-of-factly, without the weight of accusation, but they still crush me. We could have been something together. We could have been so good. How's your father? he asks. He's dying, I say.

Like *home*, the word throws me. My father's dying. Actively dying; he won't make it through the weekend, might not make it through the next twenty-four hours. In a matter of moments—in the time it would take me to fly back and forth from Seattle to Buenos Aries only a couple of times—he'll be gone. Honestly, he's probably already gone. His heart might still beat, but I have a feeling he's so far past consciousness he wouldn't open his eyes if I stood beside him and screamed. Our relationship will never evolve, and I'll forever be waiting for a declaration of his love.

How long does he have? Adam asks. I don't know, I say, The weekend?

Adam's probably beginning to understand the motivation for my call. After all, he went through something similar just a few years ago, and his connection with his father wasn't anywhere near as complicated as the one I have with mine.

Are you with him now? he asks. No, I'm here, I tell him, In Seattle. You're *here*? he breathes, and I try to explain how I landed in Bogota and couldn't make myself get on the next plane. Oh, honey, he says, the word slipping from his mouth out of habit, Where are you now? At the airport, I admit, and he tells me he's coming to get me.

Arguing with him would be absurd. I knew I'd see him; why else would I have called? Will I recognize you? I ask.

Now I watch as he makes his way through baggage claim. He hasn't spotted me yet, and I'm thankful for a second to steady myself. He's dressed for Seattle, in jeans and an overcoat and a scarf that even from a distance calls me to compliment his eyes. Years have gone by; he'll be forty-four in May, and I think about the birthdays passed, the moments I've missed but can see now in his face. He's older, his hair thinner, but his smile, when he finds me, I remember from the night we met. We reach for each other; I hold him tighter than I should, then tighter. You're so *thin*, he tells me once I've pulled myself away. I had pneumonia, I say, and he touches my arm. Even through my leather jacket, I can feel his heat.

I follow him to his car; a few inches closer and his sleeve could touch my own. One misstep and I could trip into his arms. His fingers in mine, as familiar as if I'd never left. All those times I walked beside him into our favorite restaurant, onto an airplane bound for Belize, around Kyle's pool on our way down to his boat; never has the space between us seemed more conspicuous. What happened to the BMW? I ask when he stops at the back end of a Toyota Camry and pops the trunk. Didn't make it out of Austin, he admits.

An ember of anger I thought I'd extinguished comes to life in the center of my chest. His BMW didn't make it out of Austin? The car he bought with the guy he was fucking? The car that epitomized everything wrong with our relationship?

He takes my suitcase from my hand, and I take a breath. After all, he's at the airport in the middle of the night because of me.

Are you hungry? he asks, shutting the trunk and adding, Easy enough to stop somewhere. Yeah, all right, I say, Whatever's open. Well, maybe not the 24-hour Wendy's, he says, smiling. Actually…, I start, and he groans. Don't tell me, he says, You're eating meat? My landlady makes really good beef empanadas, I admit. He laughs without the animosity I felt hearing he'd ditched the BMW.

Then again, I'm not the one who cheated.

At a 24-hour diner, I order scrambled eggs and decaf coffee. My hands tremble beneath the table, and I hold them between my knees to make them stop, watching as Adam stirs sugar into his coffee. I keep waiting to wake from this dream, for the punch line, to find myself in my studio in Buenos Aires, a wall of glass across from me. Instead, I'm asking Adam questions about Microsoft and listening to stories about his nieces and nephew. He speaks easily, casually, as if there's nothing unusual about sharing breakfast with me in the middle of the night, despite not having spoken to me in years. What did you mean, you're working with glass? he asks, and I show him the tiny lacerations on my fingers.

Our food comes. I barely touch my eggs and keep my hands cupped around my mug of coffee. I haven't removed my coat; the weather's worse than I expected. For a moment, I see Adam climbing from our pool in Austin. He doesn't bother with a towel; the sun will dry him soon enough. His skin feels warm.

As we're waiting for the check, I ask if he's seeing anyone. No, he says, and then he looks terrified, like he's caught himself in a lie. I just take a sip of coffee and wait for him to elaborate. Haltingly, he admits that he's been out a few times lately. There's a friend of a friend, or something like that. They're not serious. He's toying with his spoon as he speaks, spinning it on the table. For three years, Joel, he says, I've been going through the motions.

I think about what I've been doing the past three years. Scrambling to pay rent. Tripping on Ecstasy with a stranger in Chicago. Getting to know Henry. Traveling to Greece. Circling James and ending up in Buenos Aires. Buying a motorcycle. Telling my father that I love him. Circling James and ending up in Buenos Aires, again. Showing up for the glass day after day, no matter how tired I am, no matter how heartbroken. I'm suddenly so weary.

Joel, Adam says, and I wish I couldn't see our history when I look into his eyes. He reaches for my hand, cradles my fingers in his own. Why didn't you answer me? he asks, When I got your email, I thought— I pull away from him. Can we go? I say, I'm beat.

James / Chicago

Henry's sound asleep when I get home from Jenna's dinner. My sitter told me she could hear my phone ringing somewhere near the couch but the sound was too muffled to figure out where. I wonder who's been calling. Joel maybe. Or my sister. My plan since this morning has been to wake up my kid even if that means we're playing hot and cold at midnight. I need to talk to Joel and that's all there is to it.

Looking at the way Henry's curled up so sweet in his bed holding tight to Mr. Boo makes me waffle.

All right, so it's not just Henry. All day I've been thinking about that phone call last night and the more I think on it the more confused I feel. What if I put myself out there and Joel shoots me right down? That could happen. Hell, that's *likely* to happen. Just because I'm ready doesn't mean he'll be on board.

That's what was bothering me today while I was with Jenna. Then after dinner I drove her back to her hotel and we were talking about Sappho and Catullus, nothing personal at all and I pulled up to the curb to let her out and she said, Good luck with that woman. What woman? I asked and she blinked and then I blinked because *shit* she was talking about *Joel*. This morning I'd babbled about being at the beginning of something and she'd assumed I meant with a woman. I stared at her and she looked all embarrassed and before I could jump in with an *oh right right* she said, I'm sorry, I didn't realize...

She thought I was gay and I corrected her so quick I sounded like I was lying even though I wasn't. I swear I wasn't. I wasn't because I'm not. I know I'm not. I lived with Joel for a long time and I saw what he did, met the guys he fucked and no way did I ever want a piece of that. Even after Joel and I started sleeping together—well, mostly after we stopped—I'd catch myself studying one of my students or some guy in front of me at the grocery store and I'd try to imagine... you know. They did nothing for me. I didn't want them, simple as that but the way I felt when I thought about Joel... I'd made us happen and whatever, we might've had sex years ago but that doesn't mean I don't remember what we were like together. Well shit, obviously. Henry's living proof.

For a long time, for a good year after Joel and I quit sleeping together I didn't go on any dates. I didn't hook up with a single girl. I was trying to figure out what the hell I'd been doing with Joel, if there was something about him that had me straying temporarily from what I'd always believed was a staunch heterosexuality or if what had gone on between Joel and me meant I was something else, something I'd never much considered and wasn't at all sure I wanted to be. Having a gay roommate was one thing. Being gay myself, having to explain that to my friends, my parents, my colleagues? That was something else. However broken up I was about Joel—he likes to pretend I didn't give a shit about hurting him, that calling it quits was something easy instead of what made me fail my qualifying exams in my doctoral program—I knew I didn't have a choice. I wasn't going to be what he needed. I wasn't going to be his boyfriend.

Then I met Lizzie and she was my relief. I wanted her. I loved her. I wasn't gay. I *knew* it. Now here I am, twelve years later, wanting Joel just as bad as I ever did back then and maybe more and one insinuation from a woman who isn't even my colleague yet has me looking like a closet case. *Awkward* doesn't even begin to describe our goodbye outside Jenna's hotel.

I need to be damn sure I'm ready this time. If I tell Joel I want him (Do I? All the way home I was second-guessing myself.) and he says okay then I need to follow this thing through whatever that looks like, wherever that leads us. We're not twenty-five anymore. We've got a lot at stake, so much that instead of waking my son I go downstairs and pour myself a drink. In the living room I sit down in front of *Crossing* and take in what he thought of us. After a while I close my eyes.

Joel / Seattle

Early twentieth-century, Adam says as we pull to the curb, and I stare at his bungalow, with its peaked roof and gingerbread woodwork. You did this *yourself?* I ask, and he admits that he hired plenty of help. C'mon, he adds, Let me show you.

I follow him up a half a dozen steps to a porch large enough to hold a glider and an umbrella stand. The door looks like it's the original, and I wait as Adam slides a key in the lock. Inside, there's an agreeable slant to the hardwood floors, old school windows, furniture I don't recognize. The kitchen has glass-fronted shelves and a tiled countertop, a table in the corner with bench seating, a stove and refrigerator made to look vintage, even if they're not. A wooden cabinet holds a stackable washer and dryer, and a screen door opens onto a small back porch and even smaller backyard. But big enough for a garden, Adam allows, Maybe this spring.

He gestures me down the hallway, pausing so I can see the guest bedroom, barely large enough for a full-size bed and dresser. The bathroom might be my favorite room, with its opulent color scheme—rose and amethyst and pearl—and I linger over the crystal chandelier with pink droplets, and a claw-foot tub. Gorgeous, I tell him, and Adam winks. Want to take a bath? he asks.

The second the invitation leaves his mouth, he realizes what he's done, pulling words from the past as if nothing has happened since he first spoke them eleven years ago, as if we could slide in at opposite ends of the tub the way we did the night we met. I can feel my face emptying of blood; a gilt-edged mirror above the pedestal sink reflects my expression, pale and precarious. Joel— Adam starts. You know what? I say, I really need to sleep.

The next morning, I come to as if I've been drugged or knocked unconscious. Disoriented, head aching, I pull myself into a sitting position, then remember where I've ended up: in Seattle, in Adam's guest bedroom. I fled here last night after he asked if I wanted to take a bath. Now I look around me, at the sky heavy with rain, glimpsed from behind the curtains. There's a chill here, seeping through the windows, and I shiver beneath a coffee-colored quilt stitched with stars as intricate as snowflakes. Adam isn't here; the office, he'd said as I was turning away from him last night, and so he must be there now, in whatever meetings he couldn't cancel.

Adam. I'm in his house. I saw him just a few hours ago. He's coming back at some point, and I can see him again. Shouldn't I be in Houston, waiting for my father to die? Or in my studio, glass slipping through my fingers? I should be with James, and I search for my phone. Surely by now… But I can see with one glance that he hasn't called. Only Catherine has tried to get in touch with me; I'd left a vaguely worded message yesterday before I boarded the plane to Seattle, something about delays and cancellations, and now she wants an update. James obviously needs no such information. All those voicemails I left him yesterday and he can't bring himself to respond. I shudder a sob, then go in search of Adam's thermostat and bump up the heat.

Twenty minutes later, I've wandered to the front porch to sit in the glider, then come back inside, shaking the mist from my hair. I've stood in the middle of the living room, poked through the lawyer's bookcase against the wall opposite the television, tried out the sofa and both chairs, some kind of Goldilocks. I've looked through Adam's refrigerator and drunk a glass of water from the set of glasses I found above the dishwasher—one hidden behind a cabinet, which made me laugh. I've sat on the cushion-covered picnic bench and watched the rain drip from the gutters. Then I walked down the hall, glancing in the bedroom where I'd slept. In the bathroom, I checked out Adam's medicine cabinet and the linen cupboard where he keeps his towels, and I wandered back across the hall and returned with my toothbrush, standing in front of the sink while I brushed my teeth. I rinsed my mouth, then my face, and as I patted myself dry with a hand towel, the radiator hissed. Now I hold my chilly hands above the metal, trying to get warm.

I no longer feel the rush of rage that consumed me when we first pulled up to the house early this morning or when I stood in his bathroom and stared at his claw-foot tub, which seemed to me emblematic of everything I'd ever wanted when we were together and which he refused me again and again. That he's changed his life in the past three years—gotten rid of the car, bought and redecorated the kind of house we'd talked about buying together—leaves me tired and confused, and after a minute, I rub my hands together and turn out the bathroom light. There's one room I haven't yet explored, and though I should probably leave him his privacy, I head there anyway.

A carbon copy of the room I wanted for us, the room I envisioned. There's a quilt on the bed and a bedside lamp with fringe long and thick and pink. I find the same color in the quilt, along with greens and grays that remind me of colors I used long ago and haven't painted with since. There's an armchair in the corner by the windows, and I brush the green velvet with the tips of my fingers. A desk barely big enough for a laptop, a chestnut-colored dresser, a closet with the door ajar. I thumb through his clothes, the suits and ties and dress shirts he's been wearing for the past three years, most of which I've never seen. Sandals, tennis shoes, a pair of cycling shoes that tells me he's back on his bike or taking classes on his lunch hour. There's a bookcase, an alarm clock with an iPod docking station, a plant stretching its leaves toward the gray sky. A nightstand with a drawer: I pull that open and find a handful of change, Tylenol, a box of condoms with only a few missing. For just a moment, I picture him with the friend of a friend he mentioned last night.

I don't know why I'm here, and trying to make sense of the past twenty-four hours leaves me wondering how much say I really have about anything. I've experienced too many synchronicities in my life to make me think there isn't a bigger picture. I just can't see the final image, and the moments that have made a difference—getting paired with James for a roommate, freshman year; insisting I wasn't up for a night out and meeting Adam as I was leaving a club; making a quick run to Central Market and ending up, however circuitously, in Buenos Aires—don't feel as random as they did when I was younger.

The front door opens; I hear Adam calling my name. There's urgency in his voice, and fear. This man wants me as much as James ever has, even if he treated me just as badly. With no one do I know where I stand, not one hundred percent of the time. I can make assumptions. I can guess. There were moments my father was good to me. James redeemed himself over and over for the way he behaved that terrible winter we slept together. Adam knows he hurt me, would take back every wrong inflicted if he could.

I could say no. I could thank Adam for letting me spend the night, wish him well, and check myself into a hotel. In the absence of men, I could turn to my art. It's easy enough to find paper and a decent pencil. I've worked with less in the past, sketched on a paper napkin, scrawled on my hand. I'll use anything to release the madness inside of me, the insight, the beauty. This I can rely on; my muse has never let me down. I may have lost sight of her at times, but I've always found my way back to her. In an hour, I could be in her hands.

I was afraid you were gone, Adam says, appearing in the doorway, and his relief crashes over me. Just as I find my footing, his arms pull me under.

James / Chicago

I know what happened the second I see my cell phone. Henry's hooraying beside me, shouting and clapping because I finally found the damn thing zipped into the couch cushion and I shush him, ice spreading through my gut when I look at my screen and see how many voicemails Joel left me. Fuck. *Fuck.* Something's wrong, something bigger than what happened the other night. I start listening to his messages—*James, he's dying, I'm going to Houston. Just landed in Bogota, where are you? James, will you please fucking call me? I know you're pissed, but I need you right now. Come on, James, please*—and man, I just want to weep.

Henry hid my phone, I blurt out the second Joel answers and his *whatever* sounds so whipped I realize right then and there that the *love* I belted out when I was on the phone with my sister I could never pass off as bullshit. Your dad, I say, Is he...? Dead? Joel finishes and man, that's when I know just how badly I fucked up not waking Henry last night and demanding my phone. Joel— I start and he tells me his dad's still alive. But not for long, he adds. I'm sorry I'm not there yet, man, I say. James, he sighs, I'm not even there.

He's been rerouted from Bogota with a flight landing in Houston at 6:30 this evening. I'll be there, I tell him, I'll have Henry with me but I'm callin' the airline soon as I hang up. Please don't bring Henry, he says, Take him to Fort Worth tonight, and just come down tomorrow. Are you sure? I ask, flat out despising the thought of him landing in Houston without me. Please, he says.

Three and a half hours later Henry and I are on a flight to Texas. My boy's beside himself, thrilled with the last-minute adventure to see his granny and grandad. He chatters to me and to Mr. Boo and *oohs* and *aahs* as he looks out the window when we leave the windy city to the dark. This here isn't remotely what I was thinking when I told my sister I needed to talk to Joel. A quiet conversation with a cigarette in my hand once Henry had gone to bed, that's more what I'd planned and instead I'm flying into a funeral. Instead it looks like I've been avoiding Joel right when he needed me most.

Henry's got his thumb in his mouth and I dig around in his little backpack and find him a pacifier. Man, I packed so quick I'm probably forgetting something essential but I know I've got my cell phone and charger and I guess as long as I can get in touch with Joel that's good enough. He's on his way to Houston too and something about the thought of us both up here in the night sky makes me feel like maybe everything might be all right. Better late than never, right?

Joel / Houston

My father's breathing, but barely; the sound makes me think of the clear, unencumbered breaths I've taken through a regulator: with James, with Adam, by myself when I lived on the Mexican coast. My first time scuba diving, I went with my father. I couldn't have been more than seven years old, but I remember widening my eyes at the sound, the way I might have the first time a doctor placed a stethoscope on my chest and let me listen to my heart. *I'm alive.* In the bed beside me, my father breathes no such breath. His death rattle fills the room, makes me want to hold my hands over my ears; I keep them in my lap. I think Catherine expected me to touch him, to whisper words of encouragement or endearment. I offer nothing, save for my presence beside him. I'm waiting for him to die.

I'm not sure what Catherine's thinking, but she's tearful and tender, which reminds me that the man she's mourning isn't anything like the man I've known for almost thirty-seven years. There's too much to disregard, too many scars to overlook, disavows of love to ignore. Once, furious with James for confiding to Adam that we'd been intimate, I scoured through our years together, racking up the evidence in favor of his prosecution. In the end, I found too much friendship to write him off forever. Now, if I were to scrutinize my relationship with my father, I'd come up so short I might as well put the noose on him myself.

The demons hovering around my father's bed find this funny, and they laugh aloud. I don't laugh along with them, but I watch them, knowing they might just as easily be my father's companions in the afterlife as a fabrication of my overwrought mind. I've hit some kind of wall, though I'm not sure I could pinpoint the moment: when my father met my eye in silence, when Catherine called, when I landed in Bogota without a voicemail from James.

When I slept with Adam.

James will be here tomorrow, but not Adam, who has left no less than a half a dozen voicemails since I walked away from him twelve hours ago. I haven't answered any of them, but I glance down at the string of texts James and I have exchanged since he called this afternoon, just as I was getting into a cab in Seattle. They'll cost a fortune, but I don't care. He's in Fort Worth, spending the night with his parents, then flying to Houston tomorrow morning without Henry. He has his phone on, and he instructed me to let him know if anything happens.

Catherine's praying; I wonder if that's noteworthy. The demons don't seem to think so. They're toasting each other with fiery glasses of champagne, aware that my father's a lost cause. There's no chance for him now, not with the way his breath's clattering around, and I think about lying on the ground in that cemetery in Chicago and hearing James talk about the coin the Greeks placed in the mouths of their dead to ensure their safe ferry to the Underworld. I'm struck by the urge to fumble for a loose quarter, picture shoving it between my father's cold, dead lips.

He's fucked, and so am I.

Buenos Aires feels eons away, an Elysium of my imagination. I left in such a hurry that I abandoned the glass, have not even one sliver in my pocket. I spent the first half of today with Adam, burrowing into my past like I was digging my own grave. I don't know who I am to James, but we're not done with what happened in his kitchen last month; I'm sure of that. At this point, I'm numb, as dead as my father's going to be, sooner rather than later, judging from the party the demons have thrown in his honor.

They're dancing, macabre eyes glinting with light. Pointed tails and pitchforks, they make love to my father, ignore Catherine's beseeching hands, her keening. If I were to try to intervene, they wouldn't hear me. They're consumed with their prize, my father's soul in exchange for the pleasure of his lies, the sinking of a fist into the soft flesh of his first wife, a lit cigar and the arm of a child. My father labors for breath, and the demons celebrate with loud, raucous voices in a language impossible to understand. The heat in the room stifles. I wipe my forehead with the back of my hand.

As the soirée crescendos, Catherine excuses herself for just a minute. I want to call her back, go so far as to reach for her fingers. Pressing my hand between her own, she gives me a faint smile; she thinks I'm comforting her and whispers her appreciation. She's going to miss the finale, but she's already turning away, closing the door behind her. The demons grin, raise their claws. I stare at my father, who looks nothing like the man I remember. Unrecognizable and incapable of hurting me any longer, if I could only wipe my memory clean.

As I watch, he lets out a ragged, agonized breath. He never takes another. Around me, the demons break into applause, jabbering and gesticulating, the cacophony almost more than I can bear. They crowd closer to my father, wetting their lips with sharp tongues. Then they're tearing into him, shredding his skin with jagged nails, searching for his soul. One looks over its shoulder, spies me balled up in the corner, and grins. I squeeze my eyes shut, trying to block out their shrieks of delight; they've discovered something blacker than even they envisioned, and I make myself smaller and smaller until suddenly they're silent.

Slowly, I inch open one eye. The room's empty except for my father, who's sitting on the edge of the bed with a scotch in his hand and a head full of hair. Son of a bitch, he says.

James

All the way to Houston I've been wondering. I haven't seen Joel since I cried *love* to my sister. I could be wrong about everything. Hell, there's a part of me that almost hopes I've gotten this ass-backwards. I mean, what do I think he's going to say when I tell him a flame lights right up in the center of my chest every time I think about him like I'm the furnace and he's the fucking pilot light? Just because I'm finally figuring shit out after all this time doesn't mean he'll tell me he feels the same way. Or maybe I'd think as soon as I saw him, *Jesus, Fielding, you were way off on this one.*

I wasn't way off. I was so spot-on I can't even find a *hi* for him. He opens the front door and the second I see him something sucks the air from my lungs. All these years I've been digging and what I finally found doesn't look anything like I expected. Instead I'm staring at starlight. I look at him shining in front of me and I feel the same way I felt last summer when the first rays of sun in over two thousand years saw that mosaic. All this time he's been right in front of me.

Thanks for coming, he says like I'm nothing more than the next-door neighbor before I can catch my breath and man, my heart just *sinks*. He's too checked out to realize what's glittering between us and I decide then and there to show him. Not now, not when he's taking me over to Catherine where I mumble my condolences knowing Joel's standing right beside me and can hear every lie I'm muttering about being sorry the bastard's finally gone, but soon. In the meantime I'll do everything I can to help him. Because I don't care if he's got dry eyes, I don't care if he's wearing some expensive sweater he probably bought this morning. I know this guy and he's not here.

Over the next couple hours he talks with Catherine's friends and handles phone calls from his dad's colleagues, smooth the way he was taught to be. That sweater he's wearing? Cashmere. His daddy would be proud. I might be the only one who knows I'm watching a charade and man, I'm aching to tell him that he doesn't have to pretend with me. I won't judge him if he'd rather be celebrating same as I'll understand if he's feeling this more than he thought he might. Want me to get you a drink? I ask, thinking maybe he'll loosen up a little and let down his defenses. No, thank you, he says like he's my customer at El Arroyo or something. How about some food? I ask, You hungry?

All day people have been dropping off food, lasagnas and salads and a ham I shoved in the spare fridge in the garage because the other one's already overflowing. There's got to be something here he can eat but he just shakes his head without looking up from where he and Catherine are writing the obituary. Man, if he keeps this up, this shiny façade, he's in for a seismic shift and it's not going to be pretty.

I leave it a while, listening along with Joel while Catherine reminisces. Every so often she breaks down and cries and Joel waits all patient for her to get herself together again. At this rate his dad's obituary won't make the paper tomorrow. I keep expecting Joel to get tired of hearing about how great the guy was but he holds it together until Catherine starts listing the pallbearers. That's when his jaw tightens and I don't blame him. I go into the kitchen and make him a plate with food I think he'll eat, salads and fruit and a handful of macadamia nuts from some fancy jar. When I set it beside him I get a look that gives me an idea of where we're headed before this is all over. I said I wasn't hungry, he reminds me. You gotta eat, Joel, I say in a low voice, If you wanna keep this same pace, you gotta eat. He hesitates then pops a nut in his mouth. I feel a big old twinge of relief. He'll be able to go a while longer and maybe I can get him alone, get him talking so he's not carrying this all by himself.

Hell, I'd carry it for him if I could.

Joel

Death steals my energy but withholds sleep. I've gotten no rest since I arrived in Houston, and despite having to deal with the preparations for my father's visitation and funeral—despite the visitation itself earlier tonight—I'm wide awake. Every time I think I'll be able to settle down, a different image floats through my consciousness: the chandelier in Adam's bathroom; my father's sickbed, stripped bare; Johnson McGarrity, my father's former boss, who retired years ago and walks now with a slight limp, his fingers gnarled from arthritis. I shook hands with him tonight; I shook hands with many of my father's colleagues. Some of them I've known for years. They came to my father's wedding back in '96. They came to my mother's funeral in '92.

I'm handling myself better this time around. I didn't flee the funeral home tonight; I haven't snuck any scotch. I'm not creating a scene. I've stepped into my father's shoes, do everything Catherine asks and anticipate what she doesn't. I know she's hurting. So I helped write the obituary, made the final decision about a casket, ordered the flowers. I've agreed to be a pallbearer. There's no request I've denied, and if nothing else, I'm grateful that tomorrow night this will all be over.

I might be a little less apprehensive if Adam would stop calling. He leaves voicemails telling me he wants to book the next flight to Houston. I'm half-afraid he might, and I should probably call him just to make sure that doesn't happen. Instead, I haven't responded to him at all. I can't put the words together, and as the hours pass, his messages become more carefully constructed, his voice more frantic. I don't know how to tell him he's making everything worse.

Then there's James. I believe his story about Henry hiding his phone; I was the one who taught his son the game. When James finally got hold of me, I was in Seattle on my way to the airport, and I could hear how sick he felt over missing my calls. He scrambled to get down here, has done everything right since he arrived. If he regrets that kiss last month or any of our better conversations since, he's doing a good job of pretending otherwise. If anything, I'd say he's holding back. Something's on his mind, and I have a feeling he's waiting until after tomorrow to unload. I have a feeling that under the circumstances, he wouldn't be happy to hear I spent Thursday night in Seattle.

Under any circumstances.

A skittering sound opens my eyes, and I sit up in bed, certain I'll find a demon crouched in the corner, nails long and tail sharp. They're done with my father; now they've come for me. A glimmer of moonlight slips through a gap in the curtains but fails to illuminate the shadows. I can hear you, motherfucker, I hiss, my voice too loud for the middle of the night, and ten seconds later, James stands backlit in the doorway. My gaze darts into the empty corner; I'm more abashed than relieved to find it empty. You all right? James asks, and the question strikes me as so ridiculous, so ludicrous, that I start to laugh. Hilarity sputters from between my lips, and I clap my hand over my mouth so I don't wake Catherine, though there's little likelihood that my stepmother, downstairs in a haze of narcotics, will hear me. Dude, James says, alarmed enough to step closer, and I get myself under control, snuffing my laughter the way we doused that campfire when we took Melissa and Cathleen into the woods. Tomorrow night, I tell him, I'm going to get drunk. Okay, he says slowly, You sure that's a good idea? I give him a smile, teeth bared so wide I'm almost snarling. Positive, I say.

James

The day's as easy as anyone could rightly expect, especially given the way Joel was acting in the middle of the night like he was trying to get himself checked into a mental ward. He plans on getting trashed after the reception and I'm trying to gear myself up to join him. I'm cool cracking open a beer but I've got a feeling that's not what Joel has in mind. I need to get him out of here. I need to get him away from Houston and on a plane to Chicago.

To look at him you'd think he was just fine. He's standing right beside me dressed in a suit and tie, his hair pulled back in a short ponytail so discreet I have to remind myself it's even there. Whatever, he's got circles under his eyes. He might be a little on the pale side. If I didn't know better I'd guess he was on his way to dinner but hungover from last night's party.

At the church he lifted his dad's casket without blinking. But there's a storm brewing inside him, I can feel it. I can feel it just standing here next to him. Man, I have never in my life wanted to touch him the way I do right now. Just a hand on his shoulder. Just so he has *something*.

The timing here sucks.

Across the open grave I can see my parents. My dad's holding Henry who's gazing at Joel like he's got some kind of bead on his thoughts. I can't even guess what he's thinking about the hole in the ground or the casket ready to be lowered the second the service ends. I wish he didn't have to see any of this shit.

Ashley didn't come but she sent flowers and a shit ton of texts asking what's going on. I kept it simple: I don't know. Henry hid my phone and Joel's dad died and now I'm working on getting him through this funeral before I start up a conversation about anything else.

I guess not everyone knew what a bastard Joel's dad was because there's a line of people here ready to pay their respects. Maybe they're mostly Catherine's friends. What do I know? Either way we're looking at a long night ahead of us. No way will these people skip the reception. I listened to Joel book the country club himself. I gave him advice on what to serve at the goddamn buffet. With that open bar we'll be getting back to Catherine's house late.

I steal a sidelong glance at Joel. He's got his head tilted like he's listening to every word the minister's saying but I don't buy that bullshit for a second. He might look the part of a grieving son but I know better.

He's pissed and he's not going to be able to hold it in forever.

Joel

I've talked to more than a hundred people, murmured *thank you* more times than I care to count. My smile feels forced, my tie like a noose. I keep going because there's no one else to handle this crowd other than Catherine, and she's walking a tightrope very few women could probably navigate. Svelte in a black dress and slender heels, she looks, nevertheless, like a wife who just lost her husband. I'm compelled to support her, especially knowing that after today, the likelihood I'll see her again with any frequency borders on slim to none.

Though there's an open bar, I haven't had a drink. Too easily, I could lose control here, as weary as I am, as unstable. I'm holding myself together until later tonight, when I plan on toasting my father with a glass of his favorite scotch. Or maybe I'll toast his death; I haven't decided yet. For the moment, I'm drinking water, which seems to be confusing James, who's on his third beer and keeps asking if he can get me anything. I'm irritated, not by his drinking but by his attention. I felt the same way the night of my mother's visitation. I need a modicum of space to process what's happening, and there are too many people to appease.

Right now, I'm headed toward Kyle and Scott, who've been nice enough to drive down from Austin. James must have gotten in touch with them over the weekend. I haven't seen them since the September before last, and there's something surreal about running into them in one of the reception rooms at River Oaks Country Club.

Come here, love, Kyle coos, opening his arms. He's dressed in a suit so somber and understated that Catherine would never recognize him. You've had a long few days, he murmurs soothingly after he releases me, and something about his intonation sets off an inner alarm. I glance at Scott; at once, I realize they've talked to Adam, and my eyes land on James, who's standing next to me and still has no idea I ended up in Seattle last week. I think I've changed my mind about that drink, I tell him, and that's all the encouragement he needs. He heads for the bar, and I turn back to Kyle and Scott. You talked to Adam, I say. Honey, Kyle moans, What were you *thinking*? I had a hard time convincing him not to come here today, Scott adds, and my heart bucks in my chest. Please, I say, Tell me he's not on a plane. He's not on a plane, Scott assures me, But I have a phone full of texts asking about you.

I try to back away, bumping into the demon that crawled out from under my bed this morning and has been following me around ever since. He grins, revealing sharp, black teeth. Why don't you come up to Austin for a few days? Scott suggests, Once you're finished here. I can't, I tell him, automatically glancing in James's direction. Kyle follows my gaze. Girlfriend, he warns, Don't you dare start up with him again.

The demon winks, like we're in on some kind of joke. Desperate for an escape, I scour the room and latch onto James's parents. They've kept their distance today, spent most of their time corralling Henry, who's sucking on his fingers. He must have lost his pacifier, and out of habit, I find myself patting my pockets in case I have an extra. I have to go, I say to Kyle and Scott, throwing a *thank you for coming* over my shoulder, and though they protest, I don't stop. The demon trots along behind me.

Joel, Mrs. Fielding says, holding out her arms, and I let myself be hugged, then turn to Henry, who's in his grandfather's arms. How's it going? I ask him, touching his cheek, and he takes his fingers from his mouth. I wanna cookie, he whines, sounding every bit as forlorn as I feel. Well, that's easy enough to find, I say, realizing too late that we're only serving cake.

He doesn't need a cookie, James tells me, walking up with a couple of beers. Henry scowls at his father. He's amped up enough, James adds to me, or maybe to his parents, He doesn't need the sugar. You don't need another beer, I say, taking note of the extra bottle in his hands, But I don't see that stopping you.

James's parents exchange glances, like they've been warned ahead of time about my demeanor and now have the evidence of my emotional state right in front of them. James gives his head a slight shake, like he's telling them not to say anything. Impatient, I take Henry right from his grandfather's arms, opting out of the beer James brought me. Let's get you a cookie, I say to his son.

Sometimes I forget how it feels to hold Henry. He's so solid, packed with warmth, and I tighten my arms around him as I head into the hall. You lose your pacifier, buddy? I ask Henry, and he nods, his eyes gleaming with tears. I bet he missed his nap today, and there's no way he's not feeling the tension here. You think a cookie will help? I ask. He nods again, without taking his fingers from his mouth. I'll have to wash his hands before I can let him eat anything, and I stop one of the waiters and ask him to point us in the direction of the kitchen, where Henry scores a heart-shaped sugar cookie scattered with sprinkles. He's all smiles as he washes his hands in the same sink the chefs use, insists on walking along beside me as we head back to the reception room. I take a breath, the first intentional breath I've taken all day. We have another hour here at most. I can make it another hour, surely.

My phone rings at the thought, and I close my eyes. I don't have to answer Adam's call. I don't have to listen to his voicemail, some variation of *I miss you, I want you, I love you.* I'm breaking his heart, and I watch Henry scrape the sprinkles from his cookie and drop them one by one to the carpet. A trail? I ask, and he nods, squatting down to examine where one of the sprinkles blends in with the pattern. Then he gazes behind him with a woeful expression. I can't see them, he says. That's okay, I tell him, I remember where to go.

James

Joel holds his shit together until Catherine shuts herself up in her bedroom with a prescription for Ambien. Then he starts to pace. Through the living room, into the kitchen, back into the living room… Man, I know that whatever suggestion I make—for food or rest or conversation—he's not going to meet with a smile. Look, I finally say since I'm stupid and can't help myself, Why don't we go for a run? A run, he repeats like he's never heard the word in his life. Might make you feel better, I mumble and he claps his hand on my shoulder hard enough to hurt. No, he muses, No, I don't want to go for a run, James. He takes two steps then turns to face me with his hands locked behind his head. I think I'm ready for that drink, he says and this time he means it.

I trail him into his dad's office where he takes a decanter of scotch from the bookshelf and pours us each a double before he sits behind the desk. I'm not so sure I like the look of him in his daddy's chair and I stay on my feet until he orders me to sit down. I don't think he'll get to these, he jokes, tapping a stack of papers, Do you?

I don't laugh and he looks up at me, a smile jerking the corners of his mouth. Oh c'mon, he says, Where's your sense of humor? Sitting back, he presses the tips of his fingers together. He looks just like his dad and after a minute he picks up his scotch and turns the glass from side to side like he's trying to figure out what he wants to do next. To my father, he finally announces, extending his drink in my direction and after a second I clink his scotch with mine.

I don't much feel like savoring but I take an obedient sip and hold the liquor in my mouth before I swallow. You know what's missing, he says, winking at me and when I shake my head he looks at the humidor. No, I tell him right away, knowing where he's going. Well, where's your sense of adventure, James? he asks, Aren't you *curious?*

Aw man. That *hurts.*

Let's see, he murmurs, polishing off the rest of his scotch and rubbing his hands together. He opens the humidor and runs his index finger back and forth across his dad's collection. Now *this*, he tells me, picking out a Cohiba and holding the cigar just under his nose, Takes me back. Stop this shit right now, Joel, I say but he snips the end off the cigar and finds a silver lighter. Three quick draws and a gray cloud drifts toward the ceiling.

From across the desk he hands me the cigar in a way that says he's not going to take no for an answer. Trapped I raise it to my mouth as he pours himself another drink. Smoke burns my throat and I make the mistake of trying to chase the taste with the scotch and end up coughing. He takes the cigar like we're passing a joint back and forth. Here, he announces, holding the tip an inch from his palm, I could probably take the pain. He looks at me to make sure I get what he's trying to say. I get it all right. I'm fucking horrified. Here, he continues, switching hands, It might hurt so much I won't be able to work. He shifts his eyes in my direction. Do you think I have the balls? he asks.

I've got a feeling the wrong answer will land us in the ER. Yes, I try. You're wrong, he tells me. Then he leans across the desk. Or you're lying, he adds. I guess I'm wrong, I say. I guess you are, he agrees after a minute, dropping back and reaching for his drink. For just a second I think he's winding down.

Then he looks up at me and I can see he's just getting started.

Joel

The more I drink, the more the demon in the corner settles down. He's been after me all day, trying to catch my eye; now I'm being smart. A double and a single of my father's favorite scotch and that demon has gotten nice and quiet. He's curled up in the corner now, my own incorrigible pet. Heat waves emanate from his body, and I loosen my tie and unbutton my collar. Is it just me, or is it hot in here?

I'm smoking one of my father's cigars, the scent every bit as familiar as the scotch I'm pouring into one of the heavy crystal glasses he kept in his office. Another? I ask James, but he shakes his head. My father had this guy pegged all wrong. The day they met I glimpsed the gleam in my father's eye: James had pledged a fraternity. He had straight A's. He looked like the sort of guy who could get any girl he wanted. What a joke that he wanted me.

Not enough, though. Never enough to tell me. Never enough not to care what anyone else thought.

Isn't that why I hung up on him last week? *What do you want from me?* I'd asked him, and what did he say? *I don't know.*

Of course, since then, he's made excuses. He told me his sister phoned right after I ended our call. By the time they finished talking, he knew I'd be asleep. Henry hid his phone. James would've called me from his office the next day, but he's the head of the search committee for some professor his department wants to hire, and he was responsible for entertaining the candidate. My head spins thinking about all the pieces that have gone into the puzzle that make up this moment, this moment where I'm sitting at my father's desk across from this guy I've known since freshman year.

I knock the ash from my cigar, not caring where it falls. Did you get enough? I ask, offering what's left to James, and he takes it too eagerly, as if he's afraid I was serious about burning a hole in the palm of my hand when there's nothing, nothing I'd ever do to jeopardize my work. I glare at the demon in the corner, who's fast asleep. Nothing, I tell it, Do you hear me?

The demon doesn't move, but James looks at me with consternation. You're wasting the cigar, I chide, and to appease me, he holds it to his lips. I watch him through the smoke the way I'd watch porn, aroused and detached at the same time. Stop, he says in a low voice. Stop watching you? I ask, hardening right up in spite of myself.

The demon opens its eyes. I glare in its direction, and it grins back, just a little, just enough. Fuck *off*, I say, taking a sloppy sip of scotch I'm hoping will chase it away.

Too late, I realize I have James looking over his shoulder, as if he's expecting to find someone standing in the doorway. Who're you talking to? he asks. No one, I mutter. The heat in here stifles, and I wipe my brow with the back of my arm. I think we should call it a night, James decides. When we're having so much fun? I ask.

Those words come out a little slurred, and I clear my throat and eye the demon, dismayed to find it on its feet. It's watching me, waiting; I know what it wants, what it's hoping I'll say. Helplessly, I look across the desk at James. Why did I fall for him, all those years ago? Or didn't I have a choice? You're my father's fault, I tell him, and the demon laughs. What're you talking about? James asks.

Now that just pisses me off. He's accused me more than once of being a masochist. Who else would I have chosen? And now here I am, sitting in my father's office with my very own demon licking its blistered lips. How can James not realize the part he played? Talk to me, he says, and this time the demon and I laugh together. Talk to you? I repeat, You want me to tell you what I'm thinking?

At first, I'm merely amused by the trepidation crossing his expression, but the second he steels himself and nods, I feel another prick of desire. From the corner of my eye, I see the demon cock its head. *Curious.* I think you'd feel better if you talked to me, James says. That's your answer for everything, isn't it, I agree, Except for when it counts.

Now he looks chastened; good. If he'd answered the question I asked when we were on the phone last week, I wouldn't have hung up on him. If his sister had called and we'd still been talking, he would've let her roll to voicemail. We would've figured this out before we got off the phone. Instead, he's trying to tell me that I should open up when that's all I've done lately.

Fuck this. I lean forward and take him in. Flaws and imperfections, he was still what I wanted that summer in '95 after he came home from Greece, bronzed and brazen, a tattoo of the sun blazing on his hip. I couldn't figure him out, and that was part of the appeal. Now I've put the pieces of this mosaic together. He doesn't want me, but he doesn't want anyone else to have me. He wants me, but he's too afraid to tell me. He fucks me, but he doesn't want anyone to know. He loves me, and he hates himself as a result.

The demon's panting, tail pointed toward the ceiling. Saliva drips from its jaws, spatters on my father's expensive Persian rug. I can smell its foul breath from here, and I dump some more scotch in my glass, hoping the liquor's scent will help. I don't think you need to drink any more, man, James says, and I narrow my eyes. You're not my father, I remind him. That's right, he says, That's why I don't like seeing you do this to yourself.

My eyes flicker toward the demon, who seems interested in hearing how I'll respond. What do you think? I ask it. Who the hell are you talking to? James groans. There's a demon in the corner, I say, gesturing with my glass and sloshing some of the scotch onto the desk. James looks over his shoulder, then slowly turns back to me. Shrugging, I give the demon a small smile; our little secret. It does a dance, turns in a circle on cloven hooves. It's burning the shit out of the carpet.

Joel, James says, sounding as grave as the grave. Did you hear that? I ask the demon, As grave as the grave? *Stop*, James insists, Stop this shit right now. You don't need to worry, I tell him, I'm getting used to it. There's no fucking demon, James hisses, and I look over at the evidence to the contrary, cackling with its head thrown back. I cackle along with it until it stops and stares at me with a Machiavellian eye. James pulls at his hair. The motion trips me up, and I suddenly remember watching him once, back before we started sleeping together, raking his hand back and forth across his skull. We were high; we were always high. I watched him, and I jerked off thinking about him, and last month, he kissed me in his kitchen and ran his hands through my hair, and for a few seconds, a few seconds, everything felt right.

The snarl that stretched my face when he showed up in my bedroom doorway last night comes right back to me. I'll tell you what I want, I say, and with a howl of triumph, the demon leaps onto the desk between us.

James

It doesn't make me feel better thinking that what's happening here I can chalk up to a masochistic streak so deep and wide I don't think Joel will ever dig himself out. He's hallucinating, claiming he sees a demon in the corner. What the hell am I supposed to do with that? You've had enough, man, I told him when he poured himself another glass but he isn't listening to me. He's talking to an imaginary demon and I am at a complete and total loss. Running my hand through my hair, I start thinking about my options and that's when he fixes his eyes on me. They're hot and wild and then he smiles same as he did last night when I heard him talking to himself in his room. Or hell, maybe he was talking to the demon he swears he's seeing now.

You want to know what I want? he asks. Yes, I say, relieved, *Yes*. He'll tell me and I'll give it him and we can end this night once and for all. You're *sure*? he asks all slithery and sly.

I balk. Yes-s, I falter and he leans forward.

I want you to fuck me, he says, Right here, in my father's office.

Tears spring to my eyes. He doesn't think I'll turn him down. He thinks I'll do what he says same as I swallowed his daddy's scotch, same as I smoked his daddy's cigar, that some crazy combination of guilt and sympathy will make me do what he wants even though agreeing will jeopardize everything we've worked the past decade to get back, every chance we've got of moving forward.

You want to make it up to me, James? he adds, inviting me to plummet into guilt and revenge and regret right along with him, Here's your chance. *No,* I say and fuck if he doesn't look seriously taken aback like there's no way he could've heard me right. What do you mean, *no*? he asks. I mean, I say, gritting my teeth, I'm not gonna join you in this fucked up rendition of how-can-I-screw-myself-over-this-time.

That tension I've been sensing ever since I got to Houston shimmies right on up to the surface of his skin and before I can stop him he raises his glass. Joel! I cry but I'm too late. He brings the glass down hard and his hand opens right up. Blood pours from his palm. All of a sudden he looks more terrified than I've seen him since sophomore year when he got that phone call about his mom. I can hear what he's thinking. Without his hand he can't work and without his work he's got a whole lot of nothing.

I leap to my feet as blood runs down his wrist and soaks the sleeve of his shirt. He's cupping one hand under the other and it's not making a damn bit of difference. C'mon, I insist, Come with me. I lead him into the bathroom off of his dad's office where I take a monogrammed towel and wrap it around his hand. Hold that tight, I tell him, trying not to panic at the way the towel's already soaking right through. Shut up, he's mumbling, Shut up. *Perfect.* He's still talking to a fucking demon. I turn on the faucet. Let's take a look, okay? I say.

He's going to need stitches. I know that before I pull away the towel. No way he's getting off without a trip to the ER tonight, not with what's seeping between his fingers. He's holding his hand tight and when I finally pry it open *oh fuck* he sways on his feet. I grab onto him. All right, I say, keeping my voice nice and calm same as when Henry fell from the monkey bars last summer, We're just gonna run over to the ER, all right?

He doesn't fight me and I rewrap his hand with a fresh towel and walk him to the front door where I tell him to sit at the bottom of the stairs with his hand elevated so he doesn't bleed all over the damn place. I run upstairs to get my keys, taking care to keep my steps quiet so I don't wake Catherine. Man, this night cannot get any worse.

Ready? I ask, hauling him to his feet and I lead him out to my rental car where I have to clip his seatbelt myself. Where's the nearest ER, Joel? I ask but he doesn't answer.

I'll go downtown. There's got to be a hospital downtown.

I head in that direction. Joel's staring out the window, moving his mouth like he's talking even though I can't hear a sound. *Goddamn.* You okay, Joel? I ask but he doesn't answer. Man, they're going to take one look at this guy when we get to the ER and want to admit him. Joel, I say, *Joel.* He turns and somewhere in his expression I try to find him. There's no demon, I tell him, Do you hear me?

He smiles.

I do not believe this night.

And I don't know where I'm going. If he can't snap out of it long enough to point me in the right direction I'll have to pull over and call 911. Joel, I say, but he moans. I'm going to be sick, he mumbles and I swerve over to the edge of the freeway so quick that cars all around us start laying on their horns. I unclasp his seatbelt and reach across him to open his door and he stumbles from the car up to the edge of the overpass. Scrambling after him I stop him before he can hurl himself over the railing. All right, I say, turning him toward the car and I have to jump back so I don't get puke all over my shoes. I keep my arm around him until he's finished. Man, that towel's soaked with blood. I've got to get him to the hospital or he's never going to paint again.

Better? I ask once we're back in the car and I'm pulling onto the freeway and to my relief he nods. Do you have any water? he asks. I pull out what's left of the bottle I got yesterday at the funeral home and open the top for him. Take the next exit, he says and I look over at him. He really does seem a little better. Maybe he just had to get some of that alcohol out of his system. You'll probably need stitches, I warn, hoping he's not looking at surgery too. I don't have insurance, he reminds me. I'll take care of it, I tell him.

At the hospital we're ushered right on through, probably since that towel's dribbling blood all over the floor. Joel's not talking much, answering questions with so little interest I finally go ahead and take over. I know him well enough to fill in the blanks anyway. Can we get a specialist in here? I ask the intake nurse. Let's see what the doctor says, she tells me.

The doctor calls in a specialist, some guy named Boatright. I keep repeating what happened with the smashed glass, that Joel just buried his dad but it's the long-ass lines running from Joel's wrists to his elbows, the ones he carved ten years ago that have someone from psychiatric asking questions. That Joel's eyes look downright dead isn't doing him any favors. Pull it together, man, I warn when we get a minute alone, Or they're never gonna let you walk outta here.

We're sitting side by side on the bed when Dr. Boatright tells us Joel doesn't need surgery. I hear Joel's breath leave his mouth and my arm goes right around him. This isn't the first time we've waited for a diagnosis together. You're sure, I say to the doctor, You're one hundred percent sure. But Dr. Boatright has only been cautious because of the painting. There's a nick in Joel's flexor tendon but Dr. Boatright's confident that'll heal in time. Fifteen stitches, four weeks in a splint and in six to eight weeks Joel will be fine. Are you hearing this? I say to Joel, Do you understand?

He doesn't answer. My arm doesn't move.

Joel

The demon has taken up residence in the back seat of James's rental car, and the windows fog with its hot breath. My hand's wrapped in gauze; I've taken so many steps backward that I don't think I'll ever find my way home again. I've swallowed a couple of Hydrocodone, not so much because my hand hurts, but because I'm hoping the pills will make the demon go away. Instead, it scrabbles back and forth across the seat, panting as we get closer to my father's house. I have no illusion that when we go inside to pack—I told James as we were leaving the hospital that there's no way I'm spending another night under my father's roof—the demon won't follow me. At the hospital, it crouched at the foot of my bed, left claw marks on the sheets. I almost told James, but the doctors wanted to keep me overnight, and I didn't want him agreeing with them. I didn't need to be admitted. I just need to get out of Houston.

It's possible the demon can't leave the city.

I have every intention of going inside, of packing my clothes and cleaning the blood from my father's desk, but James pulls up to the house, and I start shaking my head. I can't seem to stop. He watches me with a sober expression; somewhere under the fog of my anxiety, I feel a pang of self-recrimination for putting him in this position. I'll take care of it, he finally says, and I slump against the seat with relief. Maybe these pills will start to work, and I can sleep. Maybe by the time he comes back, the demon will be gone.

Instead, it scrambles out after James. Stop! I cry too late for James to hear, but the demon's not following him into the house. I watch as it scales the brick, clinging with its claws until it reaches the roof. I peer through the windshield and spy it perched on the edge, a gargoyle in reverse. Who knows what evil it's inviting inside, and I'm just about to plunge into the night to warn James when the driver's side door opens and my father sits down beside me.

Sucking in my breath, I fumble for the door, but no matter how hard I pull on the handle, I can't get it open. The temperature in the car skyrockets, and I glance over my shoulder, still jerking the handle. Unconcerned, my father sips his scotch. Frowning, I take a closer look. The glass has been broken, then patched back together. Cracks crawl through the crystal, and I wonder at the pattern, or if I'm imagining one. How the liquor isn't seeping through the fissures, I can't imagine.

My father clears his throat. You're looking..., he says, taking me in and trailing off, as if there's no word in the English language that could adequately describe the state of disarray in which he's currently found me. I glance down at myself, at my blood-stained shirt, at my hand wound with gauze. I've had a rough night, I mumble. Obviously, my father agrees, and I feel a flash of anger wrapped up in shame. I keep my mouth shut, though; I don't know who—or what—I'm dealing with here, and I take a quick glance at the rooftop, where the demon swings its legs as if it's a child sitting in a too-tall chair.

Why are you here? I ask, and my father winks. I didn't want to leave without saying goodbye, he tells me. I guess I don't have to ask where you're going, I mutter, and his smile thins. So much for trying not to antagonize him. Actually, he muses, It's not so bad. He glances at his reflection in the rearview mirror and laughs. I mean, look at me, he says, I haven't looked this good in years!

He's right; he could pass for forty, which puts him right about the age he was when he memorialized the day that I skipped school in favor of the beach. Through my sleeve, I touch the scar from that long-ago cigar, but he's still looking at his reflection. Not a bad way to spend eternity, he's murmuring. As I watch, he holds a vain hand to his hair, then turns to me. Hell isn't without its disadvantages, of course, he confides, The heat can be unbearable. He grins. But I can broil a steak like *that*, he says, snapping his fingers. He waits for my reaction, gives me a good-natured cuff on the arm. What do you say? he asks, Would you like to join me? In hell? I say, and he holds his glass of scotch up to the moonlight, then breaks off a piece of crystal. This should do the job, he tells me.

I take the crystal in my hand and gaze at its jagged edges. As with everything else, my father spared no expense when it came to his barware; I'm looking at a slice of Baccarat from a double old-fashioned. Even in the bare light of a half-moon, its glimmer captivates.

That's no box cutter, my father adds, as if there's something less off-putting about a suicide with a polished execution. I hesitate, turning the crystal over and over between my fingers. My father glances at the sky, which holds just a hint of dawn. I can sense his impatience, and even after all these years, I don't want to anger him. I roll up my sleeves. I can still see the scars from my last attempt. All I have to do is follow the lines.

You do it, I offer, holding out the crystal. Believe me, he says, If it were that simple... He glances up at the demon on the roof, then turns back to me with an expression gentler than any I ever saw from him when he was alive. Honestly, Joel, he sighs, What's keeping you here? James, I say, confused, Adam... My father waves away my excuses, spilling scotch on his trousers and looking suddenly furious about the mishap. For once in your miserable life, he snarls as I shrink away from him, Do something right!

With a sob, I press the tip of the crystal into my wrist. James opens the door.

James / 30,000 feet above sea level

I know Joel's not himself because he's barely acknowledging Henry. Even during his last trip to Chicago he could handle my son. But it's all me in the airport, all me on the plane, never mind that I've gotten almost no sleep in the past thirty-six hours. I know Joel's shaken up and hurting and a little drugged on top of everything else but I'm so tired I feel like I'm going to be sick. The last place I want to be right now is thirty thousand feet in the air but I knew there was no way Joel could stay in Texas. That was abundantly clear. I'm not even sure how he's going to manage Chicago.

He ended up with a prescription for Hydrocodone I wasn't happy about filling because he was already catatonic enough that psych insisted on talking to him again before he was discharged. So much adrenaline had flooded my system by that time that I just started outright arguing with the guy. Joel had just buried his dad, he'd broken a glass, I was right there, goddamn it and I know what I saw. His suicide attempt was ten *years* ago, Jesus fucking *Christ*. Joel barely noticed my tirade. I swear to God I wanted to kick him so he'd reanimate. I couldn't leave him there alone and I couldn't stay much longer in Houston. I'd like to hear something from you, Joel, the guy from psych finally said. Man, I hated the way he used Joel's name like they were something familiar and Joel must've had the same feeling because the way he slit his eyes reminded me of the rattlesnake my uncle and I found on his ranch when I was a kid. My uncle stepped in front of me in just enough time to take the bite. He almost died; I would've. The guy from psych looked like he wouldn't fare much better. If you're worried about my threat level, Dr. Dalton, Joel said, shocking the shit out of me by remembering the guy's name, I'd advise you against admitting me.

Thirty minutes later I filled Joel's prescription at a 24-hour pharmacy and drove back to his dad's house where Joel started shaking his head before I could even shut off the engine. I can't go in there, he confessed and that's how I ended up mopping up the blood in the bathroom and cleaning the mess on his dad's desk. By the time I got our bags packed, left a note for Catherine and lugged everything downstairs the sky was turning light. I got in the car expecting to find Joel asleep but he looked like he'd spent the night with the devil himself. What's wrong? I asked and he started laughing, the kind of laugh that chills your bones right on down to the marrow. Get me the fuck out of here, James, he said and I did.

I wanna get *up*, Henry says beside me. I know you do, buddy, I agree, I do too. He cups the edges of the armrests in his little palms and rocks back and forth. You want to make the plane go faster, I tell him and for a second my commiseration helps ease his frustration but I can't keep up the conscious parenting for long and when I back off pretending to fly the plane along with him he starts crying. Joel doesn't even look at him. He's sitting in the aisle seat and I'm wedged here in the middle since Henry wanted to look out the window. Now that it's night there's nothing to see anyway.

Henry's wailing gets louder and I scrunch down in my seat so I can talk to him. He hushes up once he's got my attention but the second I straighten he starts again. Joel shoves away from his seat so fast I think he's sick. Or hell, maybe he's trying to escape from that demon.

I want Joel, Henry whimpers, trying to squirm out from under his seatbelt. I point up at the light. The pilot wants us to stay in our seats, I tell him and Henry scowls. Joel's not in his goddamn seat so why does he have to buckle up? Joel's sad right now, I tell him. Henry gets that faraway look in his eyes which means he's trying to figure things out. Sometimes you get sad, I remind him and he nods, his eyes still somewhere else. I crane around the aisle seat to place Joel's progress. He looks like he'd crawl out of his skin and just leave it behind if he could.

His daddy died, Henry says matter-of-factly. That's right, I agree, muffling a sigh. I wanna get *off*, Henry pouts, his eyes filling with tears and I tell him I get it, I want to get off too. His little mouth quivers and I end up taking off his seatbelt and pulling him into my lap. He flings his arms around my neck and I pat his back.

Joel

There was a chance the demon wouldn't be able to get on the plane, but no such luck. It's my new best friend, rode in the backseat on our way to pick up Henry from the hotel where he was staying with James's parents, then curled up at my feet as I tried to sleep on the way to the airport. On the plane, the demon slinks up and down the aisle, drops to its haunches and crawls under the seats until it pops up beside me with an obstreperous grin. I try ignoring it; at first, it's amused. It thinks we're playing a game, and it gets in my face, tries to make me react. When I close my eyes, it clamps its claw on my thigh. I jerk upright, my leg burning from its touch. You all right? James asks, and I get to my feet without answering.

The flight attendants don't want me wandering the length of the plane, and I can hardly tell them why I'm on the move. *Well, you see, Satan sent one of his minions to follow me…* If James hadn't taken over at the emergency room last night, I have a feeling that doctor would have admitted me on the spot. I'd be sedated now, which would be its own kind of hell. I'm having a hard enough time handling the Hydrocodone we picked up on the way back to my father's house. I don't want to lose control.

I have to keep an eye on the demon.

Sir, I need you to return to your seat, a flight attendant says, and I jerk a thumb in the direction of the lavatory. She presses her lips together but nods, either because of the bandage wrapped around my hand or because of the fire in my eyes. I make my way to the back of the plane, looking over my shoulder for the demon, who skips along behind me like a childhood bully. I can smell it from here. How can no one else?

Locking myself in the bathroom, I close the lid on the toilet seat and sit with my head in my hands. In one hand, actually; the other throbs. The demon tried to cram itself in here with me, but I scooted in so fast I slammed the door on one of its hooves. Its shriek shook the plane, but I managed to get the door closed and locked. It's angry; I can hear its quick breath on the other side of the door.

I could've gone right from Houston to Buenos Aires. I could've told James that I needed time to recover, needed space. But I'm James's demon. From year to year, I follow him. Even when I know better, even though he hurts me. I need him, or maybe I just need him to want me. Now he might be in a place where he's willing to take a risk. Not enough of one, probably. He has too many hang-ups. That's something I have to remember, because the past few days he's been James the way I always wanted: patient and attentive, without the possessive bullshit I always mistook for interest. Instead, he's looking at me in a way that once upon a time I could barely imagine. I'm afraid to let myself believe he can follow through.

At the other end of the spectrum, I have Adam, who will likely leave me another voicemail before this plane lands. What would he say if I told him about the demon lying in wait for me on the other side of the door? Adam wanted to come to Houston for the funeral; a word and he would have booked a flight. He almost came without invitation. Closing my eyes, I think about our last moments together, his hand tracing slow circles on my bare back as I sat on the edge of his bed and spoke with Catherine, who'd jolted me out of a sleep so sumptuous I'd almost sobbed when I recognized my reality. Naked, he followed me into the bathroom, where I stood under his beautiful chandelier and cried. In his arms, we'd never for one moment been away from each other. Let me come with you, he whispered, but I was already pulling away from him.

Those circles I painted my last year in Austin held a prophecy I'm just now beginning to discern. Millions of men in the world and I keep coming back to Adam and James. Why do they have such a hold on me?

Someone's knocking. The demon? I picture its claw curled into a fist, one pointed ear pressed against the door. The thought amuses me, and I burst forth with a laugh, then press my good hand against my mouth.

I have to figure out a way to escape.

James / Chicago

That nap at the end of our flight screws up Henry's bedtime. When we finally get home I crawl into bed next to him, figuring he'll fall asleep faster if I'm right there. Every time I think he's made it and I try to steal away, his eyes fly open. No no no, Daddy, he protests, Not yet. So I screw my eyes shut and will myself to relax, to get into this here moment and not think about Joel downstairs. He hasn't opened his mouth since we left my folks' hotel this afternoon, didn't say one word on the plane. His eyes have the same faraway look Henry's had earlier.

We were young when Joel's mom died halfway through our sophomore year. He'd gone to Houston for Christmas and I'd gone to Fort Worth and I don't know what happened but he was back in Austin before the new year. I know because I called him at his parents' house—this was before he had a car phone—and his dad told me Joel was already gone. When I tried our house in Austin Joel answered all right but I could tell something was off. I probably asked if everything was cool and I'm sure he gave me some bullshit reassurance I took as truth because whatever, I was home for the holidays and by that time I'd gotten used to Joel's moods blowing up like a coastal storm. He'd settle down.

Then I saw for myself what he'd been doing. Big old canvases covered with paint, his mom staring out at me with wicked eyes, hair spitting snakes like she was some kind of Medusa. In one painting she was crushing a bird. Dude, I breathed and he spun around to face me, his brush flicking a glob of green that just missed the Redwings I'd gotten for Christmas. For a second I thought he was going to tell me to get out of his studio. That would've been a first. Instead he gave me a fucked up smile. Let me show you what I've done, he said.

Up close I could see the fingerprints fading on his neck.

A couple weeks later he got the call from his dad and we made that awful drive to Houston and that's how I found myself kneeling with my arms around him in his mom's bloody bathroom. The aftermath was predictable, months of skipped classes and too much beer. He wouldn't paint either and I finally cleaned his studio myself, thinking maybe he just couldn't stand seeing what he'd done before she died. I stacked every single one of those paintings backwards against the wall and propped a fresh canvas on his easel. Almost a year passed before he touched it.

I'm not going to fuck up with my boy. I know I'll make mistakes. Hell, I've already made them. But my kid will not end up like Joel, so upended from his dad's death he doesn't know whether to grieve or celebrate. I curl a little closer to my son, match his breath, make sure we're skin to skin. The second we connect I can feel him relaxing and I hang around a few extra minutes to be sure he's asleep before I slip out from under his blankets.

Downstairs I flick on the monitor. Through the window I can just make out Joel on the front porch. For a second I think he's smoking and I almost hope that's the case since I could use a cigarette of my own. But all I'm seeing is his cold breath and I guess I'd be downright cruel to take a pack of Marlboros out there now. After the past few days there's no way he'd turn me down.

The phrase sticks in my head. *There's no way he'd turn me down.* The weariness I felt a little while ago vanishes, supplanted by a dose of good old-fashioned anxiety. This isn't happening the way I expected. I was thinking he'd come up here because he wanted to see me. Worst-case scenario he'd tack Chicago on the end of another trip to see his dad. We'd have time for a beer. I'd be nervous but absolutely fucking sure in a way I couldn't be that first time around, not without a big ass joint in my hand.

I wasn't planning on his dad dying first. I didn't factor in fifteen stitches and a prescription for pain medication. I didn't expect his marathon insomnia.

I do not want him misinterpreting my motivation here.

When I step outside he barely looks at me. He isn't wearing a coat but I don't think he feels the cold. I touch his arm then the fingertips of his left hand, waiting for him to wince. Nothing. If he spoke right now I think he'd shatter.

I want to hold him together. I knew it the first day I met him when I felt something pull tight between us. We were young and stupid but I could feel the chaos under his surface and I wanted to calm it down. For a long time he let me. He let me be the one and I let myself go too far before I was ready.

I don't want to fuck up again. We need to move at the right pace. We're glacier I know. But I don't want him looking at me the way he did last month like my name might as well be Judas.

I'm still touching his fingers and I drop my hand. I need to ease in nice and slow. I'll be whatever he wants tonight. I don't have to be anything more than his friend. There's plenty of time.

Hey Joel? I say and he lifts his eyes. But barely; I might've found him half-asleep and I see him suddenly the way I did years ago. In my bed naked and accessible. Here's my point of entry and damn if I don't barrel right past my own advice.

He catches me up, mouth open matching mine, *God.* That's what I've been wanting since he left and we stumble on back until we hit the door. My hands have hold of his hair same as last time, my tongue deep deep deeper *like this* you couldn't get a c-note between us when he pulls his mouth away and scans the porch like he's looking for something. *Please don't tell me you see a demon.* Inside, he says.

He doesn't have to tell me twice. I yank open the door and my arm trembles in its socket and chatters on down through my fingers then back up to my skull. We barely make it inside before he has me up against the door my hands under his shirt my mouth all over that pulse in his neck, *God*. Wait, wait, he murmurs, Henry. I whip around but Henry's sound asleep two stories up. Maybe Joel just doesn't want him coming down to find us all tangled up together. I lean in and go for his mouth slow slow slower *like the swing* hand on the back of his neck. Upstairs, he whispers.

He gets there first and I shut the door behind us. My bed's a wreck since I left town in such a hurry. The only light comes from the lamp on the bedside table. Now that we're up here I don't know what to do, I don't know where to put my eyes but every time I ditch them he pulls them back up again. Knock off a decade and I'd be looking for another toke on that joint.

Instead I put his name in my mouth and *bam*, he shuts the distance between us.

His kiss has the weight of so many years. This time he doesn't ask what we're doing. He doesn't ask if this is really happening. This right here feels ancient and he kisses me like he's been doing it for centuries. I fall past a history I knew better than to believe we'd buried. There's no time to think about whether or not Henry's still asleep, no time to wonder if I have what it takes to be everything to Joel this time around. There's no time at all.

And that's just one kiss. By the time he pulls me toward the bed I don't care about anything. Not what this means, not where we go from here, not how I'm going to explain myself to my friends and family, none of the shit that clouded my perception the first time. It's not even the sex I want and *God* do I want the sex. It's Joel I want. I want Joel and I'm long past denying it.

He goes down on me and I don't make it all the way back to the surface. I never do, not for months. Everything's muted like I'm breathing underwater, sunshine shuttering through the waves like that day in Mexico when we were twenty years old and he wanted me to go scuba diving. Only when I knew we were pulling up and out did I start to appreciate what I'd spent the previous thirty minutes missing.

The metaphor isn't lost on me and I turn my head to catch his expression. I guess I want to see what I'm feeling mirrored back to me because *God* that was good. And so long coming.

But he's not looking at me. He's looking like it's near midnight and he's damn sure there's not going to be a last-minute call from the governor. I've seen his expression on a girl before, one who regretted giving it up the second we finished. Back then I got defensive and distant and I could go the same way here but realize just in time what I've done. Months—hell, years of buildup—and I decide *tonight's* the night to make something happen. Tonight when he's going on zero sleep, when he's still coming down from his dad's death, when he's looking at weeks without the use of his hand. Tonight barely twenty-four hours after he offered me a cigar and told me to fuck him in his daddy's office, when he's been talking about seeing demons.

And we're right where we left off, me taking whatever I can get without a hint of reciprocity. Fuck me. I'm twenty-five all over again.

I've got to fix this and I pull him toward me and kiss him like we're just starting. I kiss him until I feel him shift. I kiss him until I'm ready to do this all over again, *God*. I rein myself in: *his turn*. I take my mouth away from him long enough to unbuckle his belt, unzip his jeans and man, my hands have never felt so steady.

Joel

Peeling open my eyes, I snake my gaze around the room, searching every corner and suppressing the urge to look under the bed. Head cocked, I listen for the demon's claws, then slide my foot out from under the covers to test the temperature. The air's chilly; the demon's gone. It disappeared the second James kissed me. Up until that moment, there'd been no hiding from it. On James's front porch, the demon had swung itself around and around the newel post, grinning wider every time it spotted me. Then James kissed me, and for the first time since the day of my father's funeral, I couldn't see the demon anymore. I locked the door behind us, but the demon didn't rap on the windows and howl its frustration; I wasn't taking any chances. I took James inside, and I went down on him, and I haven't seen the demon since.

Instead, I have absolutely and thoroughly fucked myself, which was probably the demon's intention from the beginning.

For now, James sleeps. I stare at him in the light from the bedside lamp, at his parted lips, the flutter of movement beneath his eyelids. The scent of cigarettes clings to his skin, smoke with a shot of sex. In his dreams, he doesn't have to be afraid. I could whisper his name, and he'd answer. If I kissed him now, he'd respond out of instinct. But I know what I can expect the second he opens his eyes.

My hand aches, and I silently get to my feet. I've left my prescription on the coffee table in the living room, which was foolish, given Henry's inquisitive hands. I make my way there now, and after a few tries, I manage to pry off the lid and pick out a couple of pills. I swallow the medication and drop down with my phone, my own ticking time bomb. I'll have to call Adam eventually, but for now, I'll play the voicemail he left while I was sleeping.

Five days after the death of my father, five hours after I traded sex for solace, I sit in the dark in James's living room and listen to Adam cry.

James

Henry's in his booster seat right up against the table, spearing scrambled eggs with a fork and keeping up a constant monologue about Rufus who glowered at us when we got home last night but I guess has finally decided to forgive us. He's sitting on the kitchen counter, twitching his tail too close to my coffee. I've barely had a chance to take a sip. Last night I crashed without setting my alarm and when I woke up this morning I took one look at the clock and knew I'd have to hustle.

Even so I took a second. Joel was asleep beside me and I stared at him a while then lifted the covers like a teenager. I guess I just wanted to prove to myself that I hadn't been dreaming. I've got a quick memory of mumbling to him in the middle of the night—he must've been hurting, must've gotten up for his medicine. This morning I took a look at the groove between his eyebrows and the blue circles under his eyes and decided not to shake him awake.

But I wanted to wake him. God, I wanted to wake him.

The thought makes the blood pool in my crotch but there's no time to savor it. I still need to pack Henry's lunch. I hate to send him to preschool this morning but I've got to get to campus and there's no way I can leave him with Joel, not now. I throw crackers and cheese and the last of the grapes into Henry's lunch box. I'm going to need to get to the store on top of everything else.

I'm hungwy, Henry whines and I look at his empty plate. How 'bout askin' nicely, buddy? I suggest and he scowls at me. He's grumpy and overtired and I'm guessing I can look forward to a meltdown by the time I get him home from preschool this afternoon.

I want to spend time with Joel. I want to make sure he's okay with what happened. Last night he slid from my hands without opening his eyes and fell back against the pillow and I was the one who ended up reaching for my shirt and wiping him off after that hand job. I couldn't believe he let me. The gesture was tender like you wouldn't believe and I half-expected him to yank away from me. Man, there was so much I wanted to say. But I couldn't get anything out and he kept his eyes closed and after a while I just laid on down beside him.

I'm so lost in thought I still haven't gotten Henry's eggs and he's banging his fork against the table in retaliation. Jumping into motion I scrape the last of breakfast onto his plate. If he's hungry after he finishes these he might be out of luck. Daddy made eggs, he says. That's right, I answer mildly then realize he's talking to Joel. My face flames at the sight of him and I start blabbering about how did he sleep and how's his hand and does he want coffee. He raises his eyebrows. Getting himself a glass of water, he turns around and leans back against the sink. He looks better than he did last night but not by much.

Henry's singing that song about Rufus and a trail into the woods and I shush him and tell him to finish up his eggs so we can get to preschool. I feel so damn awkward. I don't even know what to do with my hands and I end up rearranging the contents of Henry's lunch just to keep them busy. Joel watches me like he knows exactly what I'm doing. I'm screwing this up already and as if he wants to be sure I get the message he jerks back when I ease up next to him. Don't you have to get going? he asks.

Well yeah. But shit.

Joel

I'm listening to Adam's voicemail again. I hate him for crying. I don't want him to love me anymore. I don't want to love him back.

I want him to have never cheated on me in the first place.

James was ridiculous this morning. Flushed and foolish and barely able to look me in the eye. Then he leaned in, right in front of Henry. Don't you have to get to work? I asked.

I don't think we can come back from this again.

And yet that kiss after Christmas... Isn't it at least possible that something's different? That James is different? That kiss in his kitchen—he wasn't stoned.

He didn't fuck me in my father's office either.

I turn off my phone. I still haven't eaten, and that's probably not wise. I need this hand to heal. The sooner I heal, the sooner I can work. I'm so close; I know the feeling. At night, the glass takes up my dreams.

Or it did before my father died. I haven't slept much since.

Right here James and I kissed, up against this sink. If I erase the past week, I can almost believe something could happen. His mouth on mine last month, so unexpected and hungry I couldn't help but respond. The hangdog way he loped around the next morning before my flight, less like he knew he'd screwed up and more like he was crushed that I was leaving. The panic I could hear in his voicemails when I was sick and the first conversation we had after I felt better. Everything he's done since he found his phone, how quickly he dropped everything to get to Houston when he heard about my father.

The trip to the ER.

And last night, after he came. We had plenty of precedent for him to fall right asleep, and instead, he kissed me. Instead, he unbuttoned my jeans. He was sober. He jerked me off sober.

If I hadn't come downstairs this morning with such false bravado, what might I have seen? I'd anticipated him dodging my gaze, but I figured he'd make some excuse about having to get to campus even earlier than he'd told me last night. Instead, he stumbled all over himself asking me how I'd slept. Instead, he tried to kiss me. What would've happened if I'd grabbed hold of his arms and kissed him back?

For the moment, I've forgotten about Adam, and I'm just starting to think that I'm wrong about James's motivation when I hear someone open the front door.

Don't fucking *tell* me that's him.

James

I tried my best but man, I cannot stay away. Since I left the house this morning I haven't been able to concentrate on a single thing. Standing in my Field Methods course I'm distracted and disengaged and I finally just let my students go twenty minutes early. I figure I've got just enough time to sneak home for an hour before I need to get back for my graduate seminar. If I hadn't already missed most of this week I'd cancel that class too.

I'm worried. I'm worried and I don't want to call because if Joel managed to fall asleep I don't want the phone waking him up. He needs the rest. But after what happened between us last night and with his hand all wrapped up... I want to check on him. Hell, I just want to *see* him, to lay my eyes on him and know he's not looking like he did the other night. *Like a lunatic who just ditched his doctors.*

Whatever, I want him upstairs in my bed. How am I not supposed to at least be thinking about that? We've been waiting a long time. Yeah, I want him to be okay. Yeah, I want to make sure he's sane. And I'd be lying if I said I wasn't interested in last night on repeat.

I find him in the kitchen where he's leaning against the counter like he's been waiting for me since this morning. *Sweet.* Hey, I say, stepping toward him with a smile and he backhands me with a scowl. I stop where I'm standing. What're you doing here, James? he asks. Makin' sure you're all right, I say. You could've called, he points out and I tell him I wanted to see for myself. You have me for twenty-one minutes, I add, looking at my watch and giving my smile another go. Then we better make that blowjob fast, he says.

I know I'm new at this and all but he sounds pissed and I shift my weight, not sure what I'm supposed to do next. Are you sayin'...? I ask, You wanna...?

Man, I haven't even gotten the sentence out of my mouth and he's stepping in my direction. Hey, I say, starting a smile from scratch. My hands take his waist and pull him toward me. Is this what you want? he asks in a voice like that long-ago Christmas. I murmur a yes and he moves his mouth close to my ear, his breath setting fires all over my skin until I can't see straight, *Jesus.* Fuck you, he whispers. W-what? I sputter as he shoves away from me. You need me to catch you up? he says, Less than a week after my father died, I might not want to *drop to my knees in your kitchen* and suck you off on your lunch hour. Jesus, I protest. You didn't come to check on me, James, he says, We've been here before, remember?

Aw *shit*, Joel. Kick us right back to 1996. Go ahead. Pretend like we haven't changed at all in the past twelve years. Erase all the progress we've made. Let's make this all about the ways I've let you down.

I didn't come home lookin' for a blowjob, I tell him. No? he says, Then what're we doing here?

Well hell. I'm still trying to figure that out myself. That's all I've been thinking about since he left after the holidays. I don't know, I admit, I guess we're feelin' this out. That's the best you can do? he says incredulously, *We're feeling this out?* Why does that have to be a bad thing? I mumble. Because the last time you wanted to feel this out, I got *fucked*, he reminds me, Or have you forgotten?

Man, I didn't force his hand all those years ago. I can't help that he fell in love with me and decided to keep that a secret. He could've stopped us before we got started by telling me the truth.

I am not responsible for what happened in that bathroom on Pearl.

But he's shaking and all I can think is *I did this. This right here is my fault.*

I remember, I confess and he crumples like that BMW I totaled the summer before we slept together. *Bam,* and we're flying down some back road outside of Austin, the wind in his hair. *Even then.*

My hand hurts, he says, My hand *hurts* and… What? I ask. I can't shower, he tells me. Why not? I ask and he holds up his hand like I'm a dumbass.

I get a gallon-size Ziplock. Stretching a rubber band wide I crimp the bag around his wrist. There, I say, Go take a bath.

While he's upstairs I pry a couple slices of bread from the loaf in the freezer and make a grilled cheese. I slice the last apple and peel a couple carrots then cut them in sticks. I should've thought about lunch earlier, I guess. There's no way he could've done this himself.

I have everything ready by the time he comes downstairs. Eat some lunch, I tell him, hunting around for my keys. Don't go, he says and I look over at him. With his hair wet he looks like he just pulled himself out of Barton Springs. Please, he adds in a low voice. All right, I say, Just let me make a call.

Joel

Twenty minutes later, I regret asking James to stay. He's not doing anything wrong; he's just sitting across from me as I pick at the sandwich he made. I'm not hungry, but he's hoarding my pills until I get something in my stomach. I can take care of myself, I told him, and he was smart enough not to argue. He hasn't always been so cautious.

Don't go, I said, and that was all he needed to hear. One call and he'd canceled his afternoon class. In a way, I feel guilty. That last night in Houston put my mother's suicide to shame. Haven't I caused James enough drama? I don't need to be keeping him from campus too.

Last Friday, I was in Seattle. Last Friday—I do a quick mental calculation after I glance at the clock—I was in Adam's bed. One week since I've seen him, since I've talked to him, since I've slept with him, and the only evidence I have of the time I spent with him are the voicemails he started sending thirty minutes after I left. I can recite them by heart.

I love you. I miss you. Come back.

Maybe I just need to sleep, and I get to my feet, grabbing for the chair with my good hand when I'm hit with a head rush. Whoa, James says, rising halfway to his feet. I'm fine, I mumble, but when I tell him I'm going to lie down for a while, he insists on walking me up the stairs. I crawl into bed, shaking my head at his offer to change the sheets. He gets me water, hands me my pills. You want me to stay or…? he asks, and I wave him away. *All those nights he read me to sleep when I had pneumonia.* Just let me rest, I say, but the second he goes downstairs, I snake my phone from my back pocket. Adam's not the only one who left me voicemails. I'm sure Kyle will unleash a tongue lashing when he finds out I'm in Chicago, but he's also likely to have spoken with Adam.

Girlfriend, he sighs when he answers, as if the mere fact that I've finally called him is cause for lamentation. I can hear the slippers he wears slapping against his highly polished floors. I have a feeling he's going in search of Scott, who sometimes works from home. Where are you? he asks. Chicago, I admit, and he groans.

I tell him I didn't have a choice, that I had to leave Houston after I sliced my hand. He actually sounds relieved to hear about my injury, and I have to refrain from telling him that fifteen stitches in my palm and a prescription for Hydrocodone didn't stop James from making a move or me from reciprocating. Kyle, I start, hesitating, and he says, Of course we've heard from him, Joel.

I close my eyes. I can't bear to look at my hand anyway, wrapped in gauze like a gift gone awry. I haven't talked to him, I confess. We're well aware of that, sweetheart, he says. No one expects you to call him, Joel, Scott adds, and I realize I'm on speaker. Adam expects me to call, I point out, and Scott tells me I'm probably right. He doesn't want to give up hope, he says, and his words bring tears to my eyes. I can't go back, I whisper. Of course you can't, Kyle agrees. Scott? I ask when he's quiet. That's not for us to decide, Joel, he tells me. But you think it's an option, I conclude. Do you? he asks.

When I ended up in Seattle, I halfway believed in some sort of divine intervention, a benevolent hand guiding me in the direction of a future I'd previously assumed to be dead. James had abandoned me—how else was I supposed to interpret his silence?—and that plane to Seattle seemed a sign that I wasn't alone. I might still be angry. I might still feel betrayed. Adam wanted me anyway. For three years, he said, he's been going through the motions. Whatever doubt I had when those words were spoken vanished when I saw where he's living. I'm surprised that second bedroom wasn't outfitted with an easel.

Then I heard the anguish in James's voice when he realized he'd missed my calls. As soon as he understood I needed him, he flew to Houston. Adam would have done the same; he offered. But I couldn't have navigated my father's funeral and Adam at the same time. With James, I knew what to expect—or I thought I did, until this afternoon. The kiss on his front porch last night, the way he sputtered all over himself in the kitchen this morning, that infuriating *I guess we're feeling this out...* well, that's just James. The *I remember* a little while ago, the plastic bag he crimped matter-of-factly around my wrist, the lunch he made... Instead of beating it back to campus, he followed me upstairs and offered me clean sheets.

I have too much history with these men. I have too many memories.

I tell Kyle and Scott I'll talk to them later. When I get to the bottom of the stairs, James looks up. Can't sleep? he asks. I shake my head, and he leans forward to set his laptop on the coffee table. Let's take a look at your hand, he says. Too soon, I mumble, but he's already leading me into the kitchen and depositing me in the same chair I vacated less than an hour ago. He unwinds the gauze as I stare off to the side; I'm not ready for what he might uncover. The first time I looked at my arms after my suicide attempt, I almost passed out.

Better than I expected, he tells me, his voice so pragmatic I can't help but look for myself. I'm mangled; there's no doubt about that. But compared to what I could be dealing with today, I'm not doing too badly. Sit tight, he says, and I wait while he cleans my palm, then rewraps my hand with a fresh piece of gauze, splint intact. When he's finished, I lay my head on my arm. After a minute—he wouldn't be James if he didn't hesitate—he runs his hand through my hair

James

I let him come to me. No way am I going to make the mistake of approaching him, not after what happened when I came home from campus for lunch. Whatever, it's not as if I haven't touched him. I walked him upstairs and got him into bed same as I would've if we hadn't done anything more than sleep our first night back from Houston. I slid my fingers through his hair when he laid his head down right there in front of me at the table after I cleaned his hand. Anything else? I'm not about to try.

So we had a quiet afternoon and I ran to get my kid from preschool and since by that time I could eat a whole pizza by my own damn self I ordered two large pies plus a big old salad for Joel. Then I waited to see if he'd open a bottle of wine. He shouldn't be drinking with the Hydrocodone but that didn't mean he wouldn't try. The first night we slept together back in '96 and pretty much every other time after that... Beer or pot, that'd do the trick and we could stop thinking about what we were doing.

I could stop thinking.

Henry went to bed early since he's been shortchanged on sleep pretty much every day for the past week and when I came downstairs just now I saw Joel without a wine glass staring at his phone. My guess is that Kyle's been giving him a hard time about being here. Kyle acted all grateful and shit that I called to tell him about Joel's dad but he cornered me at the reception after the funeral and asked what the hell I thought I was doing. Takin' care of my friend, I told him, Same as you. You need to give him some breathing room, he insisted. *I need a break, James. I need a break from you.* You don't know what you're talkin' about, I told him. I've known you a long time, he reminded me, I know more than you think.

You all right? I ask Joel and he shuts his phone then walks up and kisses me. No prelude, no seduction— Or hell, maybe that's what the last eighteen and a half years have been. He kisses me and my arms go up and around him so tight his shirt rides above his jeans. Then we're stumbling up the stairs and falling on my bed and for the first time since I shut us down twelve years ago he lets me back in.

Joel

I can stop any time I want.

I say these words over and over to myself, the same way I did when I was using cocaine or smoking cigarettes or sleeping with Jess, the guy who reviewed my first show with such deprecation. I can stop any time I want, I think every time I kiss him. I don't understand why he lets me. Twelve years ago, his lips eluded me; he'd fuck me, but he wouldn't kiss me. Now his mouth matches mine. I can stop any time I want, I think as I pull his shirt over his head. He has more hair on his chest than he used to. He has more hair on his chest than Adam does. Between my fingers, against my cheek: softer than his beard, which scratches my skin. I can stop any time I want, I think as I unzip his jeans and shove out of my own. We're faster now that we're naked, our breath audible, our skin hot. His groan grazes my ear. We move like we're on borrowed time.

We're not using condoms. Dude, do I *need* one? he'd asked, looking alarmed when I first wondered if he had any on hand. By that time, he'd gone down on me, inexpertly and with a self-consciousness that reminded me too much of that holiday season in '96, though in those days he would've no sooner considered giving me a blowjob than outing us to our friends. I suppose I should take his willingness as improvement. Instead, his anxiety stirred an ancient pot of rejection and resentment. By the time I mentioned condoms, I felt the need to defend myself. Yeah, James, I muttered, I'm seething with STDs. Embarrassed, he folded his arms across his chest. Well, why'd you ask? he wanted to know, and I mumbled something about habit. We didn't need a condom.

Since then, his uneasiness hasn't abated. He has no problem foregoing the condoms; he's just uncomfortable in general, worried that he's not measuring up to some stupid standard he implies I'm hiding from him. Erase his discomfiture, and the sex isn't bad. Bad sex I'd be able to give up. Instead, I convince him to sit Henry in front of the television. I wake him up in the middle of the night because I'm not sleeping anyway. Addiction or not, I keep going back for more.

Fraught with insecurity, I think as we untangle ourselves Sunday night. That's how I'd describe sex with James, and I press my temples with my thumb and forefinger, realizing as I do the way he'll interpret the gesture. Every day for the past three, I've answered the same question. *Was that okay?* I'm tired of answering him. I'm tired of assuaging his self-doubt, which probably isn't fair of me, given how hard he's trying. Maybe I'm tired of seeing just how hard he's trying. Maybe I don't believe I deserve what he's giving me. How can I, when every night after he falls asleep, I go downstairs and listen to Adam? I play his voicemails again and again.

Except the one he left me this morning. That one I've heard only once.

So was that...? James asks. I give him a look scathing enough to shut him up, and for one solid minute, he doesn't open his mouth. Then he props himself on his elbow, his hair tumbling toward his face and making him look like he's twenty-five all over again, which doesn't help. Look, he says in a low, low voice I have to crane to hear, This is good for me.

I should be better able to appreciate what he's admitting. There was a time he couldn't say these words.

I want this to be good for you, too, he adds. It *is* good, I say, though the words, ground between my teeth, sound less like a compliment and more like defamation. I watch him frisk my expression, like he's trying to find evidence that I'm lying. If you tell me what you want..., he finally starts, and I throw back the covers. You know what I want, James? I say, I want you to stop *talking* this to death, the way you do everything else.

Slamming the bathroom door behind me, I turn on the shower and wrap plastic around my wrist. Before the water even has a chance to heat, I'm leaning my forehead against the icy tile. As the water warms, I close my eyes.

I'm not being fair. I'm not giving James the attention I could, and my father's death isn't to blame. If it wasn't for Adam's voice, I'd swear I dreamed seeing him. But I have his messages, which sound more wretched with every passing day.

I'm not going back to him. I'm *not*.

But his voice. His voice stays with me, clings to my fingers when there's someone else I should be touching, clings to my tongue when I'm kissing James. I can't shake him loose, and even after all this time, I don't know that I want to. *Move on*, I told him just before I left him more than three years ago. How well have I followed my own advice?

I haven't told James about my detour to Seattle or any of Adam's calls. As far as he's concerned, I'm here, and I'm not, which seems to me a far graver error than never showing up at all. Given our past, how could he not want reassurance? Given my behavior, how could he not be intimidated?

Maybe if I hadn't ended up in Seattle, maybe if I hadn't given credence to the wisp of a dream as I stood at a ticket counter in Bogota, maybe if I'd gone to Houston the way I'd planned...

Maybe if James had answered the fucking phone.

I get out of the shower and reach for my cell. Sitting on the edge of James's bed, I listen to Adam's last voicemail. He tells me I have a choice to make. He knows the past couple of weeks have been difficult for me; that was easy enough for him to see in Seattle. He knows he hurt me, and he'll ask for my forgiveness every day for the rest of his life. He understands if I'm not ready, and he's happy to wait for me, to take it slowly. But I've been gone for more than a week, and I haven't returned any of his calls. He's given me just about all the space he can. He needs to hear from me by the end of the day. If I don't call, he doesn't want to hear from me again.

Getting dressed, I think about the hours before my father died. Rain slid down the windows at Adam's house, and when he stepped toward me, I offered no resistance. If my phone hadn't rung hours later, if Catherine hadn't called to tell me she wasn't sure my father would make it through the night, I might not have left.

Of course, at the time, I thought James wasn't speaking to me. If his sister hadn't called right after I'd hung up on him, if Henry hadn't hidden his phone, if I'd been put on a flight to any city other than Seattle... Curiosity didn't kill us. Chance did.

Or maybe I'm refusing to see what's in front of me. James isn't just trying. He's wide open, ready and attentive. I'm the one wavering and for what? Adam and I had something beautiful, and he slowly and methodically destroyed us. I'm not saying there wasn't context; there was plenty. But Adam knew what he was doing. He knew what he was doing, and he hurt us anyway. James has just been afraid.

I find him downstairs in front of a basketball game. I bet if I got close, I'd smell the cigarette he snuck while I was in the shower, and I sit down beside him and reach for his beer. I don't want the drink; I want the gesture, and when I've taken half a swallow, I give back the bottle and shift a little closer, until our arms touch. He smells like smoke and cold wind and beer. He smells like the swing on our front porch on Pearl Street. I breathe in the memory. You smell good, I tell him, offering the compliment in lieu of an apology. Thanks, he says, and he shrugs so casually I decide to try another. I like the way you kiss me, I admit. His eyes flicker, but he plays it cool. Yeah? he says, How's that?

I look at him: his mess of hair and beard, his eyes a little bloodshot from the week I've given him. The aggravated pinch he wears between his eyebrows when he's frustrated with Henry or work or—let's be honest— me has disappeared, as if his irritation has decided to take the rest of the night off. Or maybe he just wants to hear what I have to say, and my eyes trace him the way they've traced *Crossing* a thousand times. My painting's the backdrop, but he's right here in front of me.

Like you just discovered fire, I say.

James

We were at the beach in Padre. Five of us had made the trip: Joel and me, Peter, a couple guys I knew from grad school. I'd packed the weed myself but told Joel to grab the pipe and he forgot. I ended up feeding quarters into the vending machine outside our condo, buying one Diet Coke after another and draining every single one into the sand. We went through three cans before Joel finally managed to punch a hole in the bottom of the last one.

That makeshift bong fucked us up better than the pipe Joel forgot to pack. We passed it around early that night before we hit the beach and ended up staggering from one bonfire to another barely coherent and too high to care. We lost Peter along the way then one of my buddies from school and when the three of us who were still standing finally got back to the condo before dawn Joel asked if we were ready for another round. I'm out, my friend Malik mumbled, ducking into the room he and Robert were sharing but I followed Joel onto our balcony. Fuck me up, man, I said but he took the first hit, holding the smoke for so long I thought I'd missed his toke. Then he tilted his head back, smoke unfurling from his nose like some kind of dragon that'd been biding its time. You joining me or what, Fielding? he finally asked, his voice rough with smoke and I jerked my eyes away from those pursed lips and took the can he was offering.

He had the kind of mouth you wanted to fuck. That's what I'd been thinking as he exhaled and for a long time I buried the thought under the excuse that I'd been smoking. But the image came back to me again and again like a song lyric you want to banish from your head and keep humming under your breath anyway. *A mouth you want to fuck, a mouth you want to fuck.* For weeks even before that first trip I made to Greece, before the tension between Joel and me got so thick we had to leave the house just to breathe I'd catch myself thinking those words. Sometimes after a few too many beers and only with my eyes closed I'd go a little deeper. Eventually I knew firsthand what I'd been wondering. Like Tiresias I had my answer.

What? Joel says now but I don't tell him what I'm thinking. I don't want him getting the idea that I'm in this for what I can take. There's too much precedent. Instead I kiss him the way I wanted to in Padre. He responds same as I'd expect. Like he's been waiting for me, like he's been biding his time.

Just like that my mouth fills with fire.

Joel

My father died six weeks ago. James and I have been sleeping together for five and a half. Every morning after breakfast, once James has left for work, dropping Henry off at preschool along the way, I take a nap since I don't sleep well at night. I don't sleep well in the morning either, but I try anyway. If I'm lucky, I can shut down for an hour. If I'm not, I stay in bed. The cold's too bitter to be anywhere else.

I'm not working. There's nothing to do, no glass at my disposal except for the sliver of Baccarat my father gave me the night of his funeral. I hid it in my suitcase, and I haven't taken it out since. I don't want James confiscating it or Henry hurting himself.

I don't feel inspired. My hand's better, and I'm mere days from abandoning the splint. I could work, maybe, but I have plenty of excuses at the ready, and James doesn't ask what I'm thinking. He's giving me time to process everything I've been through the past couple of months. He's letting me get used to us, the us we are now that we've given in.

Or given up. Sometimes I'm not so sure there's a difference.

I'm agitated, and nothing much seems to soothe me. Sex, maybe. Sleep, when I can get it. Henry helps. He lives in the moment, cares only about playing a game *now*, eating a cookie *now*. If James has papers to grade or reading to finish, Henry and I make a fort in his bedroom and disappear inside with a stack of books. He still likes *Hansel and Gretel* the best and listens intently every time, even though he knows the story by heart. When I'm reading to him, I forget about my father and work and—sometimes— Adam.

He hasn't contacted me. I knew he wouldn't; Adam's a man of his word. James would scoff if he heard me make that claim, and there was a time I would have deemed that response justified. I trusted Adam, and he betrayed my love and our partnership. I still think he's principled.

If you're going to sing his praises, Kyle said in those first few days after Adam's ultimatum, Then why didn't you go back to him? But Kyle's upset not because I decided against Adam. He's angry that I'm still in Chicago. I know you're sleeping with him, he accused in that same phone call, and I didn't correct him, which isn't necessarily the same as saying the words aloud. *James and I are sleeping together. James and I are...* What? A couple? That's hard to believe since we rarely leave the house, never speak about what we are to anyone, including each other. At times, I feel like that demon got exactly what it wanted. Other times, I think I'm right where I'm supposed to be.

Even so, I'm restless. I cry privately, though the release never lasts. James comes home, and I have dinner ready. Every so often, I pick up Henry early, just because I don't want to be alone. I volunteer to put him to bed on the nights I think I have the energy to see that through. Kyle and I have a fight; he wants me to leave Chicago. Drop it, Kyle, I say, Or stop calling.

Sex with James isn't anything like what I remember from twelve years ago, or from five weeks ago. Blindfolded, I wouldn't be able to guess his name. No. He smells the same, like cigarettes and cold wind and beer. Everything else feels different, as if he finally decided to be himself. *Was that okay?* isn't a question he asks anymore.

Maybe I'm nothing like he remembers either.

I'm thirty-seven. I'm an artist *in absentia*. I'm an orphan, a former addict, a suicide saved at the last second. I've been called a pussy, a fag, a son of a bitch. I have talent and eyes like a storm—or so I've been told. My legs have run a marathon a thousand times over. I might as well have been born with a paintbrush in my hand. My arms bear the brunt of my abuse, including seven scars from my father's cigars, two from a box cutter (self-inflicted), and one in the palm of my hand (perpetrator debatable). I've been someone's trick, someone's boyfriend, someone's partner. I like the wind in my hair.

I can't count the number of men I've fucked, but I know how many I've loved.

James

My sister knows but not my folks. I guess if I wait too long Ashley's probably going to spill the secret herself. She's that excited. Ashley didn't love Lizzie so in her book I've upgraded big time. When are you telling Mom and Dad? she asked again last night and when I hesitated she was all over my shit. What's wrong with you? she demanded and I told her to chill out, that I'd tell them in my own goddamn time.

I'm not lying either. I'll tell them.

I'm just not sure *how* to tell them.

This afternoon I'm not thinking about my parents. I've ditched my office hours and left Henry at preschool and now Joel and I are wandering around a wine shop. The store's all warm and quiet with row after row of wine bottles glinting in the low winter light and I realize these are the moments we're missing shut up in the house the way we always are. Maybe we need to get out more.

I've gotten better over the years at picking a good wine but I'm nothing like Joel who probably would've been able to get a job as a *sommelier* in college. If I gave you free rein, I say, What would you buy? Let's take a look in there, he suggests, pointing toward the wine cellar where they keep the high-end bottles. Why the hell not, I say and he gives me the kind of smile he made me work for when we came back from Greece year before last. I swear seeing it now is a glimmer of sun in a torrent. He's been here with me for almost two months and he's barely feeling better. I'll buy the fucking store if I can get him to smile like that again and I yank open the door. Soon as I do, one of our board members looks right at me. Tom, I say, startled. Professor Fielding, he nods and I almost roll my eyes at the formality of his address even though whatever, by now I know how the academic game is played.

Can he tell I'm skipping my office hours? Middle of the afternoon on a Wednesday, wandering around a wine shop… I turn to Joel, who raises his eyebrows. He's waiting on an introduction and I mumble a hasty apology and make it happen. Tom and Joel shake hands and say *nice to meet you* and I add something about Tom being on the board then look at Joel.

Man, I've got no idea how to define Joel or what he means to me and I end up gazing at his wind-blown hair and chapped bottom lip as I root around for something that can possibly cover the way his smile made me feel just a few minutes ago. There's no chance of getting everything into one word, not with my heart feeling like a fucking sparkler.

We were roommates, Joel finally tells Tom, Back in college.

Well okay. Not where I was going but I guess that's how we started.

Do you live in Chicago? Tom asks him. Buenos Aires, Joel says, I'm just visiting.

Hell, I don't like the way that sounds either. *Visit* says departure. *Visit* says we're stepping back into reality. Yeah, we're going to have to work something out eventually but so far we haven't talked about where we're going from here. I've been focusing on the small wins, the nights Joel gets more than a few hours of sleep or the day last week when I got home from campus and found him meditating. I don't think he's ready to plan anything more than dinner tonight. But *just visiting?* That almost hurts.

I hear the city's quite cosmopolitan, Tom says and Joel tells him that's true, that the art scene's vibrant and thriving, the symphony world-class. I feel a rush of something that takes a second for me to recognize as pride. Like his daddy, Joel knows how to turn on the charm. He might be wrung out from lack of sleep and grief but you'd never know that from the way he's talking to Tom about the Buenos Aires opera house. Cheeks flushed, scarf loose around his neck, he's carrying this conversation. He looks good, this whatever of mine and I start thinking about a spot in the Caymans, a sandbar where my sister went snorkeling last fall. The water wasn't that deep but four hundred yards away on the other side of the sandbar the seafloor bottomed out. Six thousand feet down, she said to me, Can you imagine? Shit, I don't even like remembering that dive I took with Joel the summer after our sophomore year and back then we were only thirty feet below the waves.

The second I kissed Joel in the kitchen a week after Christmas I stopped treading water. Three months later I'm still sinking. Anything could be below me, anything at all. I just don't care anymore.

How long are you staying? Tom's asking Joel and I bring myself back to the conversation in just enough time to hear Joel say that he'll be gone by the weekend. Well, Tom says to Joel, Enjoy our city. I give him a nod and a *good to see you* then turn to Joel. You'll be gone by the weekend? I say. I had to lie, James, Joel explains, Otherwise he'll know you're fucking me.

He hasn't lowered his voice and I whip around to see if anyone heard him. Joel smiles like I've made exactly the mistake he expected. Oh, shit, he says in a mock-whisper, Am I being too loud? C'mon, Joel, I mumble. C'mon? he says. Don't, I plead, Don't do this. You're right, he agrees, Sorry, Roomie.

Roomie? The only person who ever calls me Roomie is Kyle and believe you me it's not a term of endearment. Roomie? I say as Joel yanks open the door of the wine cellar and walks away from me. I follow him, watching as he sets a bottle of wine on the counter. I didn't even see him grab it and I reach for my wallet the second I hear the total. Put that away, Joel hisses, handing over his credit card then scrawling his signature. Roomie? I repeat. Don't worry, James, he says, I know my place.

Outside the sky's clotted with clouds and the air's got a bite. I shove my hand in my coat pocket and feel for my keys. Joel gets in the car beside me, turning to drop the bottle of wine in the back as I start the car and bump up the heat. You gonna tell me what happened in there? I finally ask, blowing on my hands. Seems pretty obvious, he says. Not to me, I tell him and he laughs more bitter than the cold. Why am I doing this? he says, Why am I doing this to myself?

I look around to make sure he's not talking to that demon again but he's looking right at me. Seriously, he says, What's wrong with me? What do you mean? I ask. I might as well have been standing in front of Pujan back there, he tells me. Pujan? I repeat, confused.

I knew a guy named Pujan in grad school. He was from England, he was kind of a prick and I was forever comparing my scholarship to his mostly because his was better. I heard from someone that he died in a car wreck a few years back.

What does Pujan have to do with anything? I ask and Joel gives me an incredulous look. Are you kidding? he says and before I can answer he starts punching the dashboard. Dude, I protest but he's smashing his fist over and over again, swearing so hard I can't understand what he's saying. Something about Pujan and blowjobs and too many chances. The windows warm with his words and I finally grab his arm. His expression makes me duck. Fuck you! he screams, Fuck you, you motherfucking *monster*!

Man, I don't know what the hell happened but somewhere along the way this afternoon went very, very wrong. He's unraveling right in front of me all the way back to that moment in his dad's office when he almost ended his career. He's not strong enough to punch a hole in the dashboard, is he? And his hand. Man, he's barely healed.

I've got to do something and I even out my voice until it's smooth as the crayons Henry and I ironed between sheets of wax paper last weekend. Joel, I start, keeping it nice and simple and at first I think I've got him. He stops wailing on the dashboard and I backend his name with the kind of smile I give Henry when he's melting down before bed. You're my father, James, he says.

My stomach bottoms out.

All my life I waited for him, he says. He takes a deep breath but lets go of it too quick to do any good. I'm really tired of waiting, he whispers.

I scramble out after him when he jerks open the door. C'mon, Joel, I say, Get in the car. Fuck off, James, he warns, shaking me away and I make a quick succession of mistakes that feel dead wrong even in the moment. I take hold of his arm. He stares down at the way my hand's tightening around his bicep but for some reason I can't let go and my words come out like I don't even own them. Stop bein' a drama queen for once in your life, Joel, I say, And get in the goddamn car!

He knocks my ass down so hard he kicks my breath clean away. Whatever, he might not be running these days or practicing much yoga but he's stronger than I've been in a long time and there's nothing I can do to hold him off. Twisting, I miss the first blow but the second gives me a mouthful of blood. Joel, I choke but he's already cocking his arm.

I don't know why he doesn't hit me. I've shut my eyes and when nothing happens I finally risk a look. He's still straddling me but he's got his head buried in his hands. I can't tell if he's crying. Joel, I say, wiping the tears streaking down my own face and he moans. Why can't you leave me alone? he says.

Then he's on his feet and stumbling away from me. I hawk a clot of blood into the snow.

Joel

I have no idea how far I've walked at this point, but Chicago has fallen black. I've been wandering around for hours without paying attention to landmarks. I have no idea where the hell I am right now, and the scarf I'm wearing doesn't come close to keeping out the cold. I'm going to have to stop somewhere to warm up, and I know just what I want: a drink.

At the next corner, I find a bar. Ambient windows and striped awning, my salvation in predictable form. I can almost taste the alcohol, and my mouth fills with saliva at the promise that's waiting for me behind those doors. I'm going to get really, really drunk, then decide what I can handle next.

My hand's on the door when a passing car bleats its horn. Turning, my eye catches a storefront across the street, buried between a dry cleaners and a nail salon.

Lakefront Yoga.

Okay. Okay, maybe. I'm not sure if my hand has healed enough to put weight on my palm, especially after the punches I threw this afternoon, but what if they have a restorative class?

I make it across the street, and when the door shuts behind me, I take my first deep breath since I left James sprawled in the snow. May I help you? the receptionist asks in a voice soft and melodic. Do you have a restorative class tonight? I ask. We do, she says, But it started at seven.

It's after *seven*? How long have I been wandering around out there?

She registers my confusion and with an apologetic smile indicates the clock on the wall behind me. I don't know which feels worse, realizing that

I've been walking the streets for over four hours or knowing that in all likelihood, I'll end up back at that bar.

As if I'm being taunted, the door to the classroom opens. The students sliding their arms into their coats exude the serenity I can only find with a paintbrush in my hand or my body in motion. I want to break down right here. I came so close.

May I help you? someone asks, and I turn. He must be the instructor, a Middle Eastern guy my age with lashes so thick he might as well be wearing eyeliner. I take an instinctive step closer, inhaling at the same time. He has an energy so grounded and powerful he makes Celeste seem like a neophyte, and as I breathe, he stands a little straighter, pulling his shoulders back at the same time like he's offering me a direct line to his heart chakra. I give myself a hit before I speak. I was looking for a restorative class, I tell him, But my timing's off. Maybe, he says.

His response comes so predictably and sounds so Zen that I laugh. I'm Qamar, he says, offering his hand. Joel, I tell him, and he looks over my shoulder. I glance behind me to see the receptionist removing her coat from the back of her chair but looking uncertain about the decision. Qamar just tells her he'll take it from here.

He does. Once we're alone, he locks the door, then brings me a cup of water from the cooler and a change of clothes since I'm wearing jeans and an ice-encrusted scarf. I don't ask if he has time for whatever we're about to do, not because I don't want to draw his attention to the fact that I'm keeping him here after hours, but because I know the answer. I want to weep for my dumb luck.

I go into the restroom, where I unwind my scarf, hang my coat on the back of the door, pry off my boots, and unbutton my jeans. When I return to the reception area, dressed in borrowed clothes, Qamar beckons me toward a classroom toasted to a cozy ninety-five degrees. He has a yoga mat rolled out and ready. I'm asked to sit, and Qamar places himself across from me in the lotus position. His gaze penetrates so subtly I want to give everything up to him, every frustration and failure, every fuckup. I want to surrender it all because I don't think I can carry this shit for much longer. I have to let something go, and for now, at least, he invites me to hand myself over to these poses. I start, the process slow and painstaking. Breath by breath, I feel the first layer unfold.

I'm sitting on my heels, palms on my knees, *pranayama*, twenty breaths. They're shallow at first, tremulous. I feel completely disconnected from my center, but Qamar tells me to follow my breath, and eventually, with his quiet encouragement, I find a small peace somewhere inside. Holding on to that tiny truth in my tempest, I move into *bhujangasana*. Hooded like a cobra, arms as steady as I can get them. Qamar's talking, something my ears don't quite hear but my subconscious absorbs. Beyond the physical relief of my body stretching, my abdominal muscles lengthening, I begin to believe.

Then *upavistha konasana*, legs spread, my chest meeting the mat. The deeper I breathe, the deeper the stretch, James *deeper* Adam *deeper* my father, until Qamar invites me into *supta vajrasana*. This has never been an easy pose for me, even under the best of circumstances, but I fall backward, Qamar pressing gently on my inner thighs, opening up my pelvis and creating space in my hip socket. He exudes no sexual energy whatsoever. He's pure compassion, and I breathe, unlocking whatever I've buried here.

Ardha kurmasana. Kneeling, arms stretched long in prayer, head below my heart. Every negative thought my ego conjures somehow slips from my mind, and I bliss there for a while before I slide into *shavasana*. But Qamar hasn't finished with me. *Urdva dhanurasana*, he says, and I arch into wheel pose, navel skyward. I can feel a break in the clouds of my sacral chakra, a parting of some epic thunderstorm. Light pours through the opening, and that's when my arms start to shake. Not because I don't have the muscular strength to support myself and not because my left hand has started to cry like I've taken a cigar to my palm, though that part's true. Instead, I'm just quaking. I expect tears to roll from the corners of my eyes and slip into my hair, but I don't cry. I'm aching for this release, and the tremors come greater and greater until Qamar touches my abdomen, the heel of his hand even with my solar plexus. The shaking reverses, shudders down my torso and through my legs like an errant orgasm. I'd collapse if he didn't have hold of me.

Somehow, I get myself into *shavasana*. Aftershocks make their way down my arms. Palms up, I let myself recalibrate, and Adam bursts through the sunlight of my vision. The tears I've been saving stream from the corners of my eyes and into my hair. I don't wipe them away; they're every bit as sacred as the pose I'm holding, and I let them flow until I'm ready to work my way into a sitting position.

How do you feel? Qamar asks. I'm not sure, I admit, and he nods. Take time to integrate, he says.

For the first time since I left Buenos Aires, I feel a wink of inspiration, something subtle at the back of my skull that feels like a whisper from my muse, and on the cab ride back to James's house, I stare into my palm. My hand hurts; I'm not going to lie. I examine the way my scar disrupts my life line, my line of love. The image I had of Adam when I was in *shavasana* flickers somewhere beneath my surface; he's so much a part of my mosaic that he might as well be the mortar.

No. My work's the mortar.

Adam was the glass that shattered into a thousand pieces.

James

Joel still isn't home. I let him walk away from me outside that wine shop and by the time I got to my feet he was gone. He's dressed for the cold this time and I know he's got his wallet but that just worries me even more. He's not an idiot. He can find his way back here, he can pay for the cab. He knows my number by heart. He's staying away on purpose and I'm not exactly in a position to go looking for him, not with Henry sitting beside me. Suppose Joel was in an accident or something? That could happen.

I'm trying real hard not to think about the demon he kept seeing last month.

I'm trying real hard not to think that I hurt him so bad he—

Henry's in his pajamas, the ones with the penguins on ice skates and every so often he looks down at the front of his shirt and pats the one caught mid-fall. We're upstairs in his bedroom building a habitat for his dinosaurs. He wanted to know where Joel went and I didn't have an answer for him. We're chilly on the floor and I reach for one of his little feet and give it a squeeze.

I'm still trying to figure out what happened this afternoon. One minute Joel was throwing smiles my way and the next I was on the ground. I'm swollen and bruised and when I grabbed Henry from preschool—after I'd gone home long enough to clean myself up—I got a grimace from his teacher that reminded me I'm not looking my best. I didn't know what to tell Henry. I'm scared he's going to put two and two together and realize Joel had something to do with why my lip looks like a balloon.

Play, Daddy, Henry tells me and I reach for a handful of blocks and stack them one on top of the other. *Thonk thonk thonk.* He knows I'm not really here and I tack on this half-assed parenting moment to the others I've got to make up for, the ones he'll probably tell his therapist about when he's older, assuming he can remember them.

Almost time for bed, buddy, I say and he screws his mouth into a scowl, probably because he wants Joel reading to him same as every other night. I take a look at my watch but seeing the time doesn't make me feel any better. With the tip of my tongue I taste the corner of my mouth where Joel's fist did the most damage. Henry reaches out to touch my face. Gentle, buddy, I warn, pulling back and he gives me a soft pat like I'm the penguin on his pjs. I manage not to wince.

After he finally falls asleep—three books later—I go downstairs to clean up the kitchen. Hell, who am I kidding? I need a cigarette and I crack the window and light up and *God* the nicotine helps. A beer will too but I'll have to stop myself at one. I guess I need to be ready to drive if Joel calls and can't find his way home. Or if I get a call that something happened to him.

Nothing happened to him, *Jesus.* He just stopped somewhere for dinner, that's all. Or he met up with someone.

Now that turns my gut right there, the thought of him meeting somebody. When he came up to see Henry for the first time when Lizzie and I had that fight… He left a day early claiming he was heading for the airport but he ended up in Boystown where he went to some club and picked up some guy and—

I guzzle some of my beer and turn the faucet on until the water's steaming up the window above the sink. I keep thinking about what happened this afternoon. We were doing just fine until we ran into Tom. Whatever, we were doing just fine until I had to explain Joel. That introduction's never been trouble except when there's something between us. Then I wonder about who I am and what people think and we start spiraling faster and faster and I keep trying to grab onto something to slow us down but Joel's the only thing I'm holding and he makes me so dizzy I can't even see. This time though… this time was different.

I know how I feel. I just can't find a word that defines us.

Once I fill the dishwasher I start on the pizza pan, taking breaks for quick drags of my cigarette. I'm wondering what Pujan has to do with all this. I barely knew the guy. I didn't even like him. We shared an office along with a couple other grad students. I don't think we ever once socialized. He was a prick. He had a British accent and—

Bam. I've been telling myself I'm just trying to finish my syllabus but really I'm avoiding Joel. That's why I'm on campus. That's why I haven't gone home even though I'm the only one in the graduate student offices this late at night. I don't want to go home and then Joel shows up in the doorway and kneels down and as I'm trying to peel him away from me I realize why he's here. For the first time since his mom died I've forgotten the date. Shit, I mutter and then he's tugging at my jeans and I'm telling him no but with zero conviction and right in my office he goes down on me and I don't want to give this up, not now, not ever. Come home, he says when I'm finished and I get my bag and he opens the door of my office and here's Pujan. So you're the *roommate*, he says to Joel and I almost throw up. Let's go, Joel mumbles, grabbing my arm and I stumble after him and find myself face to face with the chair of my dissertation committee. This guy right here could pass or fail me in March when I take my qualifying exams and I swear I can't breathe. Working late? he asks, raising his eyebrows when I don't answer him and I hear Pujan say in that British accent, I believe he's overheated.

Pujan. All this time I've remembered running into my professor but Pujan's the one who caught us. Pujan's the one who found us out. Aren't we something good? Joel asked later that night and that's when I told him I was done.

Joel

I find James in the kitchen washing dishes, the aroma of a dinner cooked without my presence lingering in the air. With his back to me and the sound of running water, he doesn't know I'm here. I watch him; thanks to Qamar, I'm no longer balling my hands into fists. Smoke from a cigarette burning in an ashtray on the counter curls toward a cracked window above the sink. James, I finally say, and he turns.

He's the one who ends up crying. I pull out a chair as he dries his hands, but he doesn't join me at the table. Instead, he leans back against the sink. Pujan heard us in my office, he volunteers. So, I say, unable to keep the bitterness from my voice, You remember. I forgot about Pujan, he admits, But I can still see my professor. He shakes his head at the memory. Do you know how you make me feel when you say shit like that? I ask.

He hangs his head. Even when I'm not trying, he says, I end up hurting you. So sometimes you're trying? I ask, and he gives me a grim smile. Sometimes, he confesses. Well, I say, looking at my swollen knuckles, That makes two of us.

We fall silent. I unwind my scarf from around my neck.

Today when we ran into Tom, he says, I didn't know how to introduce you. I noticed, I say flatly. I didn't know how to introduce you, Joel, he explains, Because you're more than any word I can find.

That's poetic enough to shut me up.

I need a cigarette, he mumbles, realizing the one in the ashtray has just about burned itself out. I watch him rip the foil from a fresh pack. He tamps the box against the counter, then extracts a cigarette. Inhaling, he winces, then touches the corner of his mouth where it wears my wrath. A haze settles over the kitchen like we've stepped back in time.

I don't know how to introduce you, he says, I don't know how to talk about you or explain you or be with you when we pick up Henry from preschool. He shakes his head. I don't know how to tell my parents, he adds. That seems par for the course, I mumble. And in light of the past few months, he says, That seems unfair.

I'm tempted to apologize, but I want to see where he's going with this. So I sit, trying to be as open and receptive as I was with Qamar. It isn't easy. Every word James dishes up comes with a side of shame.

That kiss, he says, That kiss when you were here after Christmas... He looks at me like he wants to be sure I know what he means. I remember, I tell him, and he says, That wasn't planned.

Well, that's not news to me. I can tell the difference between spontaneity and calculation. Spontaneity was that hit of water to my chest, his hands moving through my hair. Calculation was the bag of pot he brought home the first time we slept together.

I kissed you, he says, And for a month, I couldn't think about anything else.

Neither could I. Elías comes to mind and parks there for a second, but even that last night with him, I couldn't stop thinking about James, couldn't stop wondering if we could be different this time around. The question kept me up at night, belly-crawled its way into my dreams, turned up when I was working. If Catherine hadn't called, if my father had lasted just a few more weeks, where would we be now? If I'd made this trip without the yoke of death around me, would we be having this conversation? Or would we have discovered that even under the best of circumstances we aren't cut out for each other?

I'm tired of pretending I don't want you, Joel, he says.

I feel like I'm watching my life in slow motion. For years, I wanted these words. Now that they've been spoken, I don't know what to do with them.

He waits, but whatever's in my head isn't shaking loose.

Maybe I'm too late, he says.

He needs to see me slide into a smile, needs me to tell him he's wrong. Instead, I'm second- and third-guessing myself, and tears turn up in his eyes. They bring me no relief; I'm horrified to have caused them. I'm sorry, Joel, he whispers, You have no idea.

I almost let him go. But at the last second, I put out my arm as he walks past me. I don't meet his eyes; in some ways, it's easier to unbuckle his belt. Didn't I ask him to do that himself, years ago on the phone?

I have his jeans unbuttoned, the zipper between my fingers. I can put all of my attention into my hands. I can tell him with my tongue what he needs to hear. I can let him in this way, because I don't know if I can come up with the words.

His zipper comes down, and he catches his breath. I slide my hands under the waistband of his boxers and ease one side over his hip. His tattoo still has color, and I trace its outline with my thumb. The first time I saw his tattoo, I fell to my knees. I never imagined I'd have the opportunity again and again.

Is that what he's giving me? An opportunity to change where I thought we were headed? Earlier tonight, I wasn't sure if I could ever come back here.

I give up and kiss his sun.

James

I didn't think he'd give me another chance. When I turned around and saw him standing in the kitchen I figured he was done. Well, maybe not at first but I came to that conclusion when I laid out everything I was feeling and then some and he just stared at me like *too little, too fucking late*. That's when I started blinking back tears and I don't know, maybe that's what got him. I walked away and he held me back and next thing I know he had his mouth all over me. When we were through I braced myself same as he probably did back in '97 when we went out to celebrate the news that he'd gotten his first show and I should've stopped him and didn't. *This was a mistake.* But he didn't say a word. Instead he touched my mouth where it hurt. I'm sorry, he said, and I brought his forehead to mine.

Since then we've been all right, more than all right. Took you long enough, Ashley laughs when I get her on the phone. I tell Joel my sister wants to talk to him then bulls-eye the second he realizes she knows. He turns to me with his eyebrows raised and all right, so maybe my face feels hot. I start folding Henry's laundry and pretend I'm not listening to Joel's end of the conversation even though I'm analyzing every word in case he's pissed. The closest he comes is *James has always been slow* served up in a voice so thinly veiled even the cat knows what he means. Slow, I grump when he finally hangs up and he says, Your slow just about killed me, James.

That's near enough to truth to trip me up. I stop stacking Henry's clothes like I'm fixing to apologize but what am I supposed to say? Sorry I took so long to get here? All these years later I still have a hard time seeing the scars on his arms. One thing I'll say about Adam Atwater. He deserves a big old thank you for loving Joel as much as he did because if he hadn't gone to our house on Pearl the day before New Year's Eve back in '98, if he hadn't followed whatever gut impulse told him to open the door when no one answered he never would've found Joel in that bathtub and I wouldn't be standing here with Joel right now.

Joel glances up at me. Not literally, James, he says, frowning. Well..., I mumble, gesturing in the direction of his scars. He stares down at his arms then back up at me. Is that what you think? he asks and I feel a glimmer of something that feels an awful lot like freedom. You said..., I start, When you got back from Mexico you said...

He didn't say anything I guess. I told him I knew he blamed me for what had happened and he didn't say a word and that was all the indictment I needed. I guess I've been hauling that around for years. He puts his palm over his mouth same as I did when we showed up in Houston after his mom died. That night I was the one who ran after him, who heard his knees hit the floor, who knelt down beside him in the middle of all that blood and took him in my arms and that's what he's doing now, stepping toward me and wrapping me up. One hand on the back of my head with his mouth to my ear and over and over until the words get through to me he says it wasn't my fault. Over and over until the words get through to me.

I keep trying to get to the bottom of him. All those years of field work and man, there's nothing anywhere in this world that compares to what I'm discovering right here. I'm at the beginning of some brilliant excavation where there's no end to the treasure I'm going to uncover. I take his hand, the left one, the one he hurt, the one I've found holding a paintbrush more times than I can count. Kissing his palm I work my way up, taking my time so I know every inch of the scar that runs from his wrist to his elbow.

I figure I'm not the first.

I bet I'm the last.

Joel

The weather's softening, and I pull Henry out of preschool early and take him to the park. He likes the slide, collects pebbles and dribbles them along the sidewalk on the way back to the house. I'm patient with him, let him linger over the neighborhood cat sitting in the sun and the trail of ants circling a gumdrop. Are you hungry? I ask once we're home.

I sketch while he has his snack. I'll draw anything he wants, and usually, that means scenes from *Hansel and Gretel.* I've perfected the house, with its gingerbread roof and candied columns, drawn Gretel shoving the witch into the oven more times than I can count. When James gets home, Henry shows him what I've done, and I listen to James enthuse as if I've accomplished something monumental. Maybe I have. Only in the past few weeks has my hand felt steady enough to pick up a pencil.

I'm missing the glass. We're going to have to talk about that at some point, about what we're going to do. I've sent a carefully worded email to my benefactor, explaining my absence and apologizing. A few months ago, I might have worried how I'd manage financially without a stipend. Now my circumstances have changed. My father has been generous. For the first time since Adam and I split up, I can paint without worrying about money.

Ironically, I have a half a dozen shows scheduled for this fall, mostly in the States. If the reviews are positive, I'll be solvent even without my inheritance. Either way, I'm going to be traveling often enough that Buenos Aires seems an inconvenient hub. James doesn't have the same flexibility; he has tenure and plans for more fieldwork. I'm the one who's going to have to move.

Every so often, I wonder what I'm doing. James and I are lost in a labyrinth of our own making. Would we leave if we could? I'm not so sure. Something keeps us coming back. A circular narrative: that's what James called us the other night. I've said worse.

I try not to think about Adam or his appearance at the end of my first session with Qamar. He's a part of my mosaic, a part of my past; I need to look to the future. Still, the impulse to reach out to him… Sometimes I feel as if I'm denying my own breath or the beat of my heart. Instead, I focus on James and Henry and the glass I'll bring back with me at the end of the summer. I see Qamar once a week. I run when the sun breaks free of the clouds. James's parents call, and I try not to hold it against any of us when the conversation runs dry. James and I have had years to get used to us. They're just getting started.

James isn't what I expected this time around. For so long, he could only go so far, and that's why I heard him hesitate at that wine shop and hastened to a conclusion he's been proving wrong ever since. I don't know what changed. Less than two years ago, we stood in the shadows of that campfire on Crete. Now he's unreserved and unapologetic. He's no longer self-conscious. I'm no longer on the defensive. I've stopped wondering when he's going to change his mind. I don't think he will.

One night, I sketch him, the first time I've sketched anything for anyone other than Henry since I hurt my hand. James sprawls on the couch, one foot on the coffee table, *Crossing* the context. When he turns his eyes in my direction, I tell him to hold still. For years, I asked him to sit for me; he hardly ever turned me down. Now I draw him: hair thick, eyes deep, mouth full. And something else, a directness in his gaze I've never seen from him. What do you need from me? he asks. Nothing, I say, You're perfect.

James

We're done with the demons. We're not looking back anymore. We're not talking about how we got here or beating ourselves up for crossing lines. We're somewhere we've never been and for the first time I'm not scared shitless about what that means. I don't care who knows. Everyone knows, including my folks. Turns out they have a *live and let live* attitude about everyone but their son. I'm concerned, my mom admitted, releasing a sigh I wish she would've kept to herself. Whatever, I guess they're trying. They talk to Joel mostly because I told them if they couldn't they shouldn't bother calling at all.

Joel's better and that's because of us. I'm sure the yoga therapy's helping. I know he's different in the hour after he comes back from a run. I like that he's drawing again even if he's focused on fairy tales. He talks about bringing the glass here at the end of the summer. After Greece, I remind him. After Greece, he agrees.

Eight weeks starting in July. This time will be different. Everything's different. At least you're not lying to yourself, Lizzie said on the phone when she called to check in on Henry and I told her it wasn't so much that I'd been lying all those years. I just needed time, same as those canvases Joel builds. Everything that's happened in the close to two decades since we first met? We just had to gesso the canvas. Now's when we get to paint.

Henry's a part of this too. Every day I watch him with Joel and what they've got growing between them and I want to drop to my knees I'm so grateful. This boy always deserved more than me. I'm still his number one, there's no doubt about that. But Joel's so close behind I might as well have hand-picked him myself. Hell, maybe I did. Maybe he was always the one I had in mind. Maybe somewhere deep down inside, Lizzie knew she wasn't supposed to be anything more than the surrogate.

One afternoon we take Henry to the beach. Chicago's still a little cold and windy but my boy's bundled up and the sun's giving us a hint of what's coming. The sky's as brilliant as the lake's as brilliant as Joel's eyes before he drops his shades down over them. He's kicked back on the blanket we brought and I look at him lying there and *bam*, I'm in Mexico the summer after our sophomore year. So far he's gotten laid and I've had a panic attack in the pool. About the only thing I've got going for me is the way he looked when I gave him shit about the dive master who took us on my first dive ever. He was hittin' on you, I said and Joel tried to play it cool. Maybe, he mumbled. Dude, I smirked, He was practically on his knees.

I probably shouldn't have laughed. I know Joel's gay and I know what keeping that a secret is doing to him but man, I feel like such a pussy on this trip. I can't even pay my own damn way and even though I spend most of my life looking out for Joel, in that moment after our dive I felt a streak so mean I was ashamed of myself. That turn you on or somethin'? I asked and he started struggling. I knew what he wanted to say but I suddenly did not want him coming out to me just because I'd coerced him and I willed his mouth to stay shut. Problem was that when he did I felt his failure like it was mine. He couldn't manage any more than a *fuck you* and I muttered *you really had me goin' there* and it wasn't until later that night after a few tequila shots that we got our equilibrium back.

This morning we're hungover and we stumble out to the beach early. The sun comes up hot and sticky and I figure the best way to get rid of my headache is to start drinking. Between the two of us we take down half a dozen daiquiris before noon. I'm swimming without setting foot in the water but Joel's holding his own. He can handle his liquor way better than I can and after a while he shoves away from his lounge chair and cuts a neat dive into the pool. He comes out dripping and I glare at him through my shades. I'm suddenly sick of him breaking the rules and getting away with it.

Whatever, so his mom looked down the wrong end of a .38. He also has a summer so blank he had to drag me to Mexico just to break up the monotony. He doesn't have a problem footing the bill. His heart didn't start flying around in his throat at the thought of diving thirty feet deep. I watch him towel himself off and watch the girl on the other side of the pool watch Joel and I watch the smile he throws her way and I fucking *hate* him. He can get her no problem. That smile and one drink and he'll be winking at me over his shoulder as he walks that girl in her itty-bitty bikini back to our room. He doesn't even *want* her and he's still got a better shot at her than I do. God, that pisses me off and I slurp up the last of my drink and grunt when he asks if I want another one. Another daiquiri on his daddy's dime. The only thought that comes even close to taking the edge off my jealousy is *yeah but he sucks dick*. However put together he seems, I know what he has going on under the bullshit. He might look at that pretty girl and he might fuck that pretty girl but what he really wants is the dive master from yesterday.

I feel a big old smile spread across my face, all smug and satisfied and that's when he turns to me. He isn't wearing sunglasses and I've got a clear shot at his eyes. Hey, he says, Thanks for coming down here with me. I mumble something about being his tagalong since he's paying for every damn thing and man, he gives me a look so serious it cuts right through the booze. He doesn't even have to say anything. I just know same as if he'd said the words. He doesn't know what he'd do without me, and love and desire and guilt and pride tangle up tight in my heart.

I love you, I blurt out right here on the Chicago shore and Joel takes off his shades. His eyes look crystal calm. Yeah, he says, I know you do.

Joel

I have a good day, the best I've had in a long time. I've seen Qamar, gone for a run, sat outside thinking about the glass. The sun sends prisms across my closed eyes, reminds me of a time I can't quite remember. All these moments in my memory, and the only one I want to reach for has James standing on a beach, saying my name in the wind. At Barton Springs, in Mexico, on North Avenue Beach right here in Chicago. I feel cleansed, emptied of everything except the light. The idea of seeing a demon if I open my eyes seems as preposterous as where we've ended up. Nineteen years in the making, that's what we are. Nineteen years and we've finally stopped circling.

I pick up Henry from preschool. At home, I hull strawberries and we gorge on the fruit, then go in the backyard to inspect the birdhouse James put up a couple of months ago. We can hear peeping from the inside, and I take Henry in my arms and get close enough for him to see but stay far enough away for safety. What do you think they're saying to each other? I ask, and he thinks hard. They hungwy, he finally concludes. They're going to eat worms for dinner, I tell him, And bugs for dessert. He giggles, his lips stained strawberry like my own.

James finds us upstairs when he gets home from campus. There you are, he says, and he might be talking about me or he might be talking about

Henry, but it doesn't matter. We're all in this together, and I tell him we should take advantage of the weather and walk the few blocks to a café I first found two summers ago, when I came up here to help James before he left for Greece. He agrees, and we head out, Henry wandering just ahead of us. Halfway down the block, the light illuminates a piece of glass caught in a corner of the sidewalk, as red as my heart and cracked along one side. I bend down to claim it. Something you can use? James asks, and I slide my finger along the edges. I know what I've found, but I shrug. Maybe, I say.

The moon rises on our way home, brightening alongside the stars. The wind has picked up, and James holds Henry close to his chest to keep him warm. He's tired from his day, and we tuck him into bed. What about you? James asks me. What do you think? I say.

Afterwards, I can't sleep. At first, I blame the moon, then my day. I didn't run far enough; I shouldn't have sat for such a long time on the back porch. Or we've gone to bed too early, despite giving ourselves plenty of time to savor what we started. Beside me, James sleeps with his arm thrown above his head; I could wake him, and we could begin again. Instead, I take slow breaths I measure against James's. In tandem, we sleep.

Bike between my legs, the ground a blur beneath me. And his hands, his hands on my waist, fingers grazing the shirt under my leather jacket. The wind cold in my hair, thick flakes of snow sifting from the sky like confetti. Then the headlights, the impact, the tear of his body from mine like muscle from bone. A surge of electricity, more incredible than any orgasm I've had. Then...

I'm outside on the back porch, and I'm not sure how I got here. I don't remember getting out of bed. The night's quiet and cold, the stars as brittle as shards of glass. I'd put the temperature at a brisk forty-five degrees, warm enough for someone used to springtime in Chicago, but I'm shivering. The dream that chased me downstairs still has hold of me; I can feel his arms around my waist, then the moment I'm torn away from him. My sob spills into the silence, and I sink to the top step and rest my head on my knees. *Just a dream,* but the abyss of his absence feels like nothing I can withstand. I close my eyes, trying to find my way back to the warmth of the sun on my skin. Slowly, slowly, the dream releases its hold, and I finally raise my head, as certain as I was yesterday that I won't find a demon waiting for me.

I'm not counting on my mother.

James

I know as soon as I open my eyes that today's going to be as good as yesterday and maybe even better. I can hear the TV downstairs and Joel making something in the kitchen, maybe pancakes or waffles and my stomach starts rumbling. I'm still too lazy to haul my ass out of bed just yet and I stretch my arms over my head. Man, I've slept longer than usual for a Saturday morning and I guess I have Joel to thank. I hope Henry didn't get him up too early.

Last night was good. Hell, last night was better than good and I'm not talking about the sex. Or whatever, not just about the sex. I've stopped trying to understand what's happening between us and stopped trying to control it and maybe that's why I feel like I'm in some kind of free fall. All I can say is fine by me. Fine by me because this here momentum feels way better than anything else has ever felt in my life, ever.

Joel found a piece of glass on the way to dinner last night. Somethin' you can use? I asked even though I already knew the answer. He always has the same tell when he's onto something good, doesn't matter whether it's his work or a guy. A quick aversion of the eyes *one two three* then a twitch on the side of his mouth like he got hold of a tiny fishhook. I saw it for the first time our freshman year when we were sitting in a circle with the other guys in our dorm, introducing ourselves to the R.A. I'm an artist, Joel said and I watched him drop his eyes *one two three* then try to hold onto his smile. That gap between his gaze and his grin got me the way Greece eventually did. I wanted to find out more and once I figured out he had the same quirk when it came to my pledge brother I couldn't stop thinking about where he was in that space.

That's how I knew, by the way. Before I brought home that bag of pot, before we slept together. I got home from Greece after my first year in grad school and everything felt the same as always. Better even, since I'd been away all summer and that made me appreciate what I'd been missing, including Joel. My semester started up again and Joel was doing his thing in his studio and sleeping with a guy who made me grind my teeth, he was so fucking stupid and finally they split up and we had Halloween to ourselves. We headed to Sixth Street to hear a band and we caught up with a friend of ours, smoking and drinking. Peter was telling us about his new girlfriend and I tapped my cigarette against the edge of my ashtray and glanced at Joel. He was staring right at me but the second I looked at him his eyes fell to his beer. For some reason I found myself counting *one two three*. Then *bam*. Fishhook smile. Man, my heart went wild and I threw my gaze over to the girls dancing by the stage. Pretty, I commented all casual-like and he rolled his eyes and told me he couldn't tell them apart. Hell, neither could I but I had to move. I had to do something.

I slept with one of those girls the same night. I don't even remember her name. All I remember is Joel shutting down when I brought her back to our table and me pretending like I didn't know why. I'm not your boyfriend, man! I yelled at him when we left the bar and he tried to stop me from going home with her, I'm not your fuckin' boyfriend!

We got past that night. He flew to Mexico for a week and I calmed down enough to realize what a dick I'd been and when he got home we started a slow burn flirtation that finally ended the night I brought home some pot.

Or whatever, maybe it never ended because that's him on the stairs. Hey, I say when he opens the door but he doesn't smile. I try to peer around him to see if maybe Henry's on the stairs. He's watching *Blue's Clues*, Joel tells me. C'mere then, I say, inviting him into the bed with a look at what I've got under the covers. James..., he starts and I take a second glance at him. What's wrong? I ask.

I get a real bad feeling smack in the center of my chest when he sits on the edge of the bed and starts talking. Shut up, I finally beg, holding my head in my hands, Shut *up*. I rake my fingers through my hair to try to steady myself but I guess I come up short because I can't quit shaking. I couldn't get in touch with you, he says, I kept calling, but I couldn't get in touch with you. Henry hid my phone! I yell. I know, he says, I know that now. So you called *Adam*? I cry, The guy who *cheated* on you?

I can barely hear him as he talks about the airport in Bogota and magic 8 balls. Have you been talkin' to him this entire time? I moan. No, he says, I haven't spoken with him since I left Seattle.

Those words should make me feel better but all I can think is *why*? Why tell me now? I don't need to hear this shit. We hadn't even had sex yet. We were still trying to process that kiss in my kitchen. There's got to be a bottom line. Tell me, I say, Tell me what this means.

Maybe psych had the right idea a few months ago. Maybe I should've checked Joel into that hospital until he could get his head on straight. First he's seeing demons and now he's seeing ghosts? Listen to me, I start but he's talking about some dream he had the night before he got the call that his dad was dying. I've had it twice, James, he confesses and I figure if he's going to act like a whack job I might as well treat him like one. All right, I say, pretending to be patient and lasting about two seconds, What'd your mom have to say last night?

He's not talking sense and that's what I tell him. He's not talking sense, he needs some sleep, I'll take Henry and he can just spend the day in bed or go for a run or call that yoga guy or I'll take him to see someone right now, I'll find someone to watch Henry and I can take him to talk to someone. I don't need a psychiatrist, he tells me. You need somethin', Joel, I say and man, when he doesn't answer tears well up in my eyes. I blink them away but they keep coming. You're not leavin', I say, grabbing onto him, You're not leavin'! James, he whispers and I shove him away from me.

Joel

I spend the morning with Henry because James can't. He's a wreck, and I'm to blame; or maybe I'm finished finding fault. I don't want to hurt him. I hate hurting him, but ever since I saw my mother, I feel as if I've opened the throttle on my bike. I'm hurtling down a highway, and I'm just going to have to finish the ride.

That doesn't mean I'm not aching to go upstairs and tell him I made a mistake. I keep catching my breath, looking at Henry and trying to imagine a life where I don't see him every day. He gives me pause, sends me into the middle of last night all over again. My mother, sitting on the edge of her tombstone in James's backyard and swinging her legs like a girl. Mom? I said, catching her mid-laugh, and she swung around to look at me. Her hair fell thick and dark over her shoulders. I got to my feet, thinking she'd disappear when I approached. *I'm dreaming,* I thought, *I'm still dreaming,* and I pinched my arm, then winced.

James tells me I'm crazy. Part of me thinks he's right. With one word, I could put everything back in place. We could have the day we planned, the one we talked about last night as we were lying together in bed. We could play with Henry or open a bottle of wine or get a sitter and spend the rest of the afternoon alone. But I'm leaving in a few hours; I've already packed my bag. I'm not going to watch this, James said, slamming the door to his office, and he's been in there ever since.

I've called a cab. I have a four o'clock flight to Seattle. Adam doesn't know I'm coming; or maybe he does. Maybe my mother saw to that, too. You were talking to demons a few months ago, James reminded me, and I didn't help my case when I said: Just one. Will you listen to yourself? he asked, but that's the problem. I am listening. He just doesn't want to hear what I'm saying.

Henry, I say, and James's son looks up at me. We're drawing together, though he's far more interested in what I'm sketching—the gingerbread house again—than the paper in front of him. He looks so sweet today, with his curly hair and those big eyes staring back at me. I've told him I'm going away for a while. When will you come home? he asked. I don't know, I admitted, and he flung himself into my arms with so much force I almost changed my mind. He's calmer now; he likes the pictures I draw for him. Be nice to your Dad tonight, I say. I'm always nice, he confides, and I smile.

James

I've been waiting all afternoon for Joel to tell me he's been fucking with me. You're lyin', I said this morning when he told me he'd already booked a flight, You're *lyin'*. No way would he just up and leave without giving me any warning. What we've pieced together over the past few months—hell, who we've become over the past nineteen years—means something. I mean something, Henry means something. Even if Joel doesn't want to be with me he wouldn't wake up and leave the *same goddamn day*. How can you do this? I asked this morning. I didn't come to this decision lightly, he said. You came to this decision overnight! I cried.

James, he says now on the other side of the door. I know why he's knocking. I've looked out the window and fuck if there's not a cab sitting in front of the house, waiting to take him away from me after all and man, the reality of what's about to happen lays me flat. How can I shut this down when I thought we were just getting started?

James, he says again, Please.

Fuck him. Fuck him for letting me love him.

James, I have to go, he says and I lean my forehead against the door. The tears I started crying this morning haven't let up all day and they drip from my swollen eyes and snake into my beard. I keep quiet, hoping he'll change his mind.

Instead he walks away.

I wait until I can't and then I throw open the door and barrel down the stairs past Henry sitting in front of the television with his pacifier and onto the front porch *don't let me be too late don't let me be too late don't let me—* Joel! I shout.

He comes back, taking the steps two at a time. With his hand on the back of my neck his forehead touching mine his mouth this close I think maybe we'll be fine. Don't go, I whisper and he tucks something in my hand, his eyes glittering with so many tears I'm staring at starlight. I might as well be in front of that wall in his studio.

Then he's gone. When his cab turns the corner I open my palm. The glass he found last night winks up at me.

Joel / Seattle

I sit in the glider on Adam's front porch as rain falls from the sky. In Chicago, James will be finishing dinner, giving Henry his bath. I know because I know, not because we've spoken. There won't be words, not for months. Not unless I'm not supposed to be here, and I don't for a second believe I'm not.

This front porch, this glider, the dust beneath my fingers as I wait for Adam to come home: my presence here seems less like a choice and more like destiny. Last night, my mother played with her hair, braiding a long rope over her shoulder. She'd invited me to sit beside her, patting her headstone as if we'd found ourselves at the same garden party and she'd saved me a seat. I half-expected her to offer me a glass of champagne. Adam..., she said, Do you still love him? I glanced up at the second story window, on the other side of which James slept oblivious to the reunion taking place in his backyard. Even my nod felt like a betrayal. My mother smiled, like I'd answered a trick question she hadn't been sure I'd get right. Co-dependent, she concluded, looking up at the window, and I shook my head, frustrated that she didn't understand. James and I have always been something complicated. For years, we've been circling, and now, finally, we've found our center. How can I refuse what he's offering?

Adam *cheated* on me, Mom, I tell her. He cheated on you, she says, James cheated on Elizabeth... She slides me a sidelong look, and my mouth opens. Phone sex— I start. Doesn't mean shit, she finishes, using the same words James did when I called him the day after Christmas in 2005. That he lowered his voice so his wife wouldn't hear him told me otherwise; for weeks, I wrestled with what we'd done. I'd just left the man I loved for having an affair, and James and I... There was a difference, and I kept looking for the line. James and I had been drunk, or that's what I'd always believed; we'd been a thousand miles away from each other; that phone call was an isolated incident. We were friends, we had a history that spanned fifteen years, I'd been wretched with grief...

My mother slid from her tombstone and took a few barefoot steps in the spring grass. She didn't seem to mind the cold, and I watched as she tilted her head to the stars, not a care in the world. For a moment, I felt waylaid by anger. You left me alone with him, Mom, I reminded her. Details, she murmured, shrugging. You left me alone with him! I cried, and she turned to face me. Who would you be if I hadn't? she asked.

I'll never know. I'll never know what my life might have been like if my mother had protected me from my father's cigars, if she hadn't fed herself a recriminating bullet the night before classes started after Winter Break my sophomore year in college. Her suicide brought James and me closer together, determined the direction of my work. If she hadn't died, I wouldn't have followed in her footsteps with a weapon of my own. Would I even be able to call myself an artist?

Your father used to hate your histrionics, she added, and I stared at her in disbelief. Are you fucking kidding me? I said. Her smile caught me out, and infuriated, I got to my feet and stalked across the yard. Don't you want to know why I'm here? she called. No, I said over my shoulder, taking the back steps in twos, and for the first time in more than seventeen years, my mother touched me.

The glider slides back and forth, the Seattle twilight coming sooner than I expected. Adam's still not here, but I'm not worried. I gave James the glass, but I still feel its shape in my hand. If I close my eyes, I can see its place in my mosaic. You're almost finished, my mother told me last night, and I could see my reflection in her eyes. I'm close, I agreed. Closer than you think, she said.

Adam's Camry pulls to the curb. His door opening, the thrust of his umbrella into the rain, his quick steps: he's not expecting me, after all. On the porch, he lowers his umbrella, flinging drops of water that hit my bare arms. Adam, I say.

February 1996

Jennifer Hritz

James / Austin

I feel like I'm on the wrong end of a Remington .270, a deer standing stock-still in the center of some guy's scope. Instinct tells me to bolt but fear holds me fast. *I don't mind a little complication.* I don't know how long we sit there staring at each other through the haze of Joel's cigarette after I say those words but the hook in his smile just might sink me. Then there's knocking at the door and Joel drops his eyes back to his sketch. Get that, will you? he murmurs and you can bet your ass I'm grateful for the distraction.

There's a girl on our front porch posing as a Girl Scout. Man, if my little sister ever wore fuck me lipstick like this I'd wash her face myself. Yeah? I say all gruff, trying to ballpark her age but she doesn't bother answering. Instead she looks over my shoulder like she's casing the place then steps on forward like I've invited her in. Right quick I block her path. Can I help you? I ask. Let her in, man, Joel says behind me.

The girl gives me a smug little smile I don't much like but I let her inside anyway. Didn't her momma teach her any better? I wouldn't want my little sister wandering into some stranger's house. I watch her take a look around the living room, her eyes stalling first on the tabby and then the wall Joel painted.

Want a beer? Joel asks her. Sure, she says but I give Joel a look like *the hell you're gonna give this girl a beer.* He rolls his eyes and asks her what's up instead. *What's up* like they're the best of friends and she says *same old,* making herself right at home in the barstool beside him even though no one offered her a seat. He nods like he's taking her seriously. What the hell is going on here?

Do you want to buy some cookies? she asks Joel, opening up the raggedy-ass bag she's carrying and pulling out a box of Thin Mints. Are you really a Girl Scout? I interrupt and she narrows eyes lined with so much black she looks fucking feral. Yeah, I'm a Girl Scout, she tells me, So what?

I'm guessing she's fifteen. Fifteen years old and sitting at our bar with her eye on Joel's beer like she's fixing to steal a swig. Isn't this how good men go to jail? Am I going to find her daddy on our front porch later tonight with a shotgun in his hand? Aren't you a little old to be a Girl Scout? I ask. Aren't you a little rude? she snaps.

Man, the *sass* on this girl. Meanwhile Joel's taking out his wallet and handing her a ten. I reach for the Thin Mints but she snatches it away then hands it to Joel all reverential-like. Calm as you please he opens the end. Want one? he asks and she takes the cookie and bites off an itty-bitty piece. They're better if you freeze 'em, I offer.

I see the covert look Joel gives her and I see the way she mashes her lips together as she tries not to smile. Can I? she asks, pointing at the cigarette Joel shakes from his pack. I fold my arms across my chest. Shit, with that Marlboro in her mouth she seems a lot older. Got a light? she simpers and Joel leans forward. There's no stopping her smile now, not with that cigarette between her lips and the beer she's sneaking. Give me the pack, I order and Joel tosses me the Marlboros. With my cigarette hanging from my lips I drag my thumb across my lighter. Nothing happens. *Flick flick flick* and Joel lets out a big old laugh. The Girl Scout joins him and I scowl. A little help? I bitch but Joel and I can't seem to get our cigarettes lined up and finally he just grabs my hand and holds it steady.

Ever since last fall, ever since that night we went to see Soulhat down on Sixth Street and I realized what I'm dealing with here I've been wondering. First way in the back of my mind, so far back I could blame the beer I was drinking but lately I've been bandying *what ifs* back and forth until I cave and bump Joel with my shoulder or knock his knee with mine. I guess I know what I'm doing to him all right and if I could kick my own ass I would because this mood of his today? That's me. That's all me and how the hell am I supposed to finish what I started?

I take his light, the tips of our Marlboros burning between us and I give him a real deep smile I know I shouldn't and that's when the Girl Scout starts coughing smoke from her virgin lungs. You okay, kid? I ask and she bursts into tears. Just like that, Joel's leading her outside onto the front porch and settling down beside her on the swing in the dark as she cries. I peer at them through the window. She doesn't look fifteen anymore. She might as well be my little sister.

They're not talking but something's happening between them and she finally wipes away the last of her tears and gets to her feet. Joel follows her to the top of the steps and gives her a hug and I figure he'll come inside as soon as he sees her off but instead he sits back down in our swing.

Well hell.

What was that all about? I ask, banging open the door and when he shrugs I keep at him until he tells me she lives down the street and got locked out of her house a few weeks ago. He sat with her a while since he'd just finished a run. What's her name? I ask, dropping down beside him and he sighs like I'm maybe giving him too much grief about the minor who just smoked our cigarettes and drank our beer. Amanda, he says. Why's she cryin'? I ask and for a while I think he isn't going to answer me. He's quiet so long I start to think about the prep work I still have for class tomorrow. Somehow we wasted the whole afternoon and I glance over at him ready to make a crack about what happens when I try to match him beer for beer on a weeknight when he looks right at me. Man, I wonder how long he can keep me curious. I don't know, James, he says, Haven't you ever had hold of something you didn't want to let go?

Smoke and Glass

DISCUSSION QUESTIONS

1. How does the opening scene of *Smoke and Glass* prepare the reader for the narrative in Part One? Do you see any similarities between the mosaic Joel constructs in Part Two and the scenes in Part One?

2. How do you feel about James? Readers of *The Crossing* and *I, too, Have Suffered in the Garden* quite possibly have an idealized version of this character. How does he measure up on a reading of this novel?

3. Talk about the scenes where James finds himself thinking about previous intimate moments with Joel. Has he been harboring feelings for Joel all these years? Does he have a purely physical attraction for Joel? Or is he simply remembering what has transpired between the two of them over the course of their relationship?

4. What role does Henry play in the novel? Do you think James is a good father? Is Elizabeth a good mother? What about Joel's relationship with Henry?

5. How do you explain the kiss in James's kitchen? Why does James initiate the kiss? Why does Joel push him away?

6. Joel has clearly had a difficult time getting over his breakup with Adam. How do you feel about Joel's lingering feelings for his former partner? Do you find yourself impatient with him for not moving on? What changes for Joel once he sees Adam in Seattle? Why do you think he leaves Adam once again and refuses to respond to his calls, including his ultimatum? Why does he return to Adam at the end of the novel?

7. What do you make of Joel's relationship with his father? How do you feel when Joel shows up in Houston to care for him? For those readers familiar with *The Crossing*, in what ways has Joel's relationship with his father changed over the years?

8. Why do you think Joel sees demons around his father's deathbed? What do you think about the demon that starts following Joel around after his father dies? Why does the demon finally disappear?

9. What do you make of the circles Joel paints throughout the novel? How do they foreshadow and/or reflect what happens in Joel's relationships?

10. In one particularly damning scene, Joel accuses James of being his father. In what ways are these relationships similar? In what ways are they different?

11. What's your reaction to the scene where Joel discovers his mother in James's backyard? Do you think Joel really sees her? Or is she a figment of his imagination?

12. The punctuation in James's scenes differs dramatically from Joel's. Why do you think the author chose to eliminate so many of the commas in James's scenes?

13. If you're familiar with *I, too, Have Suffered in the Garden*, you know that time plays a critical role in this fictional world. How does timing affect what happens for Joel, James, and Adam?
14. Talk a bit about the novel's title. Why do you think the author chose *Smoke and Glass*? What meaning does the cover art have in relation to the title?
15. For those readers familiar with *The Crossing* and *I, too, Have Suffered in the Garden*, how does a close reading of all three novels reveal the imperfections and discrepancies inherent in memory and perspective?

ACKNOWLEDGMENTS

I'm humbled by the love and support I've received over the years, including from readers Jennifer Bloom, Amie Stone King, Susan Michalski, Catherine Vouvray, and Kim Kent.

Stephanie Estrin painted the cover for this novel, and I couldn't be more enthralled. I'm indebted to Susan Michalski, who designed the cover and helped me get this book to a shareable point. She also handed me the title! I appreciate Jay Brown's expertise regarding lobbyists in the state of Texas; any discrepancies are entirely mine. Holly Pils gave me a better understanding of motorcycles. Thank you as well to Daniel Valenzuela and Eduardo Pedroza, who helped me translate English to Spanish.

Hopeton Hay has believed in the value of this fictional world from our first introduction. Thank you for including me so often on KAZI Book Review and inviting me to speak on your diversity panels. Owen Egerton and Becka Oliver of the Writers' League of Texas, thank you for inviting me to One Page Salon and giving me the opportunity to share one of my demon scenes. Andrea Loomis, I appreciate your repeated invitations to read at West Austin Studio Tour. Steeping Room, your space offered much-needed respite and plenty of tea.

Jordanna Eyre, thank you for shifting me into connection.

Much love to my mother, who inspires me to read and read and read.

To my son, Gus: Big appreciation for putting up with a mom who counts artistic expression as her main source of sustenance.

A special thank you to all the students in my creative writing workshops, who constantly remind me of the delight to be had in writing.

And to my readers, for the patience you've exhibited as I've promised over the past few years that this novel would be finished "soon." Thank you.

THE AUTHOR

Jennifer Hritz is the author of *Smoke and Glass*, *The Crossing*, and *I, Too, Have Suffered in the Garden*. Winner of the Chris O'Malley Fiction Prize, she holds an M.A. in Literature and Language, as well as a Ph.D. in American Literature. Her short stories have been published in the *Los Angeles Review* and *The Madison Review*. She lives in Austin, Texas. Readers may visit her website at www.jenniferhritz.com.

Want to see how all started?
Keep reading for a sample of *The Crossing*.

THE CROSSING

Part One

1

October 1991

No one's at the spring this late in the season, and I stretch out on the bank, my legs crossed at the ankles as James makes his way across the rocks, his arms held out from his sides like airplane wings. We're barefoot, our shoes cast aside as easily as our afternoon class. Sun soaks our skin, and I yawn with shuttered lids, steeped in calm. At the park above us, an occasional whistle from the train punctuates the muted sound of preschoolers at play.

Fuck me, that's cold, I hear James say as he drags his toes through the water. I lean back on my elbows, watching as he braces himself, the muscles in his calves tensing. Then he's submerged, and when he breaks farther out ten seconds later, he's whooping at the chill. C'mon! he calls. Too cold, I call back, and he slams his hand through the water, like he's trying to soak me with the spray. Pussy! he shouts. At least I'm a warm pussy! I yell. He laughs and says something I don't catch before he flips over and starts a lazy backstroke.

I stare up at the sky as the wind sifts through my hair, reminding me of every dive I've ever taken, the shock of sun on my wet skin when I rise from the depths, the breeze that contradicts those very rays. I haven't been diving in almost a year, not since last Christmas, when my father forced a trip to Belize that we would've been better off canceling. The diving rivaled any I've experienced, but our accommodations reflected the country's rustic infrastructure to a degree that my father had failed to anticipate. At first, I spent a fair amount of time under the water, but my mother looked so miserable every time I left her at what I jokingly started to refer to as "our compound" that I started staying behind with her. That infuriated my father more than her refusal to accompany us on our dives, and we ended up flying home several days ahead of schedule. You're going to regret this next semester, he told me as we packed our equipment, When you're ass-deep in coursework. Diving's the one commonality we possess, the only activity we share without antagonism. That day, my father made it clear I'd ruined everything.

I glance around for James, who's never been scuba diving himself, an infraction I'm determined to correct. This past summer, I tried to persuade him to head to Mexico with me, but he never has cash, and he seemed reluctant to let me pay for the ticket myself. Instead, we spent our time at the pool, where he'd landed a job as a lifeguard, as well as a girlfriend, and I worked on my tan. At some point though, I'm going to convince him to take off with me.

Once I locate his casual freestyle, I close my eyes and give myself up to the sun. The colors I worked with all morning hold me close, and I linger over the palette in my mind, along with the canvas that's waiting for me at home. There's a part of me that can't wait to get back.

James and I live off of 29th Street, just west of Guadalupe. There's a little too much traffic, and the houses all show signs of wear, but trees arch over the sidewalks and will likely drop bushels of pecans this fall. Our house, white frame with a pine green trim, boasts a ramshackle roof and a rickety swing we frequent every evening, regardless of the weather. I love every inch of the place, couldn't care less about the sagging front porch and alarmingly low ceilings my father pointed out at the beginning of last summer, when he drove up to inspect what he'd leased at my insistence. I'm too taken with the weathered hardwood floors, the sixty-year-old windows that will leave us shaking with cold when the temperature drops. I'm too enamored of the room I call my own.

Windows line three of the walls, offering me better light than I've entertained in all the years I've been painting, and the same ancient hardwoods that greet my feet the moment I step from my bed each morning catch the kaleidoscope of colors that drips from my brush in the back room. I don't even bother to clean up. Instead, I'm reminded of what I've done, what I might be capable of doing, and when late afternoon sun casts shadows beneath my feet, I almost don't care what I've had to give up in order to get to this point.

My father finds artists frivolous and self-indulgent, and I know he's never been able to reconcile himself to the fact that he traded one in for another. My mother abandoned her work early in their relationship, but I've been holding a paintbrush since I could walk. My earliest memory, in fact, shows me plunging a thick tuft of brush into a well of scarlet, then sucking the paint off the end. My mother was appalled, but I dimly recall thinking that the color tasted exactly as I expected.

The more painting enraptured me the greater my father's resentment grew. Even now, the memory of him throwing my paints in the trash when I was six remains one of the most vivid of my childhood, and the first time I can remember him losing his temper so viciously. I honestly don't recall the offense that precipitated the event. But I do remember my father sweeping my paintings from the kitchen table and tossing them, along with my watercolors, into the trash compactor. When he flipped the switch and everything was chomped into bits, I burst into tears, then threw myself on the floor in a full-fledged tantrum. He was hauling me up by my arms when my mother rushed in and plucked me away from him. Edward, she said as I sobbed into her shoulder, How could you, how could you?

My father has an impatience for anything he can't quantify, anything he can't control. That's why when I found the house last May, I didn't play up the sun porch that could serve as my studio. Instead, I made the slightest of references to what he did to me over Spring Break.

He capitulated, like I knew he would. My Ford Explorer served the same fucking purpose.

But look what I got in return: an amazing house, big enough for James and me to each have our own bedroom, and a place for me to work as well. I've never before had so much space. This past summer, for the first time, I bought the materials I need to stretch and gesso my own canvas. There's something satisfying about shaping the frame myself, something sacred about applying the gesso with quick, even strokes. When it's finished, when the gesso's dry, I don't bother with pencil. There's a term for that, I think, some Italian word I can never remember. What if you make a mistake? James asks, and I laugh. Not because I don't make them, but because half the time they lead me somewhere I never intended, somewhere far better than I envisioned.

Sometimes James asks how I classify myself, and I almost always shrug. Abstract expressionist, he'll say, throwing out a word he knows only because he took Art Appreciation last semester, and I'll roll my eyes. I'm not looking to be categorized. Instead, I'll tell him who inspires me, who moves me, who leaves me breathless. Gorky, I'll say, Rothko, Pollock. All abstract expressionists, he'll inform me, and I'll tell him I'm not an idiot. Aren't you interested in anyone alive? he'll ask. Aren't you a History major? I'll snap back.

What surprises him, I think, doesn't seem to be the expense of what I'm doing, or the tedium of preparing my own canvas. I think more than anything, he's stunned by how easily the back room holds my attention. He catches me in there at all hours of the day and night, finds me barely able to hold a conversation because I'm so lost in the paint. I gesso canvas after canvas, undeterred by each new stretch of white.

I'm still drifting when James hits the ground beside me, shaking his head like a dog and scattering drops of spring water that hit my arms like tiny icicles. Sorry, he says, seeing me wince. He scrubs at his hair, letting his towel fall around his shoulders when he's finished and closing his eyes. Autumn light burnishes every shadow gold. I've had moments lately, when

I've felt such an intense rush of belonging I've had trouble breathing.

+ + +

James turns twenty at the end of the month. Twenty: the number feels huge, portentous, in a way that sixteen didn't, in a way eighteen never could. There's something about twenty that shimmers, even though James will still have to buy his beer tonight with a fake ID. I have four more months at nineteen myself, but I can't help thinking that somehow, turning twenty will change everything.

The morning of James's birthday, his father drives down from Fort Worth to take him to lunch. I'm quietly impressed by the interest Dr. Fielding takes in his son's life, by the way he's scheduled a day off of work to spend time with him. For my last birthday, my father sent me a monogrammed leather planner. I've known you for six months, James told me, And even I know that's not your taste. After the fact, I think he felt bad for saying anything, but it's not like his comment was some big revelation. If anything, I was more struck that this guy I roomed with, one that I barely saw for the first three months of school and spent a month away from over the holidays, knew me better than my own father.

James insists that I accompany them to lunch, so I tag along, pleased to be included but feeling at the same time completely awkward in his father's presence. Dr. Fielding is an American Studies professor, and given the current state of my grades, I'm reluctant to open my mouth. But I figure out soon enough that there's no reason for me to worry. He and James converse with little input on my behalf, and I sit there watching them, knowing that I've never experienced with my own father what I'm witnessing right in front of me. Their conversation seems so fluid, and when James pauses long enough to shove a forkful of barbeque in his mouth, his father turns to me. James tells me you're an artist, he says. Sort of, I mumble, casting a scathing glance at James, but he's already talking me up, telling his father that when we get back to the house, he should take a look at some of my work. I don't know whether to be flattered or alarmed. What're you doing? I ask in a low voice as we're walking out to the car, and he gazes back with an innocence he couldn't possibly contrive. I don't want your father combing through my shit, I tell him. Okay, he says, shrugging, acquiescing so easily that for the rest of the afternoon, long after his father has left, I'm still second-guessing myself.

We go out that night, hitting one bar after another, meeting up with friends and a few of James's fraternity brothers. There's a girl James likes, too, but I keep mostly to myself, mulling over our lunch today and my missed opportunity, thinking of what James had to say about my paintings. I wonder what would've happened if I'd invited James's father into the back room, whether his reaction would have mirrored what I imagine my own father's might be if I were to extend the same suggestion to him. My father and I would've gotten stuck on my grades, on my homework, on the classes I've been skipping. I would've been compared to James, a model student and a fraternity member to boot, characteristics my father admires and which would normally make me puke, if it hadn't been for the casual slide of James's hands in his pockets that first day we met at the beginning of freshman year, if it hadn't been for the way he hooked his gaze on mine when I confessed my aspirations mere hours after I saw him for the first time. My father's not to be trusted with the secrets I hold, with the paintings I breathe into being. I don't know if I can trust James's father either. My mother's a given, but then, she's my mother. She gave me my first brush the way she would've given over her own blood.

James is something else, something I can't wrap my head around under the best of circumstances, and which tequila renders downright impossible. He's mystifying, a puzzle exquisite in its intricacy, the one thing I want to figure out. At the same time, he's the simplest thing I know right now, my one constant other than the painting, as sure as the feel of that brush in my hand.

Or maybe I'm just drunk. I take a long, lingering drag of my cigarette; across from me, James has lost the girl, and he sucks on a cigarette of his own, an affectation for both of us that sooner than we expect will become the first thing we reach for in the morning. One by one, our friends say their goodbyes, and by last call, we're alone, licking from our lips the foam off our beers. Thanks, he says after a minute. For what? I ask, embarrassed, and he gives me a look. I shrug.

+ + +

The day before Thanksgiving, my parents' house sprawls around me, five thousand square feet of luxury. As I step into the living room, the smell knocks me back a dozen years. An outsider wouldn't think twice about the scent of vanilla wafting from the lit candles or the lingering aroma of my father's Cuban, but I feel as if whatever progress I've made distancing myself in the interest of self-preservation has already disappeared, the months I've been away feeling at the same time like the gravest sort of mistake. I embrace my mother, the thin blades of her shoulders beneath my palms like the wings of the most fragile bird. She's forty-two and still pretty, though *pretty* probably isn't the right word. Striking, maybe, in a haunted sort of way. Like something John Williams Waterhouse might have painted. I've seen her only twice since Spring Break, once in May when my semester ended and once over the summer, both trips cut short because I just can't handle the tension anymore. Now I'm worried that the strain in her voice may have everything to do with my absence. You got your hair cut, I say, and she blushes in a way that tells me I'm the only one who noticed.

We don't have much time before she expects my father home from work, and she gestures me into the kitchen, where she's preparing a meal far too elaborate for the night before a holiday. I take a doubtful look around me, at the salmon I know she's going to roast with citrus, at the almonds she'll have to toast for the rice: she's making one of my favorite meals, and I have a feeling that if I open the refrigerator, I'll find a pumpkin cheesecake she'll insist on cutting tonight. Mom, I say, We could've ordered a pizza.

She seems hurt by the suggestion and waves away my offer to help. I'd much rather talk, she says, so I give up and pull out a chair. Now, she says, offering me a smile, Tell me everything.

I provide her with an edited version of the past couple of months, skirting her hesitant question about my grades, but obviously not well enough to prevent a crease of concern from appearing on her forehead. I've been sketching some, I say to divert her attention, and she raises her eyebrows. Have you brought anything to show me? she asks. I shrug, quelling the mixture of shyness and excitement I always feel when she asks. But she shakes her head; she knows me too well. Come on, she says, Let's see.

I run upstairs. Buried under the clothes in my suitcase, I find the sketchpads I've brought, then carry them downstairs and watch from the corner of my eye as she settles herself at the table to look over what I've done. She pauses at the drawing I like best, James hunched over his Chemistry text, tugging on a handful of hair. I used to sketch him on the sly, afraid he'd be pissed if he knew what I was doing, but the first time he caught me, early our freshman year, he just stepped closer. He stared at the sketch for a while before giving me a curious glance. You're good, he said, sounding surprised, and without waiting for an invitation, he took the book from my hand and leaned back against his desk so he could start from the beginning. Now I don't even bother to hide what I'm doing. You know what you're looking at, don't you? he asked last week when he saw the sketch my mother's now examining, A four-point-oh.

I roll my eyes at the memory as my mother touches the wave in James's hair, the line of stubble along his jaw. This one has interesting texture, she says. Yeah? I say, and she nods, tapping her finger on James's collar. I like the contrast here, she says. I know exactly what she means, the rumpled softness of a tee shirt James likely pulled right from his dirty clothes next to that near-beard. I hadn't had to labor with my pencil either. The sketch just bled from my fingers, a feeling that's pretty much the best one I've found so far in this world.

My mother nods her approval, and a starburst of satisfaction starts in my chest and spreads outward from there. I value her opinion more than anyone's—and not simply because no one other than James has really seen my work. My mother was an artist herself once, and though the only reason she picks up a brush these days might be to baste a turkey, she knows what she's talking about when it comes to art. If she can find something promising in what I've sketched, then maybe I'm as good as I hope.

The back room makes all the difference, I tell her, and she says, The back room? My studio, I say, still finding myself uncomfortable with the term. Having the space to work, she agrees, and I nod. I wish you could see it, I add. Soon, she promises, though I have my doubts. My father has been to Austin only twice since I started college, and the likelihood that he'll make the trip anytime soon seems about as slim as me ending the semester with a perfect grade point, the chance that my mother would come without him even more improbable.

Mom? I say, hesitating because though I've asked her about her own work many times, she never divulges. I don't understand how she could give it up, not if she felt the same way about her work as I feel about mine. I'd rather give up my breath than my brush. But before I can tell her what I'm thinking, she's murmuring over another sketch, one from last summer. We'd just come back from the pool, and James collapsed in the shitty, threadbare chair I'd confiscated from a neighbor's trash pile, then peeled his damp shirt over his head. He still had his lifeguard whistle around his neck, and the chrome against his tan was what got me. I'd sat down right across from him with a pad of paper and a pencil. Don't I get any privacy? he asked, taking his mouth away from the phone just long enough to ask the question, and I ignored him because he let me. My pencil moved, full sweeps down the line of his torso, scrawls of loose spirals in his hair, still slick from the pool. I half-heard his voice, teasing his girlfriend as I teased out the contrast of that whistle against his skin. And his eyes: every so often, he'd glance over at me, and I worked that in, kept working that in, until his conversation ended. D'you get what you needed? he asked, Or are you going to follow me into the shower?

The front door slams shut, and I yank the books away from my mother, then slip them onto the chair next to mine. She's already on her feet, opening the oven door. Joel, she says, Would you mind setting the table?

The request comes just as my father rounds the corner, timed impeccably for his benefit. I stand and shake his hand, and he loosens the tie around his neck, looking me up and down until I straighten. Taller, he claims, though I haven't grown at all since summer. Even if I had, I wouldn't be able to look him in the eye; he'll probably always have a few inches on me. But we have the same hair, thick and dark, the same full mouth. Eyes the color of gunmetal.

Didn't your mother ask you to set the table? he asks, as if his arrival isn't responsible for delaying my response to my mother's request, and I duck into the dining room, where I find the table already set. The pool beckons just beyond the windows, glimmering in the light of a full moon. I can hear my parents in the next room; I feel a constant, low-level wariness, listening to them. But there's not even a hint of tension in the soft lilt of my mother's voice, and I lean my forehead against the glass, my eyes on the moon. Maybe I'll slip outside in the middle of the night and swim, despite the cold.

Finished already? my father asks, and I turn, then glance at the dining table where my mother has shaped the napkins into fans. But he doesn't seem to notice. Your mother, he confides, gesturing outside at the pool, Has been angling for a heater. She doesn't even swim, I say, and he says, That was *my* point.

We exchange a rare, guarded smile. I have to admit, he muses, Swimming in November has a certain appeal. Not without a heater, I tell him, and he nods. You were contemplating a night swim, though, he says, Weren't you? I frown, disliking the way he's read my mind, but he just shrugs. You've done it often enough, he adds, Over the years.

Even though he's obviously talking about something too far in the past to warrant repercussions, I tense. How do you know? I ask. I've seen you, he tells me, Once or twice. You've seen me? I say. The first time, he confides, You were fifteen.

He'd come outside for a brisk, middle-of-the-night swim, he says, only to find that I'd beaten him to the pool. He was on the verge of interrupting me—he didn't think it was safe for me to be swimming by myself at night—but then he saw me dive. Your form was flawless, he says, and I flush at the belated compliment. He watched me surface, then glide through a dozen laps, and a dozen more, without effort. Back and forth, washed in the light of a moon as full as the one we can see tonight. You finally pulled yourself out of the water and sat on the lip of the pool, he says, And for a second, I thought you saw me, but then you tilted your head back to the sky.

He's staring at the water now, as if he can see me out there. Hell, I can almost see me myself, and I take a veiled glance in his direction. He looks downright nostalgic, and when he speaks again, he sounds wistful enough to startle me. A part of me wanted to join you, he admits, But the moment was too private.

Sometimes I think I have him pegged so wrong.

Dinner's ready, my mother says, appearing in the doorway, and my father gives me a quick smile. Too cold tonight anyway, he says.